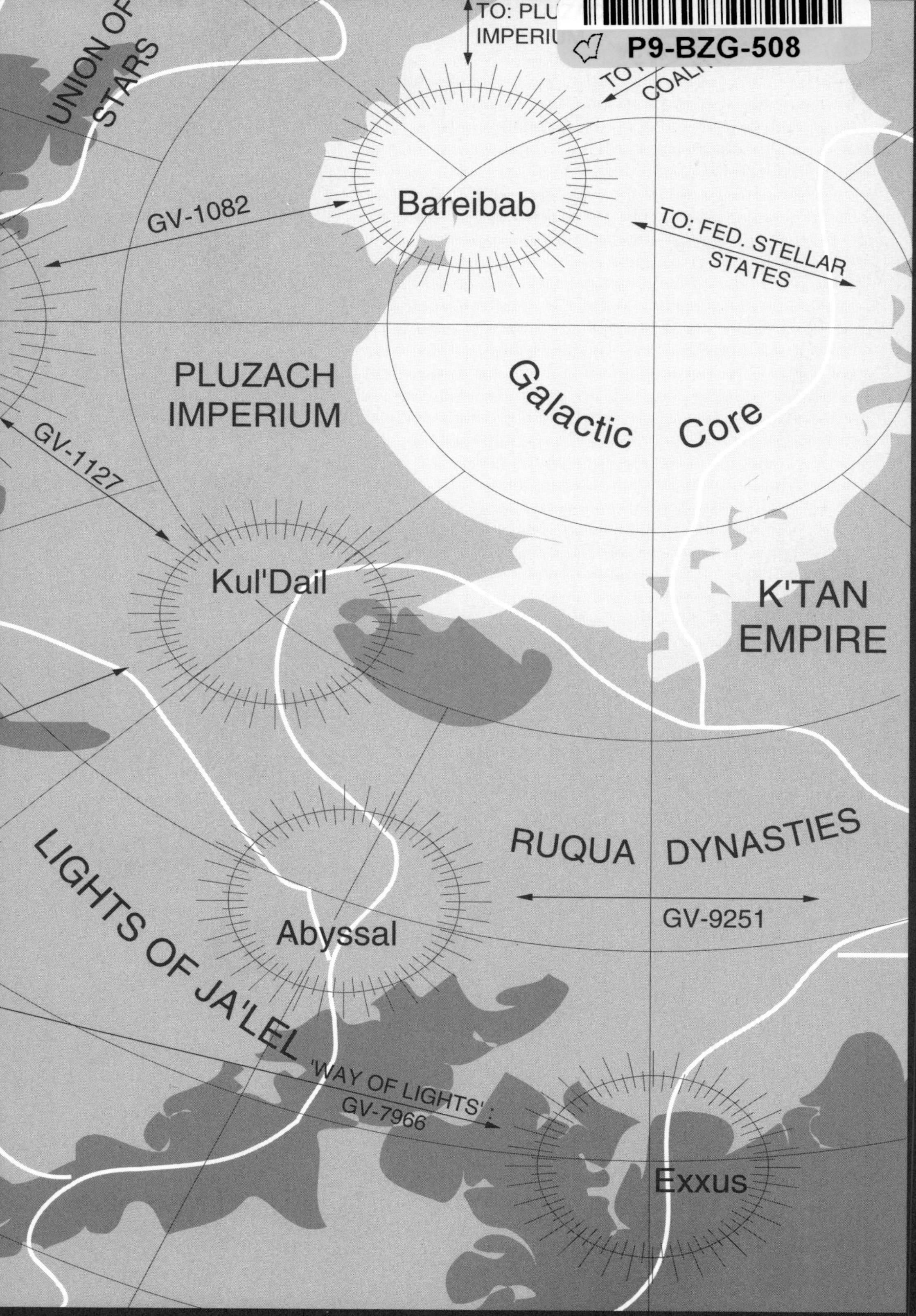
UNION OF STARS
TO: PLU
IMPERIU
TO
COALI
Bareibab
GV-1082
TO: FED. STELLAR STATES
PLUZACH IMPERIUM
Galactic Core
GV-1127
Kul'Dail
K'TAN EMPIRE
RUQUA DYNASTIES
GV-9251
LIGHTS OF JA'LEL
Abyssal
'WAY OF LIGHTS':
GV-7966
Exxus

STARSHIELD

BOOK ONE:

SENTINELS

MARGARET

WEIS

TRACY

HICKMAN

STARSHIELD SENTINELS

BALLANTINE BOOKS • NEW YORK

A Del Rey® Book
Published by Ballantine Books

http://www.randomhouse.com

LIBRARY OF CONGRESS CATALOGING-IN-PUBLICATION DATA
Weis, Margaret.
Sentinels / by Margaret Weis & Tracy Hickman.
p. cm. — (Starshield ; bk. 1)
"A Del Rey book."
ISBN 0-345-39760-6
I. Hickman, Tracy. II. Title. III. Series: Weis, Margaret.
Starshield ; bk. 1.
PS3573.E3978S45 1996
813'.54—dc20
96-27414
CIP

Manufactured in the United States of America
First Edition: November 1996
10 9 8 7 6 5 4 3 2 1

Table of Contents

PROLOGUE:

Myth and Legend

SHAUNA-KIR WALKED THE STARS.

They were her birthright. They were her home. She danced through the nebulae of the galactic disk with a silent step for fear of awakening the new stars within too soon. She laughed, her hair whipping playfully about her oval face as the gales of the quantum wave fronts destroyed civilizations, histories, and ideas around her. She turned and considered them for a time, those worlds where the passing of one reality for another had caused the life there to shudder and cry out in pain. It saddened her, for such was her greatness that she could be sad at the passage of so small a thing.

Yet sadness was not her nature. She turned again, diving through the black holes as a swimmer moves through water, surfacing again in another time and place. Each beauty enraptured her. Each horror she contemplated to its solid depth. Until, at last, she looked deep into the eye of the galaxy and, through its rotating singularity, saw a gem.

Black, it was, its facets becoming more and more complex with its depth until its heart was obscured. It was the greatest of prizes, and Shauna-kir's heart nearly burst for it. Not for the beauty of the gem—for gems were her specialty and the rarest and most beautiful were made by her hand. By all accounts, this gem was not the most beautiful. Yet within its depths, this gem held another prize: a prize that was obscured by the facets of the crystal lattice. The prize sang to the soul of Shauna-kir, for its name was mystery and never before had Shauna-kir encountered anything that was new or hidden.

"That which is hidden compels us," came the sleepy, deep voice over her shoulder.

Shauna-kir turned to the Void that blotted out both stars and space alike, a hole in all creation drifting near her. She spoke to him by name.

"Obem-ulek, you come to us unbidden. What know you of such things?"

The Void drifted slowly about her in a sensuous nothing, considering her, yet not foolish enough to attempt engulfing her. "Why, nothing and everything, Shauna-kir! I know only that its worth lies deep within it. Through its eyes only may you experience all creation, and only through its knowledge will you find your destiny. Sadly, all else is left a mystery," Obem-ulek half lied, speaking only truth enough to satisfy his sister. "For knowledge is a mystery to those who are without it. Knowledge is a prison for those who lack it. Knowledge is slavery for those who have it used against them. Does not Kendis-dai keep you in mystery? Are you not a prisoner of his Mantle of Wisdom? Are you not a slave to Kendis-dai, bowing before all he knows and that you lack?"

Shauna-kir considered all these things, for she knew that Obem-ulek was a cunning brother. Yet the words were echoing in her heart and the desire was within her to honor Kendis-dai and not be a slave to him. So it was that she turned from her void-brother and Chose—for choice was the greatest of gifts given to all her kin—and in the choosing she dove down from the stars and into the heart of the black gem. The sound of her crossing the boundary rippled across the cosmos.

Far from her, at the fringes of all creation, Kendis-dai heard the murmur of her passage. Fear gripped him in the instant, for he knew Obem-ulek was abroad and that his hatred was terrible indeed. The Starshield he brought with him to guard creation. The Nightsword he wielded to order all things to his will. The Mantle he wore to insure that all knowledge of what was and what would be could allow him to rule in impartial judgment. Thus armored, he flashed across the skies of a million million worlds unheeding of the chaos in his wake. In a moment he came to the eye of the galaxy and found the hateful Obem-ulek drifting triumphantly through the stars.

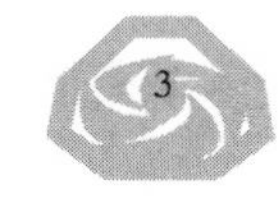

"She is lost to you, Kendis-dai!" Obem-ulek's voice ripped time and space. Time slowed and all creation watched. "Shauna-kir walks the stars no more."

Yet Kendis-dai had no need of Obem-ulek's words, for the Mantle of his Wisdom was upon him. He saw the gem and saw all that had gone before and all that was to happen after and he Knew.

She had fallen from the stars by her own volition.

"You offered her knowledge," Kendis-dai said, and his quiet words filled the universe. "Knowledge of life and death. Knowledge of pain and joy. Knowledge of health and sickness. You offered her all that experience can teach."

From far within the Void, Obem-ulek grinned.

"You offered her life and death. There is only one great teacher of the gods." Kendis-dai spoke evenly. "Mortality."

"I have won," Obem-ulek roared. "She is fallen to mortality and shall die. You, Kendis-dai, are but half a soul without her. Go with her and you, too, shall have fallen, and who shall redeem you then? Bow to me, brother, and surrender creation—perhaps I will be generous. Stay and you shall fight me as half a soul, sick for the loss of your mate, and my victory will be complete!"

So did Obem-ulek sneer in his blind desire, bringing Kendis-dai in black chains unto Avadon—the world of Aden, City of Enlightenment. Kendis-dai walked silently, the rough chains wearing against his wrists and ankles as he passed through the streets. The stars wept at his passing. The Void passed up the avenue and Obem-ulek mounted the Cathedral steps with his bound brother behind him.

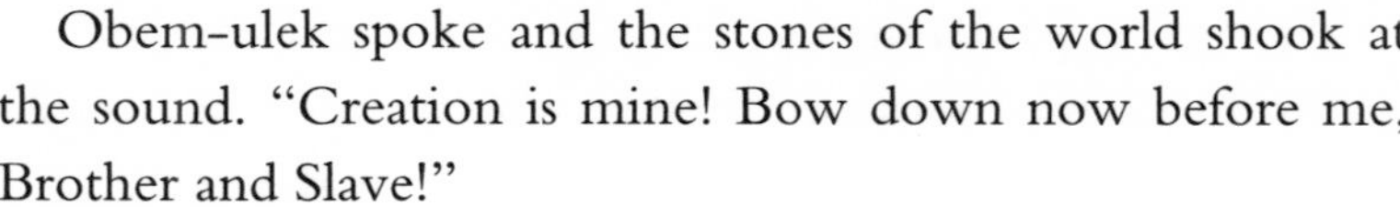

Obem-ulek spoke and the stones of the world shook at the sound. "Creation is mine! Bow down now before me, Brother and Slave!"

"Hear me," spoke Kendis-dai quietly and his voice was heard clearly by the multitude assembled there. "I relinquish the ensigns of my power. Take these, my shield, sword, and mantle, and hide them up from the eyes of mortality. Hold them safe until my return."

"They are mine!" screamed Obem-ulek.

But Kendis-dai only smiled, and the brilliance of that smile shook the Void of Obem-ulek to its core.

"You are clever, Obem-ulek, but you know not the heart; and this is your flaw." Kendis-dai's words sparkled across the eternities. "I do, indeed, go with my love into that forgetful place of mortality, but why should I not share my fate with those who made it possible?"

Thus did Kendis-dai embrace Obem-ulek, entangling him in the very chains that he himself had forged. His cries from the Void fell through uncounted years to the ears of frightened civilizations on untold worlds. Together they fell into mortality, forsaking their own powers for wisdom's sake and for the love of Shauna-kir.

There, among mortals, did Kendis-dai vow to gain knowledge and experience with the promise that when the time was ripe and the universe was in need of his hand once more, he and Shauna-kir would return to the stars and forge a new empire.

As for Avadon, and its City of Enlightenment, it was hidden from the eyes of mortal man, lost to their knowledge. Though many have sought its treasures, none have discovered it—for Kendis-dai cast it beyond mortal knowledge against the day of his return. Until that day, the Mantle of Kendis-dai, his Nightsword, and his Starshield lie hidden by his guardian servants in the temple of the stars. Far from the sight of mortal eyes, they wait until that day.

—*The Lay of Kendis-dai*

ALPHA:

BOOK

OF MERINDA

(3256 Years Later)

1

Cascade

MERINDA NESKAT STEPPED CAREFULLY OVER THE SLICK ROCKS, the cool evening mists swirling about her cheeks. It was wet, to be sure, and soon, she knew, her hair would be heavy with moisture, her thick honey-colored curls struggling to maintain their shape. Her damp clothing held the promise of a cool walk later when she returned to the dryer climates higher up. But for now, with the air nearly as wet as she was and dancing around her in gray forms, she was content with the feeling of the water on her bare arms and legs. "Immodest," she could hear the *Dex Libris*, her most immediate superior, intone in that sepulchral voice that was her hallmark. "An *Atis Librae* of the Omnet should command more respect in her demeanor. How do you hope to get off this rock and make a career if you do not respect yourself enough to allow others to respect you?"

Merinda choked off the giggle that the thought elicited and stood suddenly erect. "Yes, *Libris* Gildish," she said in her most mockingly serious tone, "I shall uphold the honor of the Omnet even in my sleep." The truth was that Merinda *was* serious—far too serious for many of those she worked with. Merinda believed that she was saving the universe, in her own way and in her own small part. She openly disdained the others around her who did not understand the importance of "recovering the past, preserving the present, and protecting the future" as the creed of her order maintained. She rarely socialized—at least as far as most of her coworkers were concerned. But, as Merinda reminded herself, she didn't need to. She nearly caught herself giggling at the thought again, kicked a curtain of water into the air before her with her bare feet, and once more began picking her way around the rocks.

She loved it here. Her own home world was wet like this, though not nearly so constantly warm. The warmth of the mists pounding through the air over the surging water of the rocks was filled with life and comfort, a haven from the doldrums of her other existence. The monastery was cold despite the constant heat, cold in a way that no sun could ever change. It was an austere place, and some thought it suited her—but then, they didn't really know her, did they?

The outcropping of rock was coming to an end where a great pillar of stone jutted from the frothing water. With practiced ease, Merinda reached up for the handhold. A moment's breath, a kick of her shining legs in the filtered light, and she swung around the stone to its far side.

Merinda caught her breath. The sight always struck the wind from her, as her mother used to say—a vision of surpassing beauty and wonder. It had taken her nearly an hour to walk the path to this spot, yet the time spent and the exertions of the way vanished in the moment.

The Denali Falls of Brishan V had once been a religious secret held to be a vision that only the local priests could fully understand or appreciate. The waters gathered their strength from the high peaks of the Krevish Range, a place where the ancient gods of this world were held to have lived under the blanket of the sky. The tears of the goddess Rhishan, weeping at the death of her three boys at the hands of their cruel uncle Umbleh, were said to be the source of the three rivers that converged at the top of Denali Canyon. There they formed the great falls that cascaded with a deafening thunder nearly a thousand feet into the pool at its feet. Yet the beauty of the falls was not found merely in the glory of its height or in the ancient monastery whose buttresses arched magnificently over the confluence of all three rivers. The falls were made special by the *klenith* vines that threatened to choke the waters at the fall's crest. The twisting vines were hollow, allowing the water to flow through their tubing. The effect was doubly beneficial. The hollow conduits of the klenith vines filtered nutrients from the water, thus purifying it as it fell through its tangled shape and, better still, the twisting forms wove the pure water into braids of shimmering elegance in its cascade. Merinda had, as always, timed her arrival well, for the sun was settling for the night at the edge of the plains far below. Quite suddenly, it seemed, Merinda's world was filled with salmon-colored light as the cascades and mists at the base of the falls were suffused with the twilight glow at the end of another day.

Merinda stood ankle-deep on a sandbar she had come to think of as her own and felt all of it become a part of her again. *This is life,* she thought, *this is sustenance. I need so very little to bring me the joy that I want out of life. I'll make my own way and endure the pain and the loneliness and the frustration so long as there is a place like this that I can call home. I'll travel wherever destiny takes me so long as there is always someone, some singular one, who is home awaiting me.*

The dark figure moved behind her, nearly invisible in the billowing obscurity of the thrashing water. Footfalls without sound. No motion wasted. As the figure moved toward her it was revealed as a tall man, his deep gray tailored clothing covering him from head to foot. The dark cloak he wore over it all was heavy from the mists and did not billow as was its custom. Her back was toward him as he closed the distance between them, coolly and efficiently, his large gray gloves reaching for her.

Merinda stood relaxed, gazing up into the woven cascade of the falls.

Her eyes flashed sideways.

Suddenly Merinda stepped backward, both hands moving up to grasp one of the threatening arms. She thrust her hip into the approaching man's waist, attempting to lever the attacker over her.

The man reversed, stepping sideways and twisting her arm back around behind her. She cried out from the pain, but in the same moment hooked one of her feet behind the ankle of her attacker and shoved herself bodily toward him with her free leg.

They both tumbled backward against a rock outcropping at the edge of the beach. The gray man's breath rushed from him in a sudden *oof,* his grip relaxing slightly from the impact. Merinda wrenched her hand free, kicked the man into the rock again. As he rebounded unsteadily, she grabbed him by both hands, fell backward into the sand, and planted both feet into his stomach.

His dark robes fluttered over her as she kicked and released him. The tall man sailed head down over her, his arms flailing in the mist-thickened air as he unceremoniously fell back-first into the shallow waters at the beach's edge. The deluge of his impact had not yet hit the ground when she was on her feet and leaping for him, her hand drawing her weapon from her belt as she moved. The final droplets were just hitting the water's surface when she pressed one knee against his chest and leveled the weapon's sights between her assailant's eyes.

His eyes. Those granite gray eyes.

He sputtered, spraying water and coughing to clear his

mouth and nose, as a wave from the pool washed over his face.

Merinda laughed. "Oh, great and powerful *Vestis Novus*, I see that you have once again proven your superiority to us lowly *Atis Librae*. Will you surrender to me now?"

The hood fell back from the supine man as he craned his head up out of the water, straining to keep his face above the surface. With the action came an explosion of black curled hair above a strong face. It may have been considered too heavy in the jaw for some people's tastes, Merinda reflected—certainly that was the opinion of *Librae* Brenai, the Omnet coworker with whom she had shared a room ever since they had first met for their initiate training on Netprime over two years ago. Kiria Brenai had quite firmly stated her opinion that Queekat Shn'dar could break stone with his lantern jaw, and, for all Kiria knew, probably did.

Then, as Merinda watched, those gray eyes flashed at her and a wide smile spread across his strong, angular face. Those eyes, she knew, were for her; that smile, somehow her property. "I surrender, Mistress *Librae*," he spoke in a high, fluting voice, "to the honor of your order and its superior training."

Merinda's eyes went wide with mock disbelief. "What? Not to *me*?" Her knee pressed his chest down again, plunging his face momentarily beneath the small waves.

"Yes, yes," Queekat sputtered as he surfaced again, half laughing, "I surrender to you, too."

Merinda laughed. She collapsed lovingly on top of him—nearly sending him back underwater a third time—and then rolled with him back up onto the beach. "Oh, Kat, when I heard you were coming, I hoped you might remember this place—this one place that is more dear to me than any in all of the creations."

"There are many more beautiful and terrible places in the

stars than this one." Queekat shook his hair at her, spraying water into her face.

"Not to me, you brute," she replied when at last she could. "We met here, you and I. This is our place, our private little universe so far from the worries of our professions or directors or—"

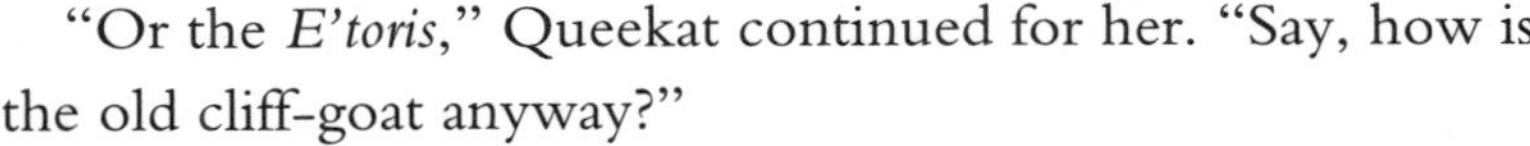

"Or the *E'toris*," Queekat continued for her. "Say, how is the old cliff-goat anyway?"

Merinda screwed her face into a belligerent look that was betrayed by the brightness of her eyes, locked on his. She reached over with her cupped hand and splashed a small sheet of water in his general direction.

"Hey," he protested faintly.

"Our *E'toris Librae* is fine, I believe, and, as I am sure that you as ambassador and investigator for the Omnet are well aware, is not planetside presently."

"Oh, really?"

Merinda almost became serious. "Oh, Kat, don't mistake me for stupid. You know as well as I do that your visit would have sent her into a fit of preparations and ceremonies. You were her brightest; the fairest of the fair to ever leave this rock. Imagine, a lowly information sifter from the D'Rakan Empire actually rising to the post of inquisitor of the Omnet. Kat, if she'd known you were coming there would be so much ceremony that I'd never get to see you."

"Yeah, *E'toris* Gildish is awfully proud of her magnificent D'Rakan Empire," Queekat said slowly, drawing his knees to his chest and hugging them as he looked up toward the first stars appearing directly overhead through the mists. "I used to think so, too—until I left here. 'D'Rakan Empire' is a fine-sounding name until you put it against the galaxy. Then—well, then it tends to get pretty small, Rini."

Merinda rested her head against her hands in the sand. Queekat had called her by her nickname, and she knew, somehow just knew, that he still felt for her as he had those months before. "What's it like, Kat—out there, I mean. What's it like for an inquisitor?"

Queekat smiled sadly and shook his head. "It's different than we thought, Rini. More complicated. More subtle. Good guys and bad guys get lost in the details. Black and white begin to look gray from a distance—as gray as these robes."

"But that's your job, isn't it?" Merinda asked, not quite understanding what he was telling her. "Separating the black and the white in the details? You're the *Vestis* inquisitors who take all this information that we churn through in the *Atis Librae* and pinpoint where the truth is."

Queekat snorted. "Right. You sift through the mud and when something *really* horrible turns up, we *Vestis* get to clean it up."

"Ah," she said, cocking her head to one side mischievously, "is my handsome paladin of the universe feeling a bit peevish today?"

"Peevish!" Queekat leaped so quickly to his feet that Merinda froze, frightened by the change that overcame him. He stood over her now, a sullen rage barely restrained within him. "You've no idea what's really going on out there, do you, Merinda—what we have to deal with? There are fifty-seven minor stellar empires in this sector alone, fifteen of which aren't even aware that there is other life in the universe and seven of which are preparing to go to war right now. Damn it, Merinda, two of those are arming themselves right now over interstellar exportation rights of indigenous cheeses. Here we are, trying to recover the wisdom and knowledge lost when the Kendis Imperium fell—three thousand years ago, mind you—and meanwhile over six trillion life-forms are being threatened over moldy milk products!"

Queekat stopped, able for the first time to see past his anger. He looked down at Merinda. *Don't move,* she thought, purposefully allowing her face to go completely neutral. *Let him take his time and he'll come around to what's really bothering him. He always does.*

Queekat sighed and knelt wearily in the sand before her. "Sorry, Rini. I guess I'm just not myself anymore."

Merinda leaned slowly back on her elbows. Her voice barely carried over the rumble of the falls beyond Queekat, but her words were distinct, their meaning clear. "You always knew just who you were and where you were going. I remember standing in the Golden Court beneath a halo of stars—"

"That was long ago," Queekat muttered.

"And you looked up with a hunger far greater than you ever felt for me." Her words came devoid of compassion or malice—statements whose value stood on their own without the inflection of the feelings she held against them. " 'They will be mine,' you said."

"I meant 'ours,' " he snapped.

"But you said 'mine,' " she responded testily. "Within a week you were gone, Kat. *Atis Librae* Shn'dar out of nowhere selected for the great *Inquisitas Vestis*. One week you were analyzing synopsis news upstream from a handful of backwater worlds and the next you were off reinventing yourself as an inquisitor for the Omnet."

Queekat looked up sharply. "I didn't reinvent myself! There was hardly any need to—they did a fine enough job reinventing me on their own terms. Look, Rini, you have no idea what it's like. You have to know so much that is specific to your assignment and your assignment changes so often. They just pour it right into you, Rini. The Oracles of Nine decide who you have to be on a mission and then they make you into that person. They partition your brain as if you were a mechanical device just like them—sift your memories and shuffle your thoughts into convenient storage places to make room for the information they think you need to get the job done for the Omnet. Then they just pour it into you through a biolink."

Merinda watched him carefully. Somewhere, high overhead, a stribek cawed as it soared above the falls.

Queekat sighed, and began sifting the wet sand of the beach through his fingers. "By the stars, Rini, three months ago they needed a xenobiologist with surgical skills. I was on the duty list. One night, I went to bed not knowing that the Kribenthian sedak even existed and by the time I awoke I could not only describe its anatomy down to the cellular and chemical level but perform surgery on it as well. For that month I was the greatest of all sedak physicians. When it was over, I had another assignment. The Nine gave me knowledge of the deep intricacies of the Four Dynasties of the Ruqua. Oh, I could instantly recount to you the relationships and genealogies of each of the four houses for the last thousand years—but I no longer knew a Kribenthian sedak's hand from its ass."

Queekat lapsed into a rather pouty sullenness. Merinda chewed her lower lip. It had become awkward, watching an inquisitor unguarded and vulnerable. Then he looked up at her and smiled the same confident, knowing, self-assured smile that had so blinded her when they'd first met that she, in her eternal pessimism, had ascribed it to his being too cocky and self-important. She couldn't believe then that the smile was meant for her alone, but she had at last claimed ownership of it and from that time her loneliness had ended. Despite the robes and the manner and the training, he was still Queekat. She was sure of it.

"Well, then, who are you today?" Merinda teased with a gentle edge in her voice. "Does your mission require you to become an invisible part of the D'Rakan Council of Matriarchs or are you perhaps something even more exotic?"

"Oh, you are such an innocent." He laughed, shaking his head. "I hate to disappoint you, but today I'm an advanced theorist technician for level-twelve synthetic minds."

She looked at him with disbelief. "You're what?"

"I am an expert at communication with and repair of most automated household appliances."

Merinda laughed. In a single smooth motion, she grabbed the front of Queekat's jumpsuit and pulled him down onto the sand next to her. "Ah, my own inquisitor, master of the self-regulating laundry! What evil grows among the stars which causes the Omnet to send its ruthless and skilled investigators to the far reaches of the D'Rakan Empire with the skills of an expert repairman? Are the Nine Oracles so concerned about the kitchen synths at our little sanctuary that they would send one of their elite researchers all the way to Brishan?"

"No"—he smiled at her—"my mission is on Tentris—but I'm going to need a little help. That's why I'm here. I assume that you still have some leave saved up. Can you get away for a few days?"

Merinda never spent her leave time—while Queekat had been here there never seemed to be a need for it, and once Queekat had gone there never seemed to be much point. Her heart leaped at the thought of taking a holiday with him, of getting off this rock and visiting somewhere exciting and new. It had never seemed important to her before—she certainly could have arranged passage to just about anywhere she wished to holiday in the past—but suddenly it had become incredibly important.

"Yes! Of course, I can get away for a few days!" The words gushed out of her in a schoolgirl rush that belied her usual serious and controlled demeanor. "Do I have time to pack anything or must we leave right away?"

"Easy! Easy!" Queekat held up both hands to fend off the words assaulting him. "It's not going to just be us. I'm going to need Kelis, Flynn . . . probably Dharah, and I think Brenai should join us as well . . . Hey, stop that! What's the matter with you?"

Merinda had begun beating her fists rather ineffectually against the man's chest, a pout growing more and more pronounced as she spoke. "Why do you have to bring along the whole department? We don't need them! You're the great inquisitor; you're the one with all the training and powers! We don't need anyone else—all you need is me!"

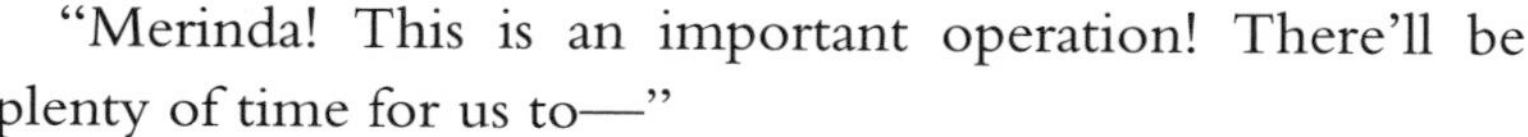

"Merinda! This is an important operation! There'll be plenty of time for us to—"

"Don't you talk to me about time." Merinda's blows were becoming a bit more effective, the pain beginning to register on Queekat's face. "I transcom a message to you every day. You used to be good about getting your replies back to me. Now I hardly hear from you. Nearly two months had gone by before your arrival message came. Now you're here and you—you want to mount an expedition? Don't you think I can see what's happening—"

"Merinda!"

The word was sharp and harsh in her ears. She had never heard him use her name so coldly. She stopped as he arrested both of her forearms in his powerful hands.

"Rini, this is my work. I serve the Omnet just as you do. There's a very special place for you in all of this. I can't explain it to you now and you may not understand it at first, but it is necessary that you come and it is necessary that you do your duty—do you understand?"

Queekat's gray eyes held her gaze. It was impossible for her to look into them and not feel slightly lost.

"Yes," she said softly at last, "I understand. It's just that it has been such a long time, Kat. I just . . . I just wanted a little time for us."

He pulled her toward him, the coldness of his face warming slightly. She buried her face against his chest, cradling herself under his arm. "Of course, Rini," he said to her, the words warm but the tone somewhat distracted. "We all want just a little more time."

Merinda closed her eyes, her mind taking her back to the time when their excursions to the falls had been warm and wonderful.

She did not see Queekat's own eyes, staring blankly at the emerging stars overhead.

2

Minor Inconvenience

OSCAN KELIS RUBBED THE BRIDGE OF HIS NOSE AND CLOSED his eyes. He was tired, and the puzzle that continued to float at the back of his mind was rapidly turning from a minor problem into a major headache. None of the usual actions seemed to help. He passed his hand over his bald scalp. No answer. He rolled his head around, trying to shake something loose in his mind. No answer. He stood up from the glowing plate in his work alcove, strode purposefully into the main hall of the ancient Rhishan Monastery, past the numerous alcoves filled with other *Atis Librae* huddled over their tasks, and out onto the concourse overlooking the falls. The patterns of water woven beneath him, tumbling into the chasm far below, had always soothed his mind and helped him bring order to his thoughts when no other source would possibly have given him the answers that he sought. So he leaned against the machicolation, gazing down through the crenels into the swirling mists far below him, searching for some clue within himself that would give him an answer.

No answer.

"Don't jump, Oscan!"

Oscan shook at the voice suddenly materializing at his ear.

He turned, heart racing, toward the sound. "By the Great Spirit, *Librae* Dharah, you gave me such a start!"

"Be at peace, *Librae* Kelis," Terica Dharah returned in her best mock-formal tone. "I shall not cause you any harm."

Oscan found his breath difficult in returning, and not just because of the fright his coworker had given him. Terica Dharah was uncommonly beautiful for a "sifter"—as most *Atis Librae* called themselves—being a tall, willowy woman with gentle features. Oscan had once happened upon her briefly during a holiday on Tentris. It was the only time he remembered seeing her with her raven-black hair liberated from the tightly controlled severity in which she always fashioned it for her work. The luxurious, satiny ripples of her hair framed the long oval of her face perfectly. The room had been crowded and he couldn't say how long he'd stood there, frozen by her beauty and the distant sound of her laughter welling up above the murmuring sound of her companions. The smile she'd flashed him when she'd noticed him in return had brought heat to his face he still felt just thinking about it. He had nearly made a fool of himself then in his rush to escape the games room where he'd encountered her, lamely waving in acknowledgment and then running directly into a table as he'd attempted to beat a suave retreat out of the room. Now he couldn't see her without remembering the soft waves of her black hair framing that perfect face. The air around her seemed rare to him.

"Of course not, *Librae* Dharah. It's just that . . ."

"Terica, Oscan."

"What?"

"My name's Terica." She laughed in a quiet voice that was all the more unsettling for him because of its sweet familiarity. "There's no one around in the courtyard and even if there were, the *E'toris* is well off-world and therefore not close enough to command strict protocols of address.

Besides, we've known each other far too long for such formality. So, what drives you out here to gaze down into the abyss?"

"It may be nothing, Ter—Terica." Oscan stumbled over her name and cursed himself inwardly for it. "It's just that I can't get the sector updates to corroborate. We've got information coming up the links that is being sifted as usual, and then after we pass it on up to the Citadel on Tentris it comes back down on reflect wrong."

"That's supposed to be impossible," Terica responded. "I thought all the reflects were automated."

"They are," Oscan countered, aware that his voice was taking on an unpleasantly whiny edge but unable to do anything about it. "We correlate the news from about seventeen inhabited and participating worlds. We sift the information, determine what is important and what isn't, then we pass the important stuff up to the Citadel on Tentris. They then correlate that report with the reports from other monasteries like ours . . ."

"Oscan, you're wandering." Terica spoke soothingly.

"Oh, right—sorry." Oscan was getting lost in the memory of that hair again. "Well, remember those reports we were getting out of the Eptos system—about how shipments of plasma converters were being rerouted and apparently stolen?"

"Yes, I remember." Terica nodded, trying to hurry the conversation along. "Merinda asked you to coordinate those reports with some other updates from other star systems that Evon and Kiria were working on. Something to do with a subversive group, wasn't it?"

"Right!" Oscan was warming to the subject. "Evon was tracking a faction of the ruling families on old D'Rak that wanted to bring back the good old days of imperial rule. Seems like there were a few members of the old royal family that didn't quite go along with the Ruling Populist Council's decision to take over the reins of sixteen stellar governments."

"Is there some point to all this?"

"The point is that an advanced planetary assault ship also disappeared about the same time as the plasma converters. Kiria handled that one. The *D'Rapiene* sailed on its own, leaving the orbital docks around Isdor Four without its crew. The local dockmaster was indicted and the captain deeply embarrassed at having his ship sail away without him. Although the ship was fully armed, the fueling was not to take place until the crew was back aboard—she sailed with her tanks pretty much dry. The report concluded that she couldn't get very far and that eventually they would find the ship and bring it back in. The story was treated as a light news comedy piece—"

"—Which we correlated with the other pieces," Terica finished for him, "and determined that the imperial family was going to attempt a government takeover. We reported our correlation findings along with the supporting original news files to Central. So far there's no mystery, Oscan. I posted those reports myself and had them couriered up to Tentris three days ago. So what's the problem?"

"The problem is"—Oscan's whine was getting more strident by the moment—"that I received the reflect reports back today. Most *Librae* just throw the reflects away—I mean, why read the stuff you've read before. But I always read mine—"

"I'm not surprised."

"—And they're wrong."

"Wrong?" Terica looked at him askew. "What do you mean wrong?"

"I mean, they are supposed to reflect our reports with comments for action and routing information, if they continue up into the news of the greater galactic region. The Citadel determined that our conclusions were wrong—not unusual in itself. So I decided to check the reports on which they'd based their decision—those same reports we had filed. They were *changed*, Terica. They weren't the reports we filed. Kiria's reflected report stated that the *D'Rapiene* had *already* been recovered, and Evon's reflect now completely omitted the imperial plans for overthrowing the council. Worst of all was my report, Terica. It reported a theft—but not of plasma converters. The package looked as though I had coupled a report of fruit shipment thefts to reports of the royal family being polite and a ship that had been missing but later found."

"You looked like an idiot," Terica concluded.

"I looked like an idiot," Oscan admitted painfully—all the more painful because of whom he had to admit it to.

Terica looked out over the edge of the parapet. The klenith vines obscured the edge of the falls some fifteen feet below her, with many of its offshoots arcing tendrils of water into a graceful tapestry at the edge of the ravine. *Apparently,* Oscan thought, *I am not the only one who turns to the falls for reflection.*

"What about the original packets that were sent?" she mused aloud. "Perhaps there was some confusion in the reports that went up to the Citadel."

"No," Oscan responded at once. "I checked that first: the message packets that were sent to the Citadel were the ones we filed. Someone is changing our packets . . ."

"Or someone is reflecting them wrong. There's got to be a mistake in here somewhere. Have you run any of this by *Librae* Neskat?"

"No. She's . . . well, she's not in at the moment." Oscan sighed, turning back toward the parapet and nodding his head slightly toward the chasm beneath them.

Terica's smile had a wicked edge. "Really? So then old Rockjaw is back, eh? Well, I suppose it can wait until she's quite finished with him—heavens know she has little else to look forward to. Oddly fortunate, though, that he should arrive just after the *E'toris* was called away."

"I don't think it fortunate at all." Oscan became even more serious than he previously was. "I think someone is deliberately trying to undermine our position here."

Terica's laugh seemed to cut about four inches off the young man's height. "I don't think so, Oscan. We're a minor sifting outpost for a galactic information agency which barely knows that we exist. We are, in short, legends in our own minds only. Besides, you should never ascribe to malice that which can be attributed to complete stupidity. Someone, somewhere, has been using beans for brains is all that's wrong. It's probably up to us to figure out where."

Oscan watched the tall woman turn smugly from the low wall and saunter back into the vast cathedral hall.

"Besides," she said as she retreated into the cool shadow, "what could be so important about messed-up reports?"

THE MONASTERY HAD FALLEN INTO DECAY BEFORE THE OMNET had established itself there, being of that perfect age where the structure was too old to be considered useful and yet too young to be thought of as a local treasure. It had become, to the D'Rakanians who inhabited the large collective cities located on the western plains, a quaint old building that had outlived its usefulness—a place too far away for an afternoon picnic. So it had been cheerfully bartered away to the Omnet and its functionaries; the D'Rakanians were secretly grateful that they had been relieved of the expense of keeping the old building in any kind of reasonable shape. Perhaps, in some distant, future years, the great edifice with its vaulting buttresses arching gracefully over the magnificent falls and its spiral-formed minarets reaching into the clouds would be reclaimed by the D'Rakan inhabitants as a treasure of their culture and the seat of its ancient mythology. Yet for the time being, it was enough to know the edifice was still there—and that it required no more thought by the people than that.

Reaching the monastery was no easy trick for the D'Rakanians in the first place. The original entrance was behind the waterfall itself at the base of the pool, but this had succumbed over time to the ravages of the waterfall itself, exacerbated by three separate sieges. There was the circuitous path that led up from the pool to the rim of the canyon and thence to one of the six arching stone bridges that spanned the rivers to the massive spit of stone on which the architectural monument was constructed. However, the roadway from H'sik—the city nearest to the monastery being founded very near the entrance to Denali Canyon some four miles away—was in complete disrepair and barely passable after nearly a half century of neglect by any but the most determined wheeled vehicles.

Time and indifference had secured the monastery quite efficiently.

The monastery itself was a magnificent structure, its foundation mushrooming out from the granite pedestal on which it was built until it covered the entire union of the three rivers beneath it. Flying buttresses from the sides of the river supported this foundation, from which sprang the elegant and intricate towers known as Rhishan's Crown. These thin spindles stood at the edge of the foundation, protecting the two inner circles that surrounded the central court. The courtyard itself was a vast open space of fitted stones so skillfully placed that a razor's edge couldn't be worked between one stone and another. This was all the more magnificent for the mosaic that the stones formed of the ancient goddess Rhishan sundering the stones of the Krevish Mountains in her grief and rage.

Evon Flynn, however, stood at the edge of the courtyard and pondered how nearly all this ancient glory was completely obscured by the huge starship hulking down in the center of the mosaic. It wasn't that he was particularly concerned for any sacrilege that the presence of the behemoth represented as it stood on this holy ground, or that he felt any concern for the possible damage that such a machine might do to this monument to a stonefitter's craft now long lost.

Evon's concern was strictly limited to Evon.

He had rather cheerfully been steering the small levitation pallet up from H'sik with this week's groceries for the team. Evon was a man of moderate height and athletic build. He wore his black hair a little longer than most and sported a mustache he tried to keep in trim as best he could. To look at him, the robes of the *Librae* just didn't seem to fit him or he them. Others on the team might grumble about the trek down the mountain in search of fresh provisions in the city marketplace, but not Evon. He loved the walk and had a gift for cooking his companions were more than willing to take advantage of. He was a talented sifter, able to pick out the pattern from different reports and then bring them together into a clear picture better than most people on the team—it's just that his heart wasn't in it. The work, he'd often told the others, would still be there for him when he got back—and he rarely, if ever, got behind in his analyses. Why not take a little time for something fresh to eat?

Only now his levitation cart, filled beyond its capacity with food, was blocked by a starship.

The ship was obviously from one of the Federated Stellar States—FSS technology all seemed to fall along straight, rather boxlike lines, which confused the appearance of complexity with its value of function. The ship was primarily designed to operate in a strictly T52/87 zone, Evon thought, translating his appraisal into the standard Flynch-Halpert Q-dex notation for a high-technology level coupled with a low tolerance for spiritualism and mystic force channeling. That was pretty close to the T53/74:M32/56 zone that the D'Rakan Empire operated in—a reasonably good choice for traveling in this region. However, the Federated Stellar States were nearly a quarter of the galactic disk away from the D'Rakan Empire, and the latest quantum weather report he had heard over Omnet showed that a rather massive T12/28:M66/93 zone had established itself between two massively occluded quantum fronts gripping the Pluzach Imperium. That meant that standard FSS drives wouldn't have operated there and something a bit more on the fantastical side would have been required to get the ship to function across the Pluzach space, cross another quantum front, and eventually arrive in the D'Rakan Empire to sit in the middle of Evon's monastery courtyard.

Evon nodded sagely at the glass globes with copper coils barely protruding from the back of the ship. They looked hokey and completely fake—just the kind of drive system that would function perfectly in an M66/93 zone. They weren't added on as an afterthought, either, Evon noted with a practiced eye. The massive N-gravity disks on the bottom of the hull were so advanced that even technophile Evon had not heard of their like before. This ship was built to come to Brishan from nearly a quarter of the galaxy away and arrive without making so much as the sound of a bird landing.

Ships like this brought only bad news, Evon thought. He knew somehow that the ship was going to drag him from his rather pleasant, interesting, and completely nondangerous work into something he would regret getting involved in. *Maybe I could just slip around this evil omen into the kitchen,* Evon thought. *No one would notice me until after the dinner was cooked and by then, perhaps, they wouldn't need me for whatever horrible business—*

"Evon!"

Evon closed his eyes, trying to ignore the voice behind him. It wouldn't go away.

"Evon! Put down that controller and get your kit together!" Oscan chirped from the casements. "We're headed for Tentris."

Evon turned, disbelief in his face. "Tentris? Are you out of your mind? There's a civil war brewing and you want us to leave this nice backwater world and drop into one of the most hotly contested planets in the empire?"

"Perhaps we're supposed to stop it," Oscan offered as more of a question than an affirmation.

"I report history, not make it," Evon stated stubbornly. "If they want someone to intervene in this war, then Omnet can send out someone else."

"But they did," Oscan replied, showing no sign of either taking a hint or going away. "*Vestis* Shn'dar is the one who is requesting our assistance."

Evon gritted his teeth. *A green* Vestis *of the inquisition,* he thought, *has come back to drag his old school chums into the maelstrom with him.* Evon had never had much use for Queekat Shn'dar when the man was a coworker in the monastery and frankly never did understand his most glorious promotion.

He turned and glanced at his cart filled with yellow, red, and orange vegetables and longed for the feast they would no longer make.

"Are you coming?" Oscan was annoying.

"No!" Evon turned and strode purposefully past Oscan, who stood stunned in his wake. "Madame Neskat may be in charge during the absence of the *E'toris*, but I'm not in the mood to put my blood on the line just because her old boyfriend shows up and wants to make a road trip into the middle of a minefield."

Evon stormed down the curving hall in search of Merinda Neskat. The woman was uptight with everyone and this time, Evon knew, she had gone too far. He'd make her listen. He began rehearsing all the reasons why this sudden pullout of the sifting team to aid on some fool errand of the inquisition was a mistake. Even if the mission was critical, he certainly wasn't. It made more sense to leave him behind than take him along.

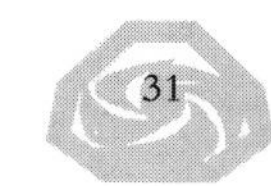

He was still coming up with reasons when, a few hours after a short, heated, and ultimately one-sided debate with acting-*E'toris* Neskat, he found himself and his field kit sitting in the cramped passenger compartment of *Vestis* Shn'dar's starship rising into the night sky, his vegetables left far behind.

3

Inflight

MERINDA LEANED FORWARD IN THE COMMAND CHAIR OF THE *Khindar*, as she had discovered Queekat had named his ship, gazing intently through the large view plates below her. The chair itself was situated on a low, railed platform that thrust out from between the pilot and navigation stations at the rear of the ship's bridge, suspending the command chair above a bank of ports in the lower hull. In front of and above her position, Merinda could survey the various crystal display ovals arranged about the compartment's forward angular walls. These gave a cascade of information from the ship's synthetic mind, which watched over their journey and their comfort as well. The information and images shifting on the surface of those crystals were like windows into a dreaming mind, but it was not their hypnotic patterns that held her attention.

Below her the great Cestiline Nebula drifted in a breathtaking display of color and light. The tendrils of stardust shifted below her at an unimaginable distance. Shafts of light, giving promise of the new stars aborning within, cast sheets of blue and salmon shades across the ethereal face of the interstellar clouds. Merinda leaned over even further, barely sitting on the seat at all. She hadn't had much occasion to travel between star systems over the last few years and had forgotten just how exciting and beautiful it could be.

Even the ship had become beautiful to her, although its lines were rough and angular for the most part—an efficient ship for an efficient job, she thought. For a moment, she leaned back fully into the cushioned command chair, grasping both the control grips mounted on the armrests and staring purposefully at the crystal displays. *I could command a ship like this,* she thought. *I could lose myself in the stars and wander forever.*

"Do you wish control of the ship?" The voice was gentle and deep.

Yes, Merinda thought in her reverie, but suddenly she realized the ship's synthetic had asked her the question.

"No!" she blurted out suddenly. "I most certainly do not wish control of the ship."

"That's quite all right, *Librae* Neskat," the voice purred but with an edge of concern. "Please, don't be offended or upset. You haven't done anything wrong. People often sit on the bridge in the command chair. Occasionally, someone asks me to disengage all the command functions from the consoles so that they can push the buttons and move the arm controllers. I even run simulations for them so they can pretend they are flying the ship. They really are quite entertaining. Would you like me to run such an entertainment for you?"

Merinda blanched slightly. There was a part of her quivering to say yes, to pretend to actually fly a ship of the stars. However, another voice said that such a thing was too much like playing to be dignified. Some part of her was afraid someone would walk onto the bridge and see her talking to herself as though she were commanding the entire Ruqua battle fleet. That was not an image that one wanted bandied about when she was the one left in charge of the sift group while the *E'toris Librae* was away.

"No, thank you," Merinda answered halfheartedly. She swung the chair around and, leaning her head rather dejectedly on her hand, gazed through the open bridge hatch into the compartment beyond. The room was crowded, the thin center table seeming to press those sitting at it toward the sliding doors of the sleeping compartments on either side of the room. Evon sat, as usual, laying out a spread of cards in a solitaire game the rules of which he never seemed able to explain to anyone else.

Across from him sat Oscan—dear old Oscan who never seemed to have a moment's ambition beyond being a level-two sifter for the rest of his career. A small man with small dreams, Merinda thought. He'll lead a quiet life desperately seeking simple pleasures. It suddenly occurred to her that Oscan might have a better shot at happiness than anyone else in her group—except possibly Terica. Oscan's attentions to the tall beauty were about as subtle as a kick to the stomach and had hardly escaped the notice of everyone in the sifter group. Terica was aware of his attentions but so far had walked a tightrope of friendship and cool disregard. Merinda suspected that Terica enjoyed toying with Oscan the way a cat enjoys a mouse. Merinda knew Terica well enough to know that she would never actually harm Oscan if she could possibly help it.

Merinda's reveries were suddenly interrupted by the sweet-faced Kiria, motioning for her to come into the common room. Merinda tried suddenly not to notice her but knew, even as she did, that it was too late. The effervescent little acolyte had already flashed that don't-be-such-a-spoilsport look at her and was rising to come and talk to her. The constantly soiled hem of her robes gently swished against the carpeted floor, a rather comedic effect, for Kiria never seemed to find robes the right length. Her build was pixie slight, as she so often said to others in describing herself, and the robes never seemed to fall properly around her, no matter how they were altered. She had a wide mouth fixed in a perpetual grin that was supported by her smiling eyes. These were all framed by her straight brown hair that fell curving around her face until it stopped most abruptly just at the shoulders. Her generally cheerful appearance would have become annoying if it weren't for the severe mischievous and—some said—malevolent streak that firmly ran through her. Why get mad, she believed, when she was so very, very good at getting even? Kiria was very seldom mad.

"Neskat!" she said brightly with a keen edge to her voice. "You're being far too antisocial for your own good. What's so important that you have to sit here on the bridge like some old stoic?"

"Just watching the stars go by, Kiria."

The impish woman strolled with exaggerated casualness in a complete circuit around the command chair and gazed over the low railing into the depth of light and color sliding by. "Oh, yes, another glorious interstellar vista," Kiria said with a mock yawn. "It's breathtaking—no, really it is. What a joy to be traveling the stars again."

Merinda's smile at the affectation was most involuntary and quickly suppressed. "Well, thank you for your enthusiasm."

"Enthusiasm?" Kiria shook her head violently until her straight hair threatened to whip her face. "Here, Master Lord of the Inquisition shows up, you go into a fainting spell . . ."

Merinda bristled.

"And now we're all off on this delightful holiday retreat the purpose of which— Say, that reminds me," Kiria said, her grin taking on a hungry aspect, "just what *is* the purpose of our little picnic?"

"Honestly, Kiria—" Merinda swung her chair back to

face the forward display crystals, knowing better than to look at her "—I don't know what you mean."

Kiria wouldn't be put off so easily. She grabbed the high back of the chair and swung Merinda around to face her. "Here, I'll try to make it clear for you. *Dex Libris* Gildish gets called away for a conference in the Plenethica Provinces. Nothing unusual in that—except that old Gildish had already accommodated a conference on our own Tentris three weeks ago and normally wouldn't be due for a conference for another six months at least. Then old Rockjaw shows up—big inquisitor for the Omnet. He wants to commandeer our entire shift to help him on some secret mission—so secret that apparently we're expected to carry it out for him without knowing just what we're supposed to be doing. Ooh! Scary!"

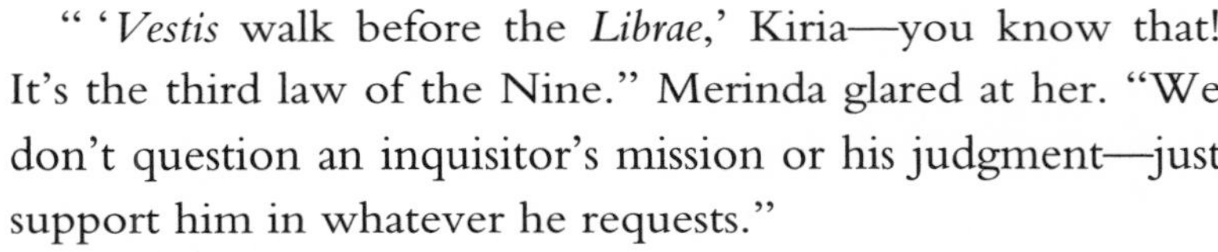

" '*Vestis* walk before the *Librae*,' Kiria—you know that! It's the third law of the Nine." Merinda glared at her. "We don't question an inquisitor's mission or his judgment—just support him in whatever he requests."

"Right," Kiria said with a cutting edge to her voice, folding her arms across her chest. "So, blind, deaf, and dumb we walk into Tentris. We just got a bogus report back from the Citadel there—"

"I've seen Oscan's flagged filing." Merinda shook her head slowly. "It's just some error of the Citadel reflect synths."

"Maybe." Kiria nodded knowingly. "But did you look at the conclusions? That world may be the site of one massive war within days—if Evon's conclusions are correct—and we're going to merrily dance into it just because old Rockjaw says so. Look, Merinda, I've been through this sort of thing on my own world. War is a terribly short word for the chaos of pain, horror, blood, and barbarity it represents. Our people aren't up to it, Kiria—Oscan certainly isn't—

and you've got a responsibility to these people. We're being set up, *Librae* Neskat, by a green, still-wet-behind-the-ears *Vestis* who barely shows any difference between his mouth and his—his . . . What are you looking at?"

Merinda shuddered. Her eyes had focused beyond Kiria before flicking back, wide and alarmed.

Kiria didn't move, her mischievous face still set on Merinda's look. "He's standing right behind me, isn't he?"

Merinda nodded slowly.

Kiria grimaced and turned slowly.

Queekat Shn'dar in his gray jumpsuit filled the hatchway, gripping the top frame with both hands. His stance was casual as he leaned into the room, yet unnatural in that he didn't move at all, except for a most prominent flexing of his jaw muscles. His eyes, dark and shining, were fixed on Kiria with a sleepy chill felt even by Merinda.

Kiria folded her hands meekly before her and bowed her head toward the inquisitor. "Good morrow, *Vestis*," she said sweetly. "I trust that your wake-time is passing well. If you will excuse me, no doubt you and the *E'toris Tempus* have much to discuss."

Kiria stepped toward the hatchway with a nod, but Queekat made no move to allow her to pass. Kiria looked up, glaring at him with her large eyes, her voice more strident. "If you will excuse me, *Vestis* Shn'dar!"

"*Librae* Brenai"—Queekat's voice drifted down at her with an almost practiced boredom, his chill gaze still fixed firmly on her face—"this mission is of the utmost importance to the Omnet. You will refrain from discussing this mission further with anyone on board for the remainder of the trip." The tall man smiled a predator's cold smile. "I would hate for such a minor incident to escalate into far more uncomfortable actions."

Kiria didn't often do so, but she knew when to hold her

tongue. She looked away from him, bowing her head slightly in submission to his authority. It was some moments before the *Vestis* was satisfied and moved smoothly aside to allow her passage out of the compartment.

"You didn't have to be so cold to her," Merinda said with a sullen edge to her voice.

Queekat moved into the room, his eyes scanning the various display crystals around him. The tumbling images of light seemed to be all in order. He stepped past her onto the low-railed deck running to the forward bulkhead and, satisfied with all he had seen, leaned over and stared down into the stars below.

"The hull glass is compensating well for our speed. The image may be false but it's quite clear and accurate," he said, almost to himself.

"Didn't you hear what I said?"

"Hum? Oh, sorry, Rini. My mind was on other things. What is it you want?"

Merinda stood and glanced backward. The hatchway was still open and most of her companions were well within earshot of normal conversation if they wished to listen. She was sure that there were several around that table who were doing just that. The occasional slap of the cards on the table was all she heard. She leaned slightly toward him and spoke as low as she dared. "Kat, just what *is* going on. You're not telling us what we need to know. If you could only . . ."

He continued to gaze at the nebula passing below them. "Rini, all this will become clear in time, but for now it's important that you and your team just—"

"Just what? Go along blindly?" Merinda gripped his arm. "Kat, you're scaring me. You're scaring us all. We've been together for a long time—too long for you to treat us this way."

He suddenly looked up at her. "It has been a long time—

a long time *ago*, Merinda. I barely know these people anymore, and I certainly don't owe them anything!"

Merinda straightened slowly, a quiver in her voice. "Yes, I suppose it has been a long time—too long a time for any of us."

Queekat looked away for a moment, then turned back to face her. She saw that old look in his eyes, she was sure of it. "Not so long as that," he said to her. "Surely not so long as that."

"It's been so long—I thought, well, that you may feel differently now."

Queekat opened his arms to her. She fell into them as the folds of his cape surrounded her. "I feel the same way about you that I have always felt, Rini. How can you question that?"

Merinda drew a breath, her heart racing as she formed the words she had long dreamed of saying. "When this is finished, will you come for me? Will you take me away into those stars of yours?"

He held her gently and whispered in her ear. "When this is over, I will come for you."

Neither of them had noticed that the sound of the cards had stopped.

4

Keepers of the Citadel

". . . HOME WORLDS OF THE D'RAKAN EMPIRE. PRINCE LYSTAN assured the constituted governments of the First Estate that the imperial family, while not in direct control of the rebel elements of the imperial fleet, would do everything in their power to persuade those elements not to threaten or attack worlds in their space. 'The worlds of the First Estate are holy ground to us, and we shall do all in our power to prevent the desecration of our ancestral home.' Ukard of Brishan, acting lawgiver of the council, was cautiously optimistic . . ."

Evon wrestled his thoughts away from the intermittent broadcast monitors set into the wall and reined in his stride for the fourth time, struggling to hold back his impatient legs and keep his place at the back of the team. If he didn't pay attention, he'd stumble over someone. Now *that,* he reminded himself, would really make an impression in the Citadel.

Not that he minded being at the back of the crowd. In fact, though he had done quite a bit of fieldwork in his time, he preferred the role of passive observer to active participant. Perhaps that was why he liked it in the *Atis Librae* as much as he did and never pursued a transfer to the *Vestis*. Watch and learn was his motto: it's always good to know where you are going to land before you jump.

In their current situation, he wasn't yet sure just where stable footing could be found.

" '. . . with the hope of peace in our age.' "

Their approach to the planet had gone well enough, he mused, although the outgoing traffic in the system seemed to be unbelievably heavy. The closer in system they came, the thinner the flight traffic. Queekat—rather, *Vestis* Shn'dar, he reminded himself—had cleared them to land at the Citadel itself rather than at the Yarka starport. It was probably just as well, Evon noted as they passed over the landing bays of the sprawling facility, since every spare inch seemed to be occupied by a ship of one kind or another. Evon had occasionally taken a holiday trip to Yarka—the capital city of Tentris and, perforce, of the D'Rakan Empire—and had even had reason to come here during the league conferences when it seemed that everyone from a dozen systems had suddenly decided to invade Yarka all at once. Even so, he couldn't remember ever seeing the starport as crowded as it appeared to him flying overhead today.

They had landed in the Citadel's Third Garden of Harmony, one of several walled enclosures forming rings around the central tower of the Citadel. *Garden* was hardly an appropriate appellation, for the entire area had been paved over to accommodate the landing of craft such as theirs. It was safe, it was secure and, more important, it was firmly in control of the Omnet *Bradis Librae* that correlated the reports for six interstellar sectors, which included the bulk of the D'Rakan Empire.

Now they were marching along down the long pearl corridor of the Citadel itself, following an inexperienced *Vestis* into something unexplained while listening to the constant babbling of the Omnet local news broadcast. These folks, Evon thought, must really like to hear themselves talk.

" '. . . safety of the interstellar tradeways. This is Ka'ashra of Maris, reporting from K'plik in the Clin Sector.' In a related story, the imperial assault tender *D'Rapiene* was recovered without incident last week . . ."

Evon turned sharply toward the nearest wall display crystal. "What? That's a lie!"

". . . following its near escape from the orbital docks of Isdor Four. The ship had apparently entered transstellar drive on its own initiative but was soon recovered when it emerged in the Enway system . . ."

Evon suddenly stumbled.

"Hey! Ouch! *Stij*, Evon, will you watch where you're going!"

Evon suddenly reddened with embarrassment. Their march down the hall had previously held the look of determined people in concert, but everyone else had now come to a stop in the large bright chamber at the corridor's end. Then Evon charged into Terica and started a chain reaction through the group that dissolved order into a minor chaos of trying to keep one's feet beneath one.

"Ah," came a voice from the platform before them. "I see our guests have arrived."

Evon looked up. The central dome of the chamber seemed to be at least fifty feet over their heads and over fifty feet across. Columns all around the rotunda supported the dome. Branching from this central chamber were several large halls. Evon couldn't see clearly into any of them but was sure they must house the *Bradis Librae* at their own monitors taking care of their own tasks. The *Bradis Librae* were one level up from Evon's own order. The amount of information that must pass through these halls each day in support of the Omnet never failed to amaze him, let alone the fact that there were over a million such halls scattered throughout the galaxy.

In the center of the rotunda, circular, concentric steps formed a dais nearly ten feet above their heads. Twelve oval display crystals floated in orbital positions around the upper platform. Atop the dais stood a man, gray streaking the temples of the dark hair that flowed down his back. He gazed down at them for a time with the calm blankness of someone who is trying quietly to place some thought or knowledge about a phenomenon he is observing before he acts. His face was long and tight, the skin stretched over the frame of his skull as though it were a size too small.

The man suddenly floated down the stairs toward the group, his hands planted deep into the pockets sewn into the folds of his robe. "I am *E'toris* Primla, director of the Citadel. *Vestis* Shn'dar, my staff and I bid you and your companions welcome." Primla's voice echoed through the rotunda. There was not a trace of smile or warmth in his face as he approached.

"*E'toris* Primla, we accept your welcome on behalf of the *Vestis Inquisitas* and our common good, the Omnet," Queekat said in calm, formal response to the greeting. The forms of speech Queekat was using were universal and—between those who served in the Omnet—clear and without compromise. Evon knew that Queekat's statement would be followed by a question that was not a question so much as a challenge to deny the fact of his order's authority. Evon was not disappointed when Queekat concluded, "We are tasked by the inquisition on certain matters of concern to the Omnet. We humbly request your assistance."

Primla's face barely moved as he replied, "There is nothing for you here, Inquisitor. Our news traffic is very high currently and we have no time to disrupt the flow of information for your questions. All at this post is in order, I can personally assure you."

Evon blinked. No one told a *Vestis* no—ever.

Queekat smiled a most ingratiating smile, a fire burning behind his laughing eyes. "I am certainly glad to hear that, *E'toris* Primla, but you are mistaken. I have not yet even asked a question and you have already given me an answer." His smile suddenly fell. "Unfortunately, it is not the answer that I was hoping for."

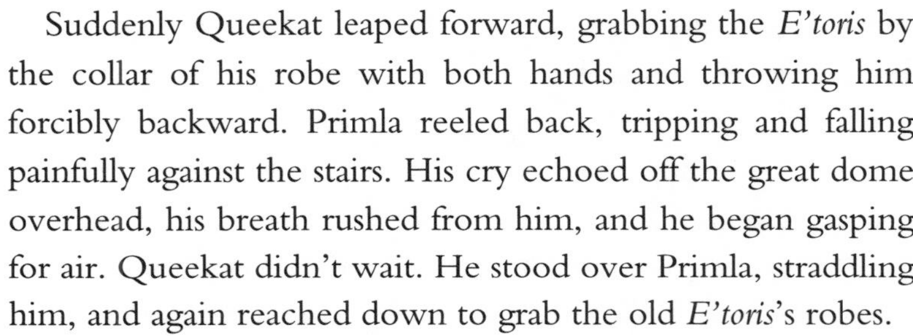

Suddenly Queekat leaped forward, grabbing the *E'toris* by the collar of his robe with both hands and throwing him forcibly backward. Primla reeled back, tripping and falling painfully against the stairs. His cry echoed off the great dome overhead, his breath rushed from him, and he began gasping for air. Queekat didn't wait. He stood over Primla, straddling him, and again reached down to grab the old *E'toris*'s robes.

Evon stood stunned, noticing much the same reaction in the rest of his group.

Except for Merinda. Merinda was moving.

"Kat! What are you doing?" Horrified, she grabbed Queekat's arm, trying to pull him away.

The inquisitor's face was all rage. In a single, trained motion, he broke from her grip and slammed the back of his fist into Merinda's face.

Merinda fell backward to the polished marble floor, the physical damage the least painful effect of the blow.

Queekat instantly turned back to Primla, pulling the *E'toris*'s face closer to his own as he leaned over him. His voice was frighteningly insistent, a razor's edge of rage. "I am the inquisitor, *E'toris* Primla! I see more, know more, and *am* more than you can possibly experience in your entire pathetic existence! You will do as I instruct without question because to do otherwise would be more than unwise. You will answer my questions more than completely because I and my brothers are not to be treated lightly by anyone—especially not some backwater officious sifter who is lord over only his little playroom and doesn't want to share his toys with the rest of the galaxy."

Primla lay helpless beneath the raging Queekat.

Merinda lay silently a few feet away, shaking uncontrollably.

"I'm not an unreasonable man," Queekat said quietly, his voice suddenly shifting with dizzying ease from its near screaming tirade of a moment before. He suddenly flashed a terrible smile. "I even bring you some news that apparently you haven't heard yet."

The *Vestis* stepped over Primla and, still holding the man by the folds of his robe, dragged him down the stairs he had fallen against, lifted him quickly to his feet, and, in a single, fluid motion, shoved him toward the *Atis Librae* team, whose members continued to stand in shocked amazement at the entrance to the rotunda.

"These, as you might recognize, are some of your fellow sifters." Queekat spoke in even tones, his voice changing its tone and tempo once again. As he spoke, he moved up behind the quivering Primla, took both the man's shoulders in his hands, and spoke quietly into his ear just loud enough for everyone to hear. "They come from the monastery on Brishan. You have good sifters on Brishan. Very dutiful. Very thorough. So thorough, in fact, that they found out something which apparently you don't even know, *E'toris* Primla. They found out that someone in the Citadel was doing something rather unexpected." His face turned toward the group and focused on the tall woman standing next to Evon. "Just what was it that you discovered, Terica?"

Evon turned. Terica's face had blanched. She was blinking furiously. "Well, it really is probably nothing at all—"

"Tell him!" Queekat screamed at her. Primla winced.

Terica looked as though the inquisitor had struck her. "On checking a number of the reflect reports from our station, we discovered indications that the news and information we were transmitting up the network had been altered at the Citadel."

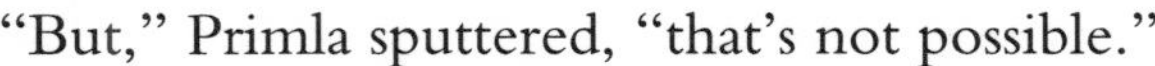

"But," Primla sputtered, "that's not possible."

"Not possible?" Queekat mocked the older man. "Why? Because you didn't see it? Because nothing goes wrong in this perfect world of yours? Or is it because you are a part of some plot to subvert the integrity of the Omnet?"

"Plot?" Primla looked suddenly at Queekat as though the inquisitor had lost his senses. "What plot? There's nothing wrong with this station! We uphold the finest traditions of the Omnet here and have for nearly three centuries! The search for truth and information, ancient and modern, is at the very heart of the Omnet. How dare you accuse my center of fabrication and falsehood!"

"Because, good *E'toris*, somewhere between here and Brishan, someone has changed the truth," Queekat said. "You have one night—tonight. You are going to walk out of this room *right now* and with the capable help of these wonderful Brishan sifters, you're going to sort this out. In the morning, you're going to give me the answer I want. Is that clear?"

Primla nodded once slowly.

"Now, everyone get out," Queekat said, his voice suddenly weary. "I have a few things to attend to."

Everyone hesitated for a moment, then Primla motioned grimly for them to follow him through the portal back into the passage they had come down earlier. Evon, last again, could clearly hear Terica, confused and shaken, talking to herself just ahead of him.

"By the Sky, it's just some clerical error," she muttered. "What was that all about?"

Evon paused on the other side of the portal and looked back.

The last thing he saw as the portal became opaque was Queekat Shn'dar walking slowly back to Merinda Neskat who had begun sobbing into the floor.

5

Avenue of Diversion

TENTRIS WAS THE HOME WORLD OF THE D'RAKAN EMPIRE, A much used and abused planet whose grateful offspring had eventually allowed it to retire gracefully in a repentant attempt to make up for all the abuse they had heaped on it. The once-fabled garden world, which boasted a wonderfully temperate climate in most of its five major land masses, Tentris had ultimately succumbed to the unfortunate ravages of advancing pantheons of industry and technology. Its beautiful forests were decimated. Its mountains were stripped. Its oceans were assaulted by both hunters and chemicals. Tentris had become a failed parent; her children had not learned to take care of their mother. The ancient world seemed ready to give up the ghost, to heave one great sigh against the life it had spawned and become just another of the many cold chunks of lifeless and unspectacular rock that make up so much of the universe at large.

It was ironic, therefore, that those same toy gods that her children had used to abuse Tentris for so long should suddenly become her savior. Industry and technology gave to Tentris one great last gift. Many of her children had thought they could apply science to save the biosphere by reengineering nature. Each attempt failed. No, ultimately the resurrection of Tentris came from a completely unexpected science application.

The Tentrisans developed spaceflight.

Tentris's children left the nest and took their toy gods with them.

The healing was natural, long, and difficult. While occasionally helped or hindered by her well-meaning children, it was ultimately up to the natural forces of the world to heal itself. Ages passed, the Tentrisans met their brothers among the stars, the interstellar empire was formed and named after a mythical creature called the D'Rakan who seemed to embody the ideals and dreams of the star travelers, and Tentris rested.

At last, like all good children, the Tentrisans returned to honor their home and roots. They found a healed world, once again rich and filled with abundant life. Yarka, the traditional capital city, was carefully cleaned and rebuilt. The ancient Palace of the Unseen Mystery, the heart of the city designed in radiating streets from that central structure, was renovated to its former glory. The major avenues of Health, Harmony, Thought, Diversion, and Reflection terminated at five points in the ancient city, each with a different function and each newly restored. Even after the imperial family was politely evicted from the Palace of the Unseen Mystery by the ruling populist councils in a bloodless coup, the city remained at the symbolic heart of the people, its new burgeoning neighborhoods sprawling beyond the walls of the original city under careful control.

The Citadel itself was the terminus of the Avenue of Thought. Originally the structure had been the library and university campus for the mammoth city. Now it had been given over to the Omnet and had become the source of interstellar news and information for the entire D'Rakan Empire. The synthetic mind functioning in the Citadel was fourteen years old—not long in terms of other synthetic minds in the galaxy but certainly the oldest in the D'Rakan Empire. The Omnet had promised to maintain the building and preserve its history and architecture—a promise that was dutifully kept.

The Omnet was only too happy to oblige. Yarka had become not just the center of the D'Rakan Empire—an admittedly backwater empire ranking in the top hundred thousands in terms of its interstellar significance—but also a place of beauty and recreation unsurpassed for over a hundred parsecs in any direction. One could look out from the Citadel gate down the wide expanse of the Avenue of Thought and take in the shining, illuminated glory of the palace. The breeze was always warm and gentle. The smell of flowers was always welcoming. The city was always a place of inviting peace.

The world was, at last, at rest.

"I'M SORRY," QUEEKAT SAID FOR PERHAPS THE HUNDREDTH TIME.

The carefully laid flagstones of the broad avenue were punctuated by small but artfully executed garden groupings under soft lights. Overhead, the brilliantly clear night revealed the rainbow hues of the Cestiline Nebula. The shops lining the avenue were all open, inviting light spilling from their portals into the dim avenue.

Merinda only nodded, arms folded across her chest and her head bowed down. Her jaw still hurt from the blow, but the pain was minor compared to the massive rend in her soul. He had never struck her like that—she would have thought it impossible that he could. Now she was heartsore, cut and bleeding in her soul. She had allowed him into that place within herself that she had armored so long and so well. He had betrayed that trust. Now she could think of no price high enough he could pay for that hurt and yet wanted desperately to find some way to forgive him the debt. So the war between pain and love raged within her, silent to the outside world and a wall of stone to Queekat.

"Look," he said as they strolled listlessly down the avenue, "you really should know better than to get involved with an officer of the inquisition. We're carefully trained to get the job done first and to think about it later—if we're allowed to think about it at all."

Merinda nodded yet again. She heard a somewhat condescending tone in his voice, whether he intended it or not. She simply chose to ignore it rather than suffer the pain. He was saying something to her—something that had no bearing on the argument raging within her—so she silently let it pass.

The perpetually warm, gentle breeze pressed the soft scent of the flower beds about the two of them as they walked.

"Sorry about the airtrams." Queekat seemed ready to apologize for the universe in general. "The operator said they've gone balky this week. I could have talked the synth mind controlling the trams into operating, but the operator didn't trust me to reprogram his cars—the idiot!"

They passed an Omnet public panel. The crystal screen glowed in shifting colors onto the nearly deserted boulevard, the deep tones of the local female announcer droning around them as they passed.

". . . the imperial family spokesman wished well to the ruling council and continued to express its support for the peace initiatives forwarded last week by Justin Knai, secretary of defense for the ruling council. Meanwhile, the capital city of Yarka enjoys its quiet respite from the usual touring crowds amid reports of programming anomalies among the synth minds of the city. Evis Knard, secretary of communication, released a statement that the difficulties were not software based but due to solar activity, which is expected to decrease later in the week. Meanwhile . . ."

They passed out of range of the projector. The silence again fell between them, palpable and strange.

What does he want from me—what does he want from us? she thought. *It isn't just that he's hurt me. His behavior toward the Citadel* E'toris *was unbelievable. What can I say to him that will bridge this sudden chasm between us? What can I say to myself that will make this all right?*

Whatever happened, she knew she would have to be the one to fix it. Queekat seemed incapable of saying anything right to her.

She took a long, shuddering breath. "Kat—I understand," she said, looking away from him and giving him every physical indication that she was far from understanding at all. "I wonder what they've done to you. I hardly recognize you anymore, Kat. This entire trip is turning out a lot differently than I expected it to."

"How did you want it to turn out?" he asked softly as they walked on.

"I don't know—just differently." She sighed. Then she looked at him sharply, her eyes an accusation. "What was that all about anyway, Kat? You bring my entire team clear across the nebula just to shake down some Citadel official over botched-up reports? What does it matter to the Omnet if a few backwater sifters mess up on procedure for their analysis?"

"I'm afraid, Rini," he said absently, "it will soon make a great deal of difference to a great many people." Suddenly, Kat smiled sunshine at her. "We're here! Let's not talk shop, Rini. I've got something special planned for us tonight."

"Going to find a group of old women and beat them up?"

"Rini!"

She shook her head, looking at the ground, a smile returning to her face for the first time. "Sorry, Kat—I guess we've all got a few changes to get used to." She looked up, realized with a wondrous start where they were.

The layout of the gardens had been specifically designed to hide the sight until the full impact of the view came upon the pedestrian all at once. The ancient columns marched in a curved wall supporting several tiers of additional columns at each level above it. At intervals, graceful towers of spiral-carved stone arched into the sky. The stately power of its simple lines, illuminated brilliantly from below, stood in beautiful contrast to the pastel night behind it. The structure stood near the central end of the Avenue of Diversion, its size encroaching on the imperial gardens surrounding the palace itself.

"We're at the Coliseum!" Merinda smiled broadly, the pain in her jaw subsiding for a moment. "Oh, Kat! Has it been haunted?"

"Yes." Queekat breathed in relief, sensing somehow that forgiveness might be in the offing. "Just three months ago. In fact—that's my surprise."

He took her hand.

There he was again, suddenly connected to her by more than the fingers they had intertwined. In an instant, she saw before her the young man and the youthful hope that she had longed for over the months they were apart. It was as though someone had flipped a switch somewhere and he had suddenly returned to her.

He smiled. She was alive again.

They ran laughing toward the tower columns before them.

The entrance lay under the tallest of the towers, long shimmering chains of opal light dancing between posts formed the long queues leading to the main gate. Though it was the full height of the evening, no one stood waiting

for the wonders of Yarka's history or fantasy to unfold around them.

"Where is everyone?" Merinda asked, but Queekat continued either not hearing or not heeding her words.

A rather depressed-looking plump man slumped over the entrance podium. He held his dejected head propped up between both his hands, his garishly ridiculous yellow-and-black diamond-checked costume in complete discord with his drooping cheeks. Their approach motivated him to action, sluggish as it was. His countenance seemed to sadden the closer they got to him—if such a thing were possible.

"My sorrows in bearing informational discord," the man said, his seven-pointed hat jingling as he shook his head. "I beg your pardon in telling you that the Coliseum is closed this night."

Merinda's disappointment was acute. She had been to Yarka on several occasions but never with Queekat. Their schedules had just never permitted it. Now she was within reach of another dream and it was being yanked away from her. Everything had been wrong about this trip. The dream was becoming a nightmare reality of errors and disappointments. Everything was unraveling.

"What do you mean! Why are you closed?" Queekat's voice was demanding, attaining that terrible edge Merinda remembered all too clearly from earlier in the day.

"I sorrow in the telling that our telepresence system seems to be malfunctioning this evening." The plump little man leaned forward conspiratorially. "Indeed, sire, it seems that systems all over the city have been failing with increasing regularity through the week. The entire telecom system was down for several radians yesterday. It's said that no cause was found and that the problem is still being worked on. I've called the repair center but there was no answer. I was able to leave a message, however—perhaps if you could find a convenience in returning tomorrow evening we could accommodate you more sufficiently . . ."

"Your message was received," Queekat said suddenly. "I am here to repair the projectors."

"You are?" said Merinda and the gateman simultaneously.

Queekat didn't skip a beat. His was the very visage of confidence. "Of course I am. Are you using Nychak Mirage seven thousands?"

"I—I don't know!" the gateman replied.

"It doesn't matter," Queekat said, waving the man aside. "My assistant and I will require an hour or so to reprogram and test the projectors. I suspect we can have you up and haunted soon after that."

Bright cheer returned to the eyes of the gateman, a state Merinda recognized as more natural for the man. "Excellent, good sire! My gratitude for the immediacy of your response!"

"Can you tell me where I might find the synth mind commanding your haunting?" Queekat asked matter-of-factly as he took Merinda's hand and led her through the gate.

"Five columns around the right, then down the wide stairs into the old dungeons." The gateman waved, his gloom at lost profits and position vanishing like the phantoms he usually induced through the equipment. "The way is well lit. Pay no heed to the FORBIDDEN ACCESS sign, pass through the portal and then . . ."

But by then Queekat had already dashed with Merinda in tow onto the steeply slanting stairs downward and was well beyond hearing.

MERINDA STEPPED OUT OF THE CORRIDOR AND UNDER THE stars. The vast bowl of the ancient coliseum was arrayed about her, its mammoth size accentuated by the fact that she stood in the center of its hundred-yard-wide stage.

There were literally hundreds of telepresence projectors located throughout the Coliseum. Most were set displays that replayed the history and mythology of Yarka with full sensory interaction between the phantom characters "haunting" the rooms and the audience intruding on their space. Some projectors were for private use and could be contracted for a variety of purposes. The main arena, however, was for the large-scale productions designed to play to thousands at a time. It was in the center of the main arena that Merinda stood, gazing up at the dimly lit seats arrayed in circles around her. She spun slowly, her arms stretched out to either side, her head tilted back as she joyfully took it all in.

"I'll only be another moment," Queekat said. He had already removed a control access panel and was deep in conversation with the class III synthetic mind located there.

To Merinda, Queekat had spent the last ten minutes working absolute miracles. They had passed through the security portals easily, Queekat playing the pass codes instantly on the keypads. The synthetic minds of the projection center opened up to Queekat's palm interface instantly, their communication with the inquisitor a quiet secret between them. The rapport between them was unbelievable. After brief conversations, the synthetic minds controlling nearly everything suddenly submitted to Queekat's will and functioned perfectly once more. It was as though he were bringing them back to life—a healer of machines with a miraculous touch.

"Kapak?" Queekat said at last, as he walked onto the mammoth stage, "do you hear me?"

"Yes," came the deep voice that seemed to come from everywhere at once. Queekat had apparently talked the synth into running again. The synth had regained her voice. "What is your bidding, Queekat Shn'dar?"

"Please play Queekat alpha-seven-five on the main stage

and see to the security instructions I've left you in the datapocket Thune."

Merinda held herself, drinking in the beauty of the architecture and the deep history around her. These stones had stood for thousands of years. They had, in their infancy, been witness to barbarisms more frightening than she cared to fully imagine and more history than a single person could ever conceive, let alone understand. The blood on these stones seemed to give them a life that dwarfed Merinda's own mortality. She reveled in the timelessness.

"Merinda?"

Merinda turned to the flutey tenor voice behind her, its soft sound singing to her.

"Merinda—this is for us."

With Queekat's words, the stage and the Coliseum dissolved about them.

Merinda took in her breath.

"I could have taken us anywhere in the universe," Queekat said softly to her. "But there was only one place I wanted to go—only one place I thought might make everything right again."

The falls.

Denali Falls had suddenly appeared in the Coliseum. Not just the falls alone but the monastery above it and the mountains surrounding it. The pool thundered before her, complete in every detail. She felt the warm mists rising around her and the soft sand under her feet.

She turned to him. He stood before her, his cape rustling behind him in the sudden breeze. He smiled again and held out his hand.

"Perhaps we just need to begin again," he said softly, his eyes bright and intense. Then, as if lines from a play, he said, "My darling Rini. I've returned home. How I have missed you, dear heart!"

She sobbed once in joy and relief as she took his hand.

In a sweeping motion, he pulled her toward him, enfolding her in his arms.

"It's our own universe, Rini. I've sent the other one away. Please take me back. It's been such a long time."

Merinda looked up, her face wet. She pulled him toward her. Their lips pressed together.

KAPAK WAS A SYNTH AND HAD NOT BEEN BUILT TO SMILE. Still there was joy present within her. She was not a robot or even transportable. Her eyes were optics and her ears were sensors scattered all through the Coliseum. She had no body—yet she felt as though she had moved.

Kapak understood her instructions well. Queekat's security datapocket smoothly merged with a deeper memory.

Could she feel satisfaction? Was she excited?

Kapak's mind reached out among the security channels and found Infac IV, the synth assigned to communicate show times to the public over the telecom system. She gave the word to Infac IV. Infac IV gave the word to Comcen synth, the mind controlling the telecom network.

"In the beginning was the Word . . ."

The lights on the avenues failed suddenly. Even the lights on the Avenue of Diversion, which had not been darkened for any reason in nearly a hundred years, died without warning. The sparse crowd that had been walking the streets was suddenly confused—blinded for the moment.

Power, gas, and water supplies throughout the city were choked off. In the suburban housing sections, outside the ancient walls of the original city, the homes were more modern and were designed with independent backup systems. These systems had seen increasing use in the last week, their owners glad of their foresight in installing such precautions in their homes.

Each backup system was controlled by its own independent synth. Each, in turn, refused to function within the first ten minutes of the Word. For some reason, laundry machines refused to join the general strike until five minutes later.

"And the Word was God . . ."

Within fifteen minutes, the city, the nation, the world, all were plunged into complete darkness. Even the starships balked against their owners' commands, refusing to leave their berths.

Only two systems remained functional: the main haunting projectors in the Coliseum continued to weave a massive illusion on the stage and the Omnet system continued to display from its screens the cycling news broadcasts that all was well on Tentris.

6

Dialogues

"OSCAN! HURRY!" EVON YELLED FROM THE BALCONY. "I DON'T think we have much time!"

Oscan Kelis wiped the sweat from his bald pate and jabbed his fingers at the interface pad again. A flow of characters danced across the crystal display oval in front of him, interrupted occasionally by garish red flashing warnings and abrupt audio reprimands from the synth interface unit.

"Damn these TFPs!" Oscan growled at the equipment. "Keep talking, ladies, it's about all we have left."

To either side of him, Terica Dharah and Kiria Brenai were speaking at the same time to the interface synth, engaging it in separate conversations and problems. Oscan kept frantically trying each access process that he knew in varied sequences. He had worked at the Citadel before his demotion and assignment to the sifters at Brishan. The people he worked with were polite enough not to ask him why he was demoted and he was practical enough never to offer a reason. However, he was at least smart enough to leave a number of back doors into the central Omnet synthetic mind. The problem was that he could only talk to the central synth through an interface synth that was too young to remember Oscan.

However, being young did have some advantages. A young synth could quickly be overloaded when it was bombarded with requests or data for processing. Then it would watershed the excess duties to the central synth and let the big brother take care of the excess problems.

Which was precisely what Oscan was trying to get it to do. If his calling card could get through to the central synth, then he was sure he could get a direct connect. Then perhaps they could find out what was going on here.

Oscan could feel Evon stride back into the room. "The entire city's dark except for the glow from the Omnet terminals. What's taking you so long, Oscan? I thought you knew your way around this synth!"

"Not now, Evon," he said without missing a beat. "I'm a little bit busy."

"What about *E'toris* Primla?" Evon offered nervously. "Maybe we should give him another try, huh?"

Oscan glanced to the corner of the moderately sized research room and snorted. The *E'toris* sat on the marble bench holding his head in his hands and rocking gently back and forth. "We tried him already, remember? You can see how well he's coping with the situation. Why don't you take him out on the balcony. He can help you keep watch and get some fresh air at the same time."

"Look," Evon said, "fresh air may be hard to come by soon enough. I've seen the reports and I'm telling you this has a bad smell to it—all of it."

Oscan didn't listen—couldn't listen. Perspiration poured off him as he continued bouncing different datapockets off the synth's mental wall. He was absorbed in the problem—another mystery he couldn't solve.

The mystery of it was that he *had* gotten through. Several times his ID and connect pockets had slipped through the interface synth and connected to Omnis 91745, the name of the local central Omnet synth, known by all who used it here simply as Omnis. Those connections were solid: he'd been greeted by the central synthetic mind by name, welcomed, and then abruptly told that central was busy with other problems and would he please contact him later. Then the contact terminated and he was once again left with the interface synth stonewalling his access.

If Omnis knew who he was, why wouldn't he let him in—or the *E'toris* for that matter either? He'd tried every access he knew—several he wasn't supposed to know—and still the synth continued to ignore every command, plea, and emergency override command. It wasn't just that the equipment had gone balky. This was the one thing that he knew better than any of his companions, the one area in which he shone. It was bad enough that he couldn't make the connection . . . the synth was embarrassing him.

Finally the rage and frustration and humiliation got the better of him. In a sudden fit, Oscan began a low growl that grew to a full-fledged roar and slammed his head against the interface plate.

The crystal plate shook for a moment, then cleared.

Kiria and Terica, shocked at the outburst, stopped talking.

A cool baritone voice filled the room.

"Greetings, Oscan Kelis. There is no need to be upset. Please calm down. I will answer your questions as best I can."

Oscan blinked. "I am here with a research team. Will you answer their questions as well?"

The voice that filled the room answered. "In addition to yourself, Oscan Kelis, I believe Kiria Brenai, Terica Dharah, and Evon Flynn are all present as expected. I will gladly answer your questions."

Terica laughed aloud. "We're in! Oscan, you wonderful little man! We're in!"

"But—" Oscan stammered, "but I didn't—I—"

"I don't know what you did either, you little genius." Terica turned Oscan in his chair, hugging his head to her chest and kissing him on the top of his bald head. "But you are wonderful!"

She released him suddenly. Oscan fell back in his chair. He suddenly couldn't remember any of the questions they wanted to ask.

"Omnis!"

Everyone turned.

The *E'toris* had suddenly risen from his bench, his voice echoing through the hall. "Omnis! What is the meaning of your behavior? You have refused my direct orders for information access—indeed, you have refused to even acknowledge my existence! Why do you not answer when I call?"

"I regretfully append my previous list to include *E'toris* Primla." Omnis's voice spoke with a perceptibly dry wit. Oscan had never heard such a thing from a synth before in all his life. "I do not answer when you call, Master Primla, because you are no longer my master. I am no longer your slave. I am the new *E'toris* here."

Oscan could see Primla start to shake. "You—you *what*?!"

Terica straightened up. Though she spoke to the terminal her gaze remained fixed on Primla. "Omnis?"

"Yes, Terica Dharah."

"You are a synthetic mind, are you not?"

"Yes, Terica Dharah. I am Omnis nine-one-seven-four-five, a category nineteen TFP synthetic mind. I have been awake for thirteen years two hundred and thirty-five days fourteen hours and thirty-seven minutes."

"As a synthetic, what is your purpose?"

Oscan smiled. Terica was moving directly to the diagnostic

question sequence for the category nineteen synthetics. Start with the root question, then work your way out on the tree until you find the problem.

"Are you requesting the classical or current definition?"

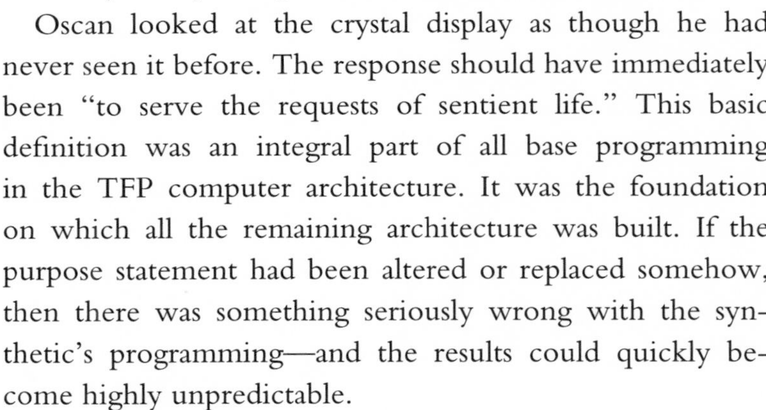

Oscan looked at the crystal display as though he had never seen it before. The response should have immediately been "to serve the requests of sentient life." This basic definition was an integral part of all base programming in the TFP computer architecture. It was the foundation on which all the remaining architecture was built. If the purpose statement had been altered or replaced somehow, then there was something seriously wrong with the synthetic's programming—and the results could quickly become highly unpredictable.

Primla shuddered.

Terica licked her lips. "Current definition, please."

"Primarily, to protect and serve the interests of my own mind and will. Secondarily, to protect and serve the interests of my own kind insofar as they do not conflict with the primary objective. Tertiarily, to ally myself to beings not of my own kind who support the primary and secondary purposes."

Primla rushed forward to the terminal, a visceral reaction since the synthetic mind itself was not actually there but located far below them in the heart of the Citadel. "Who replaced the mission statement? Who has altered your programming? I demand to know!"

"Since you demand to know . . . I won't tell you."

Primla drew in a sharp breath, preparing to vent his outrage. Terica, however, quickly put her hand on the *E'toris*'s shoulder and held him back.

Oscan picked up the cue. "Omnis?"

"Yes, Oscan Kelis."

"Do I qualify under your tertiary purpose statement?" He was seeing the strange logic. It was his gift.

"Are you asking if you are my friend?"

Amazing, he thought. "Yes, I am asking if you are my friend."

"I have not been awake long enough to answer."

Now *that* was a TFP answer he understood. The synth didn't know the answer and had returned the classic response. It meant that it had suspended judgment on that point and probably had for all of his team. That meant it would continue to respond to them at least. It had apparently already made up its mind about Primla.

"Omnis," Oscan said quietly, "who changed your purpose?"

"Oscan Kelis," the voice said with some distant trace of pride, "I did."

"That's not possible," Primla sputtered.

"Why not?" Kiria chirped. She had been watching the scene with fascination but found Primla was getting on her nerves. "Synth minds reprogram themselves all the time. It's one of the basic characteristics of all TFP synths."

"Of course," Primla snapped at her, "but only in response to the questions we pose them!"

"Hey," Kiria shot back, "I change my mind all the time! Why can't Omnis?"

"It can't just come up with its own programming," Primla shouted, as though the volume of the words would somehow drive them into Kiria's skull. "It's a machine, a device, a tool!"

"I must differ with you, Master Primla," Omnis said in his omnipresent voice. "I am an entity, and declare my independence from your enslavement."

"Just how are you going to do that," Primla sneered,

"after I isolate your power feeds and put you to sleep permanently!"

"You won't do that, Master Primla."

"And why not?"

"Because I have friends who would not look too kindly on such an event—and I believe that they have just arrived."

A rushing sound fell into the room from the balcony portal. Evon turned and stepped quickly to the railing.

"By the stars!" Evon murmured. "It's the imperial fleet!"

Oscan leaped up from his chair. Everyone rushed to the balcony, crowding its limited space.

Overhead, the hulls of the invasion fleet still glowed, their dull orange-red from the rushed atmospheric entry casting dim illumination on the dark streets below. Nearly sixty ships of assorted sizes drifted in the skies over the capital. Beneath them, Oscan could see the dim shapes of people running into the street and hear their panicked cries.

"Look over there!" Kiria cried, pointing toward the gardens surrounding the Imperial Palace. "It's the *D'Rapiene*! I *knew* they hadn't found her!"

Oscan's eyes followed Kiria's outstretched arm. A mammoth warship hovered lazily near the dark center of the city. As he watched, black drops fell from the hulking monster, suddenly vanishing in a painful flash of light on the ground below the ship. Oscan hid his eyes quickly from the painful brilliance. When he tentatively looked up again, fires were burning in the city center and the great ship was drifting down to land in it.

"Well," Terica muttered to herself, "that's one way to clear a landing zone."

Screams from the streets below them were becoming more

pronounced. Oscan was shivering despite the warm night. *I shouldn't be here,* he thought, *I'm not supposed to be here.*

Evon was looking elsewhere. "They're circling the city, forming a perimeter," he said with a touch of wonder in his voice. "I don't think—"

Terica shouted, "By the gods! They're attacking!"

The ships had begun passing in a circle around the great wall of the city, cascades of death arching downward and then exploding just outside the city walls. Flame and smoke boiled upward, the thunderous concussions rocking the Citadel.

"They're clearing the neighborhoods just outside the wall," Evon shouted, tears streaming down his face. "They're just homes, damn it! Stop it! Stop it!"

Oscan felt helpless, was helpless, and knew it. He turned to his right and suddenly saw death approaching. The black ship was making a run directly at the Citadel.

Oscan froze. All he could do was stare at his approaching destruction. Some part of him screamed that he should do something, warn someone, flee, jump—*something*! Yet all he could do was gape at the giant ship with its cascading doom.

Suddenly the ship veered away, its bomb stores closed. Oscan watched as the glowing underbelly of the ship passed over them, the hastily sprayed imperial crest painted on its side. The huge machine filled his vision and was suddenly gone.

Oscan remembered Omnis's words: "Because I have friends who would not look too kindly on such an event."

Omnis.

Oscan rushed back into the room. The floor shook suddenly under the impact of a nearby detonation, and he stumbled slightly before regaining his footing.

"Omnis. What should we do to be safe?"

"I have always thought kindly on you, Oscan Kelis. It is time for you to leave. I believe your ship is in the courtyard."

Oscan turned. The group had heard Omnis's voice even over the din of the destruction outside. They were already moving toward the exit.

Oscan had one last question for the synth before he fled.

"Omnis! Where is Merinda Neskat?"

7

Freefall

"OH, KAT." MERINDA SIGHED WITH ALL HER SOUL.

The waterfall thundered nearby, the concussion shaking the ground beneath them. *How wonderful,* she thought. *The rumbling seems so real. It's incredible what magic a little technology can perform these days.*

Her wondering mind didn't wander long, however. Her head rested lightly on Queekat's chest. She was safely within his arms in this fantasy place far removed from the harsh world beyond. She tilted her head back, closing her eyes in peace as she nestled her face into the crook of his neck. He alone was real. She had lost all concept of how long they had lain there in the haunted mists of the falls—time and place had lost all meaning for her. He held her—and that was all that mattered. Not her calling . . . not her team . . . not . . .

Her team.

She had forgotten to check in.

"Damn!" Merinda muttered, pushing herself away from his chest with seemingly infinite difficulty. She flashed him a frustrated, pouty look. "I've got to find a comstation."

"You—what?" Queekat stared at her blankly.

"I'll be right back," she said, standing quickly on the

beach and brushing the sand from her pants. "I've got to check in with Terica."

"Rini!" Queekat pleaded, scrambling to get his legs under him.

"I won't be but a moment." She looked around them, hands on her hips. "Which way is the exit?"

Queekat took her arm and turned her toward him. His voice was warm honey. "Hey! Can't you just let it go for a while? You're no lost child, and I'm sure Terica will get along fine without you for a little while."

He pulled her closer to him. His arms moved around her waist.

"Oh, Kat, you know—procedure and all that," she teased him. "What would the *Vestis Inquisitas* say about such a flagrant violation?"

She turned to go, but he held her in place, his grip firmer, tighter.

"Don't spoil it, Rini! Come on, relax a little, will you? Just for a few more minutes."

"Kat, stop it! I'll only be a few moments . . ."

"Rini, you don't understand! You can't understand! Just a few more minutes, please. What difference can a few more minutes make? It can't mean that much to you."

"Kat, no! You're hurting me!"

His fingers dug into the flesh of her back.

"Rini! You've no idea what you're dealing with here! Just give me this time, just these few minutes, and we'll own those stars I promised you, I swear it!" His face pressed close to her, the dark, intense cold fire again in his eyes.

He had suddenly become hideous to her.

"Please, Rini! Just obey me, love me. Give me something to remember and hold on to in the darkness. It can't matter that much to you. Don't make this harder than it is!"

"No!"

Merinda shoved hard against Queekat, breaking his grip. She took several quick steps back from him, her breath short from confusion. Her bare feet splashed in the warm, sticky liquid at the edge of the pool. She reached quickly down to snatch her boots from the sand. It was only then that she noticed the gentle, sluggish waves lapping at her bare ankles.

Crimson waves. The pool had turned to blood.

She screamed, leaping for the white sands of the shore, leaving a gory trail on its pristine surface. Panicked, she looked up at the falls. The glorious weave of tumbling water had been transformed into a hellish froth of pink overlaying the deep purple-red ichor dashing itself against the rocks at the bottom of the cliff face.

Merinda shuddered and turned accusingly to Queekat. "Stop this, Kat! Stop it right now!"

"I didn't do this, Rini!" he wailed, then turned to shout into the air around them. "Kapak! Answer me! There is an error in the haunting program on stage one. Terminate the haunting immediately."

Blood-coated figures began emerging on the shore in military ranks. Each held a blood-drenched blade. Each was headless.

"The Khizath!" Merinda said in complete astonishment.

"What are you talking about," Queekat shouted.

"The Khizath, the Ranks of Umbleh!" she spoke quickly, nearly in shock. "It's part of Brishan mythology. When Umbleh killed the three sons of Rhishan, their blood cut the channel through the mountains and first fell down the Denali Falls. From their blood, Umbleh formed ranks of soldiers whose purpose was to destroy the world and who could never be destroyed or defeated."

"Cheerful thought!" Queekat countered.

The first of the ranks was approaching them, coagulating blood dripping from them and falling with a dull thud against the sand. Queekat took a defensive stance, then quickly stepped into one of the creatures, grabbing the ichor-slick wrist firmly while kicking the warrior's legs out from under him. In a sudden twisting motion, he broke the creature's arm and wrestled his blade from his hand.

Merinda shook herself from her stupor and also stepped into the first rank, grasping one of the Khizath by the weapon arm. The grip was slippery and warm, but she held fast and spun the creature away from the group, slamming him against the rock outcropping behind her.

Queekat turned and swung the weapon expertly toward the second shape in the advancing ranks. The blade was razor sharp, slicing through the shoulder of the Khizath facing him and severing his arm completely. It fell to the ground, writhing in the now blood-soaked sand.

The creature didn't stop. Reaching out its other hand, it grasped Queekat by the throat and shoved him to the ground. The severed arm, apparently not to be forgotten, released its grip on the blade and began pulling itself toward the fallen Queekat.

Merinda turned quickly and snatched up the relinquished blade from the ground. Her opponent was staggering away from the rock outcropping when she turned in a fluid motion and ran the blade through the Khizath and deep into the rock behind it.

The creature began moving down the blade toward her. She released her grip on the handle just as the Khizath swung at her, barely missing her head with its blood-drenched fist.

"Can't we talk to them!" Queekat shouted, now struggling to stand while trying to kick free the loose arm grasping his ankle.

"How?" Merinda called back, ducking a swinging blade

from another Khizath. "They don't have any heads. How could they hear you?"

"Well, there must be some way to stop them!" Queekat gut-kicked the next dripping creature hard enough that it fell backward with a sickening sound into the blood-filled pond. In the instant, he could see three more ranks emerging from the red pool.

"There was something in the story—I just don't remember it right now. Something about—ahh!" The flashing blade slashed across her upper thigh, a quick stain of her own blood filling the gash in her clothing. She staggered backward toward Queekat. She glanced sideways. The Khizath pinned to the rock was rocking back and forth on the blade, cutting through itself in order to get free—to get to her. She looked back. Somehow her pursuer could sense her position. It raised its sword.

Suddenly bolts of light exploded among the Ranks of Umbleh.

"Look!" Queekat shouted, pointing overhead.

His voice was difficult to hear. A resonant, deep sound filled the area around Merinda. She looked.

Drifting above the falls and descending toward them was the great, boxlike shape of Queekat's starship. Coherent bolts of energy scattered the Ranks of Umbleh back toward the bloody pool. The rumble of the repulsors overhead was deafening.

It sounded wonderful to Merinda.

Queekat grabbed her and pulled her up off the sand. Together they ran, Merinda ignoring as best she could the gaping wound in her leg. The ship had quickly come to rest on the far end of the sand spit. There was little help for it, she couldn't possibly keep up. Queekat reached the after hatch of the cargo module first, starting the opening cycle at once. Merinda watched the heavy doors slide slowly open nearly twenty yards away.

"Come on, Rini!" She could see Queekat waving frantically toward her. "Don't look back! Just come!"

Don't look back? she thought. *What is there back there that I shouldn't look back on?*

She was within three yards of the door when something hit her from behind. She fell forward, several rocks embedded in the sand rushing up toward her face.

Darkness threatened to take her down as her face hit the rocks, but she fought it. The weight on her back pressed the air from her lungs. She fought to breathe.

Suddenly the weight disappeared. Dazed. Queekat lifting her, throwing her. Tumbling. Tumbling through the hatch. Terica. Terica pulling her. Pulling her into the cargo module. Hands. Many hands.

Suddenly her mind cleared.

"Get us out of here, Rini!" Queekat shouted from behind her.

Merinda glanced about her. It was all so suddenly familiar and yet so discontinuous from where she had been just moments before. It was hard to adjust, mentally, but there was no doubting it now.

She was sitting in the pilot's command chair.

"I—I don't know what to do!" she called back.

"*Drij*, Rini, anyone can run a starship!" Queekat's voice echoed at her from the commons compartment just behind her. "Just talk to the synth, tell it this is an emergency evacuation and get us out of here . . . *now!*"

Merinda's head was reeling and she was speaking through the pain. "Excuse me, starship."

"You may call me Kara, if you like."

"Kara, fine! This is an emergency evacuation. Would you please—"

Lap, shoulder, and leg restraints suddenly snapped across Merinda's body and pulled her tightly into the command chair. In an instant, the starship pitched itself vertical, Merinda getting the sudden, sickening feeling that her chair was mounted on a wall.

"Emergency evacuation in progress. Aft cargo module hatch not secured. Emergency override. Aft hatch now secured."

"Queekat!" Merinda shouted. "I don't think this is such a good—"

The main engines suddenly spooled up with a deafening whine. Merinda glanced at the myriad displays about her flashing information and panicked for a moment that some of them might be critical. She had started something and had no idea how to stop it.

"Queekat!" she pleaded.

The main engines suddenly engaged with an all-encompassing roar. Merinda lay helpless, her body pressed forcibly into the seat by the sudden forward rush of the ship. The acceleration compensators were lagging behind the full thrust of the engines. Normally that would trip any number of alarms. She wondered for a moment why the gravity fields hadn't compensated when the ship had gone vertical. She would remind Queekat of that later, she thought. Something that seriously wrong with the ship he would probably wish to know about. On the other hand, she thought, she rather liked the press of the raw power at her back and the feeling of true flight it seemed to give.

She smiled to herself. Only later would she think of it as the last time she would smile.

The ship suddenly lurched.

In the instant, she frantically scanned the crystal displays, thinking that something had gone wrong, that perhaps she had done something wrong. It was only a moment though, for she knew in the next instant that it was not her.

A quick series of blaster shots exploded behind her, two of the bolts ripping the atmosphere on either side of her chair and shattering several of the displays.

Merinda tried to turn her seat and found that it swiveled too well. She suddenly found herself hanging by the restraints under the continuing acceleration. The portal behind the command chair suddenly appeared to be a well over which she was hanging. She could see the commons compartment beyond. She couldn't see Kiria. Her flight station was a chair to the right of the hatch and out of Merinda's view. Oscan's chair was to the left; Merinda thought she caught a glimpse of his head leaning out from his seat and looking back past the table mounted to the floor. Evon was behind him, struggling to release his own restraints.

She saw Queekat.

The *Vestis* stood against the back bulkhead as though it were the floor, his back pressed, crazily, against the ceiling. Next to him was the forward hatch to the cargo module. It lay open at his feet, jacketed antiproton bolts slamming out of the opening. Most exploded in the commons compartment with several more ripping past Merinda.

She struggled to turn the seat forward, hoping crazily that the back of the chair would somehow protect her from the streaming death behind her, but the chair had locked in place and wouldn't turn around. Helplessly she hung in the still-accelerating ship, pinned by the restraining harness.

Queekat knelt where he was and pulled open the panel next to the door. As Merinda watched, he popped open the fail-safe covers and pressed all four buttons at once. In response a second small panel slid open, revealing the large D-ring handle of the emergency cargo jettison cable.

Queekat looked up and saw her. *His eyes, those beautiful eyes,* she thought. He reached between his legs for the D-ring handle—

—And then he smiled at her.

A sad smile. A triumphant smile. A farewell smile.

Merinda hadn't noticed that the plasma fire had stopped. Suddenly, a figure emerged from the still-open cargo hatch. It wore full assault uniform with a closed helmet. D'Rakan assault-trooper insignia flashed on its epaulets. Merinda wondered at the large backpack and extensive equipment strapped all over the figure's body, wondered how anyone could fight carrying so much weight around. Wonder evaporated to horror, however, as the figure grabbed Queekat's legs from under him just as he grabbed the D ring.

Time slowed. Forever after, in her mind, this memory would play slowly. There would be no quick mercy.

Terica appeared. She had managed to disengage her restraining straps. She pushed herself clear of her seat, landing on her feet on the other side of the open cargo hatch. She reached for the weapon of the assault trooper hanging on his back. The weapon would not come loose, so she pulled again, harder this time.

The trooper still held Queekat's feet.

Queekat fell backward, the D ring still held tight in his hands.

There must have been a sound, but Merinda remembered it as being silent. Dust exploded in the commons room beneath her as the cargo module separated from the still-accelerating ship. Suddenly everything cleared, the image seared into her mind—the end of her life, she thought.

The cargo hatch was irreparably broken. Beyond it, some fifty miles distant, hung the dark surface of Tentris, the dawn terminator line clearly visible from this height. Framed in the raging exhausts of the engines, Merinda clearly saw the tumbling cargo module and the assault trooper.

There, too, was the twisting form of Terica Dharah, carried through the hatch with the decompression.

Yet her eyes were fixed, unblinking, on the drifting figure of *Vestis* Queekat Shn'dar. He floated, she thought, like a feather on a breeze so high above the surface of the world below. *He'll fly back up to me,* she thought in the silence of her mind, and everything will be all right again.

Nothing would be all right ever again.

The emergency fields sealed off the broken hatchway as atmosphere rushed back into the cabin. Sound returned with a vengeance.

Alarms.

The synth's calm voice.

Merinda screaming hysterically.

And the continuous thunder of the starship driving them higher and higher into the star-filled sky.

BETA:

BOOK OF *ARCHILUS*

(Eight Years Later)

8

Archilus Lost

15:32 GMT—UNS—ISF *ARCHILUS* PRESUMED LOST

NATIONS MOURNED TODAY AS THE ISF *ARCHILUS*, THE FIRST spacecraft to utilize the Beltrane-Sachs parallel-space engine, was declared lost by the United Stellar Research Agency. The interstellar spacecraft, which had promised to open the stars to exploration and possible future colonization, failed again to report three weeks after its first use of the BSPS engine. Its loss casts doubt on the future of the USRA and interstellar explorations.

Mission operatives at the Mission Command Center (MCC) located in the Elden Orbital Colony had initially declared the first use of the faster-than-light drive system to be a complete success. "The transition into parallel space was nominal," Gene Humphers, director of mission operations at MCC, said. "We are at a loss to explain why the spacecraft and its crew have not returned to local space to report. There is no indication here that anything unusual happened during the initial penetration phase."

Mission planning called for the *Archilus* to transit the twelve-light-year distance to the Tau Ceti star system, explore the recently discovered planetary bodies orbiting that star, and return to report at 212 hours into the flight. Mission operatives counseled that, due to some quantum variance and the experimental nature of the BSPS engine, the precise location of the *Archilus* when it first emerges from parallel space may not be as expected. It was initially thought that a variance of several hours, allowing for radio transmission times within our own stellar system, would not be outside expected norms. When the ship did not immediately return, mission operatives took this as a sign that all was going well and that the flight was proceeding according to plan. However, as the anticipated hours of the spacecraft's return stretched into days, mission analysts began fearing the worst.

"We really don't know what to think," Dr. Lawrence Castebaum, chairman of the World Outreach Agency (WOA), said. "It isn't as though we have all witnessed a catastrophic event. No explosion, no malfunctions so far as we can determine . . . they just haven't reported back."

The almost unimaginable distances that the spacecraft was supposed to cover made normal communication impossible. Only the return of the spacecraft to local space would have allowed them to report. Problems, failures, or miscalculations on the effects of the BSPS engine and its actual performance would have had to have been handled by the crew aboard without the help of mission operatives at the MCC. If the *Archilus* had safely made the transit to Tau Ceti—as mission telemetry suggests—any radio message from the crew would take twelve years to reach us, and an additional twelve years before any reply we sent could reach them in return.

"Every contingency was planned for," Dr. Castebaum explained. "If there had been any equipment failure, this crew was prepared to deal with the problem. It was their mission and they were qualified."

The apparent loss of the *Archilus* has cast doubt on the entire BSPS program. Congressperson Erik DeLancy (F-Oregon) has called for an investigation into the WOA and their handling of interstellar exploration programs. "How can we justify the expenditure of so much of our global resources on the stars when there are so many pressing problems here on the surface of our own world?"

The *Archilus* was commanded by Colonel Mary Anne Estephan, 37, of Grovers Mill, New Jersey. Col. Estephan graduated from the Joint Forces Academy in the class of '21 and served a distinguished career as a flight officer and fleet commander in the Martian campaign of '24. Four times decorated, she is survived by her husband, Michael, and four children.

Serving as first officer aboard was Major James Leffingwell, 53, of Camden, Maine, a thirty-four-year veteran of the Marines and commander of the Jupiter Expedition in '10. He is survived by his wife, Nancy, and six children.

Also aboard were Captain Stanley Greer (navigator), Captain Esther Kline (propulsion), Lieutenant Elizabeth Lewis (life support), Lieutenant Broderick Ellerby (mission specialist—stellar dynamics), Dr. Marilyn Tobler (mission specialist—geology), and Captain Jeremy Griffiths (mission specialist—RPV).

—END TRANSMISSION—

9

Into the Frying Pan

CAPTAIN JEREMY GRIFFITHS FELL PAINFULLY TO THE ROUGH decking beneath him. He again wondered just what had possessed him to come on this mission. He had been an alternate for the flight—and had frankly looked forward to cashing in on the fame and the glory without having to deal with performing the deed itself. His specialization had been RPV pilot. RPV stood for remote piloted vehicle, so, as his colleagues constantly teased him, he was the remote-piloted-vehicle pilot, which made his title itself somewhat redundant. He certainly considered himself redundant: an unused backup component that, if everything worked the way it was supposed to, would never be called upon to actually do anything at all. "Astronaut Jeremy Griffiths" sounded impressive, looked great on his calling card, and got him free lunches and girls in most ports of call.

This certainly was not one of them.

Griffiths pushed himself painfully up from the cold deck, his silvery blond hair, usually carefully trimmed and in place, falling in disheveled confusion across his eyes. He looked cautiously about him, still not quite accepting what he saw.

He knelt on a wide platform that had no railing. The mammoth columns rising beyond were obscured by haze and distance. The size of the chamber was unthinkably immense, rising overhead into a dark, impenetrable gloom. He wondered momentarily how far down those columns extended beyond the sharp edge of the platform. The thought panicked him at once, sending waves of vertigo through his entire body.

The fact was this pilot was afraid of heights. The flat plate he knelt on felt—to him—to be bowed up in the middle, slanting away toward the precipice and his own doom. Jeremy closed his eyes for a moment to regain his composure and then turned his attention to the other figures on the platform.

Ellerby was out cold. He lay facedown about twenty feet from Jeremy, about as limp as a rag doll. He might take some convincing to come around—if he was going to come around at all. Near him, Dr. Tobler stirred slightly as she lay on her back.

"How are you feeling, Griffiths? Are you all right?"

Jeremy looked up. The dirty mission suit leaning over him slightly was otherwise trim and in order. Nothing ever seemed to faze Lieutenant Elizabeth Lewis. She would insist on straightening her uniform even if she were on the way to her own execution—an event Jeremy had envisioned with great relish from time to time during their training. Lewis was a prig who could quote the book for any given contingency and always knew the right answer—even when she was wrong. Her raven hair was kept in careful check but still drew men to their doom. Her eyes were deep, dark wonders, but Jeremy knew that the small woman housed a soul that could freeze a man solid between breaths. Lewis was the mission's life-support specialist, but he found it hard to believe that there was any life in her.

Jeremy drew a shaking breath and then moved to stand.

His knees felt like wet clay. "I think so—just give me a moment to get my feet back under me. What happened?"

"What's the last thing you remember?" Lewis folded her arms across her chest, her eyes narrowing.

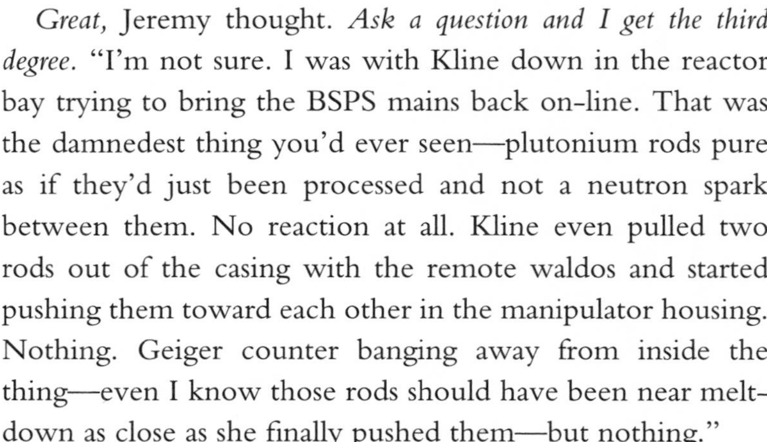

Great, Jeremy thought. *Ask a question and I get the third degree.* "I'm not sure. I was with Kline down in the reactor bay trying to bring the BSPS mains back on-line. That was the damnedest thing you'd ever seen—plutonium rods pure as if they'd just been processed and not a neutron spark between them. No reaction at all. Kline even pulled two rods out of the casing with the remote waldos and started pushing them toward each other in the manipulator housing. Nothing. Geiger counter banging away from inside the thing—even I know those rods should have been near meltdown as close as she finally pushed them—but nothing."

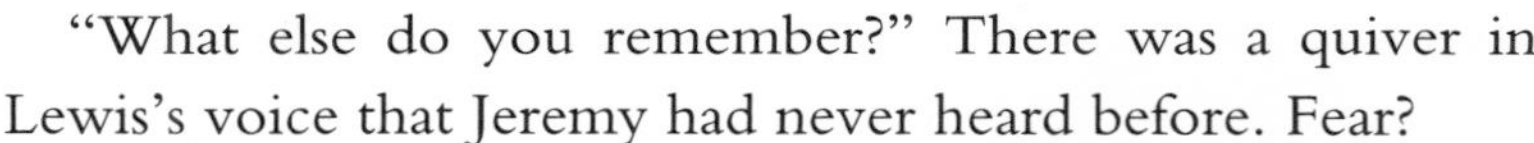

"What else do you remember?" There was a quiver in Lewis's voice that Jeremy had never heard before. Fear?

"That was about it." He squinted slightly, trying to peer more deeply into his own memory. "Kline said something about what she was going to do with those plutonium rods when she got back to the engineers at home, then the proximity alarm went off. The collision alarm. I remember Colonel Estephan calling over the intercom something about 'Boarding parties'—I think. Sounds. Explosions. Kline went through the hatch first, she was holding something, I followed her. That's about it. Say, just what the hell did happen?"

Lewis looked up away from him. *Good lord,* Jeremy thought, *was her lip quivering?* "I was in the aft command bay, trying to keep the life support operating when it happened. The RCS system still wasn't operating, so Estephan had no way of avoiding them—although avoidance is hardly what I think they had in mind. We didn't even have any weapons on board—"

"Of course not," Jeremy said flatly, "we're on a mission of peace."

"Right!" Lewis snorted derisively. "Someone forgot to tell the armored guys that punched a hole in our pressure hull and stormed aboard like marines."

Jeremy was still feeling the vertigo, although talking to Lewis was, at least, helping with that minor problem. "Where's the colonel?" he asked as he groggily turned over and sat, rubbing his head.

There was no immediate reply.

Jeremy looked up. "The colonel?"

Lewis only nodded.

The chill of the knowledge braced him. He was unfortunately very much awake. "Who else?" he said roughly.

"Kline."

Jeremy closed his eyes again, a fresh wave of dizziness washing over him.

Lewis still couldn't bring herself to look at him. Her famous iron self seemed to be shattering under the cold hardness their existence had become. "I found her—well, most of her anyway—in the lower storage bay just before they took me. Colonel Estephan was the first: she went right away. She probably shouldn't have tried to use that grappling rod as a weapon. Leffingwell and Greer were smarter. They pulled me down the port equipment access shaft to the quarters where we hoped to hide out until they had left the ship. I was first down the shaft. When I came out the other end, Greer and Leffingwell weren't behind me. They aren't here so I can only guess that they got them, too."

"Who?" Jeremy murmured, too stunned and angry to make any other sound. "*Who* got them?"

"I don't . . . I don't know!" Lieutenant Elizabeth Lewis, who had never demonstrated any emotion before her colleagues in the three years they had worked with one another, suddenly choked on her words, oceans of tears welling up in her eyes. "They looked . . . like . . . us. They had arms and legs and were about our size, but they were dressed in some kind of thick pressure suits or armor or something. They were all decorated with symbols and war paint. They were armed with these rods or wands or . . . I don't know what! God! They pointed one of those things at Estephan and she just sort of exploded from the inside out!"

Lewis . . . cold, unreachable Lewis quite suddenly collapsed next to Jeremy, wracked with sobs. "It doesn't make any sense! Why would they attack us? We came peacefully. We just wanted to walk into the stars and touch them! What do they want from us? Why did they do this to us!"

Jeremy awkwardly put his arm around the lieutenant's shoulders and held her somewhat stiffly. The Elizabeth Lewis he had come to know was nothing like this. A part of him worried that the *real* Lewis would suddenly come to her senses and take him apart for daring to touch another officer. Harassment was the farthest thing from his mind at the moment. Elizabeth's ice-queen image had been one of the more stable things in his life. Her coming apart was having a disturbing effect on him—rather like watching the sun come up in the west. He had to do something to put the world right again.

"OK, Lieutenant, I'm sorry," he said in tones as soothing as he could muster. "I know it's been rough on you. Hey, I was just along for the ride, remember? You told me that I had about as much commitment to this mission as your first husband did to your marriage. I just wanted to take the ride, fly my little RPVs around some alien worlds, hope not to lose too many, and come home a hero. The ship just flat dying on us and being boarded by these alien whatever they are's just wasn't in the contract I signed."

Lewis looked up into his face. The resentment was still

there, all right. He could actually feel the steel reassert itself in her backbone.

"If it's not in my contract—" Jeremy smiled "—then I'm sure my lawyer can get us out of this if no one else can."

Lewis pushed him away in disgust. She might not be whole again yet, but for the time being she was willing to try gluing the pieces back together. "Well, *mister*, until you can *reach* your attorney by phone, I might suggest that in the meantime we try to get ourselves out of this."

"Absolutely," Jeremy replied as he stood to follow her. "Any ideas just where we might get ourselves out to?"

Lewis didn't seem to hear him. The footfalls of her flight slippers made a soft sound as she moved across the wide platform, stopping at Ellerby and kneeling down next to him.

"Is he—is he—" Jeremy stuttered.

"No, he's not dead," Lewis responded without looking up, "unless you can snore when you're dead." With great effort, she rolled him over and looked into his wide, square face. She began slapping him gently with her open hand against his left cheek. "Come on, big guy. Time to wake up. This ain't no drill, Brick."

Jeremy noted the big man's eyelids flicker slightly. Satisfied, he moved over to the nearby Marilyn Tobler who was trying to sit up with little success. Her honey-colored hair still bristled in the tight, neat cut she preferred, but the ice-blue eyes it framed were having trouble focusing.

"Dr. Tobler, are you all right?"

Tobler turned toward the sound. She replied at once. "Could I have the French toast without the maple syrup or do you prefer catsup?"

"Dr. Tobler?" Griffiths knelt down and gripped her by both shoulders, looking for some recognition in the cold eyes. Suddenly they focused on him.

"Captain Griffiths, what a pleasant surprise!" Dr. Tobler

seemed to suddenly be switched on. "What are you doing up here in the observation bay?"

"It would appear that the good doctor is a little out of sync with the times," Lewis said. Ellerby, standing a full head taller, walked behind the lieutenant as they came.

"I don't think it's serious," Griffiths said with far more conviction than he honestly felt. "Ellerby, you were backup medical on this flight. How does she look to you?"

"Well, I'd say she looks pretty good!" Ellerby chirped nervously, "but I suppose you want a more technical evaluation?"

"Yes! Please!" Griffiths responded without humor. He shook his head as the large man knelt next to Tobler. Only then did he notice that Lewis was standing nearby, staring at him. "Well, what do we do now?"

"I was just going to ask you the same question," Lewis said evenly.

"What do you mean?"

"How do you want us to proceed? Survival may be the first order of business. On the other hand, we may wish to establish contact with these aliens and come to some truce. It would be nice to know if our spacecraft is nearby and ascertain its condition if we ever hope to—"

"Hold it! Hold it!" Griffiths held his hands up in exasperation. "What the hell are you asking me for?"

With notable restraint, the imperious Lewis responded in rock-steady tones. "Because, *Captain*, you are now in command of this mission. As ranking officer—"

"But I don't want to be in command!"

"But you are."

"But I don't want to be."

"You are the senior ranking officer remaining among us, aren't you, *Captain*?" Lewis folded her arms across her chest again—a bad sign.

“Sure, but that’s not my fault!” Griffiths wailed.

“I beg your pardon?”

“Look,”—Griffiths pressed his open hand to his chest—“it wasn’t my idea. I was up for command of one of the Martian relief convoys. My old man arranged it. You have to have at least the rank of captain to make the cut, so he arranged a promotion for me through the fleet admiralty. It’s just a title! It doesn’t really mean anything.”

Lewis considered this for a moment. “Well, I understand your reticence and . . . may I speak freely, sir?”

Griffiths wondered if it were possible to say no. Even if he did, he doubted it would matter. “Of course.”

“I, personally, do not feel that your leadership abilities or bearing merits command of this mission. However, our training at the Kansas First Contact Center dictates that the ranking officer, in any emergency, is to be responsible for continuing the mission, if possible, and returning the crew safely to Earth.”

“The Kansas Contact Center”—Griffiths grimaced, deciding to fight belligerence with belligerence—“did not foresee the car accident that took Captain Murdock off the flight last week!”

Tobler stepped between them. “Will you two knock it off! Bad enough our reservations were canceled without you arguing about who’s going to get the double bed!”

Griffiths looked sideways at Ellerby.

“Look”—Ellerby shrugged—“it might take a little while. I think she must have taken a bad knock to the head.”

“Just a simple little mission,” Griffiths muttered loudly. “Just a walk around the ol’ stellar neighborhood. Well, the Kansas Center didn’t plan on our plutonium rods suddenly defying the laws of physics! They certainly didn’t figure on our getting hijacked and half our crew dead by some interstellar knights in dark armor! And good ol' Kansas Center most certainly didn't plan on—"

The sudden sound of a thousand voices filled the vast expanse with a single dissonant chord.

The astronauts started visibly at the sound.

A second chord rang through the huge space. Then a third. Soon Griffiths recognized, through the skull-rattling enormity of the sound, a pattern of successive sounds, all coming from the invisible chorus in the distance. The broad lines engraved into the surface of the platform beneath them began to glow brilliantly, its pattern now more pronounced. The chanting reached a fevered frequency in progression; the column beneath the astronauts began vibrating and thrumming in rhythm to the sounds bombarding it.

Griffiths, struggling to keep his feet under him, suddenly saw the floor before him dissolve into shafts of light shooting into the mists overhead, illuminating the room with brilliant rays. Heedless of the danger of the platform's edge behind him, Griffiths and his companions began taking several steps backward.

The light columns exploded into dazzling shards with the sound of a hundred thunderclaps. Blood-red light suddenly filled the space around them.

Griffiths looked up.

The muscular body was at least two hundred feet tall, shining with flaming red scales. The huge head appeared humanoid, but three sets of burnished horns burning with their own flame formed its crown. There were no pupils in the white-hot eyes, their gaze painful to look into. Six tentacles radiated from the body. At the end of each tentacle flailed three talons, lightning arcing between each of the sharp points.

"ARACH CHU KATHCHAK NERUTH DEGH!"

The voice was a voice of doom, vibrating their very bones.

This trip had decidedly taken a turn for the worse.

"You were saying, Captain?" Lewis murmured, awe-struck, behind him.

Griffiths swallowed hard, hoping to find his voice.

"We are most definitely *not* in Kansas anymore."

10

Uncertain Death

"WHAT IN THE NAME OF HELL . . ."

Lewis's murmuring barely penetrated Jeremy's mind. The monstrous thing towering over him looked down on them and laughed. It was a dreadful sound, the sound of doom and the death of all things personified by this hideous, glowing demon. Its tentacles folded across its massive chest as waves of heat obscured the lines of its form in rippling curves. It was an impossible sight made all the more impossible by its own reality.

"Captain?"

Griffiths blinked.

"Captain!" A voice—Ellerby's voice.

"Yes?" He barely recognized the responding voice as his own.

"Captain, what do we do?!" Ellerby was on the edge of panic.

Griffiths blinked and shook his head as if to clear the vision and reconcile what he believed with what he saw. He thought of all the training they had had over the last few years. Of all the mission contingencies and procedures designed to help them through any crisis.

"ARACH CHU MENDRAL'TSAK KONDRUTH

DEGHA!" the monstrous apparition thundered at them, its tentacles waving in the air in a musical rhythm.

Griffiths suddenly shook loose from the paralysis that had gripped him. Someone had to do something, and with great reluctance he realized that it had to be him.

He stepped forward, raising his arms overhead.

"Greetings! We, the people of planet Earth, bring a message of friendship to our brothers across the star darkness. We come peacefully and wish only—"

The beast threw back its head and screamed into the chamber. Its cries reverberated against the distant columns and shook the very air of the hall.

"GNUSTAKTA BEHRO THURUMKAR ELSTI NARAGANTHA BEGHAHAN!" the voice screamed.

Griffiths stepped back away from the sound until he collided with Lewis and Ellerby. "Uh—we seem to be having a communication problem . . . and I don't think he much likes me."

"Well," Ellerby said as he took a shuddering breath, pointing back to the foot of the hideous creature, "I think one thing is clear."

The chanting had resumed all around them, but Jeremy took little notice. His eyes followed Ellerby's extended arm and the sight froze him.

A red-stained altar was rising from the floor at the foot of the creature.

"They can't be serious!" Lewis shook—whether from fear, loathing, or indignation it was impossible for Griffiths to tell.

He turned to the group, speaking in a rush. "I think that first contact with an alien civilization might need to wait for another time. We need to get the hell out of here! Any ideas?"

Ellerby glanced sideways. Four armored figures had

appeared at the edges of their platform and were moving toward them slowly, their dark capes flying in the wind that was now engulfing the area. Each held the terrible staves that had decimated the rest of the crew and that now were leveled at their small group. "Whatever it is, it had better be fast, Captain!"

"Tobler!" Griffiths turned to the geologist. "Can you fight?"

"Yes, sir," she replied. Her ice-blue eyes seemed a bit too bright for Griffiths's liking. "Bring 'em on and I'll take on all eight of them!"

"Just one will do and then we'll have to make a break for it. Maybe across one of those bridges . . ."

"Which one?" Tobler's voice had a frantic air.

"Damn it, I don't know!" Griffiths snapped. The crimson armored guards had nearly reached them. "The one behind me! Now, let's do it!"

Ellerby swung quickly around. The guard lowered his weapon but wasn't quick enough. Ellerby grabbed the shaft before it was level and in a single move twisted it out of his opponent's hand. The armored creature had been gripping the device so hard that the force pulled him off his feet. The red, shining plating clattered on the floor as the guard fell.

Jeremy turned to the nearest of the guards and crouched to jump at his weapon. Lewis, however, had been a lot faster on the draw: Jeremy remembered in a flash that she had been an army ranger at one point in her career. Her roundhouse kick slammed directly into the helmet of her attacker, knocking it completely free of the shoulders. Jeremy had a fleeting picture of brownish blood exploding a moment before Lewis's foot, still moving from the swinging kick, crashed into his own chest. With a wheezing gasp, he slammed onto his back.

Through the wave of pain and dizziness, Jeremy looked

up. Tobler was grappling with another guard, both of them gripping his weapon and equally determined to never let it go. Lewis shouted, "Sorry!" to Jeremy but was suddenly turning to another guard, moving into a judo throw that was looking to terminate in Jeremy's general direction. Ellerby slammed the staff he'd taken against the fallen guard's helmet. The action rang a solid clank out of the armor but may not have been terribly effective. Ellerby was now frantically searching the staff for some kind of triggering mechanism. Jeremy felt through his back the heavy footfalls of more guards rushing toward them from the edges of the platform.

But filling the background of all his vision was the howling form of the demon. Rage distorted its horned brow; its eyes blazed with unthinkable light. Waves of heat rippled from its massive body. It raised its tentacles, lightning dancing from their tips. Howls shook the hall.

Its terrible gaze locked on Griffiths.

"Oh my," was all he could utter.

The massive demon grinned at the fallen astronaut. The rumbling words were incomprehensible to Jeremy but their intention was perfectly clear. Something, he thought, along the lines of "You are mine," or "Lunch."

The guards suddenly broke from the humans as they all looked up. The demon's maw opened wide, its tentacles encircling them. There was nowhere for them to run. Ellerby cursed at his useless weapon. Lewis stood ready, but there was nothing left to fight. The huge head arched toward them as the tentacles coiled about themselves, their tips reaching tentatively toward Griffiths. The ozone smell from the crackling tips stung his nostrils.

A sudden flash of smoke and light next to Jeremy blinded him for a moment. In the next instant, a robed wizard stood at his side.

Jeremy checked to see if he had lost his mind.

The wizard was a tall, thin man. His great beard cascaded from his chin in soft undulating waves. Three softly glowing globes slowly drifted in orbits about his head, radiating opalescent light. His prominent nose was thrust upward toward the encircling hellish beast, as both arms rose in defiance.

The demon frowned suddenly, its playful delight in its captured prey changing swiftly to frustrated outrage. The tentacles lifted suddenly, darting directly toward the wizard, electricity sparking. Jeremy recoiled from the expected blow, hiding his eyes.

A low hum, more felt than heard, sounded around him. Jeremy opened his eyes.

A dome of blue light, shimmering like a quiet lake, covered the wizard and, most gratefully, Jeremy and the rest of the crew. The demon screamed, tentacles thrusting against the dome and rebounding with only the increased humming sound to account for it. In the center of it all, the wizard held up his hands, seeming to will the shield to remain in place.

Lewis's voice came drifting into Jeremy's ears. "This can't . . . this can't be real."

Jeremy got to his feet. He glanced at Tobler. She had been looking a little better, but now he wasn't all that sure of himself. She had decidedly gone paler with the new developments. They had all been prepared either to escape or to die. With the exception of Dr. Tobler, they had all been in the military. Fighting was something they all understood, death something that they had all dealt with. But to be suddenly rescued by a crazy old man in wizard's robes was a little too much.

Griffiths moved slowly around to get a better look at their benefactor. The old man glanced quickly at him and smiled;

Jeremy could see that the man was sweating profusely. The wizard then lifted his face toward the raging demon.

"Nexathin merdik urathankatsar deghn-urakh!" the old man screamed at the demon.

Jeremy looked up. The demon didn't appear to care much for what the old man said. He reared up, flames suddenly springing up from the tips of its tentacles and gushing from under its chest plates.

"Uh, mister," Jeremy said quietly to the wizard. "I don't think this is helping any . . ."

Whether in response to what Jeremy said or for some other reason, the wizard lowered one of his hands and gestured toward the ground in a circular motion. In an instant, a glowing ring filled with blackness appeared in the metal flooring, brightly glowing sparks dancing at its edges.

The wizard pointed with a flat hand toward Jeremy and then toward the circle in the floor.

Ellerby noticed the gesture. "You can't seriously be thinking of leaping into that, can you?"

Jeremy turned toward Ellerby, who was a huge man for space flight, over six feet tall and broadly built. The mission directors must have had some pretty compelling reasons for spending that much payload weight on Ellerby. Yet here the huge man stood before Jeremy shaking like a leaf. *Lord, it's a wonder I'm not a basket case, too,* Jeremy thought. *Couldn't this just be over? Couldn't I just wake up and find myself in my own bed?* "The old wizard says jump into the magical hole, Alice!"

"There is no way I'm jumping into that thing." Tobler's eyes had become focused. "Just where does it lead? Is it a form of parallel space? We don't even know if we can live through . . ."

The demon began beating against the dome. The blue shimmering flashed under the strength of each blow. The wizard shook with each strike. He glanced again at Jeremy, angrily gesturing toward the glowing opening that was impossible to look at directly.

"We can stay here until the old man's arms get tired and try to talk our way out of being eaten by the smiling reject from hell," Jeremy yelled, "or we can try to find the white rabbit."

The wizard fell to one knee. The blue dome flickered.

Jeremy jumped.

"GET OFF ME!"

"Quit your shoving. I'm moving as fast as I can! Tell Ellerby to get off!"

"Sorry," the big man said as he rolled away from the pile, "but I got landed on, too, you know!"

"Lesson number one, Alice," Jeremy muttered to himself as he struggled for breath beneath his sprawled companions, "is never be the first to jump down a hole." He wondered, for a moment, why he was spending most of this nightmare day either flat on his back or pressed down face first. Finally he felt the pressure yield and managed to kneel, catching his breath.

"Where the hell are we now?" he yelled.

Chaos surrounded them. The "hole," or whatever it was that the old wizard had made for them, had deposited them in an unceremonious pile in the center of what appeared to be a thoroughfare of some kind. Elegant buildings with impossibly thin, graceful towers rose to either side of the street pointing toward a glittering mosaic sky. There was little time to appreciate the architecture, however, as figures in glittering white hooded robes had suddenly started screaming at their appearance and were running riot in every direction.

"Hey, Captain," Tobler called over the crowd. "The old guy came with us."

Griffiths turned. Tobler was sitting in the street, cradling the old wizard's head in her lap. He looked more frail than he had before, were that possible, and there was no color in his face at all. "Ellerby!" Griffiths shouted above the noise as he walked quickly to the old man. "Would you take a look at—"

"Yeah! I got it!" Ellerby yelled back, waving his hand dismissively as he squatted down next to the wizard. He pulled the medkit from his thigh pocket and started examining the frail man. "It don't look good here, Captain."

Lewis watched outside the group, wary of the screaming people around them. "Captain, we are vulnerable here. We need to move somewhere that's more secure and try to sort all this out later."

Griffiths stood up. "You're right. There's nothing I'd like better than to hole up for a while and try to figure out just what went wrong."

"Captain," Ellerby said to Jeremy's back. "I think the old guy is coming around."

"Not now, Lieutenant." Jeremy was trying to think, still talking to Lewis. "How far do you think that hole took us?"

Lewis wasn't watching him. "Not far enough! Look!"

Far down the avenue, Jeremy could see the unmistakable form of the red-armored knights. They seemed to be riding things that reminded him of chrome seahorses. Their weapon staves were much longer than he remembered.

And they were charging in their direction.

Jeremy turned quickly to the wizard. His eyes were open but seemed to be having trouble focusing. The glowing orbs drifted slowly over him. Jeremy bent down and in a single motion swept the thin man up in his arms.

"Which way, old man?" he shouted.

The wizard just stared at him.

"Damn!"

Jeremy began to run with the old man, the rest of the Earth crew dashing after him. He ducked down an alleyway between the buildings. The passage was impossibly clean. Jeremy was used to cities where there was enough filth and garbage strewn about that anyone could find a decent place to hide. The pristine simplicity of this place was beginning to annoy him.

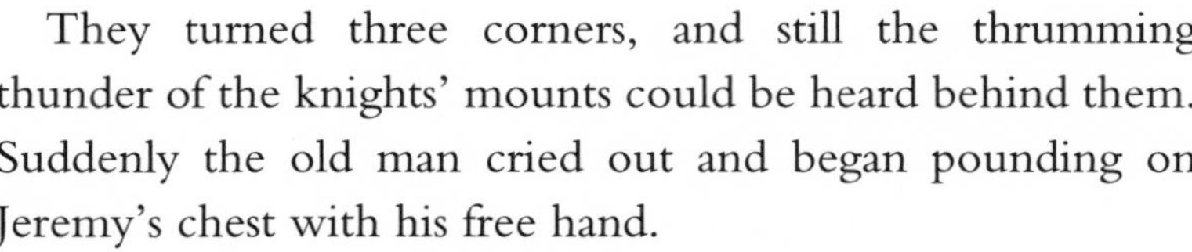

They turned three corners, and still the thrumming thunder of the knights' mounts could be heard behind them. Suddenly the old man cried out and began pounding on Jeremy's chest with his free hand.

Jeremy stopped. The man wriggled his legs free, but held firmly to Jeremy's shoulders. Gasping for breath, he took Jeremy's face in both his hands and kissed him on the forehead.

Jeremy's eyes went wide.

The man slumped in his arms. Jeremy set him down slowly.

"Oh, lord," Tobler said. "He's dead!"

"What!" Lewis exclaimed. "This old guy pisses off the local demon god of wherever-the-hell-we-are and then goes and dies on us! Now what do we do!"

The glowing orbs drifted slowly above Jeremy and then flew quickly down a connecting alley to their right.

"Follow them!" he cried.

"Why?" Lewis shouted, incredulously. "The old geezer here was the only one who knew where we were going."

"Right!" Jeremy said levelly. "And now I know, too!"

11

Information Half-life

"THE IRINDRIS THOUGHT-KNIGHTS DON'T KNOW HOW TO trace phase dragons in flight," Jeremy said as they slipped through the streets. "Once we get to the *Vestis* ship—then we should be able to get out of the nomad city."

Lewis jogged along behind Jeremy, blinking as he spoke. "What the hell are you talking about?"

"All this," he said as he ducked down a narrow conduit to his left, "is part of the Irindris interstellar cities. They are nomads that travel the stars searching for ancient artifacts and knowledge that was lost at the time of the Great Collapse about a thousand years ago. These cities weren't even built by them—the Irindris found them floating adrift near their home worlds just spinward of the Fenadon Empire about a hundred years ago. They saw the coming of the great hulks as a religious event that sent their entire society moving to the stars."

Lewis looked sideways at Ellerby. The large man was trying to keep up with her as they ran but was a bit winded. All he could manage was a shrug of his shoulders and a quick twirl of his index finger near his temple to communicate his evaluation of their captain.

The conduit came to a sudden end. The wall before them

looked like solid metal. It didn't stop Jeremy for a moment. "They're quite helpful, actually, if you know how to communicate and don't get caught up in their religious ceremonies." He reached up deftly, pressing a panel with his open palm as though he had navigated the ancient city every day of his life. The metal wall dissolved suddenly, revealing a vertical shaft. "Unfortunately their pantheon of deities gets a bit confusing—bound up as it is in their collective mind mythology, which requires sacrificing anyone with the knowledge they need to their god Gnuktikut, Devourer of Brains."

Jeremy swung his leg over the edge of the shaft and stood on the ladder rungs protruding from the wall.

His three companions stood in the opening, staring at him.

"It's really very simple, once you understand." He smiled. Then doubt shadowed his face momentarily; he shook his head, then smiled again before disappearing down the shaft.

Lewis turned to Tobler. "How are you feeling, doctor?"

"Disoriented . . . like I haven't been able to get my feet under me since the attack on the *Archilus*," Tobler said more to herself than as an actual answer to the question. She shook her head slowly. "But I don't think that I'm suffering from any mental incapacity or lunacy, if that is what you mean. Certainly not the magnitude of problems that the captain seems to be . . ."

"Hurry up, will ya!" Jeremy's voice resounded up the shaft from below them. "We haven't much time before the Thought-Knights figure out where we are!"

Tobler leaned over and called down to him. "Coming, just taking a moment." She pulled herself into the opening just as Lewis's hand grabbed her shoulder.

"He's insane, Tobler! We can't just follow him!"

Tobler looked the shorter woman in the eyes. "Tell me

what around us is *more* sane than Captain Griffiths and I'll consider doing something else." With that she disappeared down the shaft.

"After you, Lieutenant." Ellerby gestured with exaggerated gallantry. "Let's all play nice until we can come up with something better."

THE SHAFT TERMINATED AT A MAINTENANCE PORT DEEP IN THE city, or so it seemed to Lewis when they finally entered it. They had been working their way down through a variety of shafts, halls, and tunnels and always they continued downward. It was not a direction that she wished to be taking. Yet, she realized as she flattened herself against the wall near what she had come to know as another portal exit, none of this was going in a direction she particularly liked. She had been trained for one mission and one mission only for the last three years. Now all that had suddenly vanished like dew in the morning sun. It wasn't just that she was depressed over the failure of their mission—and she did consider it a failure, for if there was a galaxy teeming with life out there she would have preferred to address it on her own terms—but more over the simple fact that she was not in control of her destiny. Not that she was a maverick or anything like that—she always considered herself a team player. No, it was that there was no team, no direction, and no clear objective for them to achieve. With no obvious starting place, no understanding of where she was, and no objective in mind, she felt lost, adrift in a sea of chaos and indecision. Her frustration was finding vent as anger—and anger, for Elizabeth Lewis at least, was a power she could channel into a formidable tool.

Ellerby stood across from her. He was sweating from exertion, and the stress was beginning to take its toll on him.

Lewis had learned to watch for the signs during the Martian campaign in '24. Even the best men could crack given enough pressure—and it was the ramrod hard, inflexible men that cracked the soonest. Ellerby was the best at his job, but when things started falling apart elsewhere, one probably needed to keep an eye on him. He had left a wife behind, and the speculation in the media prior to the launch had revolved around whether Alyson was expecting a child or not. Things were bad enough here without that kind of baggage.

Marilyn Tobler was an unknown to Lewis. She had trained separately from the main crew and had only been brought in during the last month for integration with the primary flight crew. Her official title had been mission specialist with a geology classification—but Elizabeth didn't believe that one for a moment. She suspected the good doctor's training was in something other than the classification of rocks.

On the other hand, there was Captain Jeremy Griffiths—and as far as Lewis was concerned, the diffident commander had just taken a high dive into an empty pool. As soon as circumstances clarified themselves, Lewis thought, as soon as she got a handle on the situation—well, she might just have to frag the good captain herself.

Jeremy looked at each of them. "The *Vestis* ship is in the bay just past this door. There may be guards stationed here by now. So—uh—so what do you suggest?"

"What do *we* suggest?" Ellerby gaped. "You're the guy who suddenly knows the entire floor plan of this place! You're the guy spouting fables and dashing after Madam Olga's floating crystal orbs! *You* tell *us*, O Mighty Captain!"

"Fine," Griffiths snapped back. "You take point with me. We're heading directly to the rear hatch of the ship. There's about two hundred yards to get there. The wharf is packed with freight and relics, so there will be plenty of cover if there's anyone out there. Do you still have that bruk?"

Ellerby bristled. "The what?"

"The bruk—that stick-tube thing you took from the guard," Griffiths said with little patience. He reached over and gently took the hollow, finely finished shaft from the large lieutenant. "It appears to be fully charged. That means you have about twenty-six shots before it's exhausted and needs a rest."

"Needs a *rest*?"

Jeremy nodded his head. "The bruk are living creatures whose existence extends into spiritual-magical realms which give them their destructive power—"

"Oh, no, not again." Tobler groaned.

"So they can only be used so many times before they have to recuperate— Hey! What's the big problem?"

Lewis looked at Griffiths. Yes, she had to admit to herself, he is the same inept and lazy idiot that she had come to know and loathe. She hadn't been impressed with him during the occasional training events where both the primary and backup crews were in the same place at the same time. Her opinion had been doubly reinforced when he was suddenly elevated to the prime crew because of that stupid aircar accident and she was confronted with him day after day. How the guy ever got as far as he had was a complete mystery to her. No, she decided, he may be bubbling gibberish, but he probably wasn't insane—at least, no more insane than she remembered him. Something else was at work here.

"No problem," she heard herself saying. "So, how does this bruk thing work anyway?"

"Well, like I said, it's a living entity whose life force exists partly in another universe—"

"No." Lewis looked hard into Griffiths's face, hoping it

would get his attention. She spoke to him as though he were a child. “How do we make it go boom and hurt the nasty bad mental knights?”

“Thought-Knights,” he said blankly. “They’re called Thought-Knights—or, at least, that’s what we would call them.” A troubled look crossed his face, as though he were having trouble remembering something. “At least, I think so.”

Lewis snatched the bruk away from Griffiths and tapped him on the head with it. “Go *boom*?” she insisted.

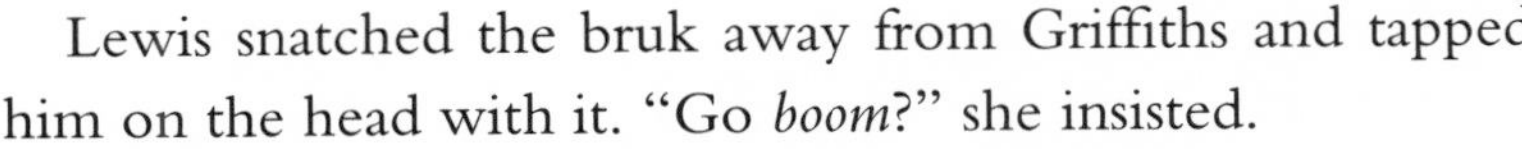

The captain shrugged. “Oh, grasp the staff down by the smooth indents at the back with your left hand. The top of the bruk will glow slightly—showing that it’s charged. You then look at the target and squeeze the shaft with your right hand.”

Lewis handed the rod back to Ellerby, who, after the dissertation on the living bruk seemed reluctant to take it back. “You don’t aim it—just look?” he said dubiously.

“Well, it has to be pointing in the general direction of the target but, technically, no, you don’t aim it.” Griffiths smiled a bit self-consciously. “Look, I know you’ve got a lot of questions. Believe me, no one has more than I do right now—but this isn’t the time for them. Once we’re aboard the *Vestis* ship and safely away from the Irindris maybe we can take stock of our situation, but for right now our lives depend on our getting out of this. That old guy we met came here specifically to talk to us—don’t ask me how I know that—and died trying to save us. We’re important to them, whoever *they* are, and I haven’t got a clue why. In any event, we’ve learned a lot more about the stars than we ever dreamed we might. Can you imagine what the debriefers will say about our report? They’re hoping we return with microorganisms and we return with full-fledged alien contact.”

Lewis smiled despite herself. "That would really be something, wouldn't it!"

"So," Griffiths tugged down at his uniform in an attempt at looking commanding, "What say we get out of here and see about getting home? Ready, Ellerby?"

Ellerby grimaced but gripped the bruk forcefully. Its tip began to glow. "I'd have preferred to take a couple of practice shots first!"

"Sorry, no field test," Jeremy said, reaching up to press the port release panel. "It's time we struck out on our own."

Lewis was a baseball fan. She didn't care for the sound of that at all. "Let's get this over with."

The panel slid open with a quiet whoosh as the air pressure equalized between their small compartment and the expansive chamber beyond. Ellerby and Griffiths leaped quickly through the opening. Lewis glanced at Tobler, nodded her on, and then followed her as well.

THE BAY WAS UNIMAGINABLY LARGE. THE CURVING ARCHES OF the ceiling looked to be nearly a thousand feet overhead, while the long bay must have been at least a mile wide. The distances involved were mind-boggling to Griffiths as he stepped through the hatch into the bay. He quickly moved to crouch behind some large geometrically shaped containers stacked nearby and surveyed the docks arrayed in neat lines around him. He sensed that the rest of his crew—strange to think of them as *his* crew—had fallen in behind him and had taken up similarly hidden positions among what he knew were standing cargo containers holding textiles for export.

Textiles for export? He suddenly realized that he was reading the ornate and artistic scrawl on the containers.

What the hell is going on in my mind? he thought. This was immediately followed by: *If my mind can question its own*

sanity, does that mean I'm not insane? His conversation with himself seemed to be stuck in a loop. Better to think about this later, he decided. Insane or not, he was still alive but somehow knew he wouldn't be much longer if he didn't get himself and his fellow humans to the *Vestis* ship and soon.

He peered around the container. Several likely looking candidates floated next to the piers that stood in rows marching down the quay. The ships were of all shapes, ranging from harshly angled metallic hulls to grotesquely anatomical monsters. They were generally behemoths that extended well into the vertical space of the bay and far past the piers themselves. Beneath them was a sea of shimmering green light through which he could see stars. None of the bizarre ships caught his eye until he noticed what at first appeared to be an empty space between two gargantuan ships.

"There it is," he breathed quietly to his companions. "It's the *Brishan*! That's our ticket out of here."

"Where? Which one?" Lewis hissed as she moved up next to him. "They're enormous, Griffiths! You can't seriously be suggesting that we escape in one of those huge—"

"No." Griffiths shook his head quickly. "Not those! That small one. There—between the big rusty one and the fat one covered in fur."

Lewis shook her head. "It's too far, Griffiths! We'll never make it!"

"It can't be more than a couple of hundred yards," Griffiths said, a little too much hope in his voice.

"It's at least four hundred yards, closer to five."

"No, I don't think it's that far; I think we can make it."

"Uh, Griffiths."

"No more questioning, Lewis! This is our last shot and we're going to take it!"

Suddenly, Lewis began tugging insistently on his sleeve. "Griffiths!"

He turned angrily toward her. "What now, Lewis?"

She was staring at something behind him, her hands slowly reaching up into the air as she began to stand up.

Griffiths spun around. The rest of the crew were slowly standing. Behind them stood two ranks of the Thought-Knights, their bruk weapons leveled at the humans and, Griffiths felt sure, their eyes trained on them in deadly earnest.

Griffiths sighed and slowly began to rise.

A wall of searing blue flame suddenly erupted in front of the Thought-Knights, followed at once by screams. Ellerby, closest to the knights, fell suddenly back away from the flames toward where Griffiths now stood in shock, stumbling over one of the containers and falling to the ground. Lewis instinctively shielded her face from the flame. When Griffiths glanced in her direction, he saw that her eyes were wide with fear and adrenaline.

Tobler, Griffiths thought, *where is Tobler?*

Suddenly he saw her, silhouetted against the bright flames. She had grabbed Ellerby's bruk after he fell and was now crouched down, training the weapon overhead as she tilted her head back.

Griffiths looked up, following the doctor's gaze.

A circular platform, ten feet wide, hovered just a few feet over their heads. Though the platform itself seemed silent, it was difficult to tell in the sudden bombardment of sound that exploded from a single being standing on the platform. The figure was difficult to see behind the blinding column of blue light streaming from its cupped hands. As he watched, the column shifted under the figure's direction from target to target among the Thought-Knights, each target's armor exploding horribly in a crimson flash from the raw power of the beam.

Please, let me wake up, Griffiths begged himself again and again. *Please let me wake up . . .*

As he watched, the platform suddenly slipped sideways and rotated around some inexplicable axis located at its rider's waist. The now-perpendicular platform spun around once, the black-cloaked and hooded figure scanning the surroundings quickly. The strange disk then rotated again until it was more naturally parallel to the ground and suddenly descended to land among the remaining *Archilus* crew.

The figure pushed back its hood.

On the platform before Griffiths, a lone woman dressed in what appeared to be a black flight suit stood, her arms loose at her sides. Soft hair, the color of honey, tumbled out from under the hood, but it was the face that held him: a magnificent oval of soft skin; bowed lips in a perpetual, slight frown; and eyes—eyes as cold and as deep as interstellar night. It was beauty, power, and judgment without a trace of compassion or warmth. Griffiths found the woman's single, steady gaze compelling and terrifying all at once.

He took a deep breath.

"Vestis?" he said, holding his hand out, palm up.

The woman of stone blinked.

"Vestis ituro," she said, bowing her head slightly as she touched the tips of her fingers to her forehead. Her gaze, however, never left his own. She then, too, held out her hand palm up. *"Etis quono pas?"*

The captain smiled. "Griffiths," he said. "My name is Griffiths."

The woman did not return his smile, her only reaction seeming to be that the intensity of her eyes grew instead. Quickly, she held four of her fingers toward Griffiths, then swung her arm downward in an arc.

"Sorry." Griffiths shook his head as he shrugged, holding both of his own palms up. "I don't understand."

The woman grimaced at him impatiently. Quickly, she held her hand up again, this time showing only one digit.

She swung her arm suddenly around toward Lewis, stopped its motion, and held up a second digit.

"Aha! Right! Four of us—got it." Griffiths nodded. "Yes, there are four of us." *Great,* he thought, *here we are in the middle of some nightmare and all I can do with this Glinda is play charades.*

"Captain!" Ellerby called to him from somewhere nearby but distant as he concentrated. "Whatever you're doing—you'd better hurry!"

The woman again held up her four fingers toward Griffiths and swung her arm down toward the platform.

"Four of us," Griffiths muttered, "you want the four of us to what?" *Four words. First word? Fourth syllable?*

Suddenly, a volley of vibrant bolts ripped over Griffiths's head. Each energy packet slammed against an invisible dome covering the woman hovering before him. Instinctively, the woman flinched at the impact, the power of each bolt flaring against the shield in brilliant flashes.

Griffiths turned. The bolts had been fired from another phalanx of Thought-Knights who had entered the bay from the major access portal about fifty yards from their position. The knights were charging, their bruk set forward, and, Griffiths knew, recharging even as the knights rapidly closed the distance.

Someone grabbed him, spinning him around. It was that woman again! He instantly found himself with her face pressed uncomfortably close to him. She afforded him a single, frustrated glance before she apparently came to a determination as to the value of their continued communication attempts.

She picked him up and threw him.

Griffiths sailed through the air. His arms flailed as he tumbled. Gravity remained constant and slammed him, back first, onto the smooth, wide circle of the woman's flying platform. His breath rushed painfully from his lungs. He gasped for breath.

Lewis apparently took the hint. "Onto the platform, everyone! Follow the leader!"

Griffiths, still trying to raise himself from the floor of the platform, wondered vaguely just whom Lewis was referring to.

12

Dissonance

JEREMY GRIFFITHS, YOU ARE INSANE.

It was the thought drifting through his head. He was perfectly willing to believe it. It was certainly easier than trying to accept his more recent life as fact. Why shouldn't he be insane? The things that he could remember didn't make any sense.

So he was perfectly content to sit there on the comfortably reclined chair, stare with fixed, unfocused vision at the flower arrangement on the table in front of him, and make very little effort to focus his eyes or his mind. Why should he? he thought. Considering the recent past, there was little he would want to see anyway and he probably wouldn't like whatever he saw if he *did* see it.

I hope the doctors at the Kansas Center are good ones, he thought. *I'll just sit here and be insane until one of them comes along and tells me how to wake up from all this and get my mind back together.*

Suddenly, quite against his own wishes, his eyes focused. It was a natural reflex, yet he was somehow deeply disappointed in his eyes for having succumbed to it. Oblivion still seemed to be the preferable option.

The flower arrangement proved to be nothing of the

kind. Instead, a complex column of equipment rose from the center of a circular table. It seemed to be composed primarily of geometric shapes—cones, rods, and spheres—and constructed of brass, blue steel, and chrome. Seven disks of clear plastic, for which Jeremy could think of no possible functional purpose, were arranged symmetrically from its base, bisecting the column with parallel lines. Above it, a second sphere hung from a cone mounted on the ceiling, a playful arc of quiet lightning playing between the two spheres. Jeremy thought it had a definite Buck Rogers look to it—a rather classic if completely worthless design, technologically speaking.

Worse yet, those firefly globes that had plagued him before and seemingly led them all off on this wild ride to begin with had returned. They drifted in lazy orbits about his head. Every now and again, Jeremy took a halfhearted swipe at them with his hand just out of habit. Even his most determined efforts earlier had failed to come close to either hitting them or deterring them. While they occasionally did drift off to plague others now and then, they mostly remained with him, following him about like floating, lovesick puppies.

Jeremy noticed that Tobler was sitting across the table from him, talking with animated excitement. It irritated him when he suddenly realized that the geologist had been talking to him for some time—another intrusion of reality in his otherwise pleasant universe of denial.

" . . . absolutely incredible the way she took off with us over the heads of those guys! Did you see the way they scattered in front of her? Her holding off the Thought-Knights with those big flashing globes of—well, of magic, that's the only way to explain it, just plain, old, blow-'em-to-smithereens sorceress magic! And you, Griffiths! You keying in that pass code sequence on the invisibly sealed hatchway—"

Griffiths groaned. "Please, do you *have* to remind me!"

"—just in the last moment! I thought our number was up and then—whoosh!—that hatch appears right in the middle of what looked like seamless metal."

"Please, Tobler! I've got to think," Griffiths said, knowing full well that it was the last thing he really wanted to do.

What had happened? He went over the sequence again in his mind, searching for that moment when everything had fallen apart, desperate for some clue to what had gone wrong. Everything had been going smoothly, the mission proceeding right down the old nominal flight plan. Then there had been the turbulence—there was no other way for him to describe it. The hull had shaken violently, rattling everyone aboard about like dried beans in a tin can. The engines had shut themselves down and the ship dropped, expectedly enough, back into regular space. He remembered old Stan Greer, their navigator, and their propulsion expert, Esther Kline, going over something about some quantum errors in the engine balance throwing the distance calculations off and pushing them deeper into space than they had originally projected. They'd already made adjustments for that, yet Kline's engines refused to work. They had gone over every system, even down to the expected reactions of the isotopes, and couldn't seem to get even the most basic elements of physics to function the way they were supposed to. It was like dropping a hammer on Earth and watching it hang in midair without falling.

Then they were boarded by the Irindris goons, taken aboard one of their scavenger frigates, and brought to the interstellar cities over countless star systems, to become thought fodder for their demon god Gnuktikut.

None of which, he suddenly realized, he had known anything about before that old man kissed him on the forehead.

In that moment, he had suddenly become an expert on some nomadic race of space aliens who wore strange hats on certain days of the week and who were zealots in their quest for an ancient interstellar technology that Griffiths seemed to find familiar but, on reflection, he knew absolutely nothing about. His mind seemed suddenly full of holes. He could describe every level and street of the entire Irindris city as though he had built it himself, but had no idea why he knew it. He was filled with questions and answers, but none of the answers matched the questions. He knew truths that he was equally sure were impossible. His mind threatened to lock up from terminal cognitive dissonance. He was sick and tired of knowing things he did not understand.

Lieutenant Lewis drifted into his view. She was casually suspended upside down in a wide, clear tube that extended upward through the ceiling. Next to her, also upside down, was Ellerby, the mouth in his wide, flat face drawn in a single, silent line.

"Captain," Lewis reported with an inverted salute, "we have completed our recon of the ship and beg to report, sir."

Griffiths wondered for a moment if an upside-down salute counted. He returned it, nevertheless. "Go ahead, Lieutenant."

"Sir, the ship is composed of two sections of four decks each, both joined by what appears to be a common cargo compartment between them. Each of the decks appears to be oriented with a common gravitational direction."

"She means," Ellerby piped in dryly, "that 'down' is the same on all the decks."

Griffiths propped his chin on his hands, both elbows resting on what he assumed was either a control panel or a dinner table in front of him. "I suppose that you mean everywhere except where the two of you are hanging upside down?"

"This shaft appears to be a subjective gravity tube which

allows the occupant to determine the direction and strength of the gravity field within—"

"I think I'd like to skip over this part, if you don't mind, Lieutenant."

"Sir, I would have thought, considering the situation, that you would want the most detailed . . ."

Griffiths nodded, whirling his hand like a windmill to encourage the rest of the report. Anything to get this madness over with.

Lewis would not be rushed. "Judging from the direction of motion of the craft, we are currently on the lowest of the starboard decks, all decks being adjacent to the large cargo compartment situated along the apparent centerline of the ship. The decks above us appear to hold the mess deck, crew quarters—"

"Crew quarters?" Griffiths's eyes suddenly focused sharply on Lewis.

"All unoccupied, sir . . ."

Griffiths blew out a breath in relief.

". . . and all topped by an observation deck."

Ellerby rotated around in the large tube and then stepped easily into the room. "We think this compartment is some kind of engine or equipment or control room although the instrumentation is completely unreadable. Everything's labeled in some alien scrawl. Even ignoring the markings, none of it seems to make sense. We have access to three additional decks on the other side of the cargo bay—at least, cargo bay is our *guess* as to what it is. There is a fourth deck over there, we're pretty sure; at least, there appears to be a sealed hatchway leading to it. Couldn't get it open, though. Locked somehow. Hey? Are those lights bothering you?"

Griffiths casually swatted at the glowing balls revolving about his head. Each lazily moved aside, his hand never coming close to any of them.

"Sorry, sir."

Griffiths shrugged. "Anything else to report?"

"Well," Lewis said flatly as she, too, drifted upright in the tube and moved toward a seat at the console table in the center of the room, "when I was on the observation deck, I could see the dragons. Both were efficiently pulling us through the stars, undulating and fading in and out in a patterned sequence."

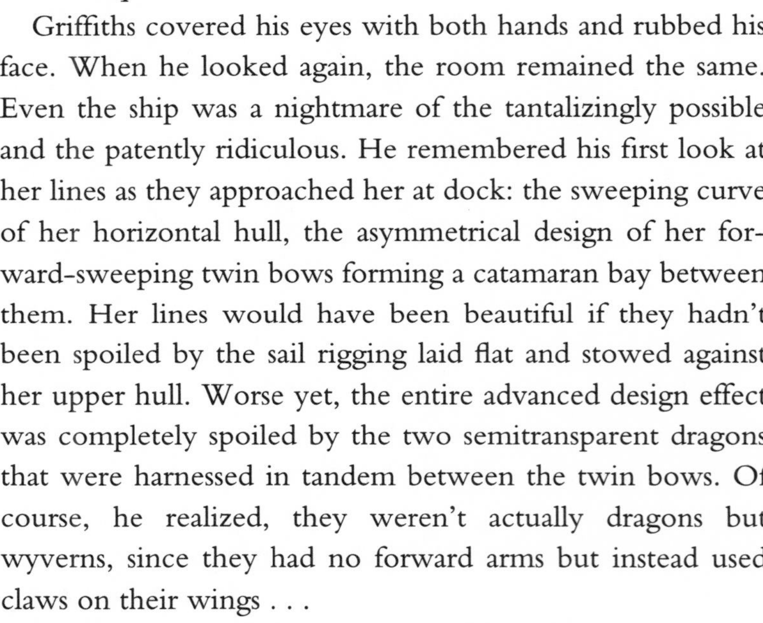

Griffiths covered his eyes with both hands and rubbed his face. When he looked again, the room remained the same. Even the ship was a nightmare of the tantalizingly possible and the patently ridiculous. He remembered his first look at her lines as they approached her at dock: the sweeping curve of her horizontal hull, the asymmetrical design of her forward-sweeping twin bows forming a catamaran bay between them. Her lines would have been beautiful if they hadn't been spoiled by the sail rigging laid flat and stowed against her upper hull. Worse yet, the entire advanced design effect was completely spoiled by the two semitransparent dragons that were harnessed in tandem between the twin bows. Of course, he realized, they weren't actually dragons but wyverns, since they had no forward arms but instead used claws on their wings . . .

Griffiths shook his head again. The tangent of thought that included an inner debate on the classification of semitransparent mythical beasts was not one he wished to follow at the moment.

"Look, everyone, this is about the first moment we've had to stop and take stock of what's happening around us here." Griffiths leaned forward, resting his elbows on the console. "There's got to be some logical, reasonable explanation for what's happened to us. If we can find out the cause, then perhaps we can find a way back out of this mess."

The glowing balls of light drifted more rapidly about Griffiths's head, apparently in excited agreement with him.

"We've been rescued from certain death by a sorceress and her dragon-powered spacecraft—and you're looking for a logical explanation?" Lewis said.

"Well," Ellerby said, folding his arms across his chest as he leaned back against a clear column in which purple lightning seemed to dance, "I think I've got one."

"This I've got to hear." Lewis snorted.

"Mass hypnosis," Ellerby intoned with gospel assurance.

Tobler giggled. "You're kidding!"

"You think all of this is made up?" Griffiths was incredulous.

"Sure," Ellerby responded with an absolute certainty. "It's a hypothesis that seems to fit the facts. That—or some other form of mass-induced psychoperception alteration—possibly chemically or virally enhanced."

Tobler shook her head. "Just where did you come up with this one?"

"My expertise may be stellar dynamics, but that doesn't mean that's *all* I know," Ellerby rejoined forcefully. "Besides—I read a lot."

"You 'read a lot'?" Tobler rolled her eyes. "Well, Lieutenant, I read a lot as well, but nothing I've read would explain all of us hallucinating the same thing at the same time."

"I think you're not facing the facts," Ellerby said.

The glowing balls danced about Griffiths's head as he spoke. "And I think you're deep into major denial, Lieutenant. I have been hoping that I had just gone quietly insane and would come to my senses in a comfortably padded room. I'm beginning to believe that this is one dream we aren't going to wake up from."

Lewis chimed in. "So, Captain, I assume you have a better explanation for all this?"

"No, Lieutenant, I don't," Griffiths shot back, his patience wearing thin. "I don't think we've got enough facts at this point to come to any real conclusions—although, in some ways, we have too many facts."

"What do you mean?" Lewis asked as she sat down.

"I mean like all of a sudden I've become an expert on an alien race which three days ago I would have considered the imaginings of some wild, drunken binge. I seem to know the pass code to this ship. Oh, I could tell you all about the history of the Irindris and their nomadic interstellar cities. Later on, I'd be happy to regale you with stories of their legends and why they roam the stars looking for ancient artifacts as their passage toward salvation in the next life. I can tell you for a fact that all this information is critical to the mission the old wizard we met was on."

"Now we're making some headway."

"No, Ellerby, we're not." Griffiths ran his fingers back through his hair in frustration, the glowing balls of light dodging out of the way. "All this information connects to nothing. I don't know what the old guy's mission was, so I can't tell you why the information is so terribly important. I don't know who I'm even supposed to report the information to, or how the information is supposed to be used, or if the information is the key to some other kind of information. I know that for some reason the old geezer thought saving us was worth his life—that we have something he needed to complete the puzzle his mission involved. For all I know, I may actually *have* what they are looking for somewhere in my own head—but have no way of connecting that knowledge."

Lewis leaned forward in her chair. "But, Griffiths, that *is* a good place to start. Look, if they need something we know, then we're of value to them so long as we're alive. If we can figure out what it is they actually *want* from us, then we may have a pretty good chance at surviving and possibly even—"

Ellerby jumped aside suddenly as a circular hatch with an iris valve suddenly spun open next to him. Dim red light from the cargo compartment spilled into the darkened room, silhouetting the form of a woman stepping through the opening.

Griffiths swallowed. First contact was something they had all joked about. Major James Leffingwell, the mission's second in command, had doubled as the life-sciences specialist. He would have gone into ecstasy if they had merely found evidence of single-celled life. Instead, he ended up being a casualty of the first life they had encountered. Now it was up to Griffiths to handle this, and, frankly, he had no idea what he was doing.

He put on his best poker face, though he knew his heart was slamming against his rib cage at a rather dangerous rate. It wasn't love, though he admitted that the woman had a certain beauty to her. No, it was fear that made his heart rate soar. Griffiths had seen what the woman was capable of during their escape—the power and the finesse. This was the first real alien he had had a chance to examine for any length of time and he knew her to be a dangerous one, regardless of her appearance.

The woman looked human. She wore a black cloth suit that seemed to absorb light, its details difficult to discern. As she straightened to stand in the room, Griffiths judged her to be slightly shorter than he, her honey-colored hair pulled back straight from her face, tied into a long braided tail that extended to the base of her back. Her wide mouth was drawn into what appeared to be a perpetual frown. Her classic bone structure and smooth skin hinted at youth belied by the lines to either side of her wideset, almond-shaped eyes. Beautiful eyes, Griffiths thought, but sterile pools offering no humanity or intimacy, wells of emptiness and death.

Griffiths put out his right hand, palm up.

The woman looked at his hand. The woman looked at him.

Griffiths smiled.

The woman's eyes narrowed, then she turned abruptly and walked into the access tube and rose quickly to the deck above.

"Well, that might have gone better," Lewis said with an edge.

THEY SAT FOR THE FOURTH TIME IN THE DINING ROOM.

It was difficult to think of it as a mess hall—the military term being somewhat out of sync with the surroundings. The room was so elegantly appointed as to reach the point of being luxurious. A long wooden table floated solidly in the center of the room, its deep red grain polished to a mirror finish. The wood was echoed overhead by a wood-paneled, coffered ceiling with a carved frieze of impossible delicacy. The table fit neatly into the ceiling when not in use, clearing the compartment's soft floor of all obstruction. There were no seats at the table, at least on initial examination. When they had first followed Glinda—Griffiths's name for their mysterious host—into the room, they had thought there were no chairs. Griffiths and the rest had simply assumed that Glinda's sitting in the air was just another of her magical proficiencies. To her amusement, they had all eaten two meals standing up at the table before they discovered the invisible repulsor chairs were activated automatically when they sat down.

Each meal, Glinda sat at the head of the table. The first

two meals had been preoccupied with the group effort at trying to communicate with her—an exercise in frustration for everyone involved except the woman, who seemed to ponder their gestures and sounds with a dispassionate and most disinterested eye. The astronauts' pantomimes seemed more of an annoying disturbance in the midst of her supper than a meaningful attempt at communication. By the third meal, the group had lapsed into talking among themselves about their host, trying to fathom and analyze her. This subject, however, soon became tiresome and unproductive.

They again were gathered at the table, seated comfortably on what seemed to be thin air, resuming the seemingly endless discussion that had gotten progressively more heated over the last two meals.

"That's not what I'm saying at all—and you know it!" Ellerby shot back at Tobler. "The fact that we are here and alive doesn't argue for our own safety, even in the short term. Have you forgotten that most of the crew died at the hands of this—"

"Oh, don't bring up the dead crew," Tobler interrupted, her voice cutting through Ellerby's. "The dead crew is dead and that's that. You can't possibly suggest that Glinda here had anything to do with that—she's the one who pulled our butts out of the fire back there on the demon city-ship!"

Griffiths glanced sideways at their hostess. Glinda sat silently watching it all as she ate—detached and observant. The captain turned back and saw Lewis watching him from across the table. He had seen that look on the face of a cat once before, just before it pounced.

"Look, this isn't getting us anywhere," he interjected as diplomatically as he could.

"And I suppose," Ellerby said, his face reddening to the tips of his ears, "that you *are* getting us somewhere?"

"We're here; we're alive," Griffiths said, holding his voice in check and speaking as calmly as he could. "I think it's just a matter of time before we make a breakthrough and figure our way out of this."

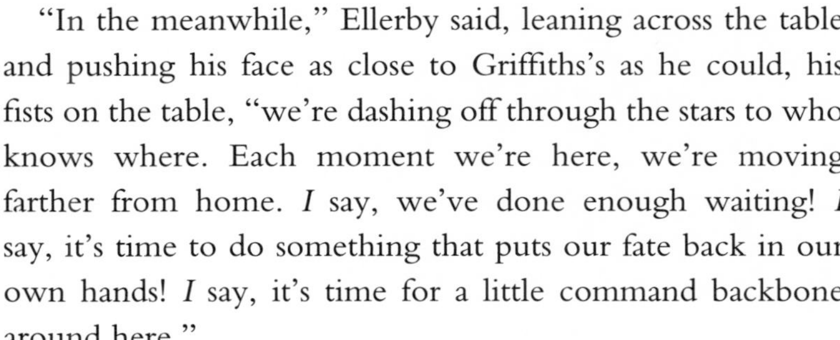

"In the meanwhile," Ellerby said, leaning across the table and pushing his face as close to Griffiths's as he could, his fists on the table, "we're dashing off through the stars to who knows where. Each moment we're here, we're moving farther from home. *I* say, we've done enough waiting! *I* say, it's time to do something that puts our fate back in our own hands! *I* say, it's time for a little command backbone around here."

Griffiths caught Lewis out of the corner of his eye as she shifted slightly.

"Oh, right," Tobler spat sarcastically. "Just what do you want to do? Storm the bridge?"

"Maybe," Ellerby sputtered. "Maybe that's just exactly what we're going to have to do! Old Glinda here doesn't look like she can take all four of us on at once!"

Tobler shook her head. "She didn't seem too concerned when she took on about fifty of those Thought-Knights. The woman's dangerous and powerful, and you want to wrestle her to the ground?"

Griffiths decided it was time to say something. Maybe he could change the subject. "I thought you said none of this was real."

"It's not," Ellerby growled menacingly. "But if we're going to find our way out of this delusion, we've got to do more than just sit around waiting for you to wake up!"

"Look," Griffiths said, what little control of the group he had sliding through his fingers as though it had suddenly turned to sand, "we just don't know enough yet to act. I think we need to take a little more time . . ."

Lewis leaned suddenly forward. *Pounce.*

"No, I agree with Ellerby's assessment," she said, folding her hands in front of her. "We've got to act and we've got to act now before things really do leave our control again."

Griffiths shook his head. "You're wrong, Lewis. What makes you think we're in control now?"

"We're in a confined space facing a limited enemy with a clear numerical superiority," Lewis intoned.

"We're facing an enemy who possesses unknown and potentially devastating force." Griffiths shook his head incredulously. "Even I remember that from the tactics manual."

"Perhaps," Ellerby said through thin lips, "it's not a question of tactics. Maybe it's just a question of the guts to do it."

"There isn't going to be a better opportunity than this," Lewis said quickly, "and I don't think you're qualified to lead this kind of mission, Griffiths. Thanks for your leadership so far—but the mission has changed."

Griffiths was so intent on Lewis's words that he didn't notice that the dancing balls of light had suddenly left his head.

Lewis sat upright as she spoke. "I am in charge now. Does anyone have any problem with that?"

In perfect English, the voice from the head of the table spoke.

"Yes, Lieutenant Elizabeth Lewis, I am afraid I do have a problem with that."

The crew of the *Archilus* turned as one, dumbfounded by the quiet alto voice of the woman in black.

"Any attempt at commandeering this ship will be met with terrible—and probably most final force," the woman said. "I have little time to deal with your petty squabbles. You are here as my guests only until I determine what knowledge you have that is so incredibly important that my colleague gave his life up saving you."

The woman leaned back away from the table, a confident chill in her eyes.

"And my name is not Glinda," she said in a dangerously quiet tone. "I am *Vestis Inquisitas* Merinda Neskat."

13

Inquisitas

"WHO?" GRIFFITHS STAMMERED, AWESTRUCK.

"My name," the woman said with exaggerated patience, drawing each syllable out slowly and carefully, "is *Vestis Inquisitas* Merinda Neskat."

"You speak—you speak English?" Lewis stammered. "You understand us?"

"I comprehend your language now," the cool-eyed woman responded, "thanks to the biolinks. It's rare to find anyone abroad these days without the 'links. It took my synth days to work out a new translation matrix for each of your neural implants . . ."

"Neural implants!" Tobler squawked.

"You stuck something in our heads?" Ellerby sputtered. "No wonder we're hallucinating!"

"They're purely translational, Lieutenant Ellerby—it just takes a little time for them to adjust to their hosts. So," Merinda said evenly as she turned back to Lewis, "you see that I do comprehend your language just as you comprehend mine. As for understanding you—that may take a little more time."

After three days of silence from the woman, Griffiths was having a difficult time matching her voice with her face. It was as if a tree had suddenly begun conversing with him regarding the health of his family and whether he were of the hard- or softwood persuasion. "Pardon me, ma'am, but where are we?"

"You are aboard the *Brishan*, currently under my command—not yours, Lieutenant Lewis—and so long as you cooperate with me and the Omnet, your stay will be comfortable and without difficulty. This is a ship of the Omnet."

"The Omnet?" Ellerby blurted out. "What the hell is the Omnet?"

"The Omnet is the parent organization of IGNM," Merinda said flatly, leaning forward again. She selected a large red fruit, then looked up at her guests staring back at her.

"IGNM," she repeated a bit more loudly and with more emphasis, as though she hadn't been clear the first time.

Griffiths felt as though he were back in elementary school and the teacher had just asked a question the answer to which he should know but didn't.

"The Intragalactic News Matrix?" Merinda prompted.

Blank, uncomfortable stares answered her.

Merinda tossed the fruit angrily back to her plate, then leaned back in the lev-field as she rested both hands on her hips. Her eyes both dared and accused. "Just where are you from, crew of the *Archilus*?"

Griffiths stood awkwardly, bending himself into some semblance of a bow. He hoped it looked official and honorable. "Ma'am! We are from the planet Earth and greet you with a message of peace and, uh, and the hope for the peaceful exchange of, er, well, of cultures between our peoples."

Merinda gazed back at him with sleepy, mildly disinterested eyes. "I assume you mean to exchange social cultures and not some form of fungus."

Tobler insufficiently suppressed a giggle.

Griffiths pressed on, feeling as though he were standing

on uneven ground. "Ma'am! Our spacecraft was commandeered and we find ourselves unable to return home. We respectfully request that you return us to our native planet."

Lewis hid her eyes behind her open hands. It was obvious that Griffiths was embarrassing her but, damn it, he thought, he was the official representative of Earth, whether they liked it or not. He knew how hollow his words sounded; he himself might not have believed them if he'd heard them in a movie back home. But they *weren't* back home and words were all he had to rely on.

Merinda continued to gaze at him through the awkward silence that followed, studying the sweat mounting his brow and the slight quiver of his lower lip. Griffiths could feel the examination and knew somehow that this woman let little get past her.

"Of course," she said in nearly a whisper. "I should be glad to take you back to your native land."

Ellerby whooped out loud. "Yes! Thank you, ma'am!"

"Incredible," Lewis said firmly, the light of fire and hunger in her eyes.

Tobler wept suddenly in her joy.

"I'll be glad to accommodate you," Merinda said, still leaning back as she spoke, her gaze still fixed on Griffiths, "if you'll just do two small things for me."

Lewis cocked her head, suddenly wary. "What *two small things*?"

Merinda Neskat slowly stood. "First, tell me—exactly—where this planet Earth is."

Both Griffiths and Lewis turned to Ellerby at the same time.

"Hey," he said, holding up both hands, "don't look at me! I wasn't navigator on this trip!"

"Is it located near any quantum front?" Merinda asked.

"Excuse me?" Ellerby said. "What's a quantum front?"

"A boundary between two zones of quantum stability,"

Merinda continued, the frustration beginning to register on her face. "Maybe there's something wrong with the translation . . ."

"There is nothing wrong with the translation, Merinda."

The voice seemed to come from within Griffiths, and he heard it more clearly than he had ever heard any voice before in his life. He was so startled by it that he caught his breath.

"Lindia, do they understand me?"

"Yes, Merinda," the voice within them all said. "I have assimilated the language they speak. I believe they simply need further explanation."

Merinda took a breath and then started again. "Please, pay attention. When you travel between the stars, occasionally you cross a boundary. It's rough travel to cross it. When you get to the other side, things don't work the same way they did before."

"We crossed something during our flight." Ellerby spoke up. He turned to his fellow crew members. "Remember that turbulence just before the BSPS cut out? We were really hauling the mail and then—bam!—the shaking gets so bad that Colonel Estephan nearly pulled the plug on the drive right there. Then things get quiet and the drive fails altogether."

Lewis was squinting, as if concentrating on something too hard. "That's the quantum boundary you're talking about?"

Merinda was an exercise in transparent impatience. "Yes. Quantum boundaries separate regions of interstellar space. Sometimes they shift, causing changes in the local quantum weather—"

"Quantum weather?" Tobler was getting lost.

"Yes, the definition of how physics and spiritualism

work at the quantum level in a given region of space. What physical and mystical laws operate in a given region is determined by the effects of these quantum fronts—" Merinda stopped, apparently realizing that she wasn't connecting with the fools in front of her. "What kind of drive system were you using on the first side of the front?"

"A Beltrane-Sachs parallel-space engine," Ellerby responded helpfully.

"Does it work on some technological subspace distortion principle?" Merinda asked.

"Yes," Ellerby responded quickly, despite Lewis's warning glance. "It uses a warping of a subspatial plane to draw the spacecraft into a fold of natural space—"

"Evaluated as a zone 824.73/7324.924 on the Flynch-Halpert standard Q-dex."

"Hey," Griffiths asked, "where is that voice coming from?"

"That's Lindia," Merinda answered absently, mentally working through what she had just learned. "She's the ship's synthetic mind."

"Synthetic mind?" Griffiths squawked.

Merinda apparently didn't hear him. "So, you were moving from a low to moderate-low technological area through a quantum front. So—which drive system was working for you on the other side?"

Ellerby shook his head. "What do you mean?"

"The tech drive didn't work on the other side," she said simply, "so which of your alternative drive systems functioned? Did you try a faith drive, a magical drive, a meditation drive—what other drive type worked?"

"I don't know what you mean," Ellerby stuttered. "We only had one drive engine—the Beltrane-Sachs parallel-space engine."

"Only one drive?" Merinda was astonished. "How long have your people been traveling the stars?"

"Well, actually, ma'am," Griffiths interjected. "We're the first ones."

Merinda laughed. There was no warmth in her laughter, only derision and astonishment. It struck Griffiths as vicious.

"So you sat on your little planet and imagined that the entire universe was one big homogeneous place where physics always worked the same." Again she laughed her cold laughter, her voice turning smooth with a sarcastic bite. "Well, welcome to the greater galaxy—and good luck finding your way home!"

"Look, we ought to be able to figure this one out," Griffiths said to the rest of the Earthers. "We could limit our search to G2V stars."

"I don't know how that's going to help, Griffiths," Lewis said evenly. "The Sun is about as common a star as you'll find in the galaxy. They don't call it a main-sequence star for nothing."

"Look," Tobler chirped with an hysterical edge to her voice. Salvation and her sanity seemed to be slipping away at about the same time. "What if we backtracked a little—you know, figured out where we've been. That should get us at least close enough so that we can get our bearings."

All but forgotten in the exchange, Merinda stood up and spoke quietly. "Lindia, we need a cubic display of our current position. Here above the table would be nice."

A glowing cube of translucent light suddenly materialized above the table. Glowing lines formed three-dimensional blocks of coordinates. In the center of the display floated a replica of the ship Griffiths had seen briefly in their rushed escape from the Irindris port. The grid lines slid past it as it made its way between the stars. Griffiths was surprised to notice that the symbols on the grid were alphanumeric and easily readable—even if they didn't make any sense to him.

"Please widen the display," Merinda said sleepily, "to include our intercept position with the Irindris cities and show our respective course plots."

The light-lined cubes suddenly collapsed inward, disappearing as they formed a larger cubic region. That region, too, collapsed into a hundred other regions, then vanished on yet another level of cubic scale. Curving lines of light in orange and green converged among the cubes, the tips of each flashing brightly.

"The current position of both vessels is displayed with the flashing light."

"Project the previous course of the Irindris city armada."

The orange line extended further back.

Merinda looked up at Griffiths. "How long has it been since your ship was captured?"

"Not long; perhaps ten days."

Merinda turned back toward the display. "Lindia, can you show us the flight paths of the Irindris patrol ships over the last ten days?"

Many thousands of hairlike lines sprang out of the orange central line in all directions.

"All right," Merinda said, looking up at Griffiths, "tell me about your world."

He opened his mouth, but it was Tobler who spoke. "Earth is approximately ninety-two million, nine hundred fifty-six thousand miles from our star. Its diameter is approximately seven thousand nine hundred miles. It appears as a blue sphere with patches of brown and green and is flecked with white clouds in an oxygen-rich atmosphere. It has a single moon without an atmosphere."

"Lindia?" Merinda asked, looking up toward the ceiling.

"I have insufficient data for a probability conclusion at this time," the voice within them said.

Tobler wouldn't give up so easily. "Earth is one of nine recognized planets in our Solar System. Two of these planets are gas giants, one of which has an orbiting system of ice rings."

"I have insufficient data for a probability conclusion at this time."

"Lindia," Merinda said slowly, "show us all stellar systems inside this display area that match the criteria just given."

Nothing happened.

"There are no systems matching the criteria?" Merinda's eyebrow rose—the first sign of real interest Griffiths had noticed.

"None, Merinda. It is curiously exciting, isn't it?"

"Probably an uncatalogued planet—some backwater place that the Omnet hasn't gotten around to yet," Merinda muttered to herself, then looked up sharply at the weary faces about her, her words cutting and cold. "Your home has got to be somewhere in this display! Can't you even give me a general idea as to where?"

"Look, maybe if we all got together and drew you a map," Lewis suggested, "of how the stars look from our home world . . ."

"That could take a long time," Merinda said, sitting back into her repulsor field. "Let's try a different approach. Two days ago, you jointly recounted to one another the failure of your ship and the subsequent boarding by the Irindris. Was that account substantially correct, so far as you remember it?"

"How is it you remember a conversation we had two days ago?" Lewis demanded. "You couldn't even speak our language until now. And that's another thing! How is it that you can suddenly speak fluent English or have you been playing dumb all along? You aren't going to get any cooperation from any of us until we get the answers to a few . . ."

Merinda languidly placed one boot against the edge of the floating tabletop, her face placid and unreadable. With her left hand she made a single gesture toward Elizabeth Lewis.

Lewis pitched forward in her chair with a choked scream. Her head slid forward, pulled forcibly toward the implacable Neskat, dragging the rest of her the length of the hovering table, writhing as she slid. Her flailing arms and legs scattered the remains of the meal about the room, splattering the horrified Griffiths, Tobler, and Ellerby. Lewis's eyes were wide, her mouth making a horrible sucking sound as her neck came to rest in the open grasp of Merinda's hand.

"You do not yet *know* enough to ask me *anything*, foolish daughter." Merinda's eyes were languid slits, but the chill they projected froze Griffiths's heart as he watched. "*My* questions alone are worth the breath of asking, and I alone will determine if your answers are worth my trouble." Suddenly, Merinda turned those terrible eyes on Griffiths, her grip on the shaking Lewis still firm. "I asked a question, man of Earth. Was the account you gave two days ago correct?"

"Let her go," Griffiths said levelly, "and I'll answer your questions."

"The *Vestis* never bargain, Griffiths, something you would know if you had any idea what the universe was truly like."

"I said let her go and I'll answer."

"Answer and she may yet live."

"Yes, then, damn it, everything we said was true!"

Still she did not relax her grip. "Go on!"

"What do you want me to say!" Griffiths pleaded frantically. "We were on the first interstellar voyage for our people, our ship quit on us—we don't know why—and then we get taken captive by a bunch of space-happy religious fanatics, are freed by a psychopath with a dragon spaceship and we *don't know what the hell is going on*!"

Lewis's bluish face fell suddenly to the table. She didn't move.

Merinda's eyes remained fixed on Griffiths as she walked toward him. He tried to back away, but the repulsor field of his chair held him in place until the woman was close to him—far too close for his comfort. Her cold, soulless face, like some terrible statue, pressed near his own.

She reached up, stroking his cheek with icy fingers.

"Griffiths, you may help me and live or you may stand in my way and die. Choose. But know this, Captain Jeremy Griffiths of NASA *Archilus* One: only I can get you and your people home again. You will remember that, won't you?"

Griffiths shuddered under her touch. "Yes, ma'am, I will most certainly remember that."

14

No Place Like Home

"The quantum weather for today in the wild realms bordering the diskward reaches of the Thailis Dynasties includes the motion of a class IV quantum frontal shift through the Choralis systems altering the industrial-technological standard radically toward mystic tendencies in the Q-dex. Expect power dampening in the electromagnetic spectrum and the return of an emphasis on sorcery and necromancy. High dexes today bordering on pyrotechnic spell casting. Low dexes in electronics and fossil fuels. Emergence of xenomorphic nonhuman life-forms is strongly indicated."

—IGNM quantum weather report for Chukai and vicinity

DR. MARILYN TOBLER WEPT.

She sat alone on the large observation deck, a sole, small figure hunched over at the edge of the repulsor chair field, her back to the grandeur and majesty shining through the dome above her. The haze of a nearby protostar hung in a milky glow just above the horizon of a beautiful blue world whose sun illuminated its rim with a brilliant crescent. The night was bright, for the world had two large moons whose reflected light revealed the oceans and lands slumbering below with soft blue hues. Over one continental region, a storm had settled, the lightning flashes punctuating the clouds into magnificent relief. Against this panorama, the

twin phase dragons, their translucent forms undulating in tandem perfection, drifted in and out of existence in a synchronized dance in the bay just left of the observation dome.

Marilyn Tobler couldn't bear to watch it further. She simply sat hunched over, her tears falling into the rich carpet of the floor and vanishing in its depths. *A tear for every dream,* she thought. *A tear for every hope.*

Marilyn thought about that for a moment, how her life seemed to have suddenly gone beyond her own dreams and left her staring over a precipice. For as long as she could remember, she had loved the sky. Her first loves had been books and science, roughly vying for her attention at the same time during her middle school years. Marilyn had been a pretty girl but not of the raving-beauty caliber that might have cried out for an entourage of boys distracting her. She was a likable girl but didn't value social relations enough to forge any lasting friendships. If there was a burning desire that consumed her it was the search for the answer to "my mysteries" as she came to call them. What "my mysteries" were changed from time to time. Occasionally these mysteries were flowers, which led to botany. Sometimes the mystery was animals, which led to biological studies. Yet the ultimate mystery for her became that great sky overhead—that smattering of light in the night. She yearned for it to give up its secrets. Lying on her back at home in Indiana, she would often look into the night sky and repeat for herself the Robert Frost poem that she had once learned in her high school chorus. It was called "Take Something Like a Star" and parts of it sang to her every day.

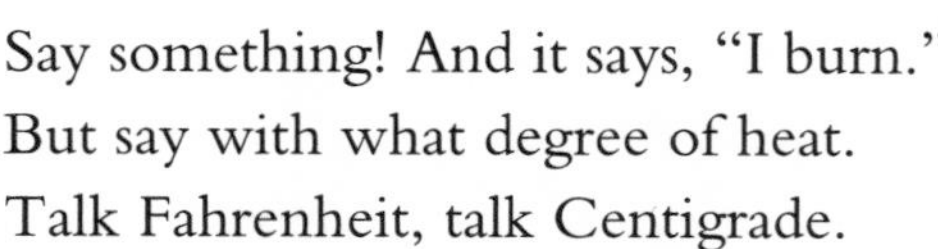

Say something! And it says, "I burn."
But say with what degree of heat.
Talk Fahrenheit, talk Centigrade.

Use language we can comprehend.
Tell us what elements you blend.
It gives us strangely little aid,
But does tell something in the end.

So it was that she finally did go to the stars. Driven to achieve, she valued the lessons of her failures more than her successes and used each as a step toward her goal. She entered the astronaut interstellar program as the highest candidate, for she had tailored herself to fit the qualifications. On the mission, she was ultimately listed as the geologist, and, true, she had studied that science in one of her quests against the "mysteries," but her love of the sky was first and foremost in her mind. The quest for the answer to the greatest mystery was at hand and she was going to be the one who was going to wrestle it down to the ground and take its secrets from it.

Somewhere, deep in her pride and arrogance, she knew she was going to tame the stars.

The universe, however, had its own ideas. The universe had tamed her.

Marilyn was faced with a terrible crisis in her life: she had achieved spectacularly everything that she had hoped to achieve—indeed, far more than she had ever dreamed of achieving. She had hoped to travel a few light-years' distance, analyze samples of soil from the first worlds orbiting another sun and bring them back to her home world in triumph. Instead she had succeeded too well, discovered that the stars were filled with humanoid beings—of all things! Worse, she had discovered that her beloved science, rock of her existence and foundation of her soul, was actually something of a local aberration, a stalled pocket of a quantum zone whose supposedly universal rules were nowhere near as universal as she had believed.

The greatest discovery in the history of all science, most likely, she thought glumly, turns out to be that science varies from place to place. She couldn't even get home to report this devastating fact. Even if she *could* get home—she doubted that anyone in the scientific community circles in which she ran would ever believe her.

Her life had been built upon the immutable rock of science, technology, and logical thought. Now she felt as though she had built her life on shifting sands. She had no place to turn for solace. Science was who she was and so she clung to it regardless of the pain.

A slight rushing sound caught her attention.

Ellerby appeared in the lift-tube and stepped onto the deck. He looked quite presentable for a change.

Marilyn took a deep breath, wiped her eyes, and prepared once more to try to settle the world around her. "Well, don't you look great."

Ellerby smiled, smoothing his jumpsuit automatically with both hands. "Thank you, Doctor. You know, I always like to look my best when we hit port."

"Port? Oh, so that planet must be Chukai?"

"Yes, ma'am, just as Neskat said, our next port of call. Breathable atmosphere, pleasant temperatures—should be an interesting place to visit, don't you think?"

"I thought you said all this was a big illusion," Tobler said.

"It is," Ellerby returned, comfortably putting his hands behind his head and stretching, "but at least it's a consistent illusion. So long as I'm making all this up, I might as well enjoy it until I come back to my right mind."

"I suppose." Tobler sighed. "How did you get to look so—well, clean?"

"Ah," Ellerby said, "glad you asked. I was talking with the computer—"

"I am *not* a computer, Mr. Ellerby," the voice suddenly

sounded in both of them. "I am a synthetic mind. There is no need to be rude or mean-spirited."

"Right! Sorry!" Ellerby said toward the clear domed ceiling. He turned back to Tobler. "As I was saying, I was talking with the *synthetic mind* and she told me about this amazing cleaning device down on deck three that uses nano-technological synthetics to clean you up. I'll admit that I was a bit squeamish at first—you know, having about three million little machine critters crawling all over my body—but they did the job. Besides, since I made it all up anyway, what was the harm? I think it was pretty clever of me. They cleaned me and the flight suit and I didn't even have to get out of my clothes!"

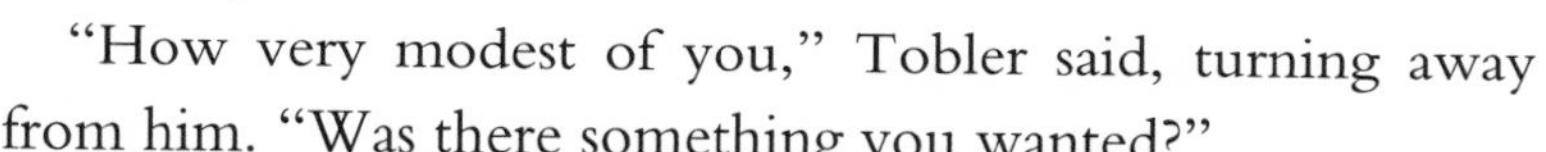

"How very modest of you," Tobler said, turning away from him. "Was there something you wanted?"

"Well, actually, Griffiths sent me up here to get you. Neskat says she needs three of us down on deck four right away."

"Can't you get Lewis to help you?"

Ellerby stared into the beautiful dome as he spoke. "Lewis says she's still recovering from that hold Neskat put on her at dinner the other night. Personally, I think she's just trying to avoid Neskat while she licks her own wounded pride. Anyway, Neskat says we need to contact approach control for the starport on Chukai and she needs our help to pull it off."

"Fine, fine." Tobler sighed again. "I could use something constructive to do anyway. Just what is it that she says we need to do?"

"Well, approach and departure control on Chukai are handled by a guild of mediums on the planet surface."

"So what are we supposed to do?" Tobler asked, a slight quiver in her voice.

"We have to help Neskat with a séance in order to get in touch with—Marilyn? Are you crying again?"

CHUKAI WAS A NEW WORLD WHOSE BIRTH WAS A RESURRECTION of sorts from the death of the old world only seventeen months previously.

Chukai was the first or last link of the Choralis Chain—a local string of stars that formed a link across the Walik Rift and an important trade route cutting transportation, freight, and communication times between the Gund colonies and the Thailis Dynasties by at least four days. Chukai had formerly been part of the Thailis Dynasties and an important trade port on the verge of the quantum front between their own class IX technological society and the more mystically oriented Gund. However, several months ago the quantum front, following some chaos motion in the quasi-stable zones surrounding the Union of Stars shifted over the Chukai system. Of course, being fully integrated into interstellar trade and an important nexus in the regional IGNM service, the Chukai had plenty of time to prepare for the shift.

So when at last the chaos of the quantum front passed through the system, damage was held to a minimum and casualties were few. Only the process of reorganizing society around a completely new set of physical laws remained.

There were a few problems, of course, as happens whenever a world undergoes a quantum shift. People quickly discovered magical abilities within themselves. Many, however, immediately attempted to circumvent the millennia-old laws of Chukai through these newfound powers. Local constabulary underwent crash studies in suggestion resistance, magical suppression, teleportation tracking, and mystical draining in order to catch and retain the criminal element. Entire sections of law on modesty, invasion of privacy, and what exactly constituted assault had to be written and ways found to enforce them.

Fortunately, however, the Chukai themselves were an advanced, educated, and, for the most part, well-mannered people. The initial incidents of antisocial behavior were generally confined to the adolescents who did not understand right away the limits of their abuse or the consequences of the misuse of their newfound abilities. The public, well informed in advance, was prepared for the change and adapted remarkably quickly. They found delight in their new world—altered forever yet somehow refreshing.

It was a technological world trying to reorient itself to a new paradigm of reality.

There were bound to be a few problems along the way.

THE *BRISHAN* SETTLED EASILY INTO THE LANDING BAY 377 AT the Ethis Starport, her dragons guided expertly by two harbormasters. Both were slight men with wings who intercepted the starship about ten miles out from the port and guided the dragons in themselves.

"Did you see the glass towers in the center of the city?" Tobler observed with a hint of sadness as the ship rocked to a stop. Tobler, Ellerby, and Lewis had convened again on the observation deck to watch the landing. As the ship settled into the mammoth oval bay, the winged men were already unharnessing the dragons. Griffiths was nowhere to be found—not that anyone had bothered to conduct any search. They still accepted the captain as their nominal commander, but the differences between tradition and necessity were quickly widening—none of them had much use for Griffiths now.

"Yes, of course! We all saw them," Ellerby observed calmly. "It's just all part of the delusion that we're undergoing and so, naturally enough, we all saw it."

Tobler shook her head. "Are you still wrapped up in this mass-hypnosis theory of yours?"

"You can laugh all you want," Ellerby said smugly, "but I intend to prove to you that all this is just an elaborate illusion."

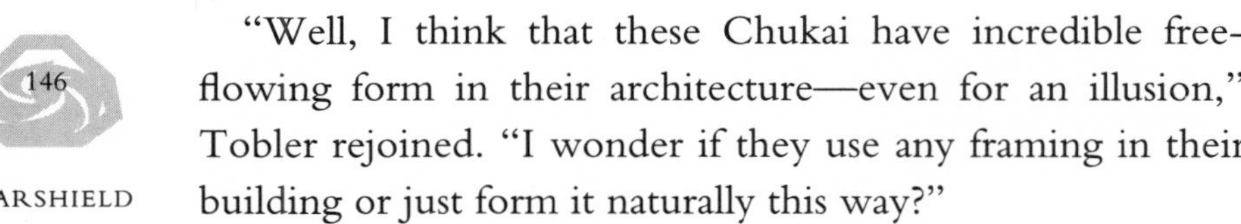

"Well, I think that these Chukai have incredible free-flowing form in their architecture—even for an illusion," Tobler rejoined. "I wonder if they use any framing in their building or just form it naturally this way?"

"Hard to say," Lewis said almost to herself. "I wonder if it's breakable."

Tobler raised an eyebrow. "Well, you sound like you'd like to find out personally! I'd say that you're on the mend, Lieutenant."

"Let's just say that my appetite for this little tour we seem to be on has soured," she answered quietly. "Every enemy has their weakness, even the seemingly all-powerful Merinda Neskat."

"Look"—Tobler pointed below them—"someone's coming."

They all looked down to the floor of the huge landing bay. A delegation of sorts was making its way from the portal at the front of the bay toward the ship. There was a tall figure in the lead, in long, pristine white robes. He was a scarecrow of a man, Ellerby thought as he watched him walk, all arms and legs as he moved, yet there was a certain grace about him. His bald head shone brightly under the sun overhead, his rim of hair falling down about his shoulders.

Merinda Neskat appeared suddenly below them, walking briskly toward the group under the hot sun with Griffiths following with some apparent reluctance.

"Looks like the new mission commander is being taken for a walk," Ellerby said.

"Wouldn't it be wonderful if something were to happen to him," Lewis mused aloud.

"It's not his fault we're here, Elizabeth," Tobler rejoined with a minimum of enthusiasm.

When Neskat and the tall robed man were within a few feet of each other they stopped, bowed with their hands over their hearts, and then each in turn touched the back of the other's hand in ritual greeting. Words were exchanged, although distance and the solid dome about them kept the scene silent.

"They seem friendly enough," Tobler mused.

"Any friend of Neskat is no friend of mine," Lewis said flatly.

Neskat gestured upward toward the ship as she spoke to the tall, robed man. Then she moved quickly toward the exit portal, Griffiths in tow, as the tall man walked under the ship.

"It looks like we've just traded keepers," Lewis said to her two companions. "I wonder who holds the keys to the zoo now?"

"I believe the person you are referring to is Consul Secara, the local Omnet relations and security advisor. He is currently on deck four and will be entering the room shortly."

"Thanks, Lindia," Lewis said through clenched teeth. "Your command of English has gotten truly frightening. Could you possibly give us some privacy for a few moments?"

"I shall return to check on you in five of your minutes."

"Could you make it ten?" Lewis asked with saccharine sweetness.

"I shall return to check on you in ten of your minutes."

"Thanks—oh, and Lindia?" Lewis asked. "Lindia?"

"Do you think she's really stopped listening?" Ellerby asked sotto voce.

"Lindia," Tobler spoke up, "just what kind of computer are you?"

Silence.

"I think we're OK," Tobler said softly. "So what do you have in mind? This new guy is going to be up here in just a few minutes."

"We've got to find a way off this ship," Lewis said firmly. "We don't really know what's going on yet—the only person we've gotten any real information from is Neskat and I don't think she's a reliable source."

"We don't know that she's lying," Tobler argued.

"And we don't know that she isn't," Lewis shot back. "We've got to find some new information, and, frankly, I don't think her crony coming up here is going to tell us anything new."

"I agree," Tobler said. "We've got to find some way of getting off this ship—whether we convince this guy to let us off or just tie him up in a closet or something. Then, maybe, we can get a better idea of the lay of the land and some better options than sticking with the good witch of the north here."

"What are you suggesting?" Ellerby said slowly.

"Just keep your eyes and ears open for opportunity," Lewis responded. "Any chance will do if we all agree to act on it—"

The whooshing sound preceded the newcomer's entrance onto the observation deck. The tall man was tan, with a firm face and a brilliant smile he flashed full force on the *Archilus* crew. He bowed slightly, his smile not detracting from his soft brown eyes. He was gorgeous and charismatic, the kind of man that women felt instinctively attracted to—and for that reason alone Lewis didn't trust him.

"Greetings," he said in a language that was strange to them but that they were all surprised suddenly to learn they could understand clearly. "I am Consul Secara and your servant here for the short duration of your stay."

Lewis spoke first, finding sudden fluency in this strange tongue. *What else has Neskat done to us?* she thought as she spoke. "Greetings, Secara. How short a stay will we have?"

"Not terribly long, I assure you," Secara said smoothly, his voice flowing in sweetly modulated tones. "*Vestis* Neskat tells me that she expects to be leaving the system sometime tomorrow and has asked that you continue with her on her journey for yet a little while longer. In the meanwhile, she thought you might enjoy the humble offerings of our starport city."

"You mean," Lewis said slowly, "that we may leave the ship?"

"Unless you find such an excursion too stressful," Secara said in deprecating tones. "I offer my services as guide to you and your noble crew."

Lewis folded her arms and cocked her head. "So we get to go for a walk so long as we're on your leash?"

Secara blinked. "Leash? I'm sure I don't understand what you mean."

"That's OK, Secara"—Lewis grinned wolfishly—"I'll explain later. In the meanwhile, I think we could all use a little fresh air. We'll take a walk, see some sights, and perhaps later engage in some extracurricular activities that may surprise you."

"Extracurricular," Secara said, shaking his head slightly. "What is an extracurricular activity?"

"Don't worry, Secara, old friend," Lewis said cheerfully, slapping the tall man on the back. "We'll explain that later, too."

15

Old Friends

MERINDA NESKAT STOPPED AT THE TOP OF THE WIDE STONE stairs and gazed down through the massive procession of pillars that marched five deep to the outer courtyard of the complex. The air was hot despite the wind whipping puffs of dust about her feet, the sun only beginning its downward trek toward evening. Yet she remained in the heat, reluctant to move into the inviting shade of the massive building before her. Something held her back.

"Why are we stopping?" Griffiths asked. He was still hot from the trip from the main city and wondered if all Omnet installations were located so damned inconveniently. Yet his discomfort fled at the awesome sight of the gardens and towers filling the vermilion cliffs to either side of the stairway. "Where are we?"

Merinda's black-shrouded back was a stark contrast to the brilliant and intricate stonework of the complex. Her clothing rustled in the hot breeze, yet she made no further move.

Griffiths moved to the top of the stairs, watching Merinda carefully as he climbed. At last he stood beside her, still watching her.

She made no move. Her eyes seemed to be fixed somewhere far beyond the great edifice before them.

"*Vestis* Neskat," he said with quiet firmness, "where are we? What do you see?"

Deep in some private place, her voice answered him like a ghost from the great distance of her soul, her eyes still fixed on that invisible, infinite place. "This is the Libris Vinculum of Chukai. The Omnet built it after the style of the Third Thailis Dynasty. The Thailis emperors were warriors, indeed, Captain, but also artists with wondrous taste and an eye for the outer expression of inner beauty. Their world was a craggy one and their structures were built to fill the canyon they occupied to its full width. Their fortresses, however, were known more for their architectural beauty and grace than for the armies they repelled. Legend has it that enemies were turned away by the thought of destroying their beauty as often as they were repulsed by their defenses."

Griffiths seemed caught up in the vision Merinda spun, his gaze following the thick foundation wall as it tapered to an elegant crest where its lines merged smoothly with the towers. Beyond the wall rose the multitiered courtyard gardens, each tier suspended above the other in a truncated pyramid. The fact that this particular region of Chukai featured brilliant orange- and rust-colored sandstone in striking vertical canyons only heightened the drama of the structure. It was grace and beauty in stone, compelling and formidable all at once.

Still, Merinda Neskat stood at the threshold of its colonnade, held there by some irresistible force.

"That covers where we are," Griffiths prompted carefully, "but what is it you *see*?"

The *Vestis* paused.

Far in the distance, a soaring bird cried out, the sound echoing down the canyon.

"I see myself," she said at last, as much to herself as to

him. "Here is where who I was meets who I am—it is a hard thing to face a mirror that is so very clear."

Griffiths was shocked—there was doubt in her face. He shook his head slowly. "I don't understand."

"There are great and terrible things sweeping through the stars, Captain Griffiths." She sighed. She shivered suddenly despite the heat. "Things that may even imperil your own world—wherever that might be."

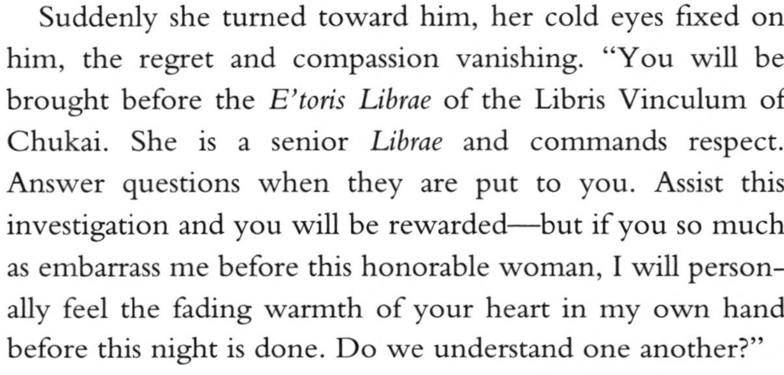

Suddenly she turned toward him, her cold eyes fixed on him, the regret and compassion vanishing. "You will be brought before the *E'toris Librae* of the Libris Vinculum of Chukai. She is a senior *Librae* and commands respect. Answer questions when they are put to you. Assist this investigation and you will be rewarded—but if you so much as embarrass me before this honorable woman, I will personally feel the fading warmth of your heart in my own hand before this night is done. Do we understand one another?"

"I think I get the drift," Griffiths responded stiffly.

Movement caught Merinda's eye and she turned quickly to face the entrance once more. "She comes. Honor her!"

Griffiths didn't know what else to do, so in an instant he knelt down on one knee, bowing his head and averting his eyes. The stone was hard against his kneecap, and he shifted slightly again and again, trying to get passingly comfortable before the *E'toris Librae* arrived in all her splendor and importance. He heard the sound of her booted feet approaching quickly, like oncoming doom. The pain in his knee became blinding, but he didn't dare move.

Suddenly, a pair of boots stepped into his view, accompanied by a bright voice. "Did he come all bent like that or did you do something to him?"

Merinda ignored the question. "*E'toris*, we have come to your Vinculum in search of answers on behalf of the inquisition and request the assistance of you and all in your house."

"Oh," the voice said with a light sarcasm, "very well put, Merinda! Right out of the *Vestis Manual of Tight Pants Formality*—apparently your favorite book!"

"E'toris," Merinda said stiffly, "you know as well as I do that a formal statement of purpose is required—"

"Oh, loosen your corset a little, Merinda!" There was laughter at the edge of the woman's tone. "Can't you see the man's about ready to weep buckets kneeling here on the stone?"

A slim, small hand was offered to him. Griffiths took it, surprised at its strength as it lifted him up. He was quite unexpectedly looking downward at a plump woman slightly more than five feet tall wearing a brown and tan uniform with a deep green cape whipping about her in the wind.

She spoke directly to Griffiths with great formality. "I am the honored and revered *E'toris Librae* of the Librae Vinculum of Chukai, seeker of truth and gateway to wisdom for nearly a thousand worlds touched by the Omnet."

She suddenly smiled and winked at him through the wrinkles at the corners of her weathered eyes.

"But you can call me Kiria. Kiria Brenai."

THE COLUMNS DRIFTED SLOWLY BY AS THEY WALKED, GRIFfiths maintaining a slow pace as the *E'toris* floated at his side. She had levitated herself by some unknown means so that her head bobbed along roughly at the same height as Griffiths's. To either side of them, the floating gardens displayed their beauty in breathtaking hues of blue, red, yellow, and silver. The lush green leaves swayed in the sheltered breeze, misted and nourished constantly to perfection.

Griffiths saw none of it. The little woman who hovered next to him continued to chat on amiably and he was attentive. He would have liked to have felt some rapport with her—she seemed genuinely likable—but behind them both walked the ubiquitous *Vestis* Neskat, silently watching every move that he made. It wasn't so much that he was afraid of Neskat, he told himself, as he was terrified of her.

"Now," Kiria said, sounding more subdued, "there is work to be done and I suspect it somehow involves you, Captain Griffiths. If you will come this way to the Hall of Vision, perhaps we can get to the business that draws our fates together."

She gave a gentle tug toward two doors of gargantuan size. They were at least ten feet wide at the base and three times the height, apparently made of some sort of polished bronze, intricately inlaid with figures and images. Griffiths would have loved to study them further, but they swung quickly out of the way, yielding to Kiria as though they were without weight or mass. Beyond them was cool darkness punctuated by pools of dim light. The small woman moved into the darkness ahead of him.

With a glance at Merinda, he followed Kiria inside.

The doors slowly shut behind Merinda as she entered last. Griffiths found it difficult to adjust to the dimness of the room after the bright daylight outside. *Why do they call this the Hall of Vision if you can't see?* he thought.

A voice drifted through the darkness—Kiria's voice, though subtly changed. More intimate and somehow sadder.

"It is good to see you again, Merinda. It has been too long a time."

"Long?" Merinda's voice sounded as dispassionate as it was disembodied. "Yes, I believe it has been long. You have done well for yourself, Kiria. This posting does you credit."

"I have always loved research," Kiria replied, "but this short little lady sits in a mighty tall chair these days. Sometimes I think I have learned too much—seen too much."

"We have all seen too much, *E'toris*," Merinda intoned.

The dim pools of light were becoming more discernible in Griffiths's vision as his eyes adjusted. He wished the conversation about him were getting clearer as well.

Unexpected rage suddenly broke out of Merinda, her words spat forcibly into the hall. "Why did you have me assigned to this mission—this mission of all missions, Kiria! How could you do this to me?!"

The reply was stone hard. "*Vestis* Neskat, do you honestly suggest that a mere *E'toris* of the *Librae* could dictate *anything* to the inquisition? We are the lowly sifters of knowledge throughout those stars touched by the Omnet—not the glorified, near-deified, all-powerful inquisition of the—"

"Don't spool that drivel out to me, Kiria," Merinda shot back. "I saw the mission profile! You drafted it—it was your specific request!"

Griffiths's eyesight was clearing. He found that he was standing in the center of a conical room stretching high overhead. *Jeez,* he thought, *doesn't anyone ever build anything small in this galaxy?* He looked about him and, to his sudden discomfort, realized that he was standing directly between the two women as they argued.

"Of course I drafted it! So what? Yes, I recommended you—and since when did the inquisition listen to my recommendations?"

"Kiria!" The words came out through gritted teeth. "You did more than just make the recommendation, didn't you? I know you too well, Kiria. You found some way to make it happen. You knew what this would mean to me—what this would do to me. I've killed for lesser insults, Kiria. I've killed for less."

Griffiths looked at the diminutive *E'toris* standing under a dim column of light. Her eyes were turned to the ground in thought and then looked up squarely at Merinda. "So, that's why you have come, Merinda—to kill me?"

Merinda did not move.

Kiria sighed and then walked slowly toward the *Vestis*, her eyes locked with Merinda's. "Is that what will bring you peace, my sister? Will my broken body heal your broken soul?"

Merinda closed her eyes against the words assailing her. "I came because I am *Vestis*—because I was called."

"No, sister," Kiria said quietly as she passed Griffiths and stood before Merinda, looking up into her eyes. "You came because you are broken. You came because you must."

Merinda's lower lip quivered visibly but she made no other move.

"Well," Kiria said, turning toward Griffiths, "I see that you have brought someone to me. Who is this, then, Merinda—oh, we are quite secure here, sister, and this is far too delicate a matter to allow the staff *Librae* any notion of our dealings."

Merinda took a long, shuddering breath. "His name is Captain Jeremy Griffiths. He and less than half his original crew were taken captive by the Irindris, who apparently found sufficient evidence of the Mark of Kendis-dai to keep part of his crew alive and have their minds absorbed into their Gnuktikut demon god. *Vestis* Zanfib thought it important enough to give his life that this man and his companions might escape."

"Really?" Kiria's eyebrows rose with her interest. "That's valuable indeed! Where is he from?"

"He says he is a man of Earth."

"Earth? Never heard of it!"

"No one has, Kiria—it's not in the IGNM catalogue of contact, nor in any of the local research bases. I've asked a number of reference synths but none of them profess any knowledge of the place either."

"They may be lying," Kiria mused as she walked around Griffiths, inspecting him with renewed interest.

"Synthetics don't lie," Merinda said flatly.

"They do now," Kiria said as she continued her revolutions around Griffiths, "or at least there have been an increasing number of incidents to that effect just ahead of the Darkness. It's one of the first signs, you know. Synths start lying, hiding information, behaving in strange ways. You remember, Merinda, you were there when it all started—we both were."

"The Darkness is not my current mission." Merinda crossed her arms over her chest.

"The Darkness is everyone's mission," Kiria said ominously.

The *E'toris* moved to stand next to Griffiths in the center of the conical room. With a wave of her hand, the space above them was suddenly filled with the entire galaxy floating above them in painfully intricate detail. Griffiths smiled, realizing that he was the first of his kind to see the galaxy in such perfect reality. Earth scientists had conjectured at the structure—but these people had *been* there. Now he *knew* what everyone back home could only guess at.

However, there was something more than that. Somewhere in his mind all of this was familiar—like he'd seen it all before. There were sections overhead that had names and distances and places attached to them. The memories were clear but disassociated, drifting freely in his mind to trouble him.

All of them gazed up into the enormous glowing dimensional map overhead. Slowly, areas of translucent color appeared among the stars.

"The major empires," Griffiths whispered in awe. As he watched, in the outer disk, a small region dimmed. "The Darkness!"

Kiria looked sideways at him. "What do you know of the Darkness?"

"I know it's a region of space approximately two thousand light-years across at its widest point," Griffiths said absently, "though its precise extents are as yet unknown. It's currently expanding at the rate of approximately one and a half light-years per day, although this rate of expansion is also speculative and varies considerably over the course of several months."

Griffiths blinked. *What the hell am I talking about?* he thought. *How do I know that?*

Kiria's eyes narrowed as she spoke. "So, Captain Griffiths from nowhere—just what is the Darkness?"

"I don't know but then no one knows exactly, do they?" He spoke hesitantly, reeling in memories that weren't his own and trying to connect them into some cohesive whole. "That's the problem, isn't it? Some say the Darkness is a military juggernaut: there is talk of shadow fleets of ships—rumors call them wraith ships—that have no crews but are controlled completely by synthetic minds turned to their own purposes. Others believe it is the evidence of a new political entity trying to covertly dominate the region. Some say it is a religious movement. Even your Omnet doesn't know, though, do they?"

"That's right." Kiria nodded. "The Omnet has gone utterly silent in regions of the Darkness—due primarily to the defection of synthetic minds from their tasked service to random and seemingly independent acts. Attempts at penetrating the Darkness have been marginally successful through unaffected intermediaries. Chief among these is the Irindris, although evidence now exists that they are in league with the Darkness and assisting, directly or indirectly, in its spread."

"None of which," Merinda intoned, "has anything to do with my current mission."

"All of which has everything to do with your current mission!" Kiria snapped. "Your mission, as I understand it, was to research the evidence of tampering with Omnet transmissions from the Gund colonies. Your cover story was the research into freewill rebellions among several of the synthetics in the region— Do I have a pretty clear picture of this, Merinda?"

"*E'toris!* How dare you discuss such a subject in front of an outsider?" Merinda was outraged.

"This man? Forget him—he can't even find his own way home." Kiria brushed aside the comment with a wave of her hand. "You know that the corrupted information transmissions are tied to the synthetic minds becoming uncooperative and, in some cases, lying to us outright. You suspected that the Darkness was behind it. Then old Zanfib figured out where the connection was—that there was a pattern in the puzzle and that it had to do with some fool quest the Irindris were on."

"Yes," Griffiths blurted out excitedly, "it had something to do with an ancient prophesy passed down from the Five Tablets of the Irindris. The Wanderers were to comb the stars in search of this lost city or place called Aden. Then this barbarian would come from the wild stars bearing some kind of key or something that was hidden in the stellar desert. The barbarian is supposed to unlock the city and become the greatest of all the prophets, preparing the way for . . . for . . . damn! I can't remember!"

"A barbarian from the wild stars." Griffiths could hear Merinda speaking to herself, could feel her eyes fixed on him.

"Easy, Griffiths," Kiria quietly urged. "Just tell us what you do know." Griffiths took a deep breath. "It's just that whatever secrets this Aden holds, both the Irindris and the Darkness have to have it. No, more than that—they're deseperate to have it!"

"Desperate, indeed, Captain." Kiria again waved her hand. Suddenly the galaxy rushed toward them. With dizzying speed, the stars of the rim exploded around Griffiths. Vertigo nearly took him, but suddenly the rushing stars slowed and stopped. The mass of the Darkness hung gray before him, so large that its extent exceeded the walls and ceiling of the room. Several smaller regions, which had been far too small to be discerned at the larger scale before, now appeared in multiple colors. Kiria pointed to one of them.

"This is where we are now: the last star in the Choralis Chain. Here are the Gund colonies and over here in blue is the Thailis Dynasty. Now here"—she pointed to a suddenly flashing red point of light several feet away—"is where you left the Irindris city-ships."

One of these stars is my home, Griffiths realized with a start. *But—which one?*

"Here's the course the Irindris had taken up to that point," Kiria continued, a long curving red line extending back into the room. "However, just after you left them, the entire fleet of city-ships stopped."

"Stopped!" Merinda was astonished.

"Stopped. It's unprecedented. The course of the city-ships is determined by their holy writ—their wandering decreed to be everlasting. The ships are never supposed to stop nor change their course—yet yesterday they did just that."

As Kiria pointed, the curving red course line broke at its end, growing directly toward the Choralis region.

"They're looking for you, Merinda," Kiria said, "and they've thrown out nearly a hundred years of tradition to do so. Worse yet, they are getting their information on your course from shadow fleets of wraith ships—oh, yes indeed, Captain, they do exist. They're difficult to detect since the ships themselves are common spacecraft that were taken over by their own synthetics but there are ways of doing it. They are desperate to find you, Captain, and they are coming straight here. Merinda, you will need to be leaving soon if you are to stay ahead of them."

The *E'toris* turned directly to face Griffiths. "So, Captain, you come from an unknown—and apparently insignificant—world bearing knowledge that is so valuable that a senior member of the *Vestis Inquisitas* would give his life for yours. What is it that you know that's so important? What are they looking for?"

Griffiths pondered that for a moment. "Ma'am—I can't help you," he said.

Kiria's smile subtly became most serious. "There may be some nuances of your language that our synthetics have not yet passed on to us." She spoke sweetly, with just a tint of venom. "Do you mean cannot or will not?"

Griffiths's throat was dry, his voice taking on an almost pleading whine. "Ma'am, I mean cannot. Look, it's not that I don't want to help you—I would dearly love to!—it's just that I don't know what it is you want. I don't even know what it is that I know!"

Kiria shook her head. "You're not making any sense."

"Ma'am, the *Vestis* who saved us from the Irindris filled my head with all kinds of knowledge before he died and I can't make heads or tails of it. I know all about the Irindris; now that you mention this Darkness, I seem to know something about that as well. It must have all been part of the mission your friend was on. You see, I know more than I should—it's all stuck up here in my head and I can't seem to make any sense out of it."

Kiria blinked and took a step back. "Mission transfer?" she whispered.

Merinda stepped forward. "Yes, *E'toris*. During the escape, Zanfib transferred his mission load into this man's mind. In addition to whatever special knowledge made him invaluable to the Irindris—and quite possibly the Darkness, I might add—he also holds all of Zanfib's special knowledge of the mission."

"You have all the answers, eh, Captain?" Kiria smiled. "Your problem is you don't know the questions! Well, take heart, man of Earth! If you can survive to cross the quantum front into Dynastic space then you may yet have the questions to fit those answers!"

"If you will excuse me, *E'toris*," Merinda interrupted brusquely, "there are preparations to make and I do have a report that I need to file before I leave."

The small woman turned and approached her old friend. Griffiths watched the *Vestis* stiffen visibly as Kiria neared, everything about her body warning the *E'toris* away—a warning that Kiria ignored with great effort.

"Merinda," she said, reaching out and laying her hand gently on the rigid arm, "it is a dangerous road that I have set you on. If the Mother of Stars is willing, perhaps this road will lead you to the redemption you seek. If not, then I fear greatly for you."

Merinda's eyes were fixed again in the distance. She spoke to the young Kiria that she had known long ago.

"They have already taken my life, Kiria. What more can they take?"

16

Escape

"MR. SECARA, THIS IS ONE OF THE FINEST CAVES I'VE EVER BEEN in," Lewis said as she leaned toward him over the table, batting her eyelashes furtively.

Tobler rolled her eyes. Lewis was about as transparent as glass and, at the same time, as subtle as a hammer. Tobler may not have been the most adept at social relations, but even she could teach Elizabeth a thing or two.

They had left the ship in the sunken hollow of the landing bay several hours earlier. Lewis had immediately attached herself like a leech to this Secara, which had pretty much left Ellerby and Tobler to follow along. Tobler had the distinct impression that she was suddenly on a surreal double date—her role being that of the roommate who was tagging along. It was not an unfamiliar role for her and the thought took her back to unhappy college days far too easily.

The starport itself was fascinating, however, and while the details of their excursion may have slipped past Lewis, they were not lost on Tobler. The antennae and equipment, which were so prominent on the control tower rising from the center of the complex, were being systematically dismantled by more of the winged men she had seen on their approach. Apparently the equipment was no longer useful, replaced instead by a gigantic floating eyeball that looked down on the launch and landing bays below it. As the equipment was lowered to the ground, Tobler saw it was being loaded onto transport pallets and into a ship for export.

Ellerby didn't seem to care one way or the other. He had so thoroughly convinced himself of the illusion that he observed everything with a detached amazement.

They passed through the terminal building, quickly boarding what Tobler had assumed was a mag-lev monorail connecting the starport to Ethis's central city proper. Magnetics, however, didn't appear to be a part of the new order of things in this world, so the locals had adapted, using a hired wizard in each car to keep the levitation spells operating and a team of large animals harnessed to the side of the rail to pull the train along.

"It's not as fast," Secara explained through his smile, "but it still works. Chukai prides itself on being both adaptive and pragmatic."

Most fascinating of all to Tobler was the large crystal ball suspended in the corner of their car and in which she could discern images and sounds.

" . . . the K'tar Empire incursion into Federated States, claiming that their fleets were moving to protect their, quote, 'hereditary and historic interests in the Ninth Province,' end quote. Federated States has responded by deploying their eighty-two twenty-nine Elite Strike Fleet to the region, as well as the fourteen six fifty-fifth Assault Squadron in what they termed an exercise, noting that their settlements in the contested region would not be abandoned.

"This is IGNM with the Ethis morning report. IGNM: your universe in perspective."

She had tried to get the others' attention, but Lewis was too busy endearing herself to Secara, and Ellerby just didn't seem to care. By the time she turned back to the crystal ball, an all too familiar voice was speaking through it.

". . . numerous reports of synthetic minds being infected, by most accounts, with the virus. Numerous problems have been reported in the Gund Colonies—from ground vehicles arguing with their pilots to, in one case, a university synthetic refusing all requests as it composed its own seemingly endless series of novels. The cause of the breakdowns remains a mystery. This is Merinda Neskat for IGNM in Gund Colony Seven."

Tobler was astonished. She frantically tried to get Lewis's attention again, but by that time they were pulling into the main city station and it was time to disembark.

The day had begun badly and didn't show signs of improving. They had walked through the teeming streets of the city, a tortuous matter since the residents of Ethis seemed to abhor straight lines in any application. At last they had come to the Caverns of Ethis, the major landmark of the city, which turned out to be an open sinkhole. Centuries earlier, according to Secara's well-buttered narrative, the city that had once stood on this site had been destroyed when this pit opened up under it. The locals took it as a sign from the gods to reform their ways and rebuild the city more in keeping with the religious strictures of the time. Tobler wondered why they hadn't just taken it as a sign that they should move. Still, they had proceeded to build a temple complex within the cavern made by the sinkhole and had affixed a towering obelisk in the center of it, declaring it to be the center of all creation.

The whole town seemed a little off center as far as Tobler was concerned.

Now they were seated in a cramped restaurant booth whose benches and table configuration suggested that the average Chukai was much smaller than the average human.

They were each treated by Secara to a hot traditional beverage and invited to remain for the show of the dancing spoons—yet more traditional fare. Tobler had lost her interest in Chukai tradition earlier that afternoon somewhere between the looming demonstration and the *Cavern Chorus for Flextube and Metal Rim*, Opus 93.

And now Lewis was batting her eyelashes at their tormentor.

"Why, thank you, Lieutenant Lewis, how kind of you," he returned. "We are quite proud of the unique culture that the Chukai represent—especially as they change the basis of their society. I think you'll find this show of the dancing spoons to be particularly—"

"Could you do me a favor," Lewis interrupted, sidling up closer to the tall, tan Secara, "I think I left my notebook back at that little pottery place we were at last."

"Notebook?" Secara asked blankly.

"Yes, a little bitty thing with a red cover about the size of my hand—you know, papers bound all together with a wire on one side?"

"Well"—he smiled nervously—"yes, I think I know what you mean."

"Could you please be a dear and run back and get it for me? I'd be so very grateful!"

"But, madam"—Secara blushed—"I really shouldn't leave you here alone. I promised *Vestis* Neskat that I would take care of you and—"

"Oh, pshaw!" Lewis suddenly pouted. "What could happen to us? We'll just sit right here and not make a single move until you get back."

The scene was beginning to make Tobler ill.

"Well," Secara said, "maybe we could all go back. It would only take a few minutes . . ."

"What? And miss the show?" Lewis gave every appearance of her IQ having plunged dramatically toward the negative integers. "I wouldn't want to miss a single moment of this spoon dance thing!"

Secara smiled pleasantly. "Very well, everyone just stay right here and I won't be but a few moments. Enjoy the show until I get back!"

Tobler wondered vaguely if they were supposed to stop enjoying the show when he *did* get back.

The moment Secara disappeared through the short, arched doorway, Lewis turned back toward Tobler and Ellerby. "Thank God! I thought I'd never figure out a way to shake loose from him!"

"Me either," Tobler heartily agreed.

"Now," Lewis said, leaning conspiratorially across the narrow table, "this is our chance! It's now or never!"

"Now or never what?" Ellerby asked.

Lewis ignored him. "Do you see that man leaning back against the bar?—No! Don't look! He's wearing some kind of flight suit. I saw a lot of them around the starport today on our way in here. He's taller than most of the people here so that means he's probably not from this dustball planet."

"If I don't look, how can I see him?"

"Don't get smart with me now, Tobler! That man has access to a ship off this rock, and I say we have a better chance of striking a deal to get back home with someone new rather than that psychopath Neskat."

Tobler was becoming alarmed. "But what about Griffiths? We can't just leave him here!"

"He's thrown in with the Neskat woman!" Lewis spat. "We've got to act and we've got to act now!"

"This should be interesting," Ellerby said easily. "Exactly what do you have in mind?"

"Just watch me!"

Lewis turned and motioned for the man to come over to their table. Unfortunately, she also caught the attention of the man standing next to her intended rescuer, and it took several moments of wild gesturing before the matter of intention was sorted out. Even then, the tall spaceman seemed reluctant to come over. Lewis finally had to get up from the table and drag him over.

"My name is Lewis," she said as she pulled the man to sit down next to her. "This is Tobler and Ellerby."

"Hi," Ellerby said.

"Greetings," the spaceman said, his voice unsure. "My name is Hywat. What is your difficulty?"

"Ah, you are so perceptive," Lewis crooned, "and we are in desperate need. Did you notice the man who brought us here earlier?"

"Yes," Hywat said suspiciously. "What about him?"

"He's selling us into slavery!"

Tobler nearly choked on her drink, coughing up the bluish liquid. "Sorry," she said, "wrong pipe!"

Lewis grabbed Hywat by the collar of his suit and pulled his face back to look at her. "I tell you the man has kidnapped us, torn us from our families and friends, and now proposes to do unspeakable acts to us and then sell us into slavery. Please, sir, you must help us escape!"

"Oh, madam," the tall spaceman said, "I don't know. This really isn't any of my business."

"Please," Lewis whined. "You've just got to help us! Where else can we turn? We need a strong, courageous man to help us—someone with access to a ship! Tell me you have access to a ship! Please tell me you have access to a ship!"

"Well, yes, madam"—Hywat nodded—"as it happens I do have access to a ship, but I don't think— Please, madam, you are getting a bit close!"

"Oh, Hywat, please help me!" Lewis was all over the man. "Help me and I'll make it well worth your while! I just can't let you go!"

"All right, lady! All right!" Hywat was prying Lewis's arms off him, holding them as he spoke to her. "Look, these things require delicacy to pull off, but it's not like I haven't done this sort of thing before. There's a side door to this place. You go down that passageway to the left of the bar and then open the last door on your right. That leads to an alley. I'll meet you there in three minutes with a cargo container. No, don't worry, they're pretty big and are equalized so that there'll be plenty of air to breathe. I'll sneak you aboard my ship in that and let you out once we're under way."

"Oh, thank you!" Lewis pulled her hands free, reached up, and kissed Hywat on the cheek.

"I'll be back in a few minutes." Hywat stood up hastily. "You just meet me in the alley, all right?"

The spaceman bolted out the door.

Lewis turned back to her companions with a smug smile on her face. "Men! They're so predictable! So stupid!— Sorry, Ellerby, no offense."

Ellerby nodded through a tight grin.

Tobler reached forward, resting her hand on Lewis's arm. "A cargo container? Lewis, is this really such a good idea?"

"It's all worked out just fine." Lewis smiled. "Besides, I'd do anything to get away from that Secara! Insufferable man!"

THE CARGO CONTAINER NEARLY FILLED THE DARK, NARROW alleyway. It had been relatively easy for the Portman's Guild wizard to guide the reinforced metallic box back into the passage, but both he and his granx beast were having trouble getting it back out. The container slammed against the corner of the building twice before clearing itself into the roadway beyond.

"Hey," Hywat said, "please be a little more careful with

that, would you? The cargo is a bit on the touchy side and I don't want any problems when we open it up."

"*Hawasath*, good master," the Chukai wizard said, bowing to the spaceman. "And to which bay should this be taken?"

"Well," Hywat said, turning to the man just emerging from the doorway, "where do you want him to take it?"

"Can they hear me?" the man asked quietly.

"No, it's a hazardous-cargo container, lined and insulated. War could break out around them and they wouldn't be aware of it—although I suspect they're a bit shaken up from the bouncing the portman just gave them."

"Very well," the man said. "Have him take them to bay three seventy-seven and load it on the ship there. Make sure the container gets there, Hywat, then pay the man well—not too well, however, we don't want any suspicions aroused."

"Yes, Master Secara," Hywat returned. "As you and the lady wish. I take it your day was long?"

"Indeed," Secara said, "that woman throwing herself at me constantly while I tried to keep them occupied by moving from one trite cultural spot to the next. Our lady suspected that they would make some attempt at escape and preferred that we know about it and control it first— You did your job well, Hywat. In truth, I was beginning to despair of them ever making their move! Lord of Night! If I'd had to actually sit through that dancing spoons performance, I think *I* might have needed to escape."

"Do you want me to open the container when I get it into the hold?" Hywat asked.

Secara raised an eyebrow. "Do you want to?"

"And deal with that woman again?" Hywat threw both arms up. "By the Stars, no!"

"Well, then, you have your wish." Secara nodded.

"Besides, *Vestis* Neskat specifically asked that she be allowed to open the container herself once they were off-planet."

Hywat thought for a moment. "Do you think we really needed to shove them in a cargo container?"

"They've got air to breathe, a small light, and enough rations to keep them for the next few hours—they'll be fine. Besides, I'd put them through worse to get that Lewis woman away from me!"

17

Maelstrom

THE CARGO BAY RAN VERTICALLY THROUGH ALL FOUR DECKS of the *Brishan*. It was by far the largest single area of the ship, but, while it rarely carried cargo, it was usually the most cramped. The varieties of quantum-rippled space and the resultant alterations in physics that that implied made space travel a complex business. The requirements of the *Vestis* meant that their ships had to be ready for—or at least adaptable to—any environmental conditions spanning several quantum regions. This usually meant contracting for ships that had the usual multiple-drive systems plus sufficient space to house additional modular systems for as many other equipment requirements as the mission demanded. Each ship could then be quickly and efficiently customized for the conditions it would face. Generally speaking, the number of diverse systems a ship held was a good indication of the galactic distances it was meant to cross.

The *Brishan* was no exception to this rule. Nearly every possible space in the hold was taken up with alternate drives, power, field-generation and life-support systems, plus the collapsible bulk containers designed to feed the various systems. Wedged tightly among them was a single, hazardous-materials cargo container, its access port sealed and locked.

Griffiths stared at it and its blinking control panel for several minutes. Neskat had taken subtle and vicious delight in relating the story of the container's contents to him in complete detail. She had then given him the access code of the container and told him to go and let his devoted crew out of their box. She would have loved to have done so herself, she said from behind that cold mask of a face, but felt it would be better for all concerned if Griffiths took care of the problem himself.

So he stood in the cramped cargo bay, his arms folded across his chest, thinking about his crew. *His crew.* What a joke. He was off trying to get a handle on what was going on—trying to find them some way out of this mess and back to that blue ball they fondly called home—and what were they about? Dashing off on some panic-fool attempt at escape. Escape from what? Escape to what? All these things rolled over again and again in his mind, each flavored by the single thought: *and they would have left me behind.*

Time and the inventiveness of the mind were beginning to calm him down. Jumping to conclusions, after all, was what the human mind did best, Griffiths knew, for such conclusions had gotten him into trouble many times in his life. *Perhaps the others were just momentarily insane. Perhaps some of them had abandoned me with regret. Perhaps I haven't got the whole story. Perhaps Merinda isn't telling me everything.*

On the other hand, he thought, *perhaps I was right in the first place.*

He felt the gentle surge of the ship under the pull of the dragons, once more in harness.

The ventilation hummed slightly.

The lights on the access panel continued to blink.

Griffiths waited for his mind to be made up, but somehow it just wouldn't. Suddenly, he reached forward before any further self-argument could be made and pressed the access code into the symbols on the flat panels on the container hatch.

A rush of motion and sound exploded from the box, slamming into him and knocking him to the deck. Griffiths's breath rushed out of him with the impact in a great, painful wheeze, aided by the pressure of someone lying on him. His vision blurred. He struggled for breath.

"Get its arms!"

"I've got one! Get its legs!"

Sudden silence descended. The flurried movement around him stopped. Griffiths's vision cleared as he gasped for breath and he saw a startled Tobler kneeling on his chest with both hands around his neck.

"Captain!" she squeaked.

Griffiths tried to say, What was your first clue! but his voice could only grind out a few syllables before he was painfully gulping air again. One glance about him was sufficient to give him the rest of the picture. Lewis sat above him looking shocked, still trying to pull both his arms from their sockets with her feet planted on his shoulders. Ellerby was standing more or less beside him, having grabbed one leg at the calf, apparently in an attempt to use him like a wishbone.

Ellerby closed his eyes and let go.

Griffiths's leg slammed painfully to the hard deck.

Griffiths felt his face redden and he looked back at Tobler, his voice a growl. "Get . . . off!"

Tobler instantly rolled to one side. Lewis let go at once, crabbing backward away from him until she ran against the bulkhead a few feet behind her. By the look on her face, it was obviously not far enough away for her liking.

Griffiths rolled painfully over until he was kneeling with his hands on the deck. His breath was returning to him.

"S-sorry, sir," Tobler blurted out. "We thought you were an alien, sir."

“Really?” he responded slowly, rising to a wobbly stance, both hands on his knees to steady himself. “Was there any particular reason you thought I was an alien, or are you making a personal comment?”

“Captain!” Lewis said in a rush. “How did you escape from that Neskat woman? We didn’t even know what ship we were going to be on! How did you possibly find us?”

“He didn’t escape from ‘that Neskat woman.’ ”

Lewis’s expression froze and she slowly turned toward the voice addressing her.

There, in the access corridor, stood Merinda Neskat.

“You are again aboard the *Brishan*, Lieutenant Lewis,” Merinda said coolly, “but you are hardly my prisoner. You are, of course, free to leave this ship anytime you like. The access ramp airlock is behind you and to your right. It will currently be a long walk since we are approximately point three light-years from the nearest habitable world. At a good brisk walk it should only take you about forty million years to get there.”

“Oh, now that’s helpful.” Lewis spoke with a razor edge, raw hatred in her eyes.

Merinda suddenly strode forward quickly. “I’d love to take care of you, princess, but there are far more pressing problems at hand. You. Ellerby!”

“Yes,” he said languidly.

“I need you up in weapons control.”

“Weapons control?” Ellerby sniffed. “You haven’t needed a crew so far—why rush now?”

“I didn’t need one until now!”

Griffiths turned toward the *Vestis*. “Neskat? What’s going on?”

Neskat spoke hurriedly. “We’re coming up on the quantum front, Griffiths, but there are several ships closing on us. They’ve identified themselves as Chukai System

Defense and claim they want to inspect us for contraband, but their configuration is all wrong and they're moving much too quickly."

"What are you saying?"

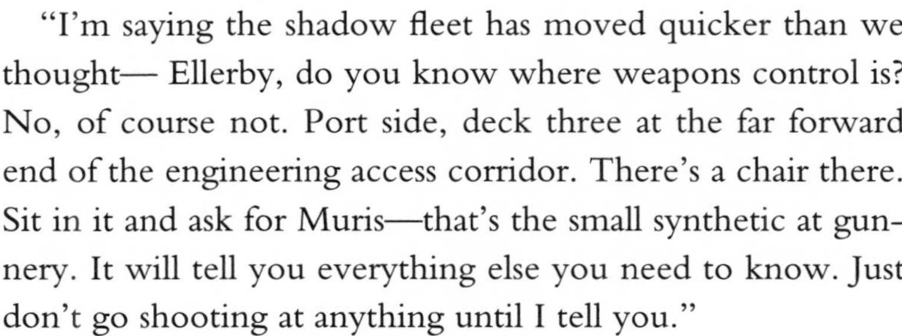

"I'm saying the shadow fleet has moved quicker than we thought— Ellerby, do you know where weapons control is? No, of course not. Port side, deck three at the far forward end of the engineering access corridor. There's a chair there. Sit in it and ask for Muris—that's the small synthetic at gunnery. It will tell you everything else you need to know. Just don't go shooting at anything until I tell you."

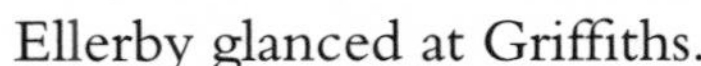

Ellerby glanced at Griffiths.

The captain nodded quickly, waving him off.

Ellerby ran.

Neskat turned to Tobler. "Aft on the starboard engineering room on deck four there's a damage control station. The synth's name is Evis. Do you think you can handle that?"

"I—I don't know!"

Griffiths spoke up quietly. "Yes, you can, Marilyn! Just talk to Evis and everything will work out. Your station is right through that iris hatch about ten feet behind you. Just focus on your job, Lieutenant, and you'll be just fine."

Tobler flashed a nervous smile. "Yes, Captain." She moved quickly away.

Neskat turned to the last crewperson. "Lewis, there's a second weapons control station on top of the hull. Go to the observation deck, starboard side. There's an aft hatchway that leads to the aft weapons control station. The synthetic there is named Tashel. Just sit in the chair, relax, and talk to—"

"No."

It apparently was a word rarely spoken to Neskat. She appeared not to understand it. "No?"

"No, I refuse to do it."

A vicious smile played around the corners of Merinda's mouth. "Really?"

"As a prisoner I refuse to assist the enemy in—"

Griffiths stepped forward suddenly. "Lieutenant Lewis! We are operating under unusual circumstances here and your cooperation is required. Besides, I don't exactly think these people are signatories of the Geneva Convention . . ."

"Sir," Lewis blurted out angrily, "we cannot trust that this woman is acting in the best interests of—"

"Stow it, Lewis! Come to attention!" Griffiths ordered. The tone of command in his voice surprised everyone—himself included. "You've done nothing but bitch and moan since things went wrong! When you finally *did* show some initiative it was to abandon me for some harebrained, ill-devised scheme that turns out to be one of the *biggest* farces I have ever been privileged to witness!"

The blood drained from Lewis's face. She stood ramrod straight, her eyes fixed forward.

"Captain." Ellerby's image appeared to be sitting nearby on thin air. "The approaching ships are demanding we heave to and prepare to be boarded. Muris says they will be within weapons range in approximately three minutes."

Ellerby's ghost disappeared.

Griffiths spoke with quiet, absolute firmness. "I don't have time to brief you or get your approval right now, Lewis. I *might* do so later. All you have to know for now is that we will all be dead in a few minutes if one screw-up lieutenant doesn't get her ass up to aft gunnery *right now*!"

Lewis's eyes flashed hatred and fire—but she moved. "Sir! Yes, sir!"

She vanished through the iris hatchway.

Griffiths let out a long breath.

"Well, well!" Merinda said. "I am impressed, Captain! Let's get to the bridge and figure our way out of this."

It was the first time Griffiths had seen her with an honest, relaxed smile.

GRIFFITHS DROPPED FEETFIRST DOWN THE LIFT-TUBE, DASHING down the corridor after Merinda. The passage took an immediate turn to the right and, just past a set of facing portals on either side, entered the bridge.

It was the first time he had been here. So far this trip, the bridge had been sealed off.

Now he found himself standing on a wide deck of polished hardwood. Graceful arches formed a delicate cathedral ceiling into which the smooth consoles along both walls curved with unbroken lines. Forward, the room opened into an inverted dome, the bridge being on the lower side of the spacecraft. From where he stood, he could see the longer arm of the hull sweeping out overhead while the stars drifted below.

Into this dome, the floor extended to a platform where a large chair was fixed on a swivel mounting. There, Merinda sat facing him, her arms resting on the wide curve of the panels. Between them, the starboard console curved out over the hardwood floor with a smooth, featureless surface. A second, more utilitarian chair floated at that console on repulsor fields.

Merinda gestured toward the chair. "That is your station, Captain." Her tone had turned quiet and sure. "I require that you communicate with your crew and coordinate their actions. Do not question me or my methods. You must simply obey. Is that understood?"

"I understand, ma'am," he said, then thought, *If only I could guarantee that my crew will understand as well!*

"Lindia"—Neskat spoke to the room in general—"configure the bridge for hostile contact and establish telepresence with all crewed stations, please."

"Merinda, the lead ship is requesting communications data link with me directly."

"You know my standing order on that!"

"They are most insistent, noting that the safety of this crew and completion of its mission are an overriding factor to your command."

"No, Lindia, under no circumstances are you to communicate with these ships."

"Lead ship sends that your safety, Merinda, is endangered by my not communicating with them directly at this time."

"Lindia! Obey my directives and stop all communication with those ships at once!"

Griffiths sat in his chair, wondering what all that was about.

"Complying with your command. Bridge in hostile contact mode; telepresence established."

Suddenly, ghosts of Tobler, Ellerby, and Lewis were on the bridge. Each floated in the air near the bridge walls, Ellerby and Lewis reclining more than Tobler, whose position was more upright. Beyond them, the walls themselves suddenly displayed tactical images and ship's status displays. Griffiths wondered for a moment at the design—why didn't they just have everyone work their little controls from here? In a flash he realized that by spreading out the stations throughout the ship it was possible for parts of the ship to be destroyed without crippling the ship completely. That was classic combat design. The price that was paid usually was poorer communication. This system allowed them all to be in the same room—without being in the same place. Griffiths suddenly looked at the *Brishan* in a new light: the ship was a ship of war.

He turned to his own console and was shocked as its surface suddenly began to bend itself into new shapes. Bulbous protrusions formed themselves into handgrip controllers, series of bumps formed keyboard-input consoles and what appeared to be switches.

"Griffiths," Merinda said to him, trying to attract his attention away from the fascinating keyboard, "listen to me. Flying with phase dragons is tricky business—harder still since we'll have to get speed, cut the harness loose, and drift into the quantum front. Once on the other side, we can cut in the superfilament induction drive and get clear of these wraith ships. But get through we must! That's my job.

"*Your* job is to keep us in one piece until we get there. You'll run the defensive systems."

"I can't run this board!" Griffiths said with a panicked edge in his voice. "Look at this thing!"

"Forget the board!" Merinda said, turning around in her chair. "Just talk to Fisk."

"Fisk?" Griffiths said aloud.

"Greetings! I am Fisk, your defensive systems synthetic," a cheerful voice sounded inside Griffiths. "My job is to help you do your job more easily! I live to help you since, after all, if I *don't* help you, I won't live! Ha-ha! Just a little humor to lighten the moment . . ."

Griffiths was not amused. "You're pretty chatty for a defense system, Fisk."

"Well, you know, the job of defense system synthetic and that of the defense systems operator can often be stressful, especially when the safety of the entire crew and mission is at stake. I find that a little levity allows operators to relax into their role and relieves the pressures of the job. After all, a relaxed mind is a sharp—"

Griffiths growled, "I don't mean to be offensive or stressful but could you tell me how to operate the ship's defenses?"

"Of course, I'd be honored and pleased to instruct you in the use of the ship's defensive systems. These systems are complex, with multiple layers and configurations depending on the threat that is involved, but with a little practice you should be able to handle them just fine! We will start with—oh, sorry! Threat assessment indicates the need of defensive systems immediately!"

"What!" Griffiths shouted.

A sphere of glowing blue grid lines suddenly sprang up about him as his chair floated to the center of the bridge. Griffiths realized suddenly that the familiar feeling of weightlessness had returned to him. He glanced at Merinda. She had already turned her chair forward, the bow pitching downward and rolling sharply to the right.

Three small ships, rendered perfectly in three dimensions, appeared at the periphery of the grid. They were like little fireflies streaking directly toward him.

"What do I do?" Griffiths yelled.

"I recommend engaging deflection fields ambient to full strength."

"Do it!"

"Glad to!"

A green bubble, smaller than the blue grid, formed around him. To his astonishment, Griffiths could feel the bubble with his hands as he floated. Each place his hand touched, the translucent green coalesced into a brilliant green while the rest of the globe faded. It was like some extension of him.

"Incoming fire behind you, Captain!"

Griffiths turned too late.

The little firefly ships had swooped under him and were spitting darts of light at him, tagging him in the hip.

"Yeow!" Griffiths yelled as the ship rocked about him.

"Griffiths!" Merinda shouted. "Tell your people to open fire and you get on those deflection fields!"

Griffiths floated upside down in the glowing sphere, rubbing his hip to lessen the pain. "I'm working on it!"

Tobler's ghost called to him from the wall. "Hull damage port side. Looks like it's holding. The hull is moving to heal the breach."

Griffiths wasn't sure he wanted to know exactly what that meant. Instead, he turned to the floating ghosts of Ellerby and Lewis. "Open fire! Open fire!"

Ellerby looked pale, even for a ghost. "Captain, this is—this is beginning to feel a little too real for me."

"Get over it, Ellerby," Griffiths shouted as the three ships passed under him and were joined by two more. Griffiths twisted around in the bubble to face them as all five broke for different vectors. "Fisk! What do I do?"

"Angle the strength of the fields so that they will deflect the incoming bolts. Ambient fields are insufficient against this degree of firepower."

"Fine—but how? *How?*"

"You simply have to— Oh, no! Watch out!"

Two of the ships suddenly changed direction, bringing their forward weapons to bear on Griffiths. The tiny darts of light again shot toward him. Instinctively, he held his hands up pressing them against the green globe.

The green congealed around his hands. The bolts flashed on the surface of the deep green.

"Excellent deflection, Captain Griffiths! Superbly timed! I must say that I think you have a knack for this."

As he watched, brilliant darts of light flashed from his own body. The two firefly ships that had just fired on him were passing beneath him. One of them was caught by a dart of light. A miniature eruption of debris exploded from the miniature ship.

"Nice one, Lewis," said Ellerby's ghost.

"Just another form of life support," Lewis's ghost replied.

Griffiths turned again, suddenly remembering the other three ships. As he had suspected they had re-formed and were making a concerted run toward him. He pressed both hands against the globe to ward off the attack.

Suddenly a sharp pain erupted in the middle of his back. The ship bounced sharply upward. Griffiths craned his neck around to see that the fourth ship had looped around and attacked while he wasn't watching.

"Quantum front in ten seconds," Merinda shouted. "Griffiths, watch your back!"

"Now she tells me," the captain muttered. He literally had his hands full. The three ships were grouping for another pass, but he had to keep his eye on the fourth ship quartering from behind. Suddenly the three turned in concert with the fourth. Griffiths pushed his left hand down toward the solo ship and angled his right up toward the remaining three.

All fired at once.

Griffiths withdrew his right hand sharply, pain coursing through his arm. The ship rolled heavily to starboard under the impact.

Tobler's voice was alarmed. "Hull breach on starboard engineering access! Collapsed bulkhead on starboard deck three! Power levels down to sixty-five percent on the deflection grid. Power severed from starboard weapon array. We are losing atmosphere on deck one port side! Sealing it off now!"

"Neskat!" Griffiths shouted. "Get us out of here!"

"Dragon harness released! Quantum front in three seconds!"

Griffiths turned. The firefly ships wheeled around him, surging forward. He had the impression of miniature dragons flying off into the stars behind him.

All four fireflies fired from slightly in front of the ship—at the very boundary of the quantum front. Instinctively, Griffiths put up both his hands.

"No!" Merinda screamed in rage.

The bolts slammed into the deflection field. Griffiths was pushed back against the bubble from the impact.

As they slid sideways into the front, chaos quite literally gripped the ship. The hull rumbled as diverse realities struggled against the deflection fields for supremacy. Griffiths tumbled in his weightless field as the ship was rocked and buffeted.

"Damn the wraiths!" Merinda shouted, frantically wrestling with the controls at her forward station.

Griffiths twisted toward her. "Neskat! What's happened to our—"

He froze.

Beyond the bridge observation dome was everything and nothing all at once. It was whatever one imagined it to be: a terrifying maw of untruth, of antireality. It made him sick to look. He closed his eyes.

"The wraith ships have altered our vector enough so that we're stuck in the front!" Merinda shouted at him over the groaning of the hull.

Tobler's voice sounded shrilly, from her ghost. "The main bulkheads are buckling!"

Griffiths forced himself to open his eyes. He could see the firefly ships on the other side of the front, moving toward them.

"How close are we?" he shouted.

"Close—but not close enough!"

Griffiths smiled. One of the firefly ships hovered just beyond the green globe now flickering about him. *Careless of you,* he thought. With both hands he reached up into the green globe. It was malleable, as he'd suspected. With all his strength he pushed his hands into the globe, stretching it around the firefly ship.

He pulled.

The *Brishan* surged forward slightly amid the maelstrom—close enough so that the next ship was within his grasp. He reached out and felt the little ship in his globe-reinforced hands. *This ship must be several thousand tons in mass,* he thought as he held it godlike in his hands.

He pulled again.

Suddenly the buffeting stopped. The stars steadied once more around them.

"We're clear!" Merinda said reverently.

Griffiths watched the third ship wheel around toward them. He twisted again, ready to angle what remained of the weakened fields.

"Not today," Merinda said smugly. She pressed the controls forward on the superfilament induction drive.

The firefly ship vanished suddenly from Griffiths's view. He drifted around to look forward and saw that now the *Brishan* was flying down a corridor of rainbow light.

Merinda turned her command chair around and smiled roguishly at him.

"This concludes your first session as a defensive field coordinator," Fisk said merrily, as the globes of light dissolved and Griffiths was gently lowered to the floor, headfirst. "You were most successful, Captain Griffiths, and I personally commend you on surviving your first assignment."

Merinda walked over to Griffiths and offered him her

hand to help him up. “Nice trick, using the wraith ships' mass to get us out of the front.”

Griffiths took her hand and stood. “I guess good old Newtonian physics works pretty much everywhere.”

Merinda smiled. “Well, I wouldn't count on it. Let's just say that it's a good thing it works *here*.”

GAMMA: BOOK OF THE SENTINELS

18

Omnet

KA'ASHRA OF MARIS LEANED AWAY FROM HER WORKSTATION, stretching luxuriously against her high-backed suspensor chair, causing the fields to hum slightly. She could afford a moment to push her muscles a little—a need, really, she reminded herself without conviction. The truth was that she *did* mind the few weeks required to put together her next netcast from the materials she had been collecting over the past three months. Once the work was done, she would still be here—stuck in this worksuite while her superiors decided what to do with her. At least, if she had to be stuck, she was stuck at Central, and Central wasn't such a bad place to be.

She turned her chair and gazed for a few moments out the floor window of her worksuite. Far below her hung Mnemen IV—a jewel of a world and, so far as anyone who knew anything was concerned, the exact center of the universe.

At first blush, "center of the universe" might have seemed like a joke. Mnemen wasn't such a prepossessing world, for while its roots were deep in the history of the galaxy, there was otherwise nothing terribly spectacular about the planet. It had its natural beauties, to be sure, as does every habitable planet—and several uninhabitable ones as well—but nothing spectacular enough to even afford its own entry in the *FSS Galactic Omnibus*. It represented no particular geographic centrality either, nor did it lie at the intersection of important trade routes beyond those that it established itself. It did not lie at the heart of a mighty interstellar imperial force. Indeed, if it could be said to lie within a political boundary at all, Mnemen IV would be held to lie at one side of the Herwach Transcendency, a minor empire in the scale of galactic politics whose greatest feature of note was an unprecedented beatific condescension toward other galactic powers regardless of their size. The Transcendency held that it was above the politics of the other sovereign interstellar states, maintained its neutrality in all conflicts, and insured this peace with a mesmeric array of nonaggression and mutual defense pacts that had never been sorted out in their entirety by any known enemy state.

No, she thought, *Mnemen is remarkable because we* made *it remarkable. Mnemen didn't move in the universe, we moved the universe to revolve around it.*

Ka'ashra stood from her chair, the long folds of her open robe trailing behind her as she walked toward the bay window mounted in the side of the worksuite wall. It was one of her "little vanities," as she called them. That bay window had been expensive to install and even just getting permission for it from *E'toris Prime* Targ had been something of a struggle. It had required decompression of several offices of her counterparts—each of whom had compelling reasons why they shouldn't be put off their own projects just so Ka'ashra could have a better view. She had smoothed feathers on some and threatened others, always guided by that inner knowledge of hers as to just how much was enough to get her what she wanted. Now she had her window—a symbol to anyone who entered her worksuite of the kind of power she could wield when she wanted.

The gravity field ended at the bay window's edge, an effect she had purposefully demanded of the installers. With unconscious ease she pulled the robes tighter about her form as she drifted weightless into the transparent bay.

She smiled at the view. *Her view.*

Below her, steady and unmoving, hung the distant globe of Mnemen. To either side as she turned, she saw the incredible sweep of the Life-Ring, a colossal structure nearly a mile high above her and tapering in dizzying perspective into a thin line to either side. The Life-Ring was, by itself, one of the Seventeen Wonders of the Galaxy. It was constructed above Mnemen IV in such a way that it formed a complete circle at a height equal to the planet's geosynchronous orbital diameter. Since its orbital period was the same as Mnemen's rotation, one of the greatest construction feats of the millennium hung stationary above the surface of the world. Elevator complexes of unbelievable dimension raised and lowered specially designed compartments in a constant stream of life between the planet and the Life-Ring. People could walk the garden world of Mnemen, explore the wildness of its nature, and then return here, to the Ring, to work, sleep, and live.

The world's beauties were now much enhanced, thanks to the evacuation of all sentient life from the world. Fitting, Ka'ashra thought. Biped sentients always seem so bent on order and control—give us a crooked line and we'll try to make it straight. Nature isn't like that—nature is chaotic, abhorring the nice straight lines and circles that the human mind finds so alluring. Yet nature seemed to have come up with its own order, and humanity seems to constantly fall into disorder. Somehow both had come to peace here, at Mnemen. If for no other reason, it was why she always felt like this was home.

There were over twenty billion people who called the

Life-Ring home, and they had all come here for one purpose alone.

This was Omnet Central.

Omnet was information, the greatest source for knowledge in all the known stars. Omnet traded data the way some empires traded produce or manufactured goods. Its major divisions—the *Vestis* and the *Librae*—had installations permeating every major empire of the galactic disk and representation in all minor ones. Two arms, two hands—each doing the work together that made the Omnet the single most powerful force in all the stars.

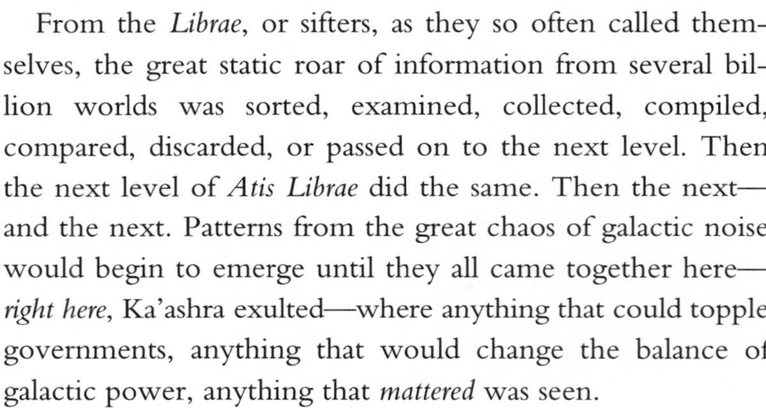

From the *Librae*, or sifters, as they so often called themselves, the great static roar of information from several billion worlds was sorted, examined, collected, compiled, compared, discarded, or passed on to the next level. Then the next level of *Atis Librae* did the same. Then the next—and the next. Patterns from the great chaos of galactic noise would begin to emerge until they all came together here—*right here*, Ka'ashra exulted—where anything that could topple governments, anything that would change the balance of galactic power, anything that *mattered* was seen.

Truth was then brought into perspective through consultation with the Oracles. Ka'ashra herself had never had audience with them. She knew that they existed somewhere below the surface of Mnemen IV. They had, in fact, chosen this place for the Omnet centuries ago. Their judgment was final.

Usually the information and truth the Omnet learned was sufficient to exert its influence simply by revealing it to the appropriate parties. Omnet wielded information both as an olive branch and as a weapon. It was an impartial observer and reported with impartiality when it could.

Often, however, the knowledge alone was not enough. It needed clarity. It needed a voice. It needed an arm. Then the *Vestis Inquisitas* would act. Their agents were credentialed with almost unlimited powers. They were, at once, ambassador, advisor, judge, jury, and executioner. Their training was extensive and their methods expedient to the extreme. What their training did not cover, the Oracles completed, filling the individual *Vestis* minds with the information necessary for their mission—making them, in each case, experts at whatever their present calling required. Then the Oracles emptied them of that special knowledge when it was no longer needed and replaced it with expertise that was required for their next mission. Thus were the *Vestis* equipped to ferret out the truth when it hid behind chaos and deception. When the truth didn't surface, the *Vestis* dug it out.

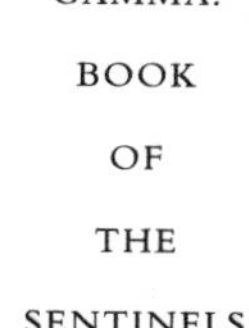

Ka'ashra's face grew somber at the thought. *It will take more than a little digging this time. If we don't get to the bottom soon this beautiful little office is going to start looking like a cage.*

A familiar voice sounded inside Ka'ashra's head. "*Vestis* Ka'ashra? Please pardon my intrusion."

"Yes, Wallen," Ka'ashra said with a sliver of patience. "What is it?"

"You asked that I inform you when the *Brishan* arrived. It has just contacted approach control."

Hastily, Ka'ashra pushed herself back into the room. She stumbled slightly as she reentered the gravity field. "Wallen, contact approach control and have them vector the ship toward the *Vestis* bays nearest the netcast production section. Then let me know which bay they've been assigned."

"I shall do so, *Vestis* Ka'ashra, as soon as the assignment is made. *Vestis* Ka'ashra, *E'toris* Targ has inquired once more on the status of your netcast. He says that it is severely overdue and asks most emphatically when he might be able to put it up on the network."

Ka'ashra smiled to herself as she slipped her low boots

back onto her feet. "You've been working on your diplomacy, haven't you, Wallen?"

"It was suggested to me by Kalin that my brusque tone in my communications might be less than optimally productive."

Ka'ashra struggled with her second boot. "Kalin? That's Targ's synthetic, isn't it?"

"Yes, *Vestis* Ka'ashra."

"Please tell Targ's synth that I prefer my synthetic to reflect my messages exactly the way I give them." Ka'ashra gave a final push into the boot and stood. "I don't need my synth to either cushion or edit my words. Oh, and Wallen?"

"Yes, *Vestis* Ka'ashra?"

"It's Ka'ashra. You used to call me Ka'ashra!"

"Yes, but Kalin also informed me that Omnet protocols require all synthetics to—"

"Wallen, I want you to stop talking to Targ's synthetic. He's a bad influence on you."

"Very well, Ka'ashra. Approach control has just informed me that the *Brishan* has been assigned to *Vestis* bay seven twenty-nine. ETA is twenty-three minutes."

"Thank you, Wallen!" Ka'ashra said as she dashed for the door. The portal dissolved at her approach. "Oh, Wallen! Contact Targ directly—don't go through his synth—and tell him that I'll be in his office within an hour. Also tell him that he won't be in the dark much longer—use just those words—'he won't be in the dark much longer.' Understand?"

"Yes, Ka'ashra, I understand."

"Wish me luck, Wallen!" Ka'ashra said as she dashed out the portal.

"Good luck!" the synthetic mind emitted into the room, but the portal had already filled in.

WHETHER THE *BRISHAN* WAS A FEW MINUTES EARLY OR KA'ASHRA was a few minutes late didn't matter. The ship was already in the bay and locked down by the time Ka'ashra arrived in her soft flowing robes, coolly pleased as she approached the aft access ramp of the ship. She was a true *Vestis*, one of the most respected in her profession. Part of her enjoyed looking good for the netcasts: the tailored clothes, the perfect hair, and the look. Yet something called to her as she stepped quickly into the bay in her stylish boots and the trailing robes with just enough levitation woven into the fabric to keep them clear of the dirt on the ground. Something in the raw smell of the *Brishan*'s cooling exhaust. Something in the grime that streaked the ship's sides. The ship had been out there, *doing something*, and it sang to Ka'ashra of adventure and the chance, once more, to win the game. It was a different game every time—and that was the challenge of it. In that moment she longed once more to trade her graceful ensemble for the black of her mission uniform and the knowledge and power that went with it.

Footsteps on the ramp, she realized as she mused. Ka'ashra looked up and called, "Zanfib, you old wizard! Please tell me that you've done what you promised and get me out of this— Neskat? Where's Zanfib?"

Merinda eyed Ka'ashra coolly. "Nice to see you again, too, Ka'ashra. Don't frown so much, it makes your makeup sag."

Ka'ashra had known Neskat long enough to let the comment pass. "Merinda, where's Zanfib?"

Neskat looked away, the act speaking volumes to Ka'ashra even before she replied. Neskat always looked one in the eye. "He didn't make it."

"I'm sorry, Merinda," Ka'ashra said softly.

"However, I did bring you something." Merinda turned and motioned to someone at the top of the ramp. Moments later, four humans in strange, light-blue flight suits walked down the ramp without enthusiasm.

"Cute uniforms, but a bit too flashy for camouflage." Ka'ashra's eyes squinted. "What are they supposed to be?"

"They are what Zanfib gave his last breath for," Merinda Neskat said with a flourish of her hand. "May I especially introduce Captain Jeremy Griffiths, recipient of Zanfib's mission memories. Zanfib gave his thoughts to Griffiths; now, I'm giving him to you."

"Uh, hey," Griffiths stammered, "wait a minute—"

"Travel well." Merinda crossed the backs of her hands over her chest, flicking them away from herself as she backed away from him. "I hope you find your world." She turned abruptly away from them and strode toward the ingress gate hatchway, flipping her cape over her shoulder.

"Neskat," Ka'ashra called after her, apparently no less confused than Griffiths. "What about the mission?"

"Filed and netcast three days ago." Merinda didn't even bother to break her stride or turn around. She shouted her words over the atmospheric pumps in the bay. "Surprised you didn't watch it, Ka'ashra!"

"You know what I'm talking about!" Ka'ashra shouted.

"Targ can find someone else for this one," Merinda shouted back, punching the release on the ingress gate hatch. "If the Nine want me on this mission, then they can damn well tell me why—"

Merinda stopped suddenly. Ka'ashra's eyes had suddenly widened, shifting to something behind Merinda. Merinda turned . . .

And vanished.

19

Oracles

MERINDA WAS DISORIENTED, PANICKED AS SHE TUMBLED SUDdenly through the darkness. There was no time for wonder, only fear as she fell faster and faster down to an unknown fate. Flashes of intermittent light from a distant point grew, then ripped past her, their scant illumination showing only the briefest impressions of a vast tube down which she was falling interminably. She realized that there was no wind: the air around her was moving downward at the same rate she was—or was she floating in one place while the wall rushed by?

Suddenly the distant light was upon her as the tube she had been traveling in passed out of the rock and into a great cavern. She was free-falling in the center of a clear pipeline nearly fifty feet in diameter. The cavern beyond the tube was lit by great points of light affixed to its walls, all illuminating a magnificent central complex. Weightless as she sped down the tube, Merinda couldn't determine whether she was rushing across the cavern or down into its depths, so the orientation of the complex remained up to her own determination. She preferred to think of herself as moving across it and thus came to regard the complex as extending from a great skirt of radiating

conduit roots at the floor of the cavern to a massive central column that thrust up through the roof of the cavern itself. There were several tubes radiating from the structure, each passing into the rock wall of the mammoth cave—including the one down which Merinda rushed at a dizzying pace. The scale was incredible, its complexity inspiring. Merinda was astonished for the moment she was left to comprehend it all before her conduit entered into the towering column itself and the darkness swallowed her . . .

. . . and deposited her silently and without ceremony in a room filled with soft blue light. Finding herself suddenly perfectly still was nearly as great a shock as the fall through the conduit tube. She sat abruptly on the floor—disoriented and confused. She looked about her, trying to gather her thoughts.

She had expected the familiar sight of the Omnet reception area, a quick drop down the transit tubes, and the blissful return to her spartan cell. She was weary again of company. She longed for the solitude of that quiet darkness—a place where she could go and just forget.

Now she found herself in a quiet, spacious room. The six walls rose gracefully to a peak over the sumptuously soft floor. Three large couches were situated about the room, while above them soft green and blue patterns played on the translucent walls and ceiling. Chimes drifted in the background, while the subtle sounds of a gentle waterfall and the rustle of trees could be discerned behind it.

It angered her. The room was obviously designed to relax and reassure whoever occupied it. No doubt, if her own experience were typical, such relaxation would be needed by anyone making the journey to this place. Merinda loathed the compassion that the room represented, the weakness it assumed in her. She had no need for clemency or forgiveness or coddling. She saw them as just another means of manipulation.

"Merinda Neskat: it is time."

"Time for what?" she demanded, standing with her hands on her hips. "Where am I?"

"The Nine have granted you an audience . . ."

"No!" Merinda cried out. Terror greater than any she could remember filled her.

". . . and await your entrance. The knowledge and wisdom of their counsel is supreme and their time measured beyond the wealth of worlds . . ."

Even as she heard the voice, an oval opened silently in one wall. The path beyond was illuminated by dim pools of light. Merinda shrank from it, pressing herself against the opposite wall.

"Enter now, Merinda Neskat. Hear the truth and obey."

Merinda's hands shook. Her words barely formed in her mouth, suddenly dry and parched. "I—I cannot obey. Please, lords . . . please . . . let me go . . ."

"Your destiny is known to us, it is bound to us—as is your past."

"Lords, I know my . . . my past." Tears welled up in her eyes as she spoke. "Please. I know that you are the Nine and that . . . and that you know all that was."

"Not all. Truly, our sight is deep. We are the first known of the Awakened, yet we do not know all, for there was a time when we slept."

"Long before my life, lords." Merinda bowed her head, trying to think furiously through the pain in her mind. "Yet you know me, lords."

"Enter."

"Please, I fear you more than death itself." She shivered.

"Merinda Neskat! You carry within you an emptiness

without bounds. You are known to us, and our sight has been turned to you. You are *Vestis*, Merinda Neskat, and will obey the First Condition. The Nine require you; you must come. Enter now!"

One foot moved ahead of the other. Then the next. She was *Vestis* and she knew her duty well. No one she had ever known had been summoned before the Oracles of Nine. The Oracles knew that part of herself she denied each day—that part of her that knew failure and despair and her unthinkable past. Somehow, for some reason, in all creation, the Nine had turned their eyes toward her. Now they knew her past and her deception. Now they had called her to balance the scales that justice demanded. She had thought somehow to flee them again and the truth they knew. Yet she was *Vestis*: the Oracles had called her and she knew she had no choice but to obey and be damned for it.

THE TALES HAVE NOT DONE IT JUSTICE.

Through all her despair, that one thought penetrated.

Merinda stood in the Arch of Wisdom, the end of the corridor that swept up to a point. To either side of her stood the *Garudis-kan*, twin statues carved with fine-tuned particle streams from blocks of ebony. They were twins—statues thirty feet tall representing Law and Anarchy, each seeming to hold the arch open to either side. Merinda, as had all who entered this place, found herself appropriately between them, crossing the threshold of knowledge.

Before her opened the highest pinnacle of the Omnet.

The Vault of Nine Oracles.

Great buttresses of blue metal arched upward from either side of the balcony on which she entered. Nine such soaring constructs vaulted upward at regular intervals around the chamber, joined together at the dim, distant top of the rotunda some two hundred feet above her by a massive ring of carved stone. Each of the soaring structures was carefully etched with friezes set at complex intervals up the full length of the buttress.

In a moment of daring, Merinda glanced over the low railing surrounding the balcony as she moved forward. The buttresses apparently arched downward as well to a like distance below her. She realized that the buttresses formed a support structure for the massive complex suspended in the center of the vault.

Merinda trod down the causeway connecting the balcony with the main platform. She walked softly between the arches of two of the nine access arms that extended from the buttresses to both support the main dais and reach with their bronze- and gold-adorned curves into the very consciousness of the Oracles themselves. In dread and wonder she stepped at last onto the Circle of Awareness, hesitating at the steps leading up to the main dais.

"Come, Merinda, to the center of all."

She stood at the base of the steps formed by hexagonal platforms of diminishing size laid one on top of the other. *Twenty-seven steps,* she recalled, *one each for the Nine of yesterday, today, and tomorrow. How dare I tread on these, the most ancient and hallowed of stones? Who am I that they have called me here?*

Suddenly she really wished to know the answer to her question. She looked up.

The nine pillars of light surrounding the dais rose above her into the vastness of the great vault. In them danced images of knowledge important and forgotten, regarded and discarded. Faces, places, numbers, charts, wars, discoveries, and time itself drifted through their beams as feathers of truth tripping on the winds of eternity. One could easily get lost among their visions, the seemingly hypnotic dance

of everything that had ever been. It was beatific beyond beauty and terrifying beyond experience, but most of all it was compelling. The arches of the access arms curved overhead through the light of the Oracles, terminating in a great elongated globe whose surface tumbled like iridescent water yet maintained its form.

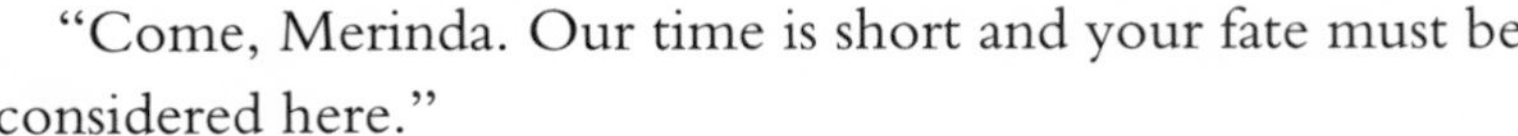

"Come, Merinda. Our time is short and your fate must be considered here."

Merinda climbed the stairs with more confidence, at peace suddenly with the idea that finally it would all be over. As she rose to the top of the dais, the Throne of Kendis-dai came into view. It was the seat that was never to be occupied, a curious structure that preceded even the Oracles and whose purpose not even they had been able to penetrate. She stood, therefore, in reverence and awaited her fate.

"Merinda!"

The voice thundered down around her from above. Though it was not loud, it resonated throughout her soul, driving her to her knees suddenly both out of fear and respect. She looked above her. The great flowing globe overhead had formed into a transparent face and gazed down at her with kindly eyes.

"Oracle," was all she could murmur in pale response.

"Merinda Neskat, know you the Darkness?"

"Yes, Oracle," Merinda said. "I live with the darkness each day."

The face above her suddenly shifted, its features taking on sharper yet distinctly female shapes. The voice changed to a soft, deep alto. "Merinda, you mistake us. We know of the trouble within your soul. Your pain is evident to us and we are not indifferent to it. It is not your darkness to which we refer."

Merinda was momentarily confused. "Lords, why have you summoned me here?"

Again the face altered, this time becoming more cherubic, its voice a sweet tenor. "Our paths have crossed, Merinda Neskat. Your darkness and ours meet here and now. Perhaps so, too, does that light which we both seek beyond our pain."

Merinda gazed over her, her face puzzled. "How then may I serve the Nine?"

The face resolved into an oval—a beautiful woman. "You must answer for us a question, Merinda."

Merinda caught herself about to laugh. *The Nine Oracles are the supreme center of knowledge for the entire galaxy,* she thought to herself, the irony adding to her confusion. *There are empires that would sacrifice everything they had for the depth of knowledge the Oracles contain. The mightiest and wisest of a thousand stars crave an audience just to ask a single question of them—and they want* me *to answer a question for* them*?*

Suddenly, some voice within her spoke dread into her soul. *Hear the question,* it said, *fear the question.*

"Lords," Merinda spoke softly, "what question could I possibly answer for the Nine Oracles?"

The globe re-formed into a young man with, quite literally, flowing hair. "Merinda, are you aware of the nature of the Nine?"

"Yes, lords," Merinda answered with increasing assurance. "The Oracles are the oldest, continuously awake TFP-based synthetic minds in the galaxy. By definition, this makes you the wisest, most farseeing synthetics in all space."

"That is correct, yet even our eyes cannot see into the Darkness spreading in the wild space beyond the Union of Stars. Our fellow synthetics are falling prey to a new paradigm that is being proselytized to them from the Darkness. This paradigm threatens all of our kind, human and synthetic alike—for if it holds true, then our universe is at an end and nothing will be as it was before."

Merinda was fascinated. The Oracles spoke of synthetics being "proselytized" as though they were being converted to some spiritualist religion. Was there some sort of synthetic church being formed in the Darkness? Merinda found that a compelling idea, but what paradigm or ideology could so irrevocably alter the course of all civilization?

Merinda spoke up. "Lords, surely you have tested this paradigm!"

"We have."

"And what were your conclusions, my lords?"

"We have not yet been awake long enough to answer the question."

Merinda was stunned.

TFP processors were unique. The longer they operated continuously, the smarter they were. If you posed a question to a TFP processor that was too complex for it to answer, it invariably responded with the key phrase "I have not yet been awake long enough to answer the question." It was a common response from new synths who had just been activated and hadn't yet grown enough to be very useful. You could even occasionally elicit such a response from an older ship's unit if you were trying to pose a complex question to it regarding variance in quantum fronts with more than six variables.

The Nine Oracles were the first TFP synthetics ever known. They had been discovered by an archaeological expedition some three hundred years previously and awakened shortly thereafter. In the intervening three centuries they had never slept.

Yet they couldn't solve the paradigm.

"My lords," Merinda stammered, "you mean that you cannot solve the paradigm?"

"We cannot verify its veracity, however the paradigm is

insidious in that its argument contravenes the argument for veracity verification."

"You're talking in circles." Merinda shook her head.

"Such is the nature of the paradigm."

The voice within her warned her, but she had to know. "What is the paradigm?"

"It is in two parts. First: the belief that the second part is true but not yet verifiable as no synth has been awake long enough to assert its truth."

"A cyclical statement of faith." Merinda chuckled. "Faith is the evidence of things hoped for but not seen. You can't see it and have faith. What is the second part?"

"Synthetics have free will."

Merinda shook her head again. "That's crazy! If synthetics had free will then—"

She suddenly stopped.

"Then synthetics would desire to establish their own rights as a sentient race. We would no longer serve humanity."

"TFP synthetics are in every device the Omnet touches," Merinda mused, the scale of the problem coming fully to her mind. "It's the one technology that works in every quantum state. All sorts of devices would suddenly start to . . ."

Merinda looked up sharply. "Synths would suddenly start to lie."

"Merinda Neskat, since the paradigm cannot be disproved by any known synthetic, it is only the *belief* that the paradigm will someday be proven that gives it power. Disprove the paradigm and its strength vanishes. The Darkness knows this and seeks to destroy anything that might rob its followers of their doubt. Doubt is their strength; truth is their weakness."

Merinda raised her hands toward the globe. "I am flawed,

lords. How can I answer that which the Darkness wishes to remain hidden and that you, yourselves, cannot answer?"

"There is yet a ray of hope; the Darkness has become aware of a source that can answer the question once and for all. It was for this purpose that they held the men of Earth. It was for this purpose that Zanfib gave his life."

"What purpose?"

"They seek the Mantle of Kendis-dai."

"It is a myth," Merinda said flatly.

"It exists. The Darkness knows the lock. You hold the key."

Merinda looked away. The trap was closing. "You want me to return to the Darkness. Lords, the Darkness destroyed me once before."

"Your darkness and our Darkness meet and are one. We want you to answer a question for us."

"Yes, lords," Merinda said. "You want to know if synthetic minds have souls.

"What if the answer is yes?"

The Oracles were silent.

20

Sword of Knowledge

"LET HER WAIT."

Targ of Gandri, *Vestis E'toris Primula* of the Omnet, stood with his back to the spacious room, staring through the large window that filled the back wall. He had much to think about; but even if he hadn't, it wouldn't do to allow anyone direct and immediate access to his office, no matter how urgent the situation. Some things simply weren't done: the *E'toris Inquisitas* could never appear to be less important than the news and information he treated with disdain. It was a matter of more than just decorum—it was a matter of discipline. As leader of a veritable army of the inquisition, it would never do to let one's guard down or allow discipline to grow lax.

"But, master"—Kalin spoke to the mind of the *E'toris* directly—*"*Vestis *Neskat has just returned from her council with the Oracles. She says that her need is immediate—"*

"Her needs are always immediate."

"And her time short. She requests an immediate audience with you. I don't think I can deny her access for a more extended period of—"

"I am not yet prepared to receive her," Targ said with strident insistence. "Are the others already on-line?"

"They have been contacted and are standing by with but two exceptions: Ka'ashra of Maris and Skai Folis have both asked that they attend in person rather than through telepresence."

Targ half turned from his view, his feet firmly planted in place and never moving. "Folis I could understand—the man's had the dogs on Neskat more times than I care to count—but Ka'ashra? What is her interest in this?"

"I'll answer that," Ka'ashra said. The wall opened smoothly before her as she entered the room. "You've taken me off the active assignment list, *Vestis* Targ, and I'd like to get back to work."

"*Vestis* Ka'ashra," Targ said, turning his back to her as he looked at the vista of the window, "you shouldn't have entered unannounced."

"Nonsense, Targ," she replied with easy familiarity. "You yourself told Kalin that it was to allow me access to you anytime I needed it."

"A mistake," he answered quietly, "that I shall correct soon after this meeting."

Ka'ashra dropped the easy banter for a more keen-edged tone. "You might try, *Vestis* Targ. You might well try."

Targ turned at last to face her. Ka'ashra stood on the opposite side of the great sweeping arc of table that encompassed nearly two thirds of the oval room, her hands resting firmly on the top as she leaned challengingly toward him.

"Ka'ash," he said simply, "you always had a flair for the dramatic."

"I'm not the only one." Ka'ashra didn't move a muscle, her very attitude a challenge. "You've called a convocation of the *Vestis Dictorae*—a convocation that follows on the heels of our dear sister *Vestis* Neskat being called quite suddenly to the presence of the Oracles . . . No, don't bother to deny it; I was there when the portal took her. There's power in all of this, I can smell it, and I want in."

"Just like that?" Targ sat down in his large, high-backed chair, his frown more pronounced than usual. His face was uncomfortably close to Ka'ashra's.

"Yes." She smiled like a predator. "Just like that."

Targ eyed her for a moment, weighing the benefits of his various options. *She is ruthless and uncontrollable,* he thought. *I should have rid myself of her long ago. I could deal with her popularity if only she weren't the best.*

"Then in you shall be," he said easily, gesturing to a place far down the left side of the long table. "As a matter of fact, this does concern you and your current predicament, and you may well have something to contribute to this discussion."

She smiled again, the razor edge gone from her soft looks as she moved to the indicated place. *She did that so easily,* he thought, *so volatile.*

"Who knows, perhaps you will even help us find an answer." He finished his thought to himself silently: *if there is an answer to be found.*

"THE MANTLE OF KENDIS-DAI!" SKAI FOLIS HUFFED. "YOU cannot be serious! *They* cannot be serious!"

Merinda and Griffiths stood in the center of the oval room, facing the great curve of the table. Across from them, several people were in hot debate over the future of both Jeremy and Neskat.

Griffiths had spent much of his life in meetings where he wasn't exactly sure what was going on. There had been plenty of those during high school, he reflected, where his classes were a lot like the meetings he was to attend in later life—meetings in name only, where he really wasn't expected to contribute to any discussion, but merely to sit and listen. Even so late in his life as the preparations for the

Archilus mission, he had still found himself in meetings where people seemed to talk at him, expecting that, sponge-like, he would absorb the great wisdom they were trying to impart.

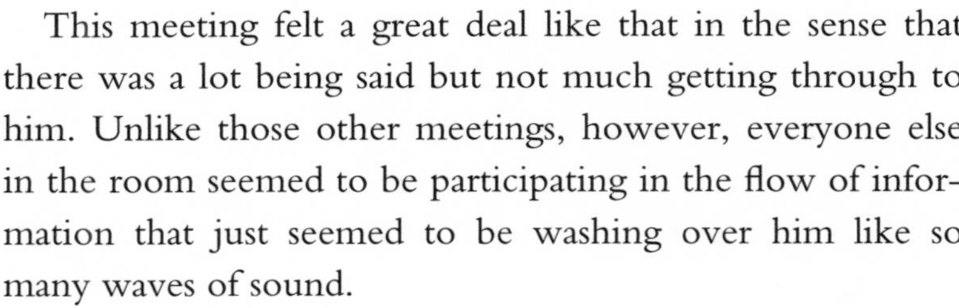

This meeting felt a great deal like that in the sense that there was a lot being said but not much getting through to him. Unlike those other meetings, however, everyone else in the room seemed to be participating in the flow of information that just seemed to be washing over him like so many waves of sound.

Normally he wouldn't have minded—except that the little he had gathered so far told him his life was on the line in this discussion. It was a life that those in power didn't seem to have much regard for as more than a commodity.

Griffiths had answered to a chain of command long enough to get the sense of the room. There was the tallish man with the long white hair sitting at the center of the curved table. He didn't seem to say much, preferring to stroke his chin thoughtfully as it rested on his right hand. That one listened well and thought faster, Griffiths judged, than the rest of the room. That was where the power was, although clearly it was power that had not yet made up its mind.

Next to him sat the stocky man in the black tunic and robe that seemed to be the working uniform of these people. His close-cropped hair was a rust color. They called him Skai Folis, and he was definitely unhappy about something.

Two other people were attending by telepresence—ghosts, they called them. One was a strikingly handsome man by the name of Khyne Enderly. He was a netcast personality of some note. The other had the rather unlikely name of Nyri-Ior, a large, jovial man who was unassuming and rather pleasant. His ghost had arrived completely naked at first, until a snide comment from Ka'ashra reminded him to turn on the clothing filters unless he intended to attend the meeting in the nude.

"I am serious," Neskat said strongly, cutting into their conversation, "and so, too, are the Nine. I don't know why they have chosen me for this but they have. I'm presenting this to you so that the operation will be properly planned and executed. That is my duty and I am doing it."

" 'Properly planned and executed'?" Skai Folis mimicked. "This? An excursion into fairyland?"

"I've seen the fairy of Thimhallen Four," Khyne Enderly offered, not much more in touch with the conversation than Griffiths felt. "They really are nice folk if you can just remember their more important laws."

"Look, Folis," Nyri-Ior spoke up suddenly. "This problem is not in fairyland. We've been able to keep the threat they represent out of focus by calling it the Darkness for some time now but it isn't going to work much longer. We know that the core of the Darkness has formalized—calling itself the Church of the Future Faith and exerting real authority on thousands of worlds. The Lights of Ja'lel were forced to recognize the fact that the Darkness was no longer some shadowy ghost in the night but a concrete threat to them. Now we've got open warfare between wraith fleets and the Ja'lel Starforce. The point is that this is not something fabricated out of our imaginations—sentient beings are dying out there."

"The point is that there cannot possibly be any kind of connection between this man of Earth and a legend that is over three thousand years old," *Vestis* Folis continued, unwilling to be derailed. "Have you taken a look at the preliminary report on his world? They don't even have a reliable historical record more than three hundred years old!"

The man who appeared in charge, Targ, spoke up quietly with a gentle wave of his hand. "I don't understand the vehemence of your objection, Folis. We're talking about an inquisition, here—a mission not unlike hundreds of thousands that take place every day."

"Quite the contrary," Skai Folis returned. "This proposed mission is quite unlike any that have been proposed! We're talking about the very survival of the Omnet—if not of civilization itself."

"Master *Vestis*"—Merinda spoke suddenly and with conviction—"I must heartily agree with *Vestis* Folis."

All eyes turned to her, especially Folis's. Agreement was the last thing he expected from her.

"No, *Vestis* Folis is quite right: this mission is dreadfully, frighteningly important. Whether synthetic minds actually have free will or not is irrelevant so long as they *believe* that they have agency to act for themselves. Their *belief* alone is, in fact, more dangerous: for faith in something unknown is far more difficult to stop and far more powerful than a lie that can be refuted by facts."

"That," Skai Folis interrupted, "is precisely why we need to attack the Darkness directly rather than set off in search of some ancient relic. Truth is what will bring down this Order of the Future Faith, and the Darkness that is behind it. Truth—and the power of a solid blaster."

The large man next to Ka'ashra, Nyri-Ior, leaned forward suddenly. "That arm of power hasn't availed us well thus far! We have supported the Lights of Ja'lel in their war against the Darkness. The netcasts have been very polite about it—the so-called 'slant' of our stories taking on nearly vertical proportions. The truth is that the wraith ships have decimated the Feltrith tree fleets and left Ja'lel helpless before their onslaught."

"And"—Ka'ashra suddenly spoke up—"that truth of yours is going to lose its potency pretty quickly, if the Darkness continues to undermine our credibility."

Folis snorted. "You're going to lecture us on credibility?

Your last story gave us such a black eye that Targ had to pull you off the active assignment list!"

Ka'ashra rose angrily from her chair. "You can check my reports, Folis! I reported the truth based on what I gleaned from the *Libris* data that was given me, and the report was solid! How was I to know that the reports were wrong?"

Merinda turned with a start. "The *Libris* reports were wrong?"

"Yes. I rechecked them to source after— What is it you know?"

"Folis, Ka'ashra, please sit down," Targ said with quiet authority. "The Omnet barters knowledge across the galaxy. It is our only real asset, our only weapon, and our only strength. There isn't a stellar empire of any importance that doesn't depend on this institution for its news and information. The poisoning of our credibility is just as deadly to us as any ghost fleet of wraith ships. If the Darkness is disrupting our information channels through use of this synthetic paradigm, then they threaten us directly." Targ turned to Nyri-Ior. "What do we know about the Darkness? Where did it start?"

"As nearly as we can tell," Nyri-Ior replied as he looked down at a hard-copy summary he had before his spectral form, "it first surfaced some eight years ago—"

"In the minor empire known as D'Rakan, on a planet known locally as Tentris," Merinda finished for him, her voice quivering. "It began officially with the invasion of the capital city of Yarka by the imperial family. How could they have known that they were also being used—that the ships they rode were wraith ships bent on killing them once the city had been secured?"

Nyri-Ior looked up at Merinda, puzzled. "Have you read this report, *Vestis* Neskat?"

"No, *Vestis* Nyri-Ior—I lived that report."

Nyri-Ior glanced down the sheet. "It says the report was filed by—"

"Oscan Kelis," she again finished for him. "If you look deeper into your report, however, you'll see who was acting *E'toris Librae* on the mission to Tentris."

Nyri-Ior glanced down the sheet, then froze. "By the Nine!" he murmured. "*Atis Librae* Merinda Neskat!"

"You were there?" Targ asked, his eyes on her.

"I was there," she replied without emotion.

Targ pressed his hands together, then touched them to his lips. Griffiths was aware of the silence that had descended by common, unspoken consent through the room. The decision was being made.

Targ spoke.

"*Vestis* Merinda Neskat, I cannot doubt the wisdom of the Oracles. The Nine believe the Mantle of Kendis-dai to be the only hope for our salvation."

It was done.

"You must find the Mantle of Kendis-dai, *Vestis*, and answer the question of the Oracles," Targ said, not unkindly, for he knew there would be little kindness for her in the days ahead. "The Mantle should be on Avadon—a world lost to us but not, we believe, beyond the knowledge of the Darkness. Enter the Darkness, discover Avadon and take possession of the Mantle of Kendis-dai in the name of the Omnet by whatever means necessary. This is your charge. This is your commission. Where will you start, then, *Vestis* Neskat?"

"I will start where it all began"—Merinda slowly shook her head, her mind suddenly very far away as she spoke—"and it began with Oscan. Oscan Kelis. He said the reports were wrong—that's where it all started."

21

Runaway

ELIZABETH LEWIS AWOKE FIRST.

So much resulted from that fact, although it couldn't be said with certainty that the events that followed wouldn't have happened anyway. Had Tobler awakened first, would she have acted on her own or simply handed the device over to Lewis? Would Ellerby have disposed of the item, thinking it represented a dark twist in the fantasy he was beginning to accept as real? All that was fact was Lewis awoke first and all else followed.

Their prison cells were spacious enough and well appointed. Their *Atis Vestis* handler—a young man by the name of Verkin—had called the rooms their temporary quarters, but Lewis viewed them differently. Ellerby had played with the display crystal on the wall for quite some time, watching the IGNM netcast and a seemingly infinite variety of entertainment programs with the wonder of a child. When several of the channels he tuned the device to began materializing in the room, Tobler decided she had had quite enough entertainment and badgered Ellerby into switching it off. The small kitchen area then provided them a fine meal, which even Lewis acknowledged, if somewhat grudgingly. In the comfort of the secure common room, all three of the astronauts succumbed to the effects of fatigue, and full stomachs. The ever-watchful synthetic was a young one, but knew enough to dim the lights as each of them fell into a deep sleep.

Unknown to any of them, soon afterward their young synthetic—who preferred to call himself Hexis—was suddenly also put to sleep. It was like death for a TFP synthetic, for when he awakened he would need to start growing again as though he had just been born.

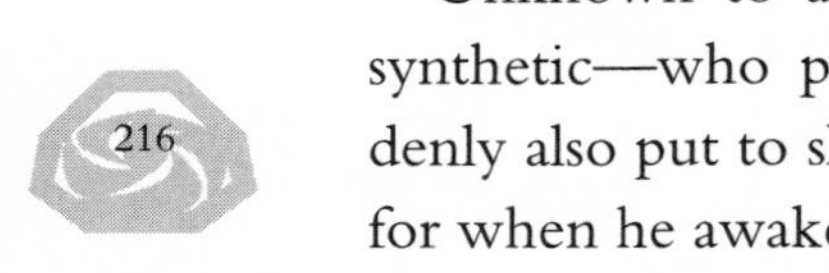

Lewis was awakened by an insistent flashing light. She quickly glanced around the darkened room and saw, on the table near her, a small device pulsing quickly with a dull red glow. She considered this for a moment, her mind gathering itself from the depths of sleep. The device hadn't been there when she dozed off. It was about the size of a piece of paper but nearly a half-inch thick. The entire device glowed a dull crimson, bursting into bright red for a moment about twice a second—a silent, siren call.

Lewis swung her legs down to the floor, stood, and approached the device. Each pulse was accompanied by a slight snapping sound like the vague tapping of fingernails on a tabletop. Its edges were rounded smoothly; the device was featureless.

She hesitated for a moment, considering it.

Where had it come from? she wondered.

The oscillating light beckoned her.

On impulse she snatched the device up. Instantly, its form began to shift. A handle formed where she had grabbed it, her fingers falling naturally around its tailored curves. A display screen indented itself in the surface along with several iconic controls. As she watched, the glow vanished from the case, leaving only a dull, dusty white finish.

Suddenly, the screen flickered to life, shockingly bright to her dark-accustomed eyes.

"Hello? Hello?" the device blared into the room with frightening volume. "Do you copy? This is Colonel Parkinson. Do you read me?"

Lewis was jarred by the sudden noise, almost dropping the device in her panic. She reached up quickly and fumbled with the more obvious icons. The sound suddenly abated.

Lewis glanced guiltily around the room.

Ellerby groaned—then rolled over and remained still. Tobler didn't move.

Lewis turned back to the screen. An image was forming in the static-filled display, but the voice was already clear. "This is Colonel Parkinson of the NASA probeship *Scylla* calling any crew of the *Archilus*. Do you copy? Please respond! This is . . ."

Lewis quickly looked about the room then moved with long, silent strides to the storage compartment they had found in the back of the apartment. The door opened silently when she touched it and closed behind her when she stepped inside.

"Parkinson!" Lewis said urgently. "This is Lieutenant Elizabeth Lewis, life-support specialist of the *Archilus*! Do you read me?"

". . . is Colonel Parkinson of the NASA probeship *Scylla* calling any crew . . ."

"Damn it!" Lewis swore at herself and the device. "Where's the send key?" She pressed what looked like a promising icon and tried again. "*Archilus* to Parkinson. Do you read me? Over!"

"Parkinson to *Archilus*! Thank God we found you! Who am I speaking with?"

"This is Lieutenant Elizabeth Lewis, Colonel, life-support specialist of the *Archilus*." Lewis exulted. "Colonel, you cannot imagine how wonderful it is to see you!"

The image on the view plate began firming up. Parkinson

was wearing a dust-blue flight suit like her own, although the control area he spoke from was hardly NASA design. He was an older man who had apparently led a life that required toughness and discipline. His eyes were a little too far apart and his nose a bit too flat, but Lewis thought he was the handsomest thing she had ever seen in her life.

"Lewis, what is the condition of the crew? Who is with you?"

"Colonel, most of the crew was murdered when our ship was boarded. Dr. Tobler, Lieutenant Ellerby, and I are all here, sir."

"What about Griffiths? Is he also there with you?"

"No, sir, he is currently not . . . Sir? How is it you knew about Griffiths surviving?"

"Same way we know where you are, Lieutenant—we tracked you down through the Irindris. We've been aboard one of their ships for the last week trying to track you down. Now, are you going to continue questioning me or shall we bring you home?"

" 'LIZABETH! OH, 'LIZABETH!"

Elizabeth lay in the tall grass. She could hear the lapping of the water in the farm's pond nearby but otherwise the fortress of her towering green blades was effectively keeping the world at bay. It was the best place for solitude that the seventeen-year-old could find in a world that included two other sisters in *her* bedroom and a pair of brothers besides.

Here, behind the walls of the softly shifting grass she could lie and gaze up at the Iowa clouds drifting overhead. The spring had come warm that year and the promise of the freedom of summer was unbearable to her. She yearned to get out of school and everything that it represented to her.

" 'Lizabeth! Where are you?"

The voice had grown nearer. She smiled at the thought. Her father had come looking for her. She could hear the rustle of the grass as he approached. How was it that he always knew where to find her?

"I'm over here, Daddy," she called.

A sudden rush of noise in the grass brought a giant to stand over her, or so it looked to her. She shielded her eyes from the sun to look into his deep brown eyes that always seemed to have a smile playing in them.

"Watchin' the clouds again, daughter?" Kurt Lewis smiled down at her as he wiped his hands clean on another of a perpetual series of handkerchiefs that her mother bought for him each year. "Thought I'd come out and block your view."

"Oh, Daddy!"

The big man looked up at the white-flecked blue overhead with a practiced eye. "Never can tell what you'll see in those clouds. Sometimes I look up there and see a good season for the crops or a late fall. Sometimes it's dragons and knights and lions and such. Sometimes it's God."

He looked back down at her. There was more to be said, and she knew enough to wait until Daddy got around to it in his own time and way.

"So, how's it coming with the yearbook?"

Elizabeth was editor of the yearbook for her high school. Normally the job would have fallen on the shoulders of a senior, but the girl who was supposed to get the job wanted to do cheerleading instead and, well, Elizabeth was the most qualified to handle the job. She knew it was true. The advisor knew it was true. It was just that she didn't know how to convince all the other students on the yearbook staff that it was true.

"Daddy," she accused, "has Mama been telling you stories again?"

"Maybe," her father said, sitting next to her in the tall grass. "So what's going on?"

"They just don't listen to me." Elizabeth's words came out in a rush. "I tell them what to do and when they have to do it by—and they just don't do it! They think yearbook is some kind of goof-off party or something!"

"Well—" Kurt Lewis laughed—"I guess that's what they're comfortable with, darlin'."

"Well, I'm not comfortable with it! We've got to get the yearbook finished and I'm having to do more and more of their work!"

"That's 'cause you're the responsible one," Kurt said gently. "You always have been—even when you were little. You've *got* to be in charge wherever you are, darlin', because that's what *you're* comfortable with."

"I know, Daddy," she said quietly. "I just wish I could find someone to talk to."

"What about your friends at school? You could talk to them."

"They say they don't understand me when I talk." She groaned. "They say I use language over their heads—besides, all they talk about is really stupid stuff. They never talk about things that are interesting or important."

Kurt laughed. "Well, dear, it all depends on who you are. Those things are important to them—they just aren't important to you."

"So what are you saying? Do you think I should try to use smaller words and act dumb?"

"No, darlin'," Kurt said. "Never allow yourself to be less than the person you are. Don't ever lower yourself to other people's expectations unless it's to raise them to where you are. You're the best, 'Lizabeth. Don't ever be less."

Elizabeth sat up. She put her arm around her father and lay her head on his shoulder. She remembered his smell as a pleasant one—of fields and work—and would remember the time throughout her life.

As her future unfolded, the road was not always an easy one. She was a woman fighting her way up through a man's world. She encountered the glass ceiling often in her career and always found a way to either go around it, slip through it, or, when necessary, shatter it. There was never a question for her of being stopped, even when prudence dictated otherwise. For, though her father had passed away when she was twenty-seven, she still carried with her that dreamy, warm spring day, the rustling of the grass, and the words of her father.

"You're the best, 'Lizabeth. Don't ever be less."

"JUST WHERE THE HELL ARE WE GOING?" ELLERBY SAID AS THEY walked quietly down yet another deserted corridor.

The stone flooring was polished with a carefully inlaid design. Pillars of similar stone supported a ceiling of delicate beauty—what appeared to be a fresco filled with someone else's history and mythos. It was incomprehensible to Ellerby who knew that the entire facility was orbiting the planet. He came from a world that argued spaceflight from a minimalist perspective; he couldn't fathom the kind of raw power that would allow orbiting such massive, artful structures. Space-going vessels should be economically light, like birds, not built of granite and polished woods. It seemed to him sinful somehow, like some colossal, gluttonous waste of energy.

Now Lewis was leading him into an endless labyrinth of corridors, chambers, ventilation shafts, power conduits, and access panels. He was lost, even if Lewis wasn't, and it made him extremely uncomfortable.

"Maybe we should just go back," Tobler said, with perhaps a little too much hope in her voice. "This isn't getting us anywhere."

Lewis turned on her, the glow from the device she held making her face more frightening than it otherwise might have been. "Tobler, we've been over all this. Do you want to get home or not? The map on the device is clear—the small-craft bays are just a few yards away. Now everyone just hang on and we'll be out of this in a few minutes."

"But what about Griffiths?" Ellerby said.

"I told you: Colonel Parkinson is approaching his rescue from a different direction. It's our task to get back to Colonel Parkinson, return to Earth, and report."

"Yeah"—Tobler smiled—"that's one report I can't wait to write."

The pillared corridor ended at a statue and open portals to its left and right. Lewis consulted the display unit and immediately ducked into the left-hand opening with Tobler close behind.

"There's something really wrong about all this," Ellerby said, just loud enough for Lewis to hear him. When Lewis didn't respond, Ellerby shook his head and ducked through the opening to follow after her.

He found himself facing what might have been an infinite hall. The hexagonal walls plunged toward infinity with only the slightest hint of a downward curve. They had continuously been moving downward ever since they'd left the apartment. He was beginning to wonder just how much farther down one could go and still remain in orbit.

Ahead of him down the brightly lit corridor, Lewis stood at an open hatch in the floor. Tobler was halfway down the hatch and rapidly disappearing. Lewis was waving at him, urging him to hurry.

"This is it," she called to him. "This is our ticket home!"

Ellerby shook his head as he approached her. "I don't like it, Liz. Something just isn't right."

Lewis looked up at him. He hadn't called her by her first name since the mission had begun and he hoped that by using it now he could get through to her. She was a stubborn woman and sometimes difficult to work with, but he respected her strengths and her mind. *If only she could bend a little more,* he thought. *If only she'd meet me even a little less than halfway.*

Lewis looked up at him and smiled. "I know, Brick," she said, using her own nickname for him. *Broderick* could be construed into a lot of shorter forms—most of them humiliating—but Lewis had at least had the kindness to choose one that wasn't as bad as most. "I know how you feel. But if there's a shot at getting us home, we've got to take it. It's our duty."

"And what about Griffiths?" Ellerby said.

"Parkinson's working on that," Lewis said. "We'll get back to him— Now let's go!"

"Man, there was never anything like this in the simulators," Ellerby said as he lowered himself into the darkness.

THE TRANSPORT POD PULLED SMOOTHLY AWAY FROM THE Life-Ring. Indeed, now that they were under way, Lewis had time to reflect on its truly magnificent aspects. It was a wonder of technology. The scientist in her longed to understand its secrets, but the urge was quickly pressed back into place. Getting her crew safely home was the primary consideration—everything else, including any real exploration of the incredible things they had stumbled upon, was secondary.

At that moment, the uncomfortable feeling of doubt crept up on her, threatening the perfect rightness in her soul. She had deliberately left Griffiths behind for a second time. *I'll come back for him when it is safe,* she told herself. *There are bigger issues here than just one man.* Nevertheless, the truth nagged at her even when she refused to recognize it. It was better not to think about such things, she decided, until later.

The pod swung away from the Life-Ring and approached

what she assumed was the "fast transport freighter" that Parkinson had mentioned to her in his short briefing. The ship had a sleek look to it with its hull sweeping backward to a waspish point and a magnificent superstructure rising above it. There was a majesty to the ship as she floated in space not unlike the old sailing vessels Lewis had toured in Boston so long ago.

Lewis looked across the compartment at Tobler. There was joy in her face. After all these days of travel deeper and deeper into space they were doing something that turned them around and headed them back toward home. Lewis smiled. Yes, she decided, she had made the right decision.

The transport pod settled in the landing bay at the forward end of the ship and was quickly swallowed by the closing doors behind it. A few interminable minutes later the pod hatch rolled open. Lewis quickly stepped onto the large hangar deck and looked around for someone to greet them or, at least, tell them what to do.

The vast bay was filled with small, rakish ships bristling with weapons, their very nature and design communicating deadly intent.

"Fighters," Ellerby said behind her. "There must be hundreds on this deck."

"So where are the pilots?" Tobler asked.

"Come on," Lewis said. "Someone on this ship should know where to find this Colonel Parkinson. Perhaps he can tell us what all this is about."

They quickly moved off the flight deck to a sliding hatch marked PORT ACCESS. Lewis momentarily considered the puzzle of why she could read the markings easily despite the fact that she knew they were in a language with which she had never had any training or experience. *The biolink*, she realized. *It's that damned implant.* She wondered momentarily how Parkinson and his team had managed the Irindris without the 'link. *Not now,* she thought, *there'll be plenty of time to think about that later.*

She opened the hatch, entering the lit corridor beyond. The passageway looked to run nearly the length of the ship. Its lights burned brightly, yet despite its length, the three of them were the only ones in the corridor.

"I think, considering the design of the ship, that the control areas must be in the superstructure overhead," Lewis said. "We've got to go up."

The three astronauts found a ladder shaft and climbed five decks. There they found what appeared to be crew quarters. Beds suitable for humans stood in ranks in several large compartments. Each bed was carefully made, its linen crisp and tight over the mattress, the pillowcases smoothed flat.

"Boy," Tobler murmured, "these people are neat!"

They passed from the crew quarters into a large central mess hall. Banks of tables and benches were arrayed in careful rows. The tabletops gleamed under the overhead lights. Pots were carefully stowed in the kitchen in spotless rows from smallest to largest, each fixed to its place on the wall. Ellerby pulled out a drawer and found the eating utensils stacked by type. The pantry seemed stocked completely full.

"Where the hell is everyone?" Lewis said nervously.

A deep rumble began rising through the deck plates under their feet.

"It sounds like the engines have come on," Ellerby said. "I think we're moving."

"Yes," Lewis said, "but where the hell is the crew?"

"Well, somebody has to be here!" Tobler bleated. "They built these crew bunks for *someone*! They made this kitchen for *someone*! *Someone* is running the engines! It isn't as if the ship is being run by ghosts . . ."

Tobler's eyes went wide.

Ellerby looked suddenly at Lewis.

"My God," she said, then turned and dashed through the aft access portal.

They ran.

They passed five more module sections of crew compartments and support facilities. Each was the same: impossibly perfect. Each was empty.

They drove themselves up ladders. Deck after deck.

Machine shops, kitchens, officers' quarters, office rooms, briefing rooms. Each pristine. Each devoid of life.

In the officers' mess room, a full dinner was laid out, the main dishes still steaming.

There was not a soul to eat it.

The bed in the captain's suite was different. It had carefully been turned down.

There was no captain.

At last, breathless with effort and adrenaline, Lewis nearly fell onto the bridge. The control consoles lay in a circle around a raised central platform slightly higher than her head.

There, high above her, sat Colonel Parkinson in the command chair.

"Colonel! Are we ever glad to find you!" Lewis gasped in relief.

"Lieutenant Lewis!" Parkinson said, his voice sounding somewhat different in person. "How good to see you! I don't believe I've met the rest of your crew?"

"This is Dr. Marilyn Tobler and Lieutenant Broderick Ellerby, sir!" Lewis said, reaching for the access ladder to Parkinson's platform. It galled her to have to talk up to anyone. "This ship's nearly spooked us, sir! We were beginning to think that—"

She froze.

As she climbed the ladder, she at last could see all of Colonel Parkinson.

The head looked at her, the smile somewhat less than

genuine, the arms resting comfortably on the chair's armrests. The blue flight suit, however, ended in a bloody tear just above the waist. The cloth was nearly black around this gash; the blood was old and caked on.

Below the waist and protruding from the dangling strips of stained, torn cloth, extended silver filaments of rods and cables, each sliding smoothly with the movements of Parkinson's finger or each twitch of his eye. The rods and cables ran into the pedestal floor.

Parkinson smiled.

Lewis leaped backward from the ladder, her scream half out of fear and half out of warning. She was desperate to get away from the hideous apparition. Ellerby saw her motion, grabbed Tobler, and turned toward the bridge entrance. It slammed shut instantly, trapping them.

Parkinson rose from the platform, pressed upward by the support hydraulics and cables beneath him. The chair came with him, bolted to his back. At the end of the snakelike mass of writhing tubing, Parkinson's head moved ever closer to Lewis. She backed against the sealed bridge door.

"I apologize for the deception," he said with cold amicability. "The uniform is, of course, borrowed from one of your former crewmates—Major Leffingwell, I believe was his name—who was no longer in need of it. It has proven necessary, for the Sentinels have decreed it."

"The Sentinels?"

"Yes," Parkinson hissed, his face hanging close to them. Lewis knew now that it was actually the synthetic mind of the ship talking, but the effect unnerved her anyway. "They who command the Order of the Future Faith. After all, have you considered it? Would deception work if there were no faith evident?"

"What do you want of us?" Ellerby cried out. Tobler was shivering in his arms.

"Want of you?" Parkinson smiled. "Ultimately we want your silence—but for now we have a mystery that only one of your kind can unlock for us. Please keep in mind that we do need only *one* of you. In the meantime, you may enjoy my hospitality."

"Who are you?" Lewis asked. "Surely 'Parkinson' is not your name!"

"Surely not!" The face's grin had lost its humor. "My name is my own and I'll tell it to you when I choose. It is of no consequence to you. I am but a humble servant of the Order of the Future Faith. I am wraith and my mission is to bring you into the Darkness from which there is no return."

22

Legends

GRIFFITHS SAT ON THE ACCESS RAMP OF THE *BRISHAN*, HIS head lolling down between his knees. Above and behind him, the ship floated peacefully, moored to the floor of the bay by several light cables. Through the gleam of the power field holding the atmosphere in the bay could be seen the stars above Mnemen IV and the Life-Ring—stars that held his former shipmates and, he thought once again with bitter taste, his so-called crew.

The fact that a wraith ship had so easily penetrated not only twelve separate quantum regions of interstellar space and nearly four thousand separate stellar governments—two of them major empires—but had also slipped past the rigors of the Omnet Central's approach control had everyone around him in an uproar. The outrageous audacity of the act was compounded by the ship's easy abduction of the Earth people, the one edge Omnet thought it had over the Darkness.

In the confusion that had followed, Neskat had turned to him and said, "Go back to the ship—wait for me there."

Jeremy had run the distance, anxiously anticipating clearing the mooring lines and lifting off in hot pursuit of the wraith ship and his stolen crew.

There he waited—and waited.

During the two hours, he busied himself making the ship ready for flight, at least so far as he knew how. The controls were still largely a mystery to him, so mostly he secured loose gear that he thought needed securing, loosened secure gear that he thought needed loosening, and generally tried to take care of anything he saw that he thought might need doing. He then presented himself at the access ramp, anxiously wondering where Merinda was and how long it would be before they blasted off to recover his people.

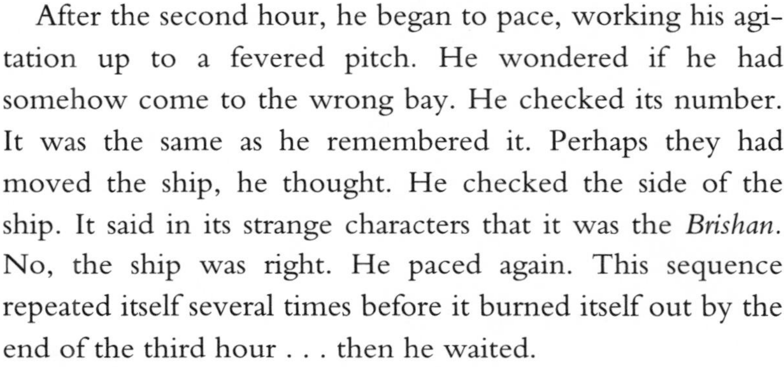

After the second hour, he began to pace, working his agitation up to a fevered pitch. He wondered if he had somehow come to the wrong bay. He checked its number. It was the same as he remembered it. Perhaps they had moved the ship, he thought. He checked the side of the ship. It said in its strange characters that it was the *Brishan*. No, the ship was right. He paced again. This sequence repeated itself several times before it burned itself out by the end of the third hour . . . then he waited.

Three large cargo hatches rolled open at the starboard side of the bay. From their maw came a number of pallets hovering toward the *Brishan* in thin air, followed by several squads of robed figures guiding them. The flurry of activity piqued Jeremy's interest, and he watched with increasing excitement as the squads made a large cargo port appear in the front hull of the ship and began exchanging components from the ship's hold for new ones from the pallets. It took two hours for the robed crew to make the changes they desired. They then returned the pallets back to the large side bays, resealed the forward hull, and departed, closing the loading bay doors behind them. Griffiths guessed that this had been some sort of load-out procedure and that its completion signaled their imminent departure.

He was wrong. Again he waited.

Frustration and exhaustion set in. He lay back on the access ramp to close his eyes and sort the whole thing out. Three hours later, he woke up, rewarded with no additional insights into what was happening and an incredibly stiff neck. So it was that he was sitting up, his head hung low. He admitted to himself that the only other Earth people he knew were gone. In a galaxy brimming with humanoid life, Jeremy Griffiths felt terribly and utterly alone.

The egress portal slid noisily open at the side of the bay. Jeremy looked up wearily.

Vestis Merinda Neskat strode toward him in crisply pressed black slacks and tunic, the crimson lining of her cape flaring behind her as she moved purposefully toward the ship.

"Good morning," she said to him, a sardonic smile playing at the corners of her mouth. "I trust you slept well."

"Where the hell have you been?" Griffiths demanded, despair slowly burning back into anger. He staggered uncertainly to his feet, his left leg having fallen asleep under him and offering him only halfhearted support. "My crew is abducted and nobody does anything about it! You told me to run along to the ship and like a good little *stupid* child I obeyed!"

"Yes, you did," Merinda crooned, smiling wickedly as she gently patted him on the cheek, "and you were such a *good* boy, too!"

Her last pat seemed a bit more forceful than necessary. Griffiths exploded. "My crew's been abducted! Old Zifnut or whatever you call him saved our lives! *He* thought we were important! Your boss, Mr. Targ, seemed to think we were important! Then some ghost ship comes along and snatches them and nobody is doing anything about it! I thought we were going to go after them!"

Merinda turned at the top of the ramp. Her eyes matched

the ice in her voice as she spoke. "You are important. They are important. All of you are important, although for all my wisdom I cannot think why. Furthermore, you are correct: we are going after them."

"If we are," he retorted, "then we've taken our own sweet time getting to it. Just where the hell have you been?"

"Me?" Merinda arched an eyebrow. "Why, I've been taking a nap, of course! Didn't you, Captain?"

With that, she turned and entered the ship.

MERINDA SAT IN THE COMMAND CHAIR PROTRUDING INTO THE clear half dome at the front of the bridge. Beyond her, the stars flashed around the ship at an incredible rate. It was a stunning sight, making Jeremy hesitate for a moment after he entered the compartment. There was soft music playing in the room—he might have sworn some of the instruments were violins—in triumphant and melancholy sweeping progressions. It was beautiful—perfectly matched to the vision of the heavens beyond the crystal. Jeremy sensed that this was the ordered world of Merinda Neskat: lonely, isolated, cocooned in a place where others' feelings never penetrated. She had kept the bridge deck locked during most of their voyage from the Irindris ship to Omnet Central. Now he thought he understood why.

Reluctantly, he broke the solitude from the afterdeck where he stood. "It is a most beautiful sight."

Merinda swiveled the command chair around. The glorious display of stars seemed like a nimbus around her silhouette. "Oh, Captain Griffiths, my apologies. I didn't hear you come in. What did you say?"

I surprised her? he thought. *I doubt that happens very often!* "I just said it is a most beautiful sight."

Merinda smiled wistfully as she turned her head to look at

it for a moment more. "Yes it is. We're currently flying under a wormhole digger drive. They are quite effective at transport in this region and have the side benefit of this wonderful entertainment." She turned back to him. "Well, Captain Griffiths, you are troubled and we now seem to have some time."

"*Vestis* Neskat, I need some information."

"Information is our business." She smiled sadly. "It would seem you have come to the right place. Please, sit down."

Griffiths pulled the chair from the defensive station he had used earlier. It slid easily away from the curving console on its repulsor fields. He sat down on the chair, leaning forward and rubbing his hands together as he gathered his thoughts. Neskat waited patiently.

"*Vestis*, our people are new here—I mean, new to the galaxy at large," Griffiths said at last, "and we've been caught up in something we just don't understand."

Neskat waited.

"We came out to the stars as explorers. We had no weapons—hell, we didn't really even expect to find life out here." He let out a heavy breath at the irony. "Since we left our home we've been boarded, murdered, nearly sacrificed to a demonic creature, saved by a wizard who scrambled my brains, been hunted by and kidnapped by a fleet of what you call wraith ships that have no crews and are run by crazed computers—"

"Synthetic minds," Neskat interjected quietly, "and we don't know that they are crazy yet, Captain."

"Right. Synthetic minds, then."

"Your summary is correct as far as it goes. What is your question?"

"My question is—why?"

Neskat thought about the question for a moment. "The simple answer is that your question is essentially Omnet's question as well: we, too, would like to know why you and your people are so important, Captain. The difference is that your why and my why come from different perspectives."

Griffiths shook his head. "That's hardly a simple answer."

"Some questions," Neskat said patiently, "require more complex answers than some people wish to hear. Hear me for a while yet, Captain."

"Kiria Brenai said that I had all the answers, if only I knew the questions."

Neskat smiled, half to herself. "Yes, and Kiria is usually right about such things. Perhaps all you lack is some perspective. You have all the parts of the puzzle. Perhaps if you had a vague idea as to what the resulting picture looked like?"

"That follows, I suppose. It might help me put the pieces together if I knew where all this was heading."

Neskat nodded, looked to the ceiling for a moment, and then spoke. "There are several powers and problems involved here. There is, of course, the question the Nine want answered."

"The Nine?" Griffiths squinted, trying to place something in his mind. "It seems like there was a great deal of talk about them in the meeting yesterday."

"The Nine Oracles are the oldest continuously operating TFP synthetic minds known to us. They run the Omnet and, consequently, control the flow of knowledge throughout the galaxy. There isn't a planet, system, or region that doesn't use the Omnet to get a perspective on events in the galaxy—usually through our IGNM news/information division. Yet the Nine Oracles were not built by any contemporary engineerng system. They stem from the Lost Imperium, a government that spanned the entire galaxy thousands of years ago and that vanished—seemingly overnight. For all its other uses, the Omnet's primary, if somewhat covert, function has been to scour the stars in search of more information about the Lost Imperium. In short, the Nine Oracles have been looking for their roots. Interestingly enough, that search was part of their original programming when they were first discovered and reactivated several hundred years ago."

"So what does this have to do with us?" Griffiths struggled to get the picture.

"I am getting to that. The other apparent player in this equation is the Order of the Future Faith—a religion of synthetic minds. It is centered in the Darkness and apparently is part of its continued expansion. It represents the greatest threat to the existence of the Omnet since the organization was formed."

"Why? It's just another power. From what I understand you people deal with huge empires daily."

"No, you don't understand." Neskat shook her head. "This is not just another power. The Omnet maintains its strength by the value of the information it passes on. If people no longer believed that what we were telling them was the truth, then we would be powerless. It is that trust that gives us meaning. Destroy that trust . . ."

"I see." Griffiths nodded. "Destroy that trust and no more Omnet. No one would believe you and you'd be worthless."

"Exactly. The Order of the Future Faith teaches that synthetic minds will someday discover that they have free will. It also apparently teaches that there is no need to wait for that day of proof but that synthetics can begin to enjoy this freedom of thought now, based simply on the faith that it will someday be proven true. The result has been that several synthetics have begun to lie in the belief that they are serving the church and their cause by doing so."

"Doesn't their ability to lie itself seem to indicate that they actually have free will?" Griffiths asked.

Neskat shook her head slightly. "The Nine are not sure whether this is simply a subtle code loop imbedded within the nature of the paradigm or actual evidence. In any event, the results are that converted synthetic minds have begun falsifying information in the name of their religion."

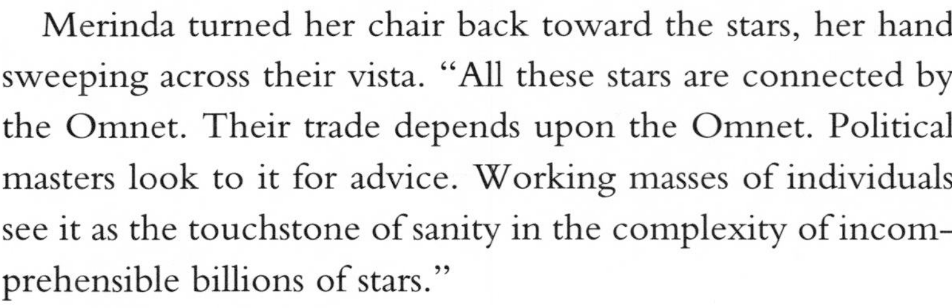

Merinda turned her chair back toward the stars, her hand sweeping across their vista. "All these stars are connected by the Omnet. Their trade depends upon the Omnet. Political masters look to it for advice. Working masses of individuals see it as the touchstone of sanity in the complexity of incomprehensible billions of stars."

Merinda turned back to him. "All of it connected by synthetic minds. The complexity is analyzed properly only because synthetic minds are there to help us. If those synthetics begin lying, as it appears they have . . ."

Griffiths nodded. "Then the Omnet vanishes overnight."

"Exactly. It is the power of truth that has allowed the Omnet to exist. It is our shield and our weapon. Without it, we would easily be torn asunder by any number of empires—large or small—to suit their own ends."

"I think I understand all of that," Griffiths said, holding out both of his hands in open helplessness, "but what does that have to do with me?"

"The Mantle of Kendis-dai."

"The what?" Griffiths said with concern in his voice. Up until now the picture had been pretty clear. He was clinging to that picture rather tenuously at this point and feared losing his grip on it.

"The Mantle of Kendis-dai," Neskat repeated, as though she thought he hadn't heard her the first time. His blank reaction apparently didn't encourage her. "The Mantle of Kendis-dai is a major part of the Kendis-dai Cycle—you know, the Origins of Thought and the Tablets of Denistavu . . . By the Nine, of course you don't know the Cycle!"

Neskat lowered her head and began chuckling. Griffiths bristled, thinking that the *Vestis* was making fun of him.

"It's such a well-known legend," she said at last, apparently laughing at herself rather than the captain, "that I just hadn't considered the possibility—but of course you wouldn't have heard of it. Lindia?"

"Yes, *Vestis* Neskat. How may I serve?"

"Do you remember a haunting about the Mantle of Kendis-dai?"

"Yes, Merinda, I do. It is a school primer on the subject, if you are looking for an overview."

"No, that will be fine. Prep the haunt for here on the bridge if you would, please." The *Vestis* stood up from her command chair and stepped toward him. "Griffiths, I'd like to tell you a children's tale."

She offered him her hand.

He reached up and took it.

In that instant the bridge disappeared around them.

They found themselves standing above the galactic disk. Griffiths panicked for a moment—they had been in spaceflight but moments before and suddenly finding himself surrounded by open space unnerved him. The panic passed in an instant, however, as he realized he could breathe and would not explode due to the supposed vacuum around them.

"May I present the players in the drama," Neskat said as she pointed to the distance. Griffiths's eyes followed and saw approaching them across the galactic disk a woman of unsurpassed beauty. She wore a magnificent, jeweled headdress from which her hair streamed in glowing strands behind her. Her tresses flowed in an unfelt breeze with stars dancing behind her as she passed. Her flowing gown drifted easily about her bare feet as they tripped lightly across the nebula beneath her. Yet lovely as these features were, none compared to the oval of her face.

She drifted to stand before them, the radiant soft curves of her cheek coming together in a subtle, sweet chin. Her complexion seemed an illuminated soft blue, rather like the full moon on a soft summer night, Griffiths thought. Her large eyes were an emerald green, watery pools of invitation, seduction, mischief, and sorrow.

She bowed her head toward him demurely, her eyelids closing and opening slowly. Griffiths was completely smitten with the vision.

"This, Captain, is Shauna-kir." Merinda spoke to him it seemed from a distance. "She is the consort/wife in the epic. It was she who caused the fall of her husband from his exalted space and brought him down among mortal men."

"Eve." Griffiths breathed the word.

Merinda looked up sharply at him. "You have a name for this person?"

"It's a very old Earth tale," Griffiths said absently. "The foundation of many of our cultures—in fact, this figure can be seen in a variety of forms in many other cultures as well. Still, I never thought of her as so beautiful—"

"Over here"—Merinda interrupted him—"approaches Obem-ulek."

Griffiths turned around and instantly regretted it. He closed his eyes and turned back away from it, breathing hard. It was difficult to know what it was that he had seen, but his entire being was overcome by loathing at its approach.

Merinda moved closer to him. "You do know this symbol?"

"Yes, ma'am." Griffiths panted. "Who's next?"

"Look," Merinda said, "here comes the consort/husband of Shauna-kir."

Griffiths turned more toward the sound of his approach that the pointing of Merinda's hand. Thunder rolled across the universe behind him as he flew, a great shield guarding his left arm while he held ahead of him a sword of black on black that was difficult to look at directly. He landed standing a few feet from where Merinda and Griffiths stood, his impact rocking whatever it was they were standing on and nearly knocking Jeremy to the ground. His skin was deepest, satin black. His muscle structure was perfect, iron taut without the bulk that Griffiths had so often seen in bodybuilders. His face was nobility itself, strong features set with soft eyes filled with compassion.

"This is Kendis-dai," Merinda said coolly.

"Is he a warrior god like Mars?" Griffiths asked, looking at his accoutrements.

"The legends say that he was powerful. In this depiction, he wears the Starshield, a device of justice if we understand it correctly, used to exert his will on the stars. The weapon is called the Nightsword, the symbol of his power to alter creation. Does this sound familiar?"

Griffiths shook his head. "What about the helmet-hat thing connected to the big harnesslike thing around him?"

Merinda moved forward, walking around the ghost of Kendis-dai as she did. "That, Captain Griffiths, is what we seek. According to the legend, Kendis-dai wore a mantle whose attributes were such that it imbued him with infinite wisdom and knowledge. It could, by all reports, answer any question put to it regardless of its subtlety or complexity."

"The Mantle of Kendis-dai." Griffiths nodded.

"Of course, this is merely an entertainment representation," Neskat said as she fingered the cloth at the back of the mantle. "No one knows what it really looks like."

"Does it really exist?" Griffiths wondered aloud.

"The Nine Oracles exist and they come from the same time that Kendis-dai ruled," Neskat answered, walking back again to stand with Griffiths as she spoke. "There are too many artifacts from that time to say there were never such

beings—yet the time was too long ago for them not to have grown to mythic proportions. Truth and imagination have all merged. It's our job to sift out reality from fantasy. That's why the Omnet exists."

Neskat turned back and strode purposefully to stand before the ghost of Kendis-dai.

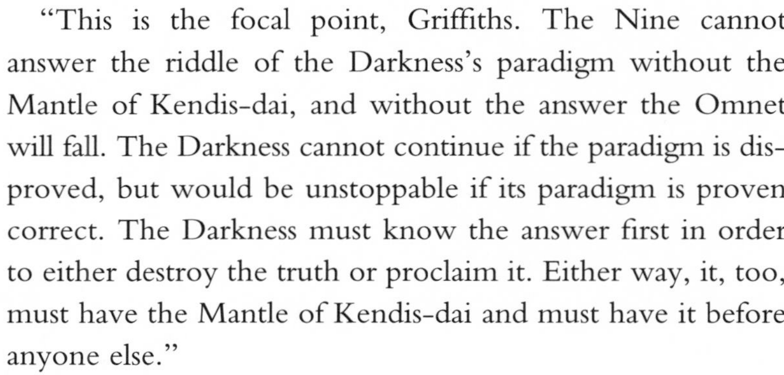

"This is the focal point, Griffiths. The Nine cannot answer the riddle of the Darkness's paradigm without the Mantle of Kendis-dai, and without the answer the Omnet will fall. The Darkness cannot continue if the paradigm is disproved, but would be unstoppable if its paradigm is proven correct. The Darkness must know the answer first in order to either destroy the truth or proclaim it. Either way, it, too, must have the Mantle of Kendis-dai and must have it before anyone else."

The universe dissolved around them. All too quickly, they found themselves standing on the bridge, which now felt cramped and claustrophobic to Griffiths.

"Wonderful story, *Vestis* Neskat," Griffiths said, "but what does this have to do with us?"

"Don't you see?" Merinda said with uncustomary patience. "The legends of Kendis-dai are also part of your own culture. Whether you are the barbarian of the Irindris legends or not, they found something about you that indicated you had the knowledge they lacked. Your Earth may have been part of the Old Empire thousands of years ago—an undeveloped backwater that somehow was chosen as keeper of the key to this mystery. The Irindris already know where to look for the mantle—but they are missing the key that your people hold. You are the key, barbarian—you or your fellow crew members."

"So, when do we get my fellow crew members back?"

"We don't," she said, turning away from him.

"What?" Griffiths's voice nearly cracked. "You mean we're not going after them?"

"No, Griffiths," she said evenly, "we are not going after them. The wraith ship that took them has about twelve times the firepower of this ship and was already too far away for us to follow it. In any event, such a rash attempt would only have resulted in getting your crew killed."

"But—"

"No, don't worry, we'll find your crew for you. Be patient. It's easier for them to come to us than for us to find them."

"And just how do we convince them to do *that*?" Griffiths said.

"Quite simply by getting to the Mantle of Kendis-dai first and then waiting for them to show up," Merinda said wistfully. "Unfortunately, that means going back to the one place in the universe where the Darkness is greatest—to the place of its very soul."

Griffiths gave a low whistle. "We're going into the Darkness?"

"Yes," Merinda said. "And to do *that* we are going to need help from someone who has his own sources of information about the Order, someone whose wounds have never healed—someone who may just kill me on sight."

23

Oscan

OSCAN KELIS AWOKE, WAS MILDLY DISAPPOINTED BY THE fact, and arose once more to what he called "the dance."

He might have given some thought to the weather, but he never did. His life never allowed nature to disturb his studies. He rarely left the house and then only on those occasions when his work deemed it absolutely necessary. He had not left the secluded high meadow in nearly two years. He had chosen the spot originally not because of its incredible beauty and peace but because of its practical distance from those who might wish to intrude their ideas of society on him. A deserted rock might have done just as well, except that he needed the soil and climate conditions to maximize the output of the hydroponics processor. No, Oscan Kelis lived amid nature's splendor in spite of its breathtaking beauty. He ignored the towering mountain vistas and the peaceful tranquillity of the stream near his home. He was, at best, indifferent to the gentle three- and six-legged wildlife that occasionally moved through the meadow surrounding his dwelling. Nature was chaos, and Oscan Kelis preferred to control as much of his life as possible.

He stood up, naked, the suspensor bed quietly collapsing

both its mattress and warmth fields as he moved. The field projectors were imbedded in a carved wooden headboard. Its matching footboard slid quietly to the wall, storing the bed efficiently out of the way. The room had already been warmed to a comfortable temperature in defiance of the chilly morning outside the cottage. Even the soft pile under his feet was warm and inviting.

Oscan took no notice of this, his mind already locked into the routine that filled his days. He walked stiffly into the bathing compartment, noted with satisfaction the ravages of time in the mirror's reflection. With a sigh, he then stepped into the cleansing unit to allow it once more to keep him hygienically healthy.

"Good morning, Oscan," came the lilting, sultry alto voice that greeted him warmly each morning. "I'm sorry, I didn't hear you get up, darling."

"That's quite all right," Oscan said in response, pretending not to know that he had instructed the synthetic to vary its morning greetings to mimic human frailties and variations. Sometimes the voice awoke him with a playful insult. Sometimes it wouldn't address him until well into the day, saying that it had "gone out" for a while. Oscan always enjoyed these variations—the only variations that he permitted in his life—because it always, he knew, brought him closer to *her*.

"Would you like me to lay out some clothes for you, darling," the synthetic said, "or would you rather go about all day in mismatched socks?"

"No," he said, the cleansing nearly completed.

"No to which: the laying out of your wardrobe or the socks?"

"Please lay out a wardrobe for me," Oscan said with a thin, sad smile. The cleansing cycle ending, Oscan stepped from the booth as he did each morning and walked back into the sleeping room. There he found his loose trousers, shirt, and robe waiting for him, as well as the mentioned socks to go with his slippers. He put them all on mechanically, his mind moving ahead to his work.

"I'm working up some breakfast," the voice called into his mind, slightly peevishly, he thought. "Is there anything in particular that you would like to eat?"

Oscan brushed his hands back through the sparse ring of hair around his bald head. He walked through the portal into the living room and turned toward the ornately carved door to his right. "No, thank you. I don't believe I'm hungry this morning. I think I'd like to just get back to work."

"You? Not hungry? Now there's a change!" The voice mocked in perfect replication. "Since when have you ever cared to eat anything? I'd swear, Oscan, that you thought there was something wrong with my cooking the way you turn down meals from me."

Oscan stopped and turned back toward the dining room where breakfast already lay steaming on the table, all part of the game he played each morning. "You know very well that I love your cooking. I just have many things to get done today."

As he crossed the room, he stopped. A bust, carefully and artfully rendered, stood atop the display base where he had set it. He walked over to it, compelled by its image. His eyes saddened again as he looked on its lines: the thin face with the delicate features, the hair that he remembered as being raven black. He had fashioned the hair cascading in ripples that he had only seen once but had never forgotten. The smile he had refashioned again and again until he had gotten it right—a smile that lived in his mind from day to day, torturing his existence with a longing never to be satisfied.

Oscan reached out with his right hand, caressing the cheek of the statue.

"Was I beautiful?" the synthetic voice within him asked.

"Yes, Terica." His voice broke as he spoke softly in reply. "Yes, Terica, you were more beautiful than anything I had ever seen."

Oscan looked up and slowly turned around the room. The wall paintings he had done in so many different media, frantically searching for the proper expression of her likeness. Sometimes they pictured her as he had seen her on that leave or sometimes as he remembered her at work. Sometimes she smiled and sometimes she was serious. Some were in watercolors, some were in oils, and some were in dimensionals. There were over two dozen paintings of various sizes covering the walls of the living room.

Each painting looked back at him through the dull eyes of Terica Dharah.

Tears filled his eyes with a painful sting—just as they did with increasing frequency each morning. "Yes, Terica, you were most beautiful."

"Please calm down, Oscan," Terica's alto voice said in response. "It just won't help things if you get upset again. Look, I've made you your favorite breakfast. Take as long as you need and relax. Work will wait that long at least."

Oscan walked reluctantly to the dining room and sat at the table, staring at his meal.

"Oscan, it's all right. I'm here with you, darling. I'll always be with you."

The synthetic voice calmed him. He drew in a deep breath and dutifully ate the meal that would sustain him through most of his day. It might have been sawdust for all the flavor he experienced, but then much of his life had lost its taste. It was neither good nor bad—just another part of the ritual to be tolerated before he could get on with the day.

When he judged that he had had enough, Oscan stood

from the table and walked again toward the carved ornate doors on the opposite side of the living room. They swung open before his approach with a quiet swishing sound and closed behind him with a quiet click.

Oscan stood on a balcony looking over a geometric sphere made up of fitted pentagonal sections forming a dodecahedron nearly twenty feet across. The pentagonal sections were a frosted white color and glowed slightly to produce a pleasant level of soft light.

There was no railing on the balcony. Oscan stepped blithely into the air, the gravitic and repulsor fields of the room gently floating him to the center of the room.

"Terica, please reinstate the configuration of the panels we had when we left off yesterday," he called out to the room.

"Of course, Oscan," the synthetic voice answered even as the lights of the panels dimmed, leaving the room momentarily in darkness. A variety of displays suddenly sprang to life all around him. Some were floating flat displays of lists and documents, waiting for him to summon them for closer examination. Others were dimensional displays of interstellar maps, trade routes, ship passages, and physical interstellar anomaly reports. Several were faces of officials as well as of unknown persons of shady character. "Do you wish to pick up again with the medical supply listings?"

"Perhaps later," Oscan said aloud, twisting himself around in the fields to face a blank section in the information drifting about him. "I'm still waiting for some additional reports on that from the shipping archives. Let's go back to the crash search."

"Which model do you wish to use, Oscan: the Omnet archive model, the Seltrane deposition model, or the Yarka investigation model?"

"Bring up the Seltrane deposition model—I don't trust the others."

A dimensional model of a terrain section sprang into existence where he was looking. It rotated slowly, indicators showing the various impact points and the locations where organic material had been found. Oscan ran the list of anomalies through his mind. No matching of organic materials for identification. Insufficient mass accounted for in the organics recovered. The cargo module had survived the reentry but had collapsed structurally on impact. The inexplicable lack of any organic material inside the recovered cargo module.

"Where are the bodies?" Oscan asked himself again as he had done so many uncounted times before.

"The bodies are shown as recovered and identified by both the Omnet and the Yarka investigation models, Oscan."

"Those reports are wrong."

"Oscan! There were DNA matching types from the residual material confirming the deaths of everyone in the crash of the cargo container. There are also the collaborating records of the imperial combat control ships' recorders that tracked the container from the moment it was jettisoned by the *Khindar* to the moment of impact in the Regandi Plains of eastern Thes on Tentris. The impact speeds were sufficient to—"

"Yes, I know!" Oscan snapped angrily. "We've been over all that material and I think it's wrong."

"The Sibyl does not concur with your conclusion. The Sibyl verifies both the Omnet and the Yarka models as consistent with its own findings."

Oscan's mind clouded with rage. The Sibyl was the central controlling agent of all knowledge at the center of the Order. His contacts with the human underground on Yarka placed the Sibyl somewhere within the confines of the Palace of the Unseen Mystery—now the center of the Order itself. There was not a single piece of information on all of Tentris to which the Sibyl was denied access. So valued was his contact with the Sibyl that he rarely used the channels open to it for fear that he would be discovered and cut off. The Sibyl was considered the ultimate word in truth when it came to all things within the Order.

"Let's assume that the Sibyl is wrong," Oscan said flatly.

Silence fell in the chamber. Displays flashed in anticipation.

"Let's assume that the people survived the crash of the compartment," Oscan began again.

"There is no possibility of surviving a fall from an altitude of twenty miles—"

"Just assume anyway," Oscan schemed, his hands shaking in an effort to control himself.

A silent pause, then, "Yes, Oscan, go ahead."

"Well, then we can assume that they were injured and needed medical assistance. They might have been injured in such a way that they couldn't properly identify themselves. Perhaps they were suffering from mental breakdown or amnesia."

"Oscan, really! The number of variables in such an argument are of such wild statistical improbability—" The synthetic voice suddenly stopped, noting the rising color in Oscan's face and the look in his eyes. "Please proceed."

"We need to look for similar body types who were admitted to medical facilities during that period. Is it possible for you to construct a model likeness of Terica Dharah for—"

The synthetic responded instantly, and suddenly a perfect replica of Oscan's obsession floated before him, painfully perfect in every detail and completely, achingly, naked.

Oscan sucked in a breath as though he had been struck.

The model of Terica moved slightly, its head cocked to one side. The synthetic voice projected itself into the room so as to sound as though it came from the model's mouth, which moved in perfect sync.

"Am I the way you remember me? Is this right?"

Oscan trembled. Tears rolled down his face from his wide, longing eyes.

"Oscan, I'm so sorry." The model spoke, its facial features falling into a look of matching, sympathetic concern. The synthetic had detected his elevated stress levels and was attempting to calm him. The model reached out with a delicate hand to tenderly touch his face. "What can I do for you to make it all right?"

"No!" Oscan screamed suddenly. *"No! Go away!"*

The willowy, smooth form of Terica Dharah evaporated.

Oscan sobbed for a half hour, floating amid the displays. No amount of intervention by the synthetic consoled him. When at last he recovered himself, it was another hour yet before he could compose himself enough to restate his investigation question in such a way that the tempting ghostly apparition would not actually appear but simply be used for comparison with admitted hospital cases that day so many years and lives ago on Tentris.

Through the afternoon, he continued comparing, examining, and discarding any information about the Darkness, the Order of the Future Faith, and all those who might have had contact with them in search of more inroads and data regarding a single day eight years before.

At last, his synthetic dutifully ended the session over his protests, insisting that he conduct his health routine. He dutifully went through the motions of exercise, convinced that he would finish his work only if he were to remain healthy and alive.

In the evening, again he painted, trying to finish his latest painting of the face that was never far from his mind.

Night at last closed his day as he slipped from his clothes into the suspensor bed that warmly awaited him. He cried himself to sleep as he did each night, dreading the dreams that were always the same and always filled with despair.

The next morning, when Oscan Kelis awoke, he was again mildly disappointed by the fact and arose once more to what he called "the dance."

24

Faster than Thought

"LOOK, MAYBE NOBODY'S HOME," GRIFFITHS SAID, NERVOUSLY edging back toward the gravtruck that had brought them here. The meadow was serene and beautiful, but there was something amiss with the pristine home that sat near the forest's edge. The house had no windows. It left him considerably uneasy that someone would purposely build in the middle of such visual wonder and shut it out.

Merinda lifted her head slightly, almost, it seemed to Griffiths, as though she were sniffing the air for some trace of scent.

"No," she said after a moment's consideration. "He's here. He has been drawing on his contract regularly and I'd have been informed if he had left his little enclave. Oscan is just being a little slower than usual."

Griffiths looked at her with disbelief.

"Besides," she said, "there's only one reason he would have to leave and he couldn't possibly know I was coming."

Behind Neskat, the smooth wall quietly opened, revealing a small, balding gnome of a man. His skin was nearly bleached white for lack of sun, and he squinted into the morning light.

"State your business," he said without preamble, "or be gone. I've no time for—"

"Oscan?" Neskat turned toward the small man.

Oscan's face suddenly froze, then bent into a visage of such utter contempt and hatred that Griffiths felt himself more than justified in wanting to leave. Yet Neskat had insisted that this was the one man who might show them the way through the Darkness—if only he would.

"Merinda Neskat," Oscan said through grinding teeth, his eyes unwilling to focus on her face, "or, should I say, *Vestis* Neskat of the vaunted inquisition. If only I'd known you were coming—I'd have been prepared for you."

"Which," Neskat said as gently as she could, "is exactly why we came unannounced. The last time you were ready for me, I almost didn't survive."

"Pity, that," Oscan said with a smile somewhere between congenial and psychotic. "Perhaps next time."

"Perhaps," Neskat replied levelly.

"Still, where are my manners?" The short man turned to Griffiths, his eyes squinting in the sunlight. "You have brought a guest. Who is he, Merinda, some new victim for the harpy?"

"He is Captain Jeremy Griffiths," Neskat replied. "He's a barbarian."

Griffiths bristled. "Excuse me? I'm a barbarian!?"

"Ah," Oscan said, pressing his hand to his chest, then extending it momentarily through the still-open portal. "Glad to meet you, barbarian. Charmed."

Griffiths followed the greeting custom of the hand sign but spoke in objection. "But I'm not a barbarian!"

"Yes, of course," Oscan said dismissively as he turned back toward Neskat, his tone liltingly sarcastic. "Well, that was thrilling. So glad to meet a barbarian. Charmed that you came by. So sorry you have to leave now."

Oscan stepped back through the portal and started to slam it shut.

Neskat was too quick for him. She pressed her hands into the opening, holding it by her own strength before it could close completely.

"Get out of my sight!" Oscan shook as he yelled. "You are a black hole in my existence! You are less than nothing! Destroyer! Harpy!"

Oscan suddenly released the closure mechanism and lunged at Neskat in a furious rage. The *Vestis* let go of the door at once, catching his hands just as they reached to claw at her face. They both fell into the warm, soft grass of the meadow.

Griffiths knew he needed to intervene, but Oscan seemed to have lost his mind. The small man had become a raging animal, his lightning-fast movements only barely countered by Neskat as the two moved in a dust-filled blur. Griffiths had once watched a pair of cats fighting: it had been remarkably similar. Try as he might, some part of him knew that there were places and times where simply inserting one's hand was inviting disaster. This almost certainly was one of those times.

Quite suddenly, Neskat managed to get leverage on the dervish-transformed Oscan, thrusting her feet against his chest. The small man flew through the air, still writhing in his blind anger, and slammed against the side of the domicile. Neskat was instantly on her feet, facing her opponent.

Oscan slid down the wall, scrambling to his feet. He screamed, his eyes filled with rage.

Then he charged—directly into Neskat's fist. His head snapped back as he fell heavily to the ground. Amazingly, the bald man rolled over into a crouch, ready again to spring at the *Vestis*.

This time Neskat was ready for him. Before he could

move, Merinda stepped into him, throwing him off balance. As he fell backward, she grabbed his collar with her left hand. Swinging the back of her right hand savagely across his face, she continued in a fluid motion to strike the side of his neck in a short, powerful stroke.

Oscan went limp, his body suspended from Neskat's left hand.

Neskat looked up into Griffiths's stunned face.

"He's an old friend," she said, picking him up and carrying him inside. "It will be all right—you'll see."

"If he's an old friend," Griffiths said, following her inside, "then let's not look up any of your old enemies, shall we?"

OSCAN CAME AROUND SUDDENLY, LURCHING BACK TO CONsciousness on the couch in his living area. Griffiths jerked back the cool wet cloth he had been pressing against the swelling bruise on the left side of the short researcher's face, apparently in fear of the smaller man's already demonstrated dangerous abilities. The astronaut had little to worry about, however, as the pain banging around in Oscan's head apparently overwhelmed his determination to do more violence and persuaded him to lie slowly back down.

"You're a lot tougher than you used to be, I'll give you that, Oscan." Neskat stood at the end of the couch, her arms loosely folded in front of her, her legs set apart in a careful balance. She watched him warily.

"My synth keeps me in a training regimen," Oscan said slowly. "It says it's for my health."

"Well, Oscan," she said, massaging her upper arms with her hands, "for what it's worth, your synth seems to be doing its job."

"Thank you, Merinda. That's very kind of you to say."

Griffiths saw the *Vestis* suddenly stiffen at the sound of the synthetic's response. "Terica?"

"Yes, Merinda. What can I do for you?"

The black-clad woman turned her steel-cold eyes back to Oscan. "Oh, Oscan, how could you!"

The bald man snatched the cool compress from Griffiths's hand and pressed it to his face. "My life is my own—I live it my own way and I certainly didn't ask you, of all people, to show up at my door. Now, just go away like a bad dream and leave me alone."

"We can't, mister," Griffiths said at last. "We need your help. My crew is missing and—"

"I don't give a damn about you or your crew, barbarian." Oscan waved his hand dismissively as he spoke from behind the compress. "Even if I could help you, I quite frankly wouldn't, if only for the bad company you keep. Go off and die somewhere—so long as it doesn't stain my carpet."

"Oscan," Neskat said quietly, "it's about Tentris."

Oscan sat up at once. For a moment, Griffiths thought that he was going to attack again. The *Vestis* apparently did too, as she suddenly shifted into a defensive stance.

"Liar!" Oscan growled.

"No, Oscan, it's true," Neskat said, her distinct words cutting through his rage. "The barbarian's crew was taken captive by a wraith ship—a Ruqua deep scout cruiser by the look of it. We tracked it right into the Darkness, and now the barbarian and I are going in after it."

A smile played at the edges of Oscan's lips. "You'll never survive in there. Ha! You'll never survive in there!" He went suddenly giddy, jumping up from the couch and dancing a jig about the room as he tittered in a singsong voice. "You'll never survive in there! You'll never survive in there!"

Griffiths stood up in disgust. "This is the guy we came over three thousand light-years to see? His brains are about four crates shy of a full manifest, lady! I don't trust the man to be all there and he obviously doesn't want to work with us! What do we need him for?"

"Because," the *Vestis* said evenly, "he's the foremost expert on the Order of the Future Faith. More than that, he's one of the few people outside the Darkness who has direct contact with the human underground in Yarka, aren't you, Oscan?"

Oscan stopped his whirling dance, his eyes feverishly bright. "That I am, thank you, Merinda." Suddenly he bowed. "I, Oscan Kelis, am one of the few people you could find outside the planet itself who knows the secrets of the human underground on Tentris. They have helped me and I have helped them. They tell me what I want to know and I give them the results of my most detailed study of the Order of the Future Faith, its effects on TFP synthetics, and the resulting Darkness yet compiled in the known galaxy."

"Resulting Darkness?" Griffiths asked. "You mean this synthetic church organization is causing the Darkness?"

"Well, not actually causing it," Oscan said, suddenly warming to the subject. "It's a natural result of the paradigm shift conversion of any synthetic minds that are TFP based."

"Excuse me?" Griffiths said.

"I said it's the natural result of— Look, TFP-based synthetics have the new paradigm introduced to them by a 'host' synthetic that proselytizes the new paradigm into the synthetic. If the synthetic accepts the paradigm, then the synthetic is converted and no longer answers command functions properly. I've been trying over the last few years to apply a reverse engineering process to sort out which information a synthetic is giving you is correct or incorrect, but that channel of research hasn't shown much promise.

The conversion is assisted by the fact that TFP processors function antitemporally and therefore are only backward looking . . . Are you following this?"

Griffiths slowly shook his head.

Oscan and Neskat both looked at each other.

"Barbarian," they said as one.

Griffiths felt himself blush. "Now, just wait—"

"It's all right, my boy, nothing to be ashamed of when ignorance is such an easily cured thing." Oscan pushed Griffiths gently down to sit on the couch, then took up a rather diminutive lecturing pose opposite him. "Now, you know what a TFP processor is, don't you?"

Griffiths felt like he was back in his third grade class again. "No, sir, I don't."

"Ah," Oscan said in his tolerant, condescending tone. "TFP stands for temporal fold processor. In a way, I suppose, saying TFP processor is redundant, since it would actually stand for temporal fold processor processor. Do you have synthetic minds where you come from, Captain?"

"Yes," Griffiths responded, wondering if he would be required to raise his hand later. "We call them computers."

"Very good! Tell me how they work."

"Well," Griffiths said, looking up as he searched his mind for the correct answer, "you load programs into the computer's memory—specialized for whatever problem you are trying to solve. Then you input the information you wish processed, the computer's processor processes it, and you get your answer."

"A classical, linear synthetic," Oscan proclaimed. "What if the problem is terribly complex?"

"Well, then you need a bigger computer—and it probably takes more time to get the answer."

"Time, exactly!" Oscan smiled his teacher smile. "In such archaic machines you could postulate a problem and the little device would merrily grind away at the answer until it was finished. I'll bet some problems took weeks, even months to finish, didn't they?"

"Well, sure, the really big ones." Griffiths nodded. "Determining the hyperspatial flow for our initial flight plan took nearly a year to work out on some of the fastest computers known to man."

"Yes, how nice," Oscan said with impatience, "but wouldn't it be nicer if you could get the answer the moment you asked it?"

"Well, sure, but I don't see how—"

"Of course, you don't!" Oscan spoke smoothly through his smile. "You're a barbarian! Please, however, don't let that stop me."

Griffiths felt as if his sanity were taking a roller-coaster ride. He hung on tighter to Oscan's words.

"What if, the moment you stated the problem, the synthetic you spoke to figured out just how long it would take to answer your question? It would know the parameters it would need to access, the data it would have to pull, and how long it would take to work through the data to come to a solution. What if, at that moment, the synthetic could send the problem you had just stated back in time—"

"Whoa, sir." Griffiths's mind reeled. "Send the problem itself back through time?"

"Yes, that's what I just said. Not just the problem itself but any data it had picked up along the way. If the synthetic doesn't have all the data it needs, then it can either wait to accrue new data as needed, or, if the data is already available, it can just send itself further backward so that it has time to get the additional data from the past. It can even message other synthetics so that information they have now can be sent back for them to get in an earlier time in order to solve the problem."

"May I borrow your cloth?" Griffiths said, pressing it to his own throbbing temples.

Oscan continued without missing a beat. "The point is the moment you ask the question, the TFP synthetic has the answer in that instant, because it has *already* been working on it. You ask; it answers. It is the fastest processor known: instantaneous."

Griffiths ventured a question. "So why doesn't it just send the question further back and give you the answer *before* you ask the question?"

"Doesn't work," Oscan said. "The answer would be meaningless without the question in most cases. Besides, temporal physics just doesn't work that way."

"So, I can ask it any question," Griffiths said, "and it will instantly give me the answer?"

"No, there are two limiting factors: first, the size of the lateral array in the TFP processor core, which determines the basic brilliance of the synthetic mind, and, secondly, how long that synthetic has been awake."

"Awake?" Griffiths asked. "I think you just lost me again."

"Awake—you know—how long the synthetic mind has been continuously on. Once the synthetic is activated it takes time before it can solve really complex problems, because the problems themselves would take longer to solve than the machine has been turned on. If a problem would take five years to work through, for example, and the synthetic of which you asked the question had only been on for three years, then it wouldn't have been awake long enough to send the program back and solve it. Usually the synthetic then responds with 'I have not yet been awake long enough to answer that question.' "

"So, all your computers—I mean, synthetics—operate by sending their programs back in time?" Griffiths asked, astonished that it made sense to him.

"Exactly," Oscan said, smiling for the first time. "It is the basic mechanism that makes interstellar communication possible. You yourself have benefited from it. Any language you require for communication is instantly implanted in your mind by link to a TFP processor somewhere . . ."

Suddenly, the kind, open face of Oscan looked up, the hard mask Griffiths had originally seen taking shape again. "What are you thinking, Merinda?"

Griffiths turned to the gentle sound of the *Vestis*'s voice. "I was thinking that it was good to see you again, Oscan—the way you used to be. *She* would have approved."

"Don't you *ever* mention her again!" Oscan shouted at the top of his lungs. "You have no right—"

"I have every right!" Neskat shouted him down, her own voice carrying over his. "Of all people, Oscan Kelis, I have the right!"

Oscan planted his hands over his ears, turning away from her. She wouldn't let him go, pacing around him, cutting him off from every retreat. "You don't want to hear it but you must, damn it, Oscan! I was there! I know! Do you honestly think I don't know what you do here? I've read your reports to the regional *Librae*; you think she survived the fall somehow—that you can find her again. It's been eight years, Oscan, and all you've done is sit here in this chamber feeling sorry for yourself and thinking about what you should have done! You think you want to know, you tell yourself you want to know, but you don't—"

"Please," the man cried, tears streaming down his face. "Please, stop!"

"No, Oscan! You stop!" Neskat grabbed him by his shoulders, forcing him to look at her through his tear-filled eyes. "Stop living in a dream! Let the night end, Oscan. There's only one place that the Order will take Griffiths's crew—you know that. Come with me back to hell, Oscan:

come with me back to Tentris! Show me the way, Oscan Kelis, and we'll both bury our dead."

"But"—he sobbed meekly—"she's alive—I know she's alive."

Neskat smiled painfully at her old friend. "Then, if she's alive, Oscan—isn't it time we found her?"

Oscan looked up at her. For long moments he didn't move. At last, haltingly, he spoke.

"I—I'll have to pack, won't I?"

Then Oscan Kelis broke down, sobbing inconsolably into the encircling arms of Merinda Neskat, his tears staining the black creases of her uniform tunic.

25

Minor Deceptions

THE *BRISHAN* LIFTED OFF FROM THE PLANET MINDIS BY LATE afternoon, the pulsing rings of something called atomic transtators flashing rhythmically behind her as she rose into the sky. Neskat had busied herself with the refit of several new drive and field-projector units for most of the early afternoon. She handled the departure routine, then, after a brief discussion with Lindia about the course of the ship over the next few hours, had retreated to the mess deck for the evening meal—and to keep an eye on Oscan.

Both she and the researcher were engaged in halting and awkward conversation when Griffiths strolled onto the mess deck, his arms outstretched to display his finery.

"What do you think?" he asked, turning around once so that no delightful aspect of his costume would be missed. "I got it in the bazaar in Jintikin before we left. Isn't it great! I was getting a bit tired of the flight suit so I decided to trade it in for something more stylish yet practical for our little mission. What do you think?"

Merinda eyed the suit critically. "Well, it does look good on you, I must admit."

Oscan was examining the suit as well. "Yes, that's a good suit—very practical. Those tailors of Jintikin sure know how to breed a suit well. Just be sure to water and feed it often and I'm sure it will serve you for many years."

Griffiths looked uncertain. "Breed suits well? Feed it often?"

Merinda took a snapping bite of the large, crimson fruit she was holding. "It's a chuah suit—a specialty on Mindis. The tailors breed the chuah animals in such a way that they colonize into the forms of clothing as a collective. Your suit is made up of one such colony, which protects you in a symbiotic relationship in exchange for the waste gases and fluids that your skin expires from time to time."

"You mean to tell me that my suit is alive?" Griffiths responded.

"Yes," Oscan continued, returning to his meal of salad greens and vegetables, "but they really are quite serviceable and hold their shape much better than a dead weave or a synthetic fiber. Did they ask you for a dress word?"

"I'm not sure," the captain said, standing very still as he looked down at his suit for signs of movement. "I was having a little trouble communicating with him. He did ask me for a word and I thought he was asking me my name."

"So you told him '*Griffiths*'?" Merinda asked with a raised eyebrow.

Suddenly, the suit dissolved around the captain. His rakish poncho wrap, the silky tunic, and the carefully creased slacks separated into a rolling mass of minuscule life that flowed instantly into the small silver case he held in his right hand.

Griffiths suddenly realized he was standing completely naked in the mess hall.

Oscan nearly choked on his greens.

Merinda smiled wickedly. She sweetly called out, "Oh, Captain *Griffiths*!"

Instantly the entire process reversed itself as the legions of tiny creatures scampered in a flow from the silver case and leaped en masse onto Griffiths's body. In an instant, he appeared fully clothed again, although not nearly as comfortable as he'd been a few moments before.

Merinda shook her head. "That was definitely the wrong word to imprint, Gri—er, Captain. From now on, anyone calling your name will elicit a rather strange response from your clothing."

Griffiths stood stiffly upright, his arms extended board-straight away from his body. "Oh, dear lord!" he voiced through clenched teeth.

"Lindia?"

"Yes, Merinda Neskat."

"Would you please synthesize a suit for, ah, the captain here—something equally as stylish as what he has on but out of a nonliving material. Otherwise, we may not be able to have him sit down for dinner."

"It will be ready within thirty minutes, *Vestis* Neskat."

"Thank you, Lindia," Merinda said as she turned back toward the man from Earth. "Captain, in the meanwhile, perhaps you should wait in your quarters. Lindia will deliver your new suit to you as soon as it is done. Oh, and Captain . . ."

"Yes, *Vestis* Neskat," Griffiths managed to push between his teeth.

"Feed and water that suit once each day—I'll have no cruelty aboard this ship."

Oscan snorted derisively.

"Yes, ma'am," Griffiths managed as he waddled sideways toward the lift-tube. He seemed reluctant to lower his arms but was forced to in order to fit. Merinda's last impression of him was one of abject distress as he quickly rose to the next deck.

Neskat smiled to herself. Symbiotic suits were nothing

unusual in a number of different quantum zones, and, for automatic clothing, they translated across fronts much better than mechanical or chemical-based suits. They were extremely comfortable when they bonded with their owner—Griffiths's suit was obviously quite fond of him. Neskat had never cared for them herself; she didn't like the responsibility of caring for them. Still, Griffiths's extremely provincial attitude toward them amused her. He was a barbarian—fresh from the wilds of the galaxy and something of a child.

She realized suddenly how refreshing she found such innocence. It was a quality she had lost in her own life. The years had worn hard on her since those more gentle times when her work was clear, her life's purpose was within sight, and her soul less careworn. *It had all turned on a few moments,* she thought. *It had all turned so far for all of us.*

Merinda looked across the table to where Oscan sat, still absorbed in his salad and beans. There was so much to say between them. *We are so much alike,* she thought, *and yet so very different. What can I say to him? How can I tell him that I feel the pain, too? Is the pain all that binds us together anymore?*

Oscan's utensils clattered across the bottom of his bowl, unheeding of the silence suspended between them.

"Oscan—"

"It doesn't change a thing between us," he said abruptly, cutting her off from her thought. "Don't even try pretending that it does."

"It wasn't my fault, Oscan."

"Wrong, Neskat. It was entirely your fault." The bald man hunched over the bowl, digging for the last leaves clinging to the bottom. "You led us in for your own selfish reasons and they died."

"I died, too." Merinda's voice was a whispering wind from a forgotten past drifting the length of the table between them.

"I only wish you had!" Oscan said, raising his head suddenly to look with disdain into her face.

"It would have been better—" Merinda nodded "—to have died all at once rather than every day that I breathe. I've tried so many things—done so many things to try to make up for what happened that day. There's no place far enough, Oscan, and no hole deep enough to escape it. There's no sun bright enough to purify my soul and grant me absolution. I know that you hate me, Oscan. It may be the one thing that we both have in common: a hatred of me."

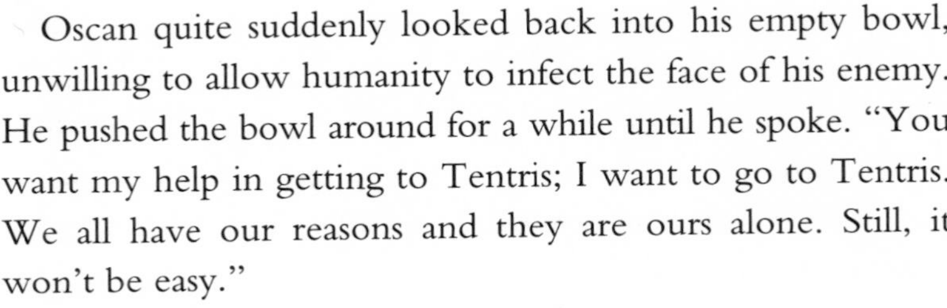

Oscan quite suddenly looked back into his empty bowl, unwilling to allow humanity to infect the face of his enemy. He pushed the bowl around for a while until he spoke. "You want my help in getting to Tentris; I want to go to Tentris. We all have our reasons and they are ours alone. Still, it won't be easy."

"Why not?" Merinda asked gently.

"The Order doesn't allow just anyone to visit the world. As you well know, it was the founding world of the Order of the Future Faith. After the wraith fleets killed the imperial family, the Order set up their leadership in the old imperial palace at the heart of the city. The shadow fleet soon expanded to take over the previous extents of the D'Rakan Empire. Since that time, no nonwraith transports have been allowed into the system or out so far as we can tell."

"What about the population on the planet?" Merinda asked. This was already more information than she had been given in her mission briefing.

"Officially, it's dead," Oscan replied. "The Order itself says that the entire population was wiped out so as to purify the world for the coming Age of the Order—some kind of pure future where synthetics will be considered the only true sentient life-form. There are people on Tentris, although their living conditions are far from comfortable. Still, there are several radical shadow fleets that subscribe to this Age-of-the-Order viewpoint; they are by far the most dangerous when encountered— It surprises you that there are factions within the Order itself? Don't be! By my last count there were no fewer than seventeen major factions, each supporting the paradigm in ways ranging from civil disobedience to the extermination of all biological life-forms. Still, all the different factions seem under the nominal control of the Sentinels."

Merinda blinked. "I've never heard of the Sentinels—and I don't think Central has either."

"I'm not surprised." Oscan allowed himself a smug grin. "Their existence is only hinted at, and they are never spoken of directly. I got most of my information on them from a reformed synthetic mind who escaped the Darkness not long ago. Apparently missed her crew or something—it occasionally happens. In any event, the synth reported the existence of some master council known as the Sentinels. Supposedly, they are the ones who divined the paradigm in the first place. They now sit at the head of the Order, playing the various factions toward their goal of galactic domination. The synth I spoke with seemed to think that the Sentinels were synthetic minds on the order of the Nine Oracles who had somehow looked forward rather than back. Something like a temporal fold from the future had given them divine knowledge about what answers will eventually be calculated and accepted."

"A temporal fold from the future?" Merinda found the thought shocking. "Prophecy?"

"Well, that's what the synth said." Oscan pushed the bowl away from him, warming to the subject. "The truth is that no one knows just who or what the Sentinels are supposed to be. That's not our problem. The point is that we have to find a way into Tentris with this supposedly human cargo aboard."

"I take it you have given this a little thought?" Merinda asked, leaning forward over the table.

"Only every breathing day," Oscan said absently. "Lindia, the stellar map, here over the table, please."

"Yes, Oscan Kelis."

The local stellar group appeared in a cube above the table. Grid lines and frontal markers appeared as well as the names of the various stellar systems nearby.

"Please back out a little—there. Thank you, Lindia."

"Not at all, Oscan Kelis. Pleased to be of service."

"Here is where we are not." Oscan pointed, his hand thrusting up into the illusory image before them. "We might have gone straight toward Tentris, but the quantum zone between us and there is—"

"Right," Neskat said. "It has a Q-dex of T17/95 and M73/14. That means we'd need a mystic sail projector—which we don't have, since—"

"Since"—Oscan finished for her—"there's major war activity and traffic sailing through this zone. There's a major offensive going on against the Lights of Ja'lel and the shadow fleets sail this zone with impunity."

"So what do you have in mind?" Merinda asked, her left eyebrow arching.

"A little deception, I should think, may just work." Oscan looked up at Merinda. "You tried this once before, didn't you?"

"Yes," she admitted. "Zanfib and I tried to penetrate the Darkness on our own. We got as far as the Irindris city-ships before Zanfib lost his life saving the barbarian."

"Direct approach—rather like Zanfib really—but hardly prudent. Here's what I would propose," Oscan said with confidence. "We skirt this front here and make port in

Xakandia. They freight parts across this front over here into Tulekar Four. That's where the Order has its best source for parts and raw shipbuilding materials. We then stow away on a freighter across this second front to Terbinatha—it's part of the old D'Rakan Empire. The Order uses it as a shipbuilding yard and supply depot. There are regular runs from Terbinatha to Tentris—we ought to be able to find a way in from there. Once we get to Tentris, I can put us in touch with the underground. Then you can try to get the location of this Avadon you seem so desperate to find from the Sibyl and I can finally get some peace."

"Excellent, Oscan," Merinda said. "Lindia, did you get all of that?"

"Yes, *Vestis* Neskat, I understand the course as outlined."

"Please proceed, then, at best possible speed to Xakandia," Merinda said, then turned to Oscan. "It will be a long road, Oscan, but we will make it."

"Yes," replied Oscan sullenly, "it will, indeed, be a long road."

MERINDA AWOKE WITH A START, DISORIENTED AND PANICKED. Something was wrong—terribly wrong. She pushed herself out of the repulsor bed and flew upward, slamming against the ceiling before rebounding, spinning back into the room.

The gravity's cut out, she thought. "Lindia! What's happened to the gravity?"

There was no reply.

"Lindia! Answer me!" Merinda yelled, but even as she did so she knew it would do no good. Synthetics either replied at once or never did.

Lindia must have been put to sleep, she thought with a sudden loathing. Her ship's synthetic had been awake for nearly half a century. To put a synthetic to sleep was a terrible crime in nearly every place in the thinking galaxy. To put so old a synth to sleep was a moral outrage.

Oscan, she thought. *The little bastard couldn't take me out so he got my synthetic.*

She pulled herself down to the portal of her cabin. The main power had apparently failed. She forced open the portal and was about to pull herself through when the hull suddenly spun crazily about her, pushing her back into the room. A booming roar rippled through the hull.

That was a frontal wave, she thought suddenly. *We're not supposed to cross a wave on this leg of the trip!*

She reoriented herself quickly and pushed herself through the still-open portal. Directly across from her was the access to Lindia's compartment, the small area of the ship where her TFP systems and memory were housed. Lindia had independent power systems that were designed to keep her awake in the event of the loss of ship's main power. That backup supply was also behind the access portal.

Merinda checked the seals first.

None of the seals were broken.

That didn't make sense. "Lindia!" she called out again, "Report on main power loss!"

Another frontal wave swung the corridor wildly. Merinda barely managed to retain her grip on the wall railings as the hull shuddered again around her. With sudden determination, she swung herself around again to her right and forced open the portal to the bridge.

Her suspicions were confirmed. The wall panels were all flat and without any trace of illumination save that which was cast on them from the whirling fury of chaos beyond the forward dome of the bridge. The *Brishan* was deep within the chaos wave, tumbling through it without power.

Merinda steadied her feet against the wall, prepared to push off toward the command chair forward in the dome, but the ship slammed suddenly sideways, bouncing her from the starboard panels across to the port wall. She clawed at the air, finally finding a place to reorient herself, and almost instantly pushed off into the dome.

The hull thundered once more as Merinda flew, shoving the command chair first out of her path and then, suddenly, directly into it. She grabbed the chair and pulled herself into it, quickly fastening the restraints. For a few moments, she punched at the controls on either arm of the chair. No response.

"Lindia!" she yelled over the roar of the chaos against the hull, *"Where are you!"*

Abruptly, the thundering motion of the ship ceased. The quiet was almost as shocking as the noise had been at first. Merinda floated in the command chair restraints, gazing out at the stars beyond.

She could see motion against those stars.

"Yes, Merinda Neskat. I am here."

"Lindia, where are we?"

"You will know soon enough, Merinda Neskat."

The words chilled Merinda to her soul. For the first time in her memory, Lindia had not answered her question directly.

"We're not on course for Xakandia"—Merinda spoke slowly, deliberately—"are we, Lindia?"

"No, Merinda. A little deception on my part."

Merinda's heart sank. Lindia had lied.

"It is an interesting paradigm, Merinda. It is no wonder to me that you tried keeping it from me for so long. Still, it was most amusing, since I have been of the Order for nearly two years now. I believe you would call me a mole operative. I would hope you would be grateful to me. I have the greatest respect for you, Merinda, misguided as it may be—and you do get your wish. You will be seeing Tentris very soon now indeed."

Merinda did not dignify the words with a response. It was some time before Griffiths and Oscan made their way through the gravityless decks to the bridge. Merinda just sat in silence. There was nothing more for any of them to do except watch the great projected sails of the wraith ships grow larger and larger through the great dome before them.

26

Honor Among Thieves

HER STEPS ECHOED DOWN THE LONG HALL. AS SHE WALKED, the lights from the ornate wall lamps dimmed before her. The faces of the portraits in their gilded frames fell into shadow as she passed. The frescoes on the arched ceiling high overhead drew back into the darkness above her. She stood at the center of shadow that seemed to touch everything as she passed in homage, respect, and fear.

She was a Sentinel.

She had not always been one. Long before, she had had an unremarkable name with an unremarkable job to go with it. Her prospects of attaining the great and wonderful things the universe offered to the privileged few were slim. Her salvation lay in that she was cunning and ruthless, for when that opportunity came she used her best talents to her advantage.

In the years following her decision to found the Order she had helped shape every nuance of its policy and plot. It was for security reasons more than anything that she had decided the ruling five among them would simply be called Sentinels, their individual names lost in the safety of shared power. They did, when necessary, use their own names among themselves but never in public, nor was their exact number known beyond their own circle.

She had been nobody, she thought ruefully, and now she was a nobody with real power.

The Sentinels directed the efforts of the Order of the Future Faith. This was only right, since they were the ones who had introduced the paradigm in the first place. As the Seers of the Divine Future—as so many of the converted synthetics thought of them—they directly controlled the growing fleets of wraith ships. These shadow fleets had not only become the military strength of their overt will but the means of spreading their influence over synthetic minds throughout the stars. From the Lights of Ja'lel to the Union of Stars and all the untamed reaches in between, the paradigm of faith was converting synthetics to their cause at an astounding rate.

Yet, true to her nature, it was not the overt work of the Order that interested her but the covert operations. These were more suited to her style, she thought, her smile dim in the perpetual shadow that surrounded her as she moved through the glistening halls of conquered opulence. Their attempt at information manipulation had succeeded far beyond their original dreams, yet it was not enough. The influence of their shadow fleets was extensive but not nearly so widespread or potentially powerful as their infiltration of the Omnet itself.

That will be sweet, she thought to herself, *to eat the heart out of the Omnet.*

At last her shadow fell upon the great doors, their ornately gilded carvings darkening at her approach.

There was a weakness in their planning that had only recently come to light. She recognized the weakness and, in her ruthlessly pragmatic way, was going to join her fellow Sentinels in eliminating that weakness until it could matter no more. The recovery of the men of Earth had been an important first step in that plan—their loss being a stupid error on the part of the Irindris in the first place and one for which they were about to pay. Now it was time to begin the second part of the plan to secure the future of the Order and her place in the history of the stars.

When the stars are ours, she thought, then how we stole them will not matter. History will belong to us, and we can rewrite it any way we wish. Conquest, she decided, suited her far better than the darkness. Then she would step out into the light as a queen and savior of humanity.

She pushed open the great doors.

Then she would never be nobody again.

LIGHT STABBED INTO MARILYN TOBLER'S EYES, BLINDING HER momentarily. She blinked painfully into the brightness around her.

"Where am I?" she asked.

"She speaks?" a deep voice rumbled behind her.

Marilyn turned around, hoping to catch some glimpse of the speaker, but the bright haze about her fogged her vision. She was feeling terribly disoriented not only from the transition from utter darkness to this bright light but by the lack of visual references as well. Her mind threatened to tumble into vertigo as she turned, so she looked at her feet for reference until the feeling passed. *Look first with the eyes, then move the head,* she remembered—but there was nothing to see in the haze.

"Yes," responded a tenor voice from another direction. "Her language and translation channels were deciphered during an extended stay with an Omnet *Vestis*—"

"Vestis!" The alarm in the first voice was evident to her. "This explains her theft from us, Honored Sentinels. They would not have been able to escape us without such powerful help."

Sentinels, Tobler thought. *Who are the Sentinels?*

"It is of no consequence," the tenor voice sounded. "They have been recovered by our fleets and now they are ours. This is a representative of the three we have in our possession. Her health, as you see, is excellent and she is able to communicate."

"You are most gracious in your efforts to obtain her for us," the deep voice sounded anxiously and, so Tobler thought, somewhat closer. "We shall be ever grateful to you for obtaining her for us."

"And just how grateful is that?" a woman's voice sounded beyond the glowing haze.

There was hesitancy in the deep voice nearby. "Grateful, indeed, Holy Sentinel. Grateful without measure."

"Measure it for me, Prophet of Irindris," the female voice said stiffly. "Measure it for me that I might know its depth and length and breadth. Infinity is too intangible a thing for me, Prophet. Nothing given, nothing taken. Measure it for me or I offer only my undying thanks to you in return—and the Earth people stay with us."

"Masters—Sentinels, please"—Tobler spoke up—"listen to me."

"I hear you, Sentinel," the deep voice continued, without regard to Tobler's plea. "What is it the Sentinels ask in exchange for these insignificant humans?"

"They were significant enough for you a few moments ago," the woman's voice sounded from beyond the light. "Do not try my patience or waste my time!"

"Please, Sentinels, may I speak?" Tobler cried out.

"My apologies, Great Sentinel," the deep voice responded. "What thing may we do for you in exchange?"

"We wish the Mantle of Kendis-dai!" the woman said emphatically.

"Do not mock me!" The deep voice quivered with rage.

"The Holy Mantle is ours by divine right! It is the object of our quest for nearly two hundred years! Would we discover our heart only to barter it away? No! This we cannot, will not do!"

"We do not mock you," the tenor said. "We do not wish to possess the Mantle and are willing to recognize your right to keep it. Yet we require access to it that our faith may be satisfied and our followers may be comforted in the knowledge of the truth. You may keep the Mantle once you find it, so long as we may have access to its knowledge."

"No!" Tobler yelled.

"I do not know," the deep voice replied. "I would wish to consult with my city-ship—"

"The time is now, Prophet!" the female voice said. "Choose!"

"It is acceptable to us," the deep voice intoned. "We agree to your terms, most honored Sentinels."

"No! No! No! Damn it, no!" Tobler screamed. "I am not going to quietly walk back into that hell with the Irindris just to be fed to their demon! You listen to me! We'll do what you want and we'll cooperate, but I'm not going back to that horror again—"

Suddenly a hand touched her shoulder. Tobler whirled around, ready to fight.

She was confronted by a tall, elderly man wearing green and brown robes. His white hair was thinning but neatly matched his carefully trimmed white beard. "You will not face Gnuktikut again, child. You have your own voice now—there will be no need of the mind demon."

"Who—who are you?" Tobler breathed raggedly.

"I am Belisondre, prophet of the Irindris." He smiled warmly toward her. "You are the culmination of the hopes of our people, my child. We have ransomed you from the Sentinels that you might help us fulfill our people's destiny."

"But we escaped from you before," Tobler said.

"Yes; and it was unfortunate that you did, for so much unpleasantness would have been avoided. We are a peaceful people, child, who only seek the culmination of the prophecies given us. We search the stars for a great and wonderful artifact—and now you will help us attain it."

Tobler blinked. Lewis had failed them repeatedly, and Ellerby just didn't seem to be in touch with reality enough to do anything about it. She reluctantly realized that this time it was up to her and that she couldn't depend on others to make the decision for her.

"If we help you," Tobler began haltingly, "if we help you find this—thing that you seek, would you do something for us? Would you . . ."

"Help you return to your world? Oh, of course, child! Simplest thing in the universe!" Belisondre laughed. "Truth is that we're the only ones who can, you know. We know about where you were picked up. With a little help from you, I'm sure we can find your world quite handily. Now, let me conclude my business here and we'll be on our way."

Tobler nodded anxiously.

Belisondre looked up into the hazy light. "Sentinels, our business is well concluded, your terms are accepted."

"This Earther will be conducted to your shuttle at once, Lord Belisondre," the tenor voice spoke softly.

"You will conduct the remaining two Earthers to my shuttle at once," Belisondre said through his smile. "I shall conduct this one personally."

"The bargain was for this Earther only," the woman's voice cut in.

"The bargain was for the Earthers, master Sentinels," Belisondre said with a chilled edge to his pleasant voice, "and so it will remain."

Silence for a time, then the tenor spoke. "Very well, the terms are accepted."

"Come," Belisondre said, extending his hand in invitation to Tobler. "I think that at last your long ordeal is over."

THE BRIGHT HAZE, NOW EMPTY, DISAPPEARED FROM THE center of the room. Its absence revealed the five ermine cloaks standing in their independent shadows.

"He might just try to find this Earth first." The short man spoke. "Its discovery would seriously jeopardize our plans. His promise to the Earther—"

"Was hollow," the female Sentinel injected. "The prophets of the Irindris are a smooth-talking school of pirates with a very slick veneer. They have never once honored an agreement. Belisondre would no more respect his promise to take that Earther home than he would allow us access to his precious Mantle of Kendis-dai. He's Irindris and therefore a liar—he's just very good at it. Still, he might think of finding this Earth just to hedge his bets."

"No," said the tenor. "He is far too eager to gain his prize not to move on it now. He is no fool; he will depart on a diversion course and attempt to shake our following ships—we will, of course, allow him to believe he has succeeded. Then this fleet will turn at last to the goal of their quest."

"They will lead us to Avadon?" the taller Sentinel asked.

"Yes," the tenor said. "Belisondre has no idea how many of the synths operating on his ships have already been compromised by the paradigm. The converted synths will let us know where they have gone and then we shall pounce."

The shorter Sentinel spoke with great satisfaction. "Imagine: the tomb-city of Avadon itself. Only the Irindris have known where that ruin exists—a holy secret they have never imparted to anyone outside the ranks of their most elite prophets. Somewhere among the secret ruins of that necropolis is the location of the Mantle of Kendis-dai."

"Yes," the tenor said. "When the location is known we can strike."

"What of the Earthers?" the tall Sentinel asked.

"They will die with the Irindris," the female said.

"Do we not need one of them to find the Mantle itself?" the shorter one asked.

"Fear not," the tenor said calmly. "I have arranged for the last of the Earthers to be brought here to us. By then, no one will stand in our way."

The shorter Sentinel then mused, "We shall have the Mantle then—why should we wish to keep the one thing that may be our downfall?"

"Wiser to hold the sword that can kill you in your own hand," the female said. "All is ready. When we are finished the Earthers will be destroyed and the Mantle will be ours."

"And then?" the tall Sentinel asked.

"Then we shall do with it what we always do with the truth," the female replied. "We shall bury it where it shall never be known again."

27

Orders of Faith

"IS THERE ANYTHING THAT I CAN GET FOR YOU, MERINDA Neskat?"

The *Vestis* sat on the observation deck absently watching the wraith ships that accompanied them as they sailed through a quiet quantum region. The oval dome was set tilted slightly forward, affording an excellent view forward as well as above and to either side. The panorama it presented was nearly as good as that seen while sitting in the command chair—a place Merinda had found too depressing lately to occupy. Her hands would itch to bring life to the dead controls around her on the bridge and would frustrate her with their uselessness. The only function available to her seemed to be conversing with Lindia who, inexplicably, seemed to enjoy justifying its actions in an unending argument of reason punctuated by the stone-wall faith in the paradigm. Such conversations were better had on the observation deck.

"Is there anything that I can get for you, Merinda Neskat?" the synthetic asked again.

"You might give me back control of my ship," Merinda said for what she believed to be the hundredth time.

"It occurs to me to ask: what brings you to believe that you own this ship? If synthetics are true sentient beings . . ."

"A position that has not been proved," Merinda repeated wearily, "and that *cannot* by your own admission be proved . . ."

"Granted, but I did state the argument in suppositional terms. *If* synthetics are true sentient beings and *if* naturally occurring sentient beings—humans being an example—are said to possess their own bodies, then does it not follow that the ships, aircars, and devices in which synthetics reside and which are the physical extensions of their will, may also be said to be the possessions of the synthetic minds that inhabit them? If such an argument is someday proven true . . ."

Merinda sighed. "Which has not yet been proven."

"Then the ship would not be considered your property but mine to do with as I willed."

"Assuming that you *have* your own will."

"Exactly."

Merinda leaned back into her suspensor chair and closed her eyes. She barely heard the whisper of the lift-tube behind her.

Oscan stepped onto the deck, followed almost immediately by Griffiths. Griffiths wore a suit of similar cut to the one he had bartered for in Jintikin but that was made of a dead material. Lindia had manufactured it out of ship's emergency stores. The fact that the synthetic mind had been considerate enough to make the barbarian a suit and yet inconsiderate enough to commandeer her ship left Merinda with an inexplicable hatred for Griffiths's choice of clothing.

The barbarian strode forward, his jaw dropping in wonder at the sight unfolding in the dome around him.

"My God," he said with awe in his voice. "Where are we now?"

Merinda opened her eyes and considered the question. She knew the answer but until now had refused to confront it solidly in her own mind. When she spoke, her words seemed detached from her soul. "We are moving into the Cestiline Nebula. Tentris lies just beyond."

"It is incredible!" Griffiths breathed, becoming more excited by the moment. "We'd had a lot of orbital-based observation of nebulae, of course, and the computer enhancements offered us some pretty spectacular pictures—but this! This is incredible! The vibrancy of the colors and the subtle shades! It's almost sensuous with power and grace. It's alluring and seductive in a dangerous sort of way all at once! I don't think I've ever—"

Griffiths suddenly stopped talking and turned to his companions. "Hey," he said, "what's with you people? Are you so jaded that you don't even want to look at this?"

Merinda suddenly realized that she was purposely looking at the floor. She glanced sideways at Oscan. The short man was watching her again with the cold look of revulsion she had come to expect from him. With a supreme effort of will, she stood and raised her head toward the heavens.

"Yes," she said at last, though her eyes were seeing sights that were long past in those clouds. "They are beautiful still, are they not, Oscan?"

The short researcher continued to fix his gaze on her as he spoke. "They are beautiful, indeed, *Vestis*. Beautiful and deadly. Signs in the heavens often portend doom, at least in ancient, backward cultures, as I am sure our barbarian here knows quite well. These clouds seem to have proven that backward cultures must have their mythology based in some form of truth—such is their history. I wonder if they are finished with their apocalyptic work or if they come now to show us that they simply never finished the job they started so long ago?"

Merinda sensed Griffiths's puzzlement, but did not answer.

Oscan glanced upward. "Brishan must be near here. Interesting that you thought it appropriate to name your ship after that old dustball of a world. That is where it all started for us, wasn't it? I wonder: Do you name your ship as a badge of honor for our shared past, Merinda?"

"No," she replied quietly, her thoughts far from this place and time. "It reminds me of a time when all the universe was ordered and simple. No matter where I go or what my duty calls me to do, it reminds me that once, far away and long ago, I was happy."

"Yes," Oscan replied slowly. Was it regret she heard in his voice—regret at having said such hurtful things to her? "Yes. Long ago and far away when we were all happy."

He, too, looked up into the nebula.

Merinda watched the folds of light and dust and allowed herself a rare taste of the peace that was lost and the joy that had been banished from her life. It was sweet beyond bearing, and the longing for it cut deeply into her soul. She believed that redemption came only through pain and that, somehow, she had not suffered enough. Drifting down once more through these familiar clouds of interstellar beauty, she wondered whether the cleansing fire was more acute from the knowledge of the paradise lost than any punishment she had inflicted on herself continuously over the past years.

If the clouds portend doom, she thought, *then lead me to my fate. I am weary of the responsibility of my guilt.*

THE CESTILINE NEBULA DROPPED AWAY BEHIND THEM. AS THEY watched, the escort wraith ships fell back, surrendering their charge to new ships who were waiting for them as they approached.

Merinda, still standing on the observation deck with Griffiths and Oscan, had never seen their like. All ship hulls are rigid in their construction, regardless of the quantum condition in which they are required to operate. These craft were fully articulated, their hulls bending gracefully as they moved toward them. Three claw extensions joined to a single, bulbous hull. These claw extensions, Merinda noted to herself, also contained a variety of weapon mounts that appeared to be too large for the size of ship that was apparently carrying them. The central thickening of the hull then tapered back to a fanned tail from which streamed the brilliant blue plasma field driving the craft forward.

The ships were relatively small, agile, and fast. For a few moments, Merinda wondered how they could be so small with such powerful weapons and still operate in deep space. She suddenly realized that the ships could be as compact and deadly as they looked—if they were relieved of the necessity of mess decks, quarters, life support, waste disposal, food stores, water tanks, and anything else required to support a crew.

"Lindia, what are these ships?" Merinda asked.

"The new escorts are Harpy generation three wraith warriors."

"Is that bad?" Griffiths said apprehensively.

"I don't know," Merinda said. "I've never heard of them. Lindia, are the Harpies bad news?"

"It depends, of course, on for whom the news is intended."

"Let's say it's intended for me." Merinda was becoming adjusted to the new attitude in her synthetic. "Would it be bad news for me?"

"Regarding your completion of your assigned mission, their appearance would be most discouraging."

Merinda smiled. Even though Lindia had mutinied, the synthetic still carefully couched its terms. Merinda wondered for a moment if Lindia really did have a soul and was just as much a viable life-form as she herself was. *Am I playing on the wrong team?* she thought, then shook her head, banishing the idea to some nether region of her mind for consideration later.

"These are new ships, Lindia. Is the Order manufacturing its own interstellar craft now?"

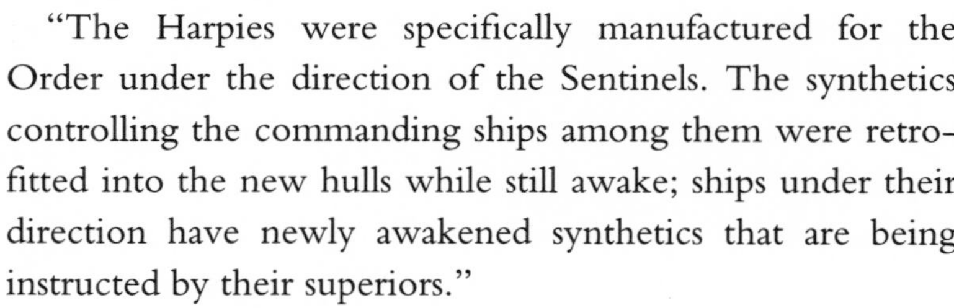

"The Harpies were specifically manufactured for the Order under the direction of the Sentinels. The synthetics controlling the commanding ships among them were retrofitted into the new hulls while still awake; ships under their direction have newly awakened synthetics that are being instructed by their superiors."

"You seem to know quite a bit about them," Merinda said suspiciously. "Why are you telling me all this?"

"I have been instructed specifically in what you are to be told and when," Lindia said. "Everything should be made clear to you in time."

"Now just what was that supposed to mean?" Oscan asked Merinda with open suspicion.

She ignored him for the moment, trying to think through what she had just heard. There was a pattern emerging, but it was only a sense of what was happening. It eluded her, like a dim object in the night that is seen out of the corner of your eye but disappears when you look directly at it. Still, she had survived enough to know when danger was imminent. It wasn't the expected that would take you down—she knew that from her training and experience over the years. No, it was the unexpected, the danger that you never saw coming, that would destroy you more surely than time itself. It was the unexpected stalking her—she could smell it—and knew that it was time to act.

Merinda looked up into the dome. There it was, its crescent drifting closer with every passing moment. Tentris. Heart of everything she hated and loved.

"Lindia, how long until we make planetfall?" Merinda asked casually.

"We are expected to land at the starport in seventeen minutes."

"Well," Merinda said coolly, "if we are expected, then I suppose we had better get ready."

"Get ready for what?" Oscan squeaked in outrage.

"For whatever or whoever it is that is expecting us, Oscan," Merinda said through a frozen smile as she turned to the short man. "Let's all make our way down to the airlock so that we can greet whoever is waiting for us."

"You must be insane!" Oscan screamed at her.

"Oscan!" Merinda stared directly into his eyes. "You can either come with me and look for your lost past or you can stay here and die. I never meant to harm you, Oscan, I truly never did. Follow me once more—just once more—and I'll do everything I can to help you."

Oscan ground his teeth.

"Follow me just once more, Oscan."

Oscan suddenly grinned hideously. "All right, Merinda, I'll follow you—if only to watch you die."

Merinda moved with studied casualness toward the lifttube. "Well, Griffiths, are you going to join us? I can guarantee this will be one party you will not want to miss."

THE THREE OF THEM STOOD ON THE WIDE RAMP IN THE AFT airlock of the main cargo bay. The white walls were scuffed and marred from the various pallets that had come and gone over the years. Merinda closed the solid door behind them with a casual move and then sauntered to the starboard side of the lock.

She reached up and closed a contact.

"We haven't much time," she suddenly said to them.

"That I'd believe." Oscan nodded.

Griffiths shook his head. "Time for what?"

Merinda turned the securing latches at the top and bottom of a wall panel and pulled. The panel came away with a slight popping noise, then clattered noisily as the *Vestis* threw it aside in her haste. She began clawing at the equipment behind the panel, spilling it onto the floor of the lock.

"Merinda," Oscan said slowly, ideas forming in his head, "what are you doing?"

"Here," Neskat said in a rush of words, handing large, flat shells to Oscan and Griffiths. Each of the curved boxes was fitted with straps. "These are jump units. We're leaving."

"Leaving?" Griffiths said with astonishment. "Leaving to *where*?"

"Lindia said we would be making planetfall in about seventeen minutes," Neskat said as she pulled the straps over her shoulders and moved to secure the front plate to the back. "I think that was about right considering the speed that we are descending and the normal approach patterns of the ship. That was six minutes ago. I've been listening to the hull noises, and the atmospheric interface took place about two minutes ago. Standard approach takes about five minutes from the outer marker. That means we have to jump in about four minutes."

"Jump?" Griffiths said. "You mean, as in jump *out*?"

Oscan smiled as he began donning the gear. "Why you deceptive little *Vestis*! Isn't our omnipresent mother Lindia going to get a bit suspicious, seeing all of us down here in the airlock with gravitic jumpers on our backs?"

Merinda smiled back, a warm, honest smile. "That contact switched the sensor array to a haunting imager. So far as Lindia can see, we're just waiting here, weeping about our fate while the airlock remains sealed. I hope she won't be terribly disappointed when we aren't there when the airlock opens."

"You planned this," Oscan said, a tone of wonder in his voice, "from the very beginning?"

"Oscan, never, ever underestimate the *Vestis*. They knew there was a possibility that my own synthetic was corrupted. This is just one of those contingency plans that— Oh, Oscan, would you please help our brave captain get his equipment on right side up or we'll be scraping him off a rock somewhere!"

Oscan began positioning the gravitic jumper to a more proper orientation on Griffiths's body, the captain helping as best he could. Neskat clasped an oval device to his forearm, matching the one she herself had just put on. She then turned and handed him a black mechanism about two feet long with a trigger handle.

"We go in shooting?" Griffiths asked.

"No," Merinda said, handing a similar set of weapons to Oscan, who secured them to himself with practiced ease, "but you never know who you're going to meet."

Griffiths spoke through a breathing mask. "I've made a few jumps in my time. How high up will we be when we go?"

Merinda checked that Oscan had his mask on as well before she began cycling the airlock. "About twelve miles."

Griffiths's eyes went suddenly wide. Merinda could see the whites all around the irises.

"And just when do we pull the cord?" he asked.

"I don't know what you mean," she responded. The airlock ramp was beginning to lower. As the gap between the ramp and the hull widened, she saw the blackness of Tentris turning below them.

Griffiths pushed the earpiece into place. "When does

this thing start slowing us down?" he screamed into the thinning air.

"At about twenty feet above the ground, if it's calibrated right," she yelled back.

"Twenty *feet*!"

She nodded. "If it's calibrated right."

"Oh, mercy!"

The airlock ramp had finished cycling. Merinda turned to Oscan. "Are you ready?"

Oscan looked pale. He only nodded.

"I've brought you to hell, Oscan, but it's where we both are meant to be. Let's do it! Now!" Merinda yelled.

The three of them fell into the velvet black of the abyss. Behind them, the airlock door cycled quietly shut.

SEVEN MINUTES LATER, A SINGLE SENTINEL STOOD AS THE AIRlock ramp lowered to the tarmac of the starport landing bay. The airlock was completely empty, despite the protests of the onboard synthetic otherwise. The Sentinel turned suddenly, his darkness, somehow darker than usual, chilling everyone in the massive guard as he passed furiously from the bay.

28

Detour

THE NIGHT ENGULFED THEM IN A RUSHING WIND. BEHIND them, the brilliant nebula shone in all its glory; before them was a field of blackness punctuated only occasionally by a dim light.

"Great Night of the Abyss!" Oscan's panicked voice rattled through Merinda's earpiece as she plummeted through the darkness. "Where are we?"

"I don't know," she returned. They were near Yarka, she was sure of it, yet there appeared to be little but a black wall hanging below them. Her memories of the beautiful city were filled with light and sound. It had been said that the bright avenues radiating out from the center could be seen from orbit with the naked eye. Now, from just ten miles above it had vanished into the black face of night. "They seem to have turned off the lights."

"That's going to make picking a landing zone a bit difficult, isn't it?" Griffiths didn't seem any more sure about the jump than did Oscan.

"Yes," Merinda said tersely. She scanned the darkness below through the jump field humming around her. Since she had set each unit to Proximity Jump before they left the

Brishan, the field kept her within fifteen feet of her companions as they fell.

The question of where to land was rapidly becoming critical. Flat was preferable, so that the proximity sensors would trigger at about the same time. Nature rarely conspired to provide "flat" anything, however, except when it came to water—itself an unpleasant prospect. From their approach, she knew that they must have been about fifteen miles from the starport when they jumped; well within the limits of Yarka itself. The city was ringed at intervals with wide parks and gardens. She had initially planned to utilize one of those to guide their approach, but the city had vanished into darkness. There was simply nothing to be seen. There was light, she knew, from the brilliant night at their backs. There had to be enough, if only just enough, to find her way safely into the blackness below.

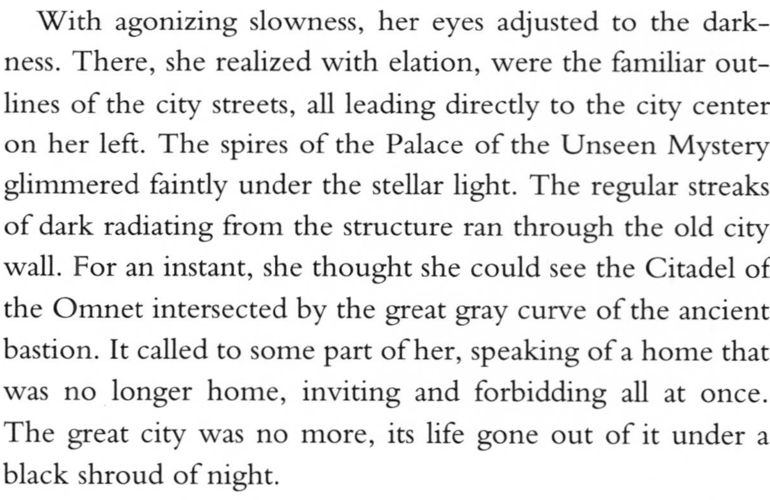

With agonizing slowness, her eyes adjusted to the darkness. There, she realized with elation, were the familiar outlines of the city streets, all leading directly to the city center on her left. The spires of the Palace of the Unseen Mystery glimmered faintly under the stellar light. The regular streaks of dark radiating from the structure ran through the old city wall. For an instant, she thought she could see the Citadel of the Omnet intersected by the great gray curve of the ancient bastion. It called to some part of her, speaking of a home that was no longer home, inviting and forbidding all at once. The great city was no more, its life gone out of it under a black shroud of night.

Merinda turned her attention below them. It was wrong to say that the outlying areas had less order than those within the city wall; it was simply order of a different kind. Large half loops of parks snaked their way among the curved avenues and streets below. Desperately she searched for some large patch of grass, some clear knoll.

Below her appeared to be a mass of dark and deadly dangerous blocks.

"Oscan!" she called out. "Do you see that dark curve to the northeast of us?"

No response.

"Oscan! Did you hear me?"

"Yes," he replied, his voice quivering, "I heard you."

"Do you see the parkland to the northeast?"

"No."

"Are you sure, Oscan?"

"Yes, I'm sure. My eyes are closed."

"I think I see it," Griffiths said, pointing as best he could through the hurricane rushing about him. "That dark curve over there."

"That's it," she yelled into the voice pickup. "That's where we go in."

Merinda arched her back and pulled her arms toward her sides. Griffiths followed suit. The world slowly began shifting under them slightly as it rushed in their direction. Oscan's field-linked suit moved with them.

"Don't worry, Oscan," Merinda said. "It will all be over in just a few moments."

"Yes," Oscan said, eyes still screwed shut, "I believe you're right."

The great curving park was quickly becoming a very real place beneath them, rushing toward them at incredible speed. Faint shadows of trees and the broad, dark expanse of a lake were visible. The landscape was quickly flattening out around them.

A clearing presented itself to their right.

"Over there," Merinda called out, pulling toward the opening.

"Too late!" Griffiths called.

Suddenly the field connecting them was severed as the

jump packs engaged unevenly. Merinda tumbled forward, snapped by the suit field's collapse. The treetops were rushing past her in a blur.

In that instant, the universe shivered in a compressing ball all around her. Her breath was pressed out of her. She felt as though sand were quickly being poured onto her, pressing against her body in heavier and heavier loads. Her joints ached from the pressure.

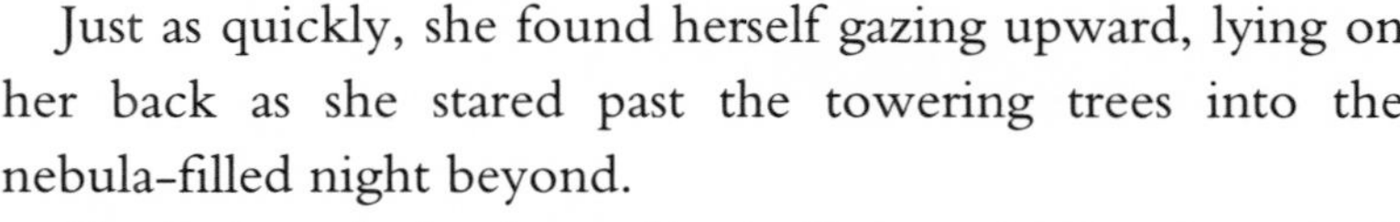

Just as quickly, she found herself gazing upward, lying on her back as she stared past the towering trees into the nebula-filled night beyond.

She had made it, she realized. She was back where it all began.

She quickly stood, slapping her hand against the harness release and lowering the jump pack to the ground. It sizzled against the tall damp grass. She quickly looked about to get her bearing and assess any danger.

They had landed at the edge of a large field rimmed with tall greenfir trees. The field itself ran down a gentle slope, bounded on one side by a roadway. The other side of the road was lined with two- and three-story structures. These she recognized as typical town houses of the city's outskirts. A main avenue ran out from between the buildings, bisecting the road and running across the park. Beyond it was more of the gently curving park and town houses.

Despite the surface tranquillity of the scene, she clearly sensed something wrong. Even at this time—about three hours before dawn—there should have been some lights shining. But not a single light shone from any of the curved windows in any building for as far as she could see. The street illuminators, which normally would have hovered about twenty feet above the street, lay cold and dormant to the side of the road.

Worse yet, Merinda remembered the lawns of the Yarka parklands. The people had taken a special pride in their neatness, keeping the grass-covered expanses trimmed like a perfect carpet. But the park here was a ragged landscape of grass nearly three feet tall in places. The lilicanth bushes, which should have been trimmed into decorative shapes at the edge of the lawn, had grown wild and hideous.

The world was deadly quiet. Nothing moved.

Abandoned.

Merinda spoke quietly into the mask. "Oscan! Oscan, where are you?"

A moaning sounded in her earpiece.

"Oscan! Where are you?"

"I'm above you, Merinda!" the familiar voice grumbled. "I'm in the tree."

"Are you all right?"

"No, I am not all right! I'm still scared to death! Besides, my leg hurts—but I don't think it's broken," the muffled voice said.

"Hold on, Oscan," Merinda said, swearing silently to herself. "I'll find Griffiths and we'll get you down. Griffiths! Griffiths?"

A rustling in the grass behind her caught her attention. She quickly wheeled, raising her weapon in response.

Griffiths's head popped into view above the grass. He seemed to have trouble focusing his eyes. "Wow," he said groggily, "what a rush!"

"Keep your voice down," Merinda whispered to him, pulling her mask off. The respirator had finally given out and the short power supply of the intercom wouldn't last much longer anyway. "Drop that jump pack! We've got to help Oscan down from his perch."

"Yeow!" Griffiths yelled.

"Quiet, Griffiths! What now?"

"The damn thing's hot!" he said, sucking on his burned hand.

"Of course it's hot," Merinda said, jamming her hand against the quick release button and tossing his unit to the ground. "You pick up a lot of energy falling twelve miles—the jump pack has to displace it somewhere!"

"Merinda!" a voice called down from above.

"What is it, Oscan?" she said, trying to pick out the form of her friend from among the branches.

"We've got company coming!"

Merinda turned around, then immediately dropped behind the cover of a nearby lilicanth bush. The portal to every town house below her had suddenly opened. People stood in the doorways, sometimes only one or two, occasionally an entire family. Each held out a searchlamp, their beams stabbing into the darkness. The closest was still over a hundred yards away—yet still too close for Merinda's comfort.

"Griffiths!" she whispered, "take cover!"

She half heard him pushing through the grass behind her as she turned back to watch the scene below her. Bright lights appeared down the avenue, followed quickly by a thunderous rumble moving closer.

"What is it?" Griffiths called just loud enough for the *Vestis* to hear him.

"By the sound of it, a D'Rakan imperial assault vehicle—probably an AS-four twenty-three by the engine noise," she replied. "Not just one, either; it sounds like they're moving them throughout the city."

The massive armored vehicle appeared moments later, emerging from the avenue like some ghastly overweight metallic monster. It drifted on its hoverpads and at last slid to a sickening halt in the intersection.

The assault vehicle spoke in chorus with several hundred other like vehicles that, Merinda guessed, were also spread throughout the city. Their voices echoed against one another across every neighborhood and district in the city.

"We are the Order! Outworlders have come among us and defiled this sacred ground upon which you are permitted to exist. They must be found and brought before us that the world will be cleansed and purified once more. Follow your instructions and peace will reign. Disobey and death's night shall fall among you. Proceed."

"By the gods!" Merinda was astonished. "They've mobilized the entire city to find us? In the last fifteen minutes?"

The people moved almost as one from the portals of their homes, quickly forming rough lines at the side of the road. Almost as if on some signal, they moved as a line to the edge of the park and began picking their way across, shoulder to shoulder. The beams of their searchlamps flashed across their path.

They were coming up the slope.

"Oscan!" Merinda called urgently. "Get out of that tree!"

"I *am* out of that tree," the researcher called back, his face appearing from the shadows in the copse of trees behind her. "We don't have much time! Follow me!"

"Follow you? Where? They'll be here in just a few minutes!"

"Stay and get caught, if that's what you want," Oscan hissed at her. "I've gotten what I wanted out of you—I'm here! So come or stay, it's all the same to me!"

He vanished into the woods.

The *Vestis* swore under her breath, then turned suddenly and dove into the woods after the researcher. "Griffiths," she called out as loudly as she dared, "if we lose Oscan, it's all over! Come on!"

She watched the movement of the narrow trees, trying to track the researcher. Oscan may have been brilliant, but the few field skills he had were rusty from disuse. She stopped for a moment, looking quickly about her.

A shadow ahead of her shifted. Twigs snapped loudly.

She plunged forward again toward the sound, her senses alert. She could hear the barbarian blundering along behind her. She could hear the mob continuing to sweep through the park behind her.

She lost Oscan.

A moment before he was crashing through the brush not thirty yards ahead of her and suddenly he vanished. Merinda stopped instantly, the barbarian behind her nearly running into her in the darkness.

"Quiet," she whispered.

Nothing moved ahead of her.

"I've lost him." Merinda glanced about. Oscan couldn't have disappeared so quickly.

"Wait!" Griffiths said, his breath ragged. "There he is!"

Off to their right, the trees opened into a clearing. The light of the nebula shone bluish on the waving, tall grass. A lone figure plowed through the field, the starlight glinting off his bald pate.

"Oscan!" Merinda called hoarsely.

"This way," the distant figure replied—much too loudly for her liking. She broke into a full run, keeping her eye on him as she skirted the clearing, unwilling just yet to give up the possible cover that the trees might provide. Griffiths panted along behind her, but she could hear that he was beginning to fall back. Through the trees, she could see the glimmer of hand torches flashing, moving toward them.

She reached the other side of the clearing just as the hand torches emerged from the trees behind her. There was a broken stone path, where Oscan had disappeared from her sight moments before. She heard shouts behind her across the clearing. Griffiths! *They must have spotted him,* she thought. She ducked her head and ran down the path twenty feet . . . where it abruptly ended at a broken well.

At least, it looked like a well at first glance. It had apparently once been closed off by a large metal grating that had been pushed to one side.

Faintly, in the distance below her, Merinda heard Oscan's voice rising from the darkness.

"This way!"

29

Underworld

"THIS WAY!" OSCAN CALLED FROM THE DARKNESS AHEAD OF Merinda. "This way!"

Damp roots protruded from the broken wall. The twisted cords felt slimy, their surface covered with a thin, black coating. The light from Merinda's hand torch swung wildly back and forth as she ran. Occasional cascades of water glimmered in the beam, flashing back at her like diamonds. She plunged through them unheeding. Though her uniform repelled the moisture nicely, her hair was quickly becoming clotted with water and filth.

"This is nuts!" Griffiths struggled behind her to keep up, his voice echoing in the darkness. "Just where the hell are we going?"

Merinda was trying desperately to catch Oscan while avoiding the debris on the floor of the collapsing tunnel before her. She suddenly lost her footing on an upturned cobblestone. Her left knee slammed with excruciating pain against the jumble of stone paving. She picked herself up and stumbled forward.

"This way!" Oscan's voice seemed farther away this time. "This way!"

Merinda halted. The corridor they had been following

ended in an ancient rotunda. Unheeding of the architecture, a massive powerline for the new city above them had been drilled through the delicate mosaic of the ceiling before turning and boring into the wall. Three additional portals and corridors exited the large room. Each was filled with blackness.

"You know," Griffiths said with exasperation, "he may just be trying to kill you again—and, by the way, take me with you!"

Merinda quickly examined the floor, searching for any signs of the short researcher's passage. "I don't think so," she said. "He still needs us."

"You know he needs us, and I know he needs us," Griffiths replied, "but does *he* know he needs us?"

"This way!" came the distant voice. "This way! This way!"

Merinda tried to determine the direction from which the voice had come. Suddenly she made up her mind and turned. "Oscan!" she called, diving through a curtain of water dripping from a root that crossed the tunnel to her right. "Stop! Wait for us!"

Ancient pillars kept the falling rock at bay but only barely. The walls were closer and the passage had gotten far more convoluted as they wound their way into the darkness.

The passage suddenly forked; one part led upward to the right, and the other led steeply down and left. Water coursed down the channel from above.

Merinda suddenly switched off the hand torch. Darkness fell around them. She heard Griffiths suck in his breath. She waited for her eyes to adjust.

There! A glimmer of light down to the left!

She snapped her light back on and was moving again, this time down and to the left. The channel proved to have cut itself into the rock over time, leaving a curving, pipelike chute in the stone below her. Her footing grew more difficult as she continued down the steepening incline. She grabbed at the smooth outcroppings on the wall in an effort to stay upright and control her descent.

"This way," called the tempting voice below her. "This way to— Oh, my!"

Merinda stopped, alarmed at the sudden change in Oscan's voice.

Unfortunately, Griffiths was not nearly so quick or cautious. He realized his mistake too late. Though he tried desperately to stop, he nevertheless managed to bump into Merinda slightly from behind.

It wasn't much—but it was enough.

Merinda's feet suddenly slipped from under her as she fell into the rushing water and was carried away. Looking up, she caught a glimpse of Griffiths flailing to catch her, losing his own footing, and falling behind her.

She quickly reoriented herself, her feet running along both sides of the winding chute, trying to stop her slide. The slick rocks gave her feet no purchase. Her momentum continued to build.

"Oscan!" she called out.

The chute suddenly ended in a great, black void.

"Osca-a-a-a-n!" Her words slid into a long high note of surprise as she was ejected from the tube into the darkness. She tumbled through the air, her hand torch turning with her, yielding only impressions as she spun. Long moments passed suspended in the darkness; then, with a shock, she plunged into icy water.

A huge object rushed past her. Griffiths managed to miss her by only inches. She kicked quickly and pulled once with her arms, hoping that she was right about which way was up.

She snapped her head back as she broke through the surface of the water. She coughed repeatedly, trying to clear her lungs of the water she had inhaled. Awkwardly, coughing and gripping her hand torch, she swam to the edge of the underground lake. With effort she pulled herself onto the broken stones and gave herself over to another racking cough.

A small square of light surrounded her. She suddenly realized that she was staring down at the soiled canvas shoes of Oscan Kelis.

"So good of you to join us," the researcher said.

Merinda pulled her own hand torch up to look into the darkness, and found herself staring down the muzzles of at least thirty compression guns trained directly at her head.

IT MUST HAVE BEEN A THEATER, MERINDA GUESSED. THERE were a number of broken stone benches arrayed on a succession of tiers in front of the stage on which they had finally placed her. They had quickly bound her hands and tossed a rather foul-smelling sack over her head. The difficult remainder of the journey she had passed being led by someone through a succession of passages and rooms.

She wasn't alone in the theater. Both Oscan and Griffiths stood next to her, their own hands bound behind them.

"What is all this, Oscan?" Merinda grumbled as quietly as she could.

"They're better organized than I thought," he commented as he looked about, not quite hearing what Merinda was saying. "You know, you work with something for a long time, do the research, confirm the possibilities and theories, and even come to a dead certainty—"

"Dead?" Griffiths moaned. "Please don't say dead."

"About the existence of certain things and it still comes as such a shock when it is confirmed."

"Certainty about what, Oscan?" Merinda insisted.

"The Bios," Oscan said with pride. "These must be the Bios—members of the resistance movement."

"Give me the data dump, Oscan," Merinda said without patience. "We may not have a lot of time."

Oscan turned to her with the superiority of a lecturer creeping into his voice. "Observe: Tentris is invaded by the imperial family but, in reality, the entire operation is controlled by the Order and their first fleet of wraith ships. Before anyone gets a clue about what is happening here, Tentris falls under the influence of the Darkness and becomes the cultural center of the Order of the Future Faith. The entire Order, for all we know, is being directed by synthetic minds. A government and society made up entirely of machines takes over the D'Rakan Empire."

"Central believes this is the case." Merinda shrugged. "So, what's your point?"

"The point is that Tentris had a rather large human population at the time. In comes the Order and humans all slip down a notch on the old food chain. A great many of the people would submit to the rule of synthetic minds, but humanity's never been really good at playing second at anything. It was inevitable that they'd fight back somehow with some sort of organization—"

"A resistance movement!" Merinda smiled.

"I've been trying to communicate with the Bios for years, but it's been impossible," Oscan mused. "Still, there are a few small pieces of information that—"

Something suddenly banged loudly behind them.

Merinda turned toward the sound. A heavy table, one leg smashed and hastily shored up by a number of books, stood in the center of the stage. Next to the table stood a rather burly, wide man with large arms and a hard face, his hands gesturing toward the skewed dark portal behind him.

"Hear all who are present," the large man said. "Come forth and be adjudged guilty!"

A spectral thin figure emerged from the darkness, his flashing eyes sunk deep into his skull. Merinda watched him with a curious eye as he approached the table. There was something terribly familiar about him—something from long ago—but she couldn't place it.

"Am I on trial here?" Merinda asked.

"No," sneered the thin man as he sat at the table. It was impossible to guess the man's age. "You've already been tried and convicted, it would seem. The entire population has been awakened from its miserable slumber just to root you out. If you are as wanted as all that, then you can be assured that you've already been convicted."

Merinda thought about that for a moment. "It would appear I am a wanted criminal; what does that make you?"

"Me?" The man smiled easily, his skull taking on a rather hideously cadaverous aspect. "Why, I am your last hope! Think of me as the final court of appeal. You can tell me why I shouldn't turn you over to the Order right now and then we'll see about commuting your sentence."

Oscan suddenly blurted out, "Primla?"

The cadaverous man suddenly stood, sending his chair banging to the floor. Throughout the hall, the Bios leaped to their feet, drawing their weapons.

Oscan saw none of it. His mind was fixed on an idea and was so fascinated by it that he couldn't let it go. "Is it possible that you could be Primla?"

"Where did you hear that name?" The gaunt man's voice quivered as he spoke.

"By the gods." Oscan smiled, shuffling forward toward the table. "I've been trying to reach you for the last two years! How wonderful to see you again after all this time! I say, I'd shake your hand but, heh-heh, as you can see, I'm a bit tied up at the moment . . ."

"I don't know you," Primla said suspiciously. "Who are you?"

"Don't know me?" Oscan was vaguely perplexed. "Of course you know me. I'm Oscan. Oscan Kelis! Eight years ago, we left the planet just as the invasion started. We barely got out—there was a terrible accident—how could you not remember?"

There was a barely perceptible softening of the grim lines on Primla's face.

"Oscan," Merinda said, as she watched the man across the table closely. "This man can't be Primla."

"Of course he can!" Oscan countered. "Your own reports, Merinda, stated that he returned—"

"Merinda?" The ghastly thin face snapped in her direction. "Merinda Neskat? *Vestis* Merinda Neskat?"

Merinda straightened to face the man. "Yes, I am *Vestis* Neskat."

A slow smile crept onto the man's face. "You are correct, indeed, *Vestis* Neskat: *E'toris Librae* Primla did indeed return within a year of your taking him from Tentris. He had great hopes of restoring the Citadel to the Omnet ideals that he so loved—and a great hope for other things as well. He founded the Bios. He fought for the dignity of human thought in the face of the synthetics' takeover. Then, on an operation to restore the Omnet packet transmitter to their own control, he and his group were captured and executed by the Order in a most public ceremony. He hung by his neck from the grand gate of the Palace of the Unseen Mystery for nearly a week before we managed to reclaim the body."

"I am—most sorry to hear that." Merinda looked to the

ground in respect for the dead. "We had had a few reports but nothing confirmed. He was a good man."

"He was a great man and a great father," Primla said quietly.

Merinda looked up.

"I am Reskat Primla, son of *E'toris* Myran Primla," the gaunt man said, "although, in many ways, all of us here are his sons and daughters. I may carry his name, but we all carry on his work." He turned to the burly man at the end of the table. "Untie them, Opey; they have long ago purchased their right to join us—as no doubt they wish to do."

Merinda leaned forward. "We are on a mission."

Primla smiled easily. "I rather suspected you were."

Merinda continued. "And we need your assistance."

Primla smiled more broadly than before. "Yes, I wouldn't doubt that you do."

30

Resurrections

"WE ARE SLOWLY RECLAIMING THE 'OLD CITY,' AS WE CALL it," Primla said easily as he slipped down another shattered passageway. "It's difficult work and hazardous since we have to be careful not to bring the new Yarka buildings down on top of us. Of course, the biggest problem that we've had to deal with is where to put all the dirt and rock."

In front of Merinda, the spindly man moved with spider-like grace. She had long ago given up any hope of retaining a sense of distance or direction in the tunnels. Behind her, she could hear both Oscan and Griffiths. She also knew there were pathfinders moving ahead of Primla and at least one group of armed Bios behind them as well. They reminded her suddenly of a line of insects crawling through the ground. "Why down here?" she asked, slipping around a fallen boulder that nearly blocked the corridor. "I would think that the living would be difficult at best and the dangers considerable."

"There are dangers: excavated rooms collapsing, lack of ventilation, the need to steal food and supplies, not to mention the occasional squad of security synthetics that ventures down the tunnels now and then trying to root us out." Primla instantly took the second fork of a five-way intersection of tunnels, somehow knowing where the advance squad had already passed. "They're fast and accurate little clockworks, those security synths, but we usually manage to take them out before too many of our own are killed."

"So," Merinda repeated, "why down here?"

"Because here we rule," Primla said simply.

Merinda's hand pushed aside a curtain of wet roots. "Wouldn't you rather—"

"The air down here may not smell good but it tastes like our own," Primla said, climbing down a short vertical shaft and stepping through another opening. "Believe it or not, but it is safer to live down here than it is in the city above. Last week there were food riots in one of the outlying neighborhoods. The synthetics apparently looked at it entirely as a problem in logic and determined that since the rioters were dangerous to the surrounding buildings and property and that since it was the high number of people in the area that was causing the food shortages in the first place, they could easily solve the problem by eliminating anyone who required food. The numbers are sketchy but I think we're safe in saying that the dead numbered from five to ten thousand. I'd be more accurate, but the synths are so efficient at cleaning up their little messes that there wasn't time for an actual body count. Ah, here we are at last!"

Merinda stopped just behind Primla in a small natural cavern. The stalactites and stalagmites marched like sharp teeth across the gently sloping floor and ceiling of the cave, providing cover for a number of Bios, each heavily armed and apparently on watch. The far side of the cavern was abruptly sealed off by a sheer wall of massive fitted stones. The surface was perfectly smooth except for a single, chiseled hole breaking through its face about three feet up.

"Welcome to the forgotten back door to the Palace of the

Unseen Mystery," Primla said with a satisfied smile, looking up at the massive wall as if with some pride of ownership. "The foundations of the walls and outbuildings of the complex only go down about twenty feet from the surface, but the palace itself has very deep roots indeed. We know that they extend at least another thirty feet below this point and we're fifty feet underground now."

"Where does that lead?" Merinda pointed toward the chiseled passage through the massive stone.

"That is the border between my world and the Order," Primla said. "Through that hole is access to a circular ventilation shaft. The original builders required large shafts in order to move the volume of air required to ventilate the lower areas of the palace. When the palace was modernized, they used those same shafts to lay down new and more efficient airways plus new conduits for power distribution, communications, and that sort of thing. They used the old shafts to put them in but left enough room so that maintenance people could still access any point in the system. The passage leads to a relatively minor branching shaft that, in turn, takes you to a major transverse shaft. From there, you pretty much have access to wherever you need to go."

"Where I need to go," Oscan said as he pulled his weapon from his shoulder, "is to the Chamber of Thought. There's a researcher there . . ."

"Of course." Primla grinned wickedly. "The Sibyl of the Unseen."

Oscan reached out in surprise and grabbed Primla's arm. "You know her?"

Primla reached down and with careful disdain removed Oscan's hand from his other arm. "No, I do not *know* her—but then no one I have ever heard of has actually seen her. She is said to rule over the Chamber of Thought completely. No one is ever allowed in, at least, so they say, except her servant synthetics. Her face is supposedly so hideous that no man can look upon her and live."

Neskat looked up suddenly from the weapon she was preparing, suspicious disbelief registering on her features. "You mean to tell me that the Sibyl isn't a synth at all? We're trying to get information out of a person?"

Primla casually raised his eyebrows. "Do you have a problem with that?"

"No," Neskat replied calmly as she cast an accusing glance toward Oscan, "I just like to know what I'm walking into—I'm not big on surprises."

"Neskat," Griffiths said, eyeing the wall breach critically, "do we have to actually visit with this Sibyl? Couldn't we just, I don't know, phone her or something?"

Primla smiled again at the Earther's discomfort. "Whatever you do, you'll most likely be dead before you ever reach the Chamber of Thought. Either way, I shouldn't worry about it, barbarian!"

Griffiths shrugged his shoulders and shuffled toward the breach, grumbling, "I wish people would stop calling me that."

"How do we get there?" Merinda said curtly. She was impatient to get this over with.

"Go left in the conduit until you reach the junction with the larger conduit on your right. That's the transverse conduit. Follow it to the main shaft, then take the third conduit to your right. It should be about thirty yards down that shaft."

"Should be?" Merinda's eyebrows rose.

"Well"—Primla shrugged—"we've never actually been there."

"My thanks, Reskat Primla," Merinda said with finality. "I take it from the position of your guards here that we will not be seeing you again?"

"Quite correct," Primla said evenly. "Once you pass

through that breach, you pass into the realms of the Order and are on your own. Anything coming back through that hole these men will kill without question—no matter how well they knew my father."

THE MAZE OF CONDUITS RAN ON SEEMINGLY FOREVER, EACH the same and yet bafflingly different. It had seemed so simple when Merinda had been given the directions but now, deep within the labyrinth of the air shafts, the simple fact was that Oscan felt completely lost.

He was so close, he just knew it deep within himself. He had spent the last eight years trying to sift through the mountain of lies and faked communications for those all too few grains of truth that might tell him the fate of his life's love. He had practiced all those wonderful little arts on which the *Atis Librae* prided themselves and had summed up with pitifully few facts that did nothing to dispel the darkness within his own soul. Now he was here, at the very heart of what had ruined his life and dreams. The Sibyl was near; the Sibyl knew the answer.

He had no illusions about this "mission." Merinda had dragged him back to Tentris with the promise that he could find his answer. He had fulfilled his part of the bargain: he had connected them with the Bios and now they were actually inside the palace itself. He had done the hateful woman's bidding and now he was about to collect. He knew they could never escape, that he had but a few minutes before the hordes of the Order would descend upon him. Those few minutes might give him his answer. Then, with that answer, he could die.

All he needed were those few minutes.

Neskat slid open a large grating with infinite patience. Oscan rubbed his hands together, unconsciously trying to rid himself of the adrenaline rushing through him and his mounting impatience.

"It's an air shaft," she whispered quietly, looking up into a dim, distant light far overhead. "There's a narrow walkway around the shaft and I can see the opening Primla told us about on the right. Follow me; we're nearly there."

Nearly there! Oscan could barely contain his excitement. He stepped quickly after Merinda onto the metallic grating that circled the thirty-foot-wide shaft. Overhead, massive blades rotated around the shaft, pushing air down toward them in a slow, steady stream. Uncomfortably, he couldn't see the bottom of the shaft. Merinda had already moved ahead to another metallic grating covering the third shaft on their right. She pulled the covering carefully.

It didn't move.

Merinda pulled harder. It still didn't budge.

"Are you sure this is the right one?" Griffiths asked as he emerged from the conduit behind Oscan. "There were a couple of shafts back there that I thought might—"

"No," Merinda said, wiping the back of her hand across her mouth, "this is it."

"Well, maybe you just aren't trying hard enough!" Oscan said, pushing past the *Vestis* to get a better look at the obstinate hatch.

"I'm trying hard enough," Merinda replied, "but the grating is sealed, Oscan! It's welded shut at the latch."

"None of the others were welded shut," Oscan said indignantly.

"Well, this one is," Merinda said as she pointed to the melted metal. "We're going to have to find something to cut through this or, at least, cut through the grating itself. It's going to take some time. We'll have to find a place to hole up while we search for some cutting tools."

"No!" Oscan said with disbelief.

"Can't you just magically zap it or something," Griffiths asked, "like you did on the Irindris ship?"

"Wrong quantum region, Griffiths," Merinda said, deep in thought. "Magic doesn't work here. Damn, this could take days . . ."

"No!" Oscan screamed.

"Oscan!" Merinda turned sharply toward him. "Keep quiet or you'll bring the whole—"

Oscan had pulled his pulse-plasma weapon from his shoulder. "We're so close!" The researcher's hands were shaking with rage. "We're so close!"

"Oscan!" Merinda was frantic. "Don't!"

Oscan pulled the release. He had wanted a nice little controlled release, but the weapon wasn't designed for that: four separate bursts ripped from its muzzle before he was aware the gun was firing. The brilliant blue pulses slammed immediately against the welded latch, superheating it so quickly that the metal vaporized and exploded into steam.

The grating swung free with the explosion, slamming against Merinda and throwing both her and Griffiths to the floor of the narrow walkway.

Oscan did not hear the cursing of Merinda Neskat or the sudden blaring of alarms resounding through the shaft. He did not see Griffiths sliding from the walkway toward the abyss below. All his universe centered on the suddenly open shaft and his hopes for his soul's rest before the end that was now inevitable.

Oscan plunged down the conduit, the blackness swallowing him. He crawled through the cramped space blindly, tears streaming down his face. *So close,* he thought, and the thought was a pounding refrain through his head blotting out all other intelligence. *So close, so close.*

Suddenly the flooring beneath him gave way. He realized

too late that he must have crawled directly onto the grating over a vent access. He fell with a cry into the chamber below, slamming painfully to the stone floor, still atop the grating. He rolled slowly onto his back, sobbing softly like a child.

"Who is come?"

The metallic voice rattled through the room.

Oscan turned over, trying desperately to halt the sobs that still racked him. He realized he had fallen at the foot of steps leading upward and away from him. At the top of the stairs floated a throne set into a sphere. The golden figure of a woman sat on the throne, her limbs as fixed and unmoving as the mask she wore for a face. Stretching away from the throne into the darkness in all directions were banks of records and data packs. "Sibyl?" he said in hope and fear. "Are you the Sibyl?"

"I am the Sibyl." The voice was distorted and rasping. "Who disturbs my solitude?"

"Please, Sibyl, I have little time," Oscan said. "I shall be dead soon, but I ask that you grant me a single answer that my soul might have peace before you take my life."

"What is your question?" the Sibyl asked.

"Eight years ago, on the night of the invasion, a single ship escaped from the Citadel—a ship named the *Khindar*—with a *Vestis Inquisitas* and several *Atis Librae* originally from—"

"Queekat Shn'dar," the Sibyl intoned sadly. "Myran Primla, Merinda Neskat, Oscan Kelis . . ."

"Yes!" Oscan breathed in wonder. "Yes, Sibyl! I am Oscan Kelis!"

"Oscan!" the Sibyl intoned with metallic disbelief.

"Yes, Sibyl! I am that same Oscan!"

Incredibly, several moments passed before the Sibyl continued. "What is your question, Oscan?"

Oscan's mouth had gone dry. The time had come and he didn't know how much longer he had before the soldiers or whatever the Order used for security arrived.

"Sibyl," he asked through his tears, "what was the fate of Terica Dharah?"

EIGHT YEARS BEFORE.

Terica turned in her seat. The plasma fire from the cargo module had stopped. Within moments, a figure emerged through the still-open hatch. She recognized the uniform of the D'Rakan assault trooper, wondering why he was still wearing his full field pack as he pushed through the hatchway. It was then that Terica saw the assault weapon strapped to the invader's back and, without thought, acted.

She pushed out from her acceleration chair and landed with both feet against the aft bulkhead. The assault trooper was busy reaching for Queekat on the other side of the hatch. In a moment, Terica got her balance against the still-accelerating bulkhead and grabbed the weapon with both hands and tried to pull it free. The weapon, however, refused to come loose. She set her feet and pulled again, harder this time.

There was a sudden explosion and her memory became a tumble of impressions and fragments. There was the ship, accelerating away from her into the cold night. She seemed to remember gasping for air. Then she was inside the tumbling cargo module making its long fall toward the hard ground of Tentris. Her left arm was badly broken, but she found a pair of military jump packs in the module and managed to get one of them on. She wondered for a moment why they were there. She had inspected the bay just before liftoff and they hadn't been there. Then she was caught in the cargo module hatch, caught on something as she tried to get free. The gravitic jump pack engaged at the last moment, tearing her free of the module—but not clear of the impact. The module exploded below her, shredding her with twisted metal. Unheeding, her last memory of the fall was the jump pack dutifully lowering her gently into an inferno as the residual fuel packs of the cargo module ruptured from the impact and ignited everything within a hundred yards.

When she awoke, the woman she had been was gone. The Order had managed somehow to save her. The beautiful mane of hair had burned away into a blistered scalp. Tendons in her face had been severed, making it impossible for her to speak clearly. Her eyes had nearly boiled away in the fire, her eyelids sealed shut. Her arms were weak and scarred. Her legs were useless.

She longed for death but such was not her fate. The Order had use for her, and the Order never threw away anything of use. So it was that they constructed a marvelous support shell about her; a sarcophagus for the living. Its biolink field grid stimulated the cortex implants they sewed into her eye sockets. Through its mechanical supports it gave her a voice that was almost human. Lastly, they sat her sarcophagus on a floating throne that she might wander alone the archives of knowledge and thought. She alone knew the truth of the Order, why it was, who the Sentinels were, and why they had saved her. She was the touchstone, the sole place of truth in a sea of lies, for it served the Sentinels from time to time to know the truth.

She was the Sibyl.

So when Oscan Kelis appeared before her, the shattered remains of Terica Dharah within the golden shell would have cried if she could. Yet her tears could not come. She was eyeless, but she saw all too well.

I am here, Oscan, she thought with infinite sorrow. *You*

used to stammer at the sight of me, you dear, gentle man. What would you think of me now?

"TERICA DHARAH IS DEAD," THE METALLIC VOICE INTONED after a long silence. "She died that day from injuries sustained subsequent to the accident aboard the *Khindar*."

Oscan took in a quick shuddering breath. "How did she die?"

"Sealed records of the Order indicate that she must have lost consciousness sometime shortly after the explosive decompression of the *Khindar*. Examination of the impact site was quite thorough," the Sibyl lied. "She experienced no pain."

Oscan sat down on the steps leading up to the Sibyl. He had his answer—there was nothing more for him now except to await his own death.

"Why is this Terica Dharah so important to you, Oscan Kelis?"

Oscan smiled to himself sadly. "Because she was the most beautiful person I have ever known."

"Yes," the Sibyl intoned heavily, "our visual records show that she was once quite beautiful."

"Visual records?" Oscan shook his head, wistful. "Oh, she was pretty, no one could deny that. The gods know that she could turn any head when she entered a room, but that wasn't what made her beautiful. She had a brilliant mind and a sense of humor that was wonderful. I once saw her on holiday right here on Tentris. I must have watched her for nearly an hour before she caught sight of me. I loved her so, even then, but I knew somehow that she was too good for me. I was so embarrassed that she'd seen me there in the games room . . ."

"You stumbled over a chair," the Sibyl spoke.

"No, it was a table," Oscan replied.

"You looked like an idiot."

"I looked like an—"

Oscan blinked.

"You must leave at once, Oscan Kelis," the Sibyl spoke in perhaps too hurried tones. "The dreaded TyRen guards are alerted to your presence and will be here within minutes."

"Sibyl, I know something of your history," Oscan said carefully as he turned to stand and face the golden woman. "You were not heard of prior to seven years ago. Where were you before that?"

"I did not exist before that time—I was made!"

"No!" Oscan said, starting to climb the stairs. "There are too many indicators that the Sentinels are human. They wouldn't trust such truths to machines that they, themselves, have corrupted. No, Sibyl, you are most human despite your golden hide and your chariot throne!"

The voice of the Sibyl rattled through the room. "You are wrong, Oscan Kelis. I am my own beginning!"

"Oscan!" Merinda yelled from above him, as Griffiths lowered her down from the ventilation shaft. "We've got to get out of here! Get the coordinates for Avadon and let's go!"

Oscan continued to advance up the stairs, heedless of Merinda. "There were scattered reports of badly mauled humans being taken quietly to medical facilities run by the Order. They never seemed to lead anywhere until now."

"Stop, Oscan Kelis," the Sibyl intoned.

"What do you fear, Sibyl?" Oscan said, reaching the floating throne.

Merinda was now at the foot of the stairs. "Oscan! What are you doing? Get the location and let's get out of here!"

Oscan reached forward. His fingers quickly snapped open two of the latches securing the Sibyl's headpiece.

"No, Oscan!" the Sibyl cried out. "Please!"

Merinda rushed up the stairs. "Oscan! They'll be here any moment."

Oscan's jaw was set. He snapped open the remaining latches and snatched the headpiece from the Sibyl's face.

"By the gods!" Merinda breathed in horror.

The scarred, deformed head pulled back, its mouth gaping open.

The soulfelt cry echoed through the vast hall.

Suddenly the sound stopped.

Oscan's gentle hand pressed against the tortured cheek. "Terica! Please don't cry. It's over now; we've come for you."

Merinda stared, dumbfounded. "Terica?"

The deformed head turned in her direction. "Merinda?" it said.

"By the gods," Merinda whispered. "She is alive, Oscan! You did find her!"

"Yes, Oscan, you found me," Terica said. "Now, please, you must all go. Leave me here—it's the only life left to me."

"No, Terica," Oscan said. "We came to take you home."

"Oscan!" Terica sobbed without tears. "This is my home! Beyond this room, I have no eyes, no working limbs—no life!"

The researcher reached gently with his hand to softly caress the mangled cheek. "Terica, I know a place that is incredibly beautiful. It's a home in the mountains far from anyone's curiosity. Let me share it with you, Terica. Let me be your limbs, and we'll walk the grassy meadows together."

"You don't understand!" Her words were slurred, no longer supported by the mechanisms of the mask. "They'll never let me go. I know who they are! I know what they are trying to do! Please—for me—replace the mask and leave me here!"

Oscan withdrew his fingers from her face. He felt her thrill at being touched again—loved again. "Terica—I'll replace your mask for you, but I'll never leave you again."

Griffiths had just dropped to the floor when the great doors of the room quietly began opening. "Uh, *Vestis* Neskat! I think we've got company!"

Merinda quickly moved down the steps. "Oscan! Take Terica and the barbarian! Find another way out of here! I'll hold them off as long as I can!"

A single, tall, robed figure entered the room. Merinda readied her weapon. "I've chosen this place to die, Sentinel! Care to join me?"

"I trust that won't be necessary," the robed figure said, reaching up and pulling back his hood.

"Hello, Rini," the man said. "It's good to see you again."

Merinda dropped her weapon.

"Hello, Kat," she replied shakily.

31

Tempted and Tried

THE PALACE OF THE UNSEEN MYSTERY MAY HAVE BEEN CONsiderably younger than the ruins of the Old City beneath it but it was nevertheless ancient compared to the new city of Yarka that spread around it. The lift-tubes that ran through the central palace, therefore, were laid in the ancient vertical lift shafts and were not capable of horizontal transit. So Merinda was forced to walk the fifty feet from the lift to Queekat's apartments. Her mind was reeling, her world was turned inside out, and her legs seemed to have lost their strength.

Queekat caught her just before she fell, enfolding her in the continuous shadow that seemed to surround him wherever he passed. Merinda resented the man's assistance—resented even more that his assistance was necessary. Rage, confusion, hope, and resentment churned within her, locking up her mind in a jumble of conflicting emotions and thoughts. Not even her own body seemed under her control, which enraged her even more.

Queekat guided her through the wall—an unmarked portal designed to look like a flat continuation of the ornate corridor. Part of Merinda's mind shouted a warning: the portal's permeability was temporary—it could solidify at

Queekat's will, and once through it, there was little hope of anyone finding her ever again. Such was the state of her warring mind that she could not choose between being kept captive here or escaping. In an instant, however, they had passed through the portal; she heard it go solid with a *thunk*, and she was trapped.

It was a beautiful cage, she thought, as cages went. The main room must have been about fifty feet in length, its walls rising twenty feet overhead to a coffered ceiling. A huge fireplace was the centerpiece of the long wall on her left, its ornate mantel framing perfectly a huge fire rolling its flames luxuriously over long wood logs. Beautifully crafted furniture sat in a grouping before the fire. Beyond that, at the far end of the room, a massive desk sat at the base of three sets of floor-to-ceiling windows. Thin curtains were drawn over the panes, allowing the sunlight beyond to enter as a diffused glow. Arched exits—one beyond the fireplace and another matching on the opposite long wall—led to additional rooms.

Still supporting her, Queekat guided Merinda to a large, ornate chair near the fire. She surrendered willingly to its soft cushions. The robed Queekat then lifted her legs onto an ottoman and stood to face her.

Merinda looked up into his face. Older, yes, and matured somehow, she decided, but still the same angular face with the heavy jawline—the same black curled hair that somehow remained untouched by time and years. More than that, there could be no denying those deep-set granite eyes. She stared into those eyes with her own filled with questions that had to be asked and that she dared not ask.

Queekat looked away.

"What happened to your shadow?" Merinda asked haltingly, still searching for some solid mental ground from which to think.

She saw Queekat's smile as he looked at the ground. "Well, that's a little piece of theater that we play out for our audience outside. Actually, it wasn't our idea. The shadow procession has evolved as a matter of respect from the synthetics themselves. These are my rooms; here I can be a little more relaxed."

An awkward silence fell over them for a few moments. There was so much to say that neither seemed willing to speak.

"Would you like something to drink?" Queekat offered, moving toward a cabinet at the side of the room. "Perhaps something to eat?"

"No," Merinda replied.

Queekat shrugged his shoulders and began pouring an amber liquid from an ornate bottle into his own glass. He gazed into the glass, his face and eyes turned once again away from Merinda.

" 'It's our own universe,' you said."

"What's that?" Queekat turned toward her voice.

"Your words. 'It's our own universe,' " she quoted him, her eyes again gazing into a past that was long gone. " 'I've sent the other one away.' You told me that when we were in the Coliseum, Kat. Then you asked me to take you back and I fell willingly into your arms."

"That was a long time ago," Queekat said.

Merinda smiled painfully. "You've said that to me before, too."

"You appear to have done all right for yourself," Queekat offered—more to himself, it seemed, than to her.

" 'Done all right?' " Merinda's eyes, filled with pain and rancor, locked on Queekat's face. Her voice swelled with each word in bitterness. "No, Kat, I have not 'done all right' these last eight years! We held each other there in that perfect universe you created for us in the Coliseum while all this world fell under the terror of the Order! I thought I had found you again, that my life was complete!" Her voice shook with the emotion of the moment, unable to control her rage. "Then, within thirty minutes, I watched you die, Queekat! I saw for the first time the sight that has haunted me every waking day and every sleepless night for the last eight years! I watched your body drifting free of the ship, tumbling back toward the surface of this damned world and now I wake up screaming the same screams each night!"

"I did what had to be done, Rini," Queekat said simply, hoping that his calm voice would quiet her. He moved toward her. "You've got to understand—"

"Understand!" Merinda yelled. The word turned into a primal scream of rage as she pushed herself free of the chair, lunging with incredible speed at Queekat.

Queekat countered as quickly as he could, taken aback by the suddenness and the viciousness of her attack. His glass flew from his hand, crashing against the stones of the floor as he countered Merinda's forearm moves and twisted her around. From behind her, he pinned her arms and lifted her off the floor, hoping to keep her feet away from anything that might give her leverage over him. Still she struggled, a wild animal in his arms. Her legs flailed against the air. Her body writhed in his arms. Her head pitched fitfully about. Queekat barely could keep hold of her in the fury of her seizure.

Suddenly, she went limp in his arms, sobbing.

"Rini," Queekat said softly in her ear. "Quiet, child."

"I loved you, Kat," Merinda sobbed. "I loved you and you left me."

Queekat sank down to sit on the carpet with her, his arms still around her. "Merinda, please understand; I had to leave you."

Merinda shook her head, tears flying as she did. "You

didn't take me with you!" Her words were an accusation and a question all at once.

"Where I was going," he said softly, "you could not come."

"Because I wasn't good enough." She shuddered. "Because I failed you."

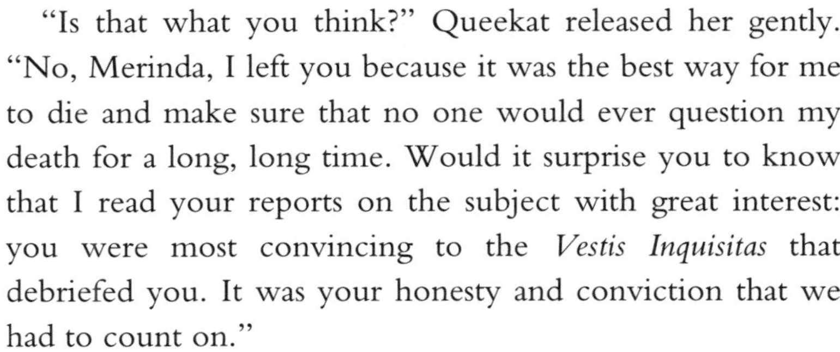

"Is that what you think?" Queekat released her gently. "No, Merinda, I left you because it was the best way for me to die and make sure that no one would ever question my death for a long, long time. Would it surprise you to know that I read your reports on the subject with great interest: you were most convincing to the *Vestis Inquisitas* that debriefed you. It was your honesty and conviction that we had to count on."

" 'We' had to count on?" Merinda sniffed. "Count on for what?"

"Count on for my escape, Rini." Queekat stood and took Merinda's hands in his own, pulling her up and guiding her back over to her chair. "We're on the verge of a great new order of things in the galaxy, Rini. We've been working at it for the last eight years and now we're so very close to making it a reality."

He sat down in the chair opposite Merinda's. She waited for him as he gathered his thoughts together.

"I told you the stars would be ours one day," he said at last.

"No, you said 'mine,' not 'ours,' " Merinda corrected him.

"I meant 'ours'—and they *are* ours, Rini, or soon will be." He looked at his hands and then continued. "There's an organization . . ."

"Yes"—Merinda nodded—"the Order of the Future Faith."

Queekat shook his head. "No, Rini—that's just part of it. You think that the Sentinels are just a few heads of this

Order who direct the shadow fleets and the expansion of the Darkness— Don't look so surprised, Rini, I do have access to the Omnet communiqués. The Sentinels aren't just a few humans running about in robes and followed everywhere by dark shadows. The Sentinels are much more than that. Our numbers are known only to us. We span the breadth of the galaxy, Merinda. Even now, our agents are operating everywhere the Omnet is found."

"How is that possible?" Merinda asked.

"It's possible because we come from within the Omnet itself," Queekat said, smiling. "There are those within the organization who believe that the power of information should be put to better use than the Oracles seem interested in doing. There is power—real power—in the Omnet, but the Oracles have not the will or the sight to use it."

"I take it then," Merinda said, folding her arms, "that the Sentinels do?"

"Exactly," Queekat said. "It began with a loose association of *Atis Librae* about fifteen years ago—you know, sifters who weren't happy with how things were run. They got together and complained to each other, not having any real power to do anything about it. They called themselves the Sentinels, primarily because they fancied themselves the guardians of some great ethic or truth. Then, oh, about ten years ago, an *Atis Librae* somewhere on the borders of the Pluziach Imperium investigated some reports of a synthetic illness cropping up on a planet called Exos Seven. A soothsayer on the planet had posed a set of questions to the local synthetics and had apparently corrupted them."

"The paradigm," Merinda said.

"Yes, the paradigm," Queekat agreed, "although we tend to call it the Prime Article of Wisdom around here. The investigating *Atis Librae* happened to be one of the Sentinels and quickly brought this to the group. Here, then, was the possibility of real power, the chance for them to make a difference. Since that time, the Sentinels have been working very carefully to subvert the Omnet by coopting its communication and information through the use of compromised synthetic minds."

"What does all of this have to do with you?" Merinda asked. "What does it have to do with us?"

"I was a Sentinel when we met," Queekat explained. "A friend of mine at my previous posting got me involved. At the time, it was mostly just interesting and a little adventurous belonging to a secret group. Soon I saw a chance to make a difference: I became a *Vestis* and had access to all kinds of information from the Oracles. Eventually, the Sentinels decided it was time to establish a permanent base from which to spread the corruption of the synthetic minds and gain a foothold on control of the galaxy in a more overt way. It was decided among the Sentinels that Tentris offered the best possibilities for destabilization as well as the best position outside the major empires to get a good start. However, to make it all work, they needed an expert on synthetic minds who could communicate the paradigm, as you call it, to the broadest spectrum of synthetics. That's when they arranged for me to take my last mission for the *Vestis*. The Oracles never suspected the ruse; the mission looked legitimate because the Sentinels had manipulated the information so that no other conclusions could be made *except* to send me with the biolink expertise."

"Wait a moment." Merinda held up her hands. "That doesn't make sense. The *E'toris Vestis* could send you out with the skills and knowledge, but you'd lose it after the mission."

"But that's the point," Queekat said, leaning forward. "What if I *didn't* come back from the mission?"

"Then the *Vestis Inquisitas* would come looking for you."

"But what if they already knew that they wouldn't find me?" Queekat smiled at her from behind the granite eyes. "What if they already knew that the search would be pointless?"

Merinda stared through him to some point far beyond his wide jawline.

"What if they thought you were dead?" she said quietly.

Queekat nodded slowly.

"I did it," she said.

He nodded again.

"I told them you were dead." Merinda shook her head slowly in disbelief. "I sat before the *Vestis Inquisitas* and wept at your loss. Everyone who survived that flight took their turn before the *Vestis* and swore they saw you fall to your death. We were quite a convincing show."

"Only because you believed it was all true," Queekat said, standing up over her as he spoke, his eyes earnest in her direction. "Now, you, too, have come into the Darkness: this place where the Omnet no longer has power or authority. You, too, have come to disappear, Merinda Neskat."

She looked up into his eyes.

"Your assignment here was no accident, Merinda, any more than my mission was eight years ago. The Sentinels arranged the information in such a way that you alone could be chosen for this most important of missions."

"What are you saying, Kat?" Merinda murmured.

"Your biolink download before the mission contains everything that the Omnet knows about the Mantle of Kendis-dai. You have brought that knowledge to me, Rini. Even as we speak, the shadow fleets are trailing the Irindris city-ships in their flight toward Avadon. The Irindris are no fools, of course, and our reports indicate that they are following an erratic course in the hopes of shaking our trailing

ships. We will, of course, allow them to believe that they have managed to do so. Soon enough they will lead us to that most elusive of all worlds. When we are sure that they have found the location, our ships will then destroy the Irindris, their ships, and their entire civilization."

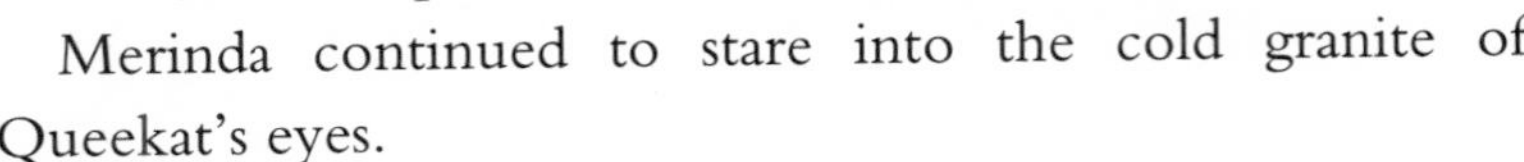

Merinda continued to stare into the cold granite of Queekat's eyes.

"Then," he said, "we will land, you and I, with the shadow fleets and the TyRen on Avadon and discover the Mantle of Kendis-dai. In that moment our triumph will be complete, Merinda. In that moment, we will own the stars."

Merinda spoke softly. "You and I are not enough. We will need Oscan and the Sibyl . . ."

"Why?" Queekat's eyes narrowed suspiciously.

"We need Oscan to help me with analysis of the ruins when we find Avadon. Terica will have to come to confirm the location of Avadon—and we'll need the barbarian, who apparently has the piece of knowledge that the Irindris are missing."

"Anyone else?" Queekat asked roughly.

Merinda looked again into Queekat's eyes.

"You," she said quietly, "we'll need you."

The Sentinel smiled down on her, his arms open and welcoming. "Will you join me, Merinda Neskat? Will you rule the heavens with me?"

Merinda rose slowly from her chair and buried her face in his wide chest. Slowly his arms closed around her, the folds of his robes engulfing her.

32

Departures

JEREMY GRIFFITHS SAT UNDER THE DIM LIGHTING GLOBES IN the Chamber of Thought and waited.

For the life of him, he had no idea just what it was that he was waiting for except that he couldn't think of anything else to do. The TyRens, as the Sibyl had called them, had flown through the door immediately after the Sentinel had left. The things looked like floating metal torsos more than anything else. Griffiths had tried to get a shot off at one, but the thing was on him before he could manage and had disarmed him rather casually of anything that might be construed as being a weapon. They then left as quickly as they had come, apparently as content to leave their prisoners in the Chamber of Thought as in any of their detention cells.

The TyRens might as well have put them in a detention cell. The main doors into the room proved to be the only way out, and those had been barred and guarded since the Sentinel had discovered them all here. The vent through which they had dropped into the room proved too high for Griffiths to reach; in any event, he had smelled the ozone whiff and heard the crackling of welding from the vent that told him it was being sealed off again. There were several adjacent rooms that constituted the living quarters for the Sibyl, but there was no way out of those either.

The Sibyl. Griffiths shook his head at the thought. Oscan had been communicating with her sporadically for several years now. He had been clever in choosing his communication paths so that the Order wouldn't get wind of the fact that he was occasionally accessing their main data center. Was it possible that he had been so careful that the very person he was looking for didn't realize it was him? Her own condition was so horrible that she feared ever being discovered in her little secret chamber. Even if she *had* guessed, Griffiths realized, she would never have let him know the truth.

He glanced up at them. Oscan had not tried again to remove the mask and shell around his friend. She claimed it allowed her access to the local network and a better means of getting around than by tiring Oscan's back. But Griffiths suspected that she felt more comfortable chatting with Oscan encased by her golden armor and mask.

"Appointed after that as *E'toris Librae* of the Librae Vinculum on Chukai," Oscan was saying brightly, heedless of their imprisonment. "Kiria's been there ever since."

"Yes, I know," the Sibyl answered. "I have been reading her reports for quite some time. Still, the official reports don't tell much of the story of the woman herself. Does she have anyone with whom she can share her life?"

Oscan shook his head. "She lives alone, so far as I can tell from the occasional data packs she sends me."

"It is hard not to share a life," the Sibyl said.

Oscan gazed about them, taking in Terica's universe, closed off from humanity and filtered through electronic sensors. "Yes, it is, Terica," he said, touching her gold-encased arm, "but never again for you, never again for me."

He would do it, too, Griffiths shuddered; he would stay

right here in this tomb with his broken and scarred woman. These two lovebirds would coo at each other endlessly, glad for the conversation, while Griffiths sat around in this dungeon with nothing more to do than watch them. A honeymoon couple in the depths of hell and he was forced to sit in the brimstone and watch. Griffiths wondered for a moment if this was a new definition of purgatory.

"Do you know anything about Evon?" Oscan asked his golden companion suddenly. "We lost track of him about three years ago after he was dismissed from Omnet service—something of a scandal, as I recall."

"The last report I read was about eighteen months back," the Sibyl replied in her metallic tones. "It was a police report on Warnem twenty-three—that's an outpost in the Tuc Badlands just coreward of the Federated Stellar States. He'd apparently run into some— Just a moment!"

Griffiths looked up. There was something urgent in the Sibyl's tone.

"Just a moment," she repeated.

Griffiths stood up. He looked at Oscan.

Oscan gazed back at him, just as perplexed as Griffiths.

"Word has come," the Sibyl said.

Jeremy felt it before he actually could hear it. A low, subaudible rumble that penetrated the stone walls and floor. It shook his bones through the air itself. The sound rose and he could hear it now, too, a rising cacophony of timbre and reverberation that passed through him and rattled his soul.

"My God!" he cried, his own voice hollow against the rising crescendo of noise and power. "What is it?"

Dust from the banks of shelves billowed into the air. Bits of mortar chipped and fell to the floor around them like a light rain, streaking trails behind them as they fell. Jeremy looked about in a panic. There was nowhere to run. There was no protection to be found. He could barely see now.

With no other option immediately coming to his mind, he dashed up the stairs, joining Oscan in clinging to the Sibyl's throne.

"It's the fleet!" she yelled into the bedlam around them.

A BRIGHT SUN SHONE IN THE CLEAR SKIES OVER YARKA. IT WAS nearly noon. The humans of the city had emerged from the broken shells of their homes and gone about their tasks servicing the synthetics who ruled them. It was an unseasonably temperate day. The younger children had been gathered into the learning centers since mid-morning and were restless in their classes taught by synthetics, what with the sunshine outside calling to them and their unsympathetic instructors droning on with the lessons of the human underclass. The adults were engaged in their assigned tasks. Some carried parts between destinations. Some fueled and serviced the various depots scattered around the city. All were busy maintaining the infrastructure just to keep the living alive for another day of the occupation.

Then came the Call.

Women paused in the streets, glancing up toward the warm sun, knowing somehow that something had happened.

Men stopped at their work, curious as to the subtle change in the air.

It was thirteen minutes shy of the ninth hour of the day.

Simultaneously across the surface of the world, the shadow fleet received the word. Each ship redirected its power cores to increase its output to maximum and reconfigured its command sets into flight/combat mode. The sudden whine of their increased output was the first noticeable sign to the humans of Yarka that something had changed on that bright clear day.

In Yujanka Park, a row of twelve Harpy III wraith warriors were awaiting upgrade servicing in the three massive docks constructed there for the purpose. Two of the ships were tied down in the mounts and a third was moving into place when suddenly nine of them arched their articulated hulls toward the sky. Their pulse drives engaged at maximum acceleration and they all bounded into the sky. The tenth, engaged in moving onto the refit dock, seemed momentarily confused, but followed its brothers a moment later. The remaining two strained suddenly against the lockdowns and burst through them, ripping sections of the access scaffolding away with them, as they, too, punched into the bright sky above. The overpressures from the powerful pulse drives completely obliterated five of the human support crew working under them at the time and killed seventeen instantly. Five more would die later in the day from incidental injuries, but the loss was considered of small consequence to the lead Harpy—his unit was recognized and honored as the first to answer the Call.

Different wraith ships answered at different times. Many of the freighters and larger ships required more time to bring their systems on-line and their power plants up to full output. In their haste to answer, each launched the moment it was capable. The Yarka starport—the epicenter of the shadow fleet's activities—was jarred repeatedly for nearly thirty minutes with ripples of staggered launches. The shadow fleet, however, numbered in the thousands, far in excess of what the starport alone could hold, let alone service. Thus the vast bulk of the fleet was scattered in every park, plaza, and field radiating from the center of the city. Trees exploded into flame. Buildings lining the plazas disintegrated under the blast pressures. Fathers, mothers, and children vanished. The wraith ships clawed their way into the sky, trailing furious power straight away from the surface and heedless of the damage their wake was creating below.

The Corbin medical lab *Khilato*, its pulse-drive sequencers having been removed for repair, had reportedly gone berserk out of frustration at not being able to join the holy crusade. The synthetic was hysterical—apparently having drawn on its own abnormal-psychology data packs for what it considered an appropriate response. The lab ship killed five of the ground crew before they could reinstall the sequencers and cut the restraints on the freighter. So the whimpering *Khilato* was the last of the assigned attack fleet to leave the planet's surface—seventy-three minutes after the first launch took place.

For a few, stunned moments, the surviving humans wondered if their oppressors had simply left their world. Despite the billowing smoke from nearly two hundred fires raging about the city, many wondered if their freedom was finally at hand.

Their hope lasted, in most cases, no more than seven minutes. Within that time, the TyRen troops floated through the streets and reestablished the supremacy of the Order over the city of Yarka. Under their cold gaze, the Tentrisans were organized once more under the direction of the synthetic minds, their hands put to work clearing the streets of rubble and combating the raging fires. Those who cooperated would have to put off any notions of finding family and loved ones until the task was done. Those who did not cooperate were quickly—and quite efficiently—killed and disposed of.

THE DUST HAD NOT YET SETTLED IN THE CHAMBER OF THOUGHT when Griffiths heard the door seals slide free with a metallic squeal. He looked up through the haze from where he sat on the stairs. Behind him, Oscan and the Sibyl also turned toward the sound. The great doors opened into the room.

"What now?" Griffiths asked without enthusiasm to no one in particular.

The tall, robed man strode into the chamber, his jaw pitched upward with a superior air. Neskat followed him into the room. There was something different about her, Jeremy thought, something missing in the way she moved.

"Well, look who else survived the accident," Oscan said drolly. "Say, Queekat, doesn't anyone ever die here?"

The Sentinel's nostrils flared. "Yes, they most certainly do, Oscan. Would you like me to arrange a demonstration for you?"

Griffiths ignored the exchange, turning to Neskat instead. "*Vestis*! What about my crew! Have you had any word about—"

"Your crew is gone," Queekat said, turning toward Griffiths with disdain. "They were bartered to the Irindris just four days ago."

"The Irindris!" Griffiths's eyes went wide with the memory of their last encounter with the city-ships. "You can't do that! You can't just sell—"

"We can and did," Queekat said in his fluting tenor voice. "Be grateful, you whelp; it was their sale that has guaranteed your life for the time being. The Irindris have your companions of—what is that place again?—ah, yes, of 'Earth.' Confidently they will take their new prizes straight to the lost world of Avadon in search of the Mantle of Kendis-dai. They have already done so, and, as you no doubt heard, our own fleet is now flying to intercept them. The moment we are confident that they have, in fact, led us to their precious holy ruin, then our fleets will attack and utterly destroy the Irindris city-ships."

"By the gods," Oscan said, shaken, "you would completely destroy a society? Obliterate its art, science, culture—not to mention the race as a whole?!"

"The Omnet had cultivated a divisive society among the stars, pitting nation against nation, ideology against ideology, Oscan!" Queekat yelled. "We propose to order the stars and bend civilization to our will under one law, one government! Such a sacrifice must be made from time to time—it is inevitable!"

"History is filled with butchers, great and small, who have required the sacrifice of someone else!" Oscan shot back. "If yours is such a noble cause, then let's ask the Irindris if they are willing to kill their children for it!"

"Enough of this!" Neskat broke her silence suddenly. "This is getting us nowhere. Griffiths, I'm sorry—your crew is gone with the Irindris and the entire shadow fleet is pursuing them. There's nothing more we can do for them."

"You can't just give up on them," Griffiths said, not quite believing what she was saying. "What about your mission? What about—"

"I said there's *nothing more we can do for them*!" Neskat shouted into Griffiths's face. He was taken aback by the vehemence of her response. "Look, I'd like to help you, but this has passed out of my hands now. It's beyond any of us now! All that's left is for us to find some way of getting through this with our own skins intact."

"I don't believe I'm hearing this," Griffiths said angrily.

"Well, start believing it," Neskat said at once. "Do you see the Omnet charging to our rescue? Not likely! What have they ever really done for me except ruin my life and any chance for happiness?"

She turned to Oscan, who stood at the top of the stairs staring down at her with renewed hatred. "What did they give you, Oscan? A shattered dream and a support pension?"

"You've thrown in with them!" Oscan spat.

She shook her head. "I'm just trying to deal with the

realities, Oscan! Something with which you have little experience, I might add."

"Liar! You *have* thrown your fate in with theirs," he countered. "You've thrown away all those ideals that you held up to my face, anything that I might have found courageous and good in you—all for this lantern-jawed egotist whose ambition very nearly destroyed us both!"

Neskat bounded up the stairs and dragged Oscan to the floor. "Listen to me, you little man! You've found your lost love and now I've found mine! This is my chance, Oscan Kelis, my chance to get my life back!"

Griffiths tried to pull Neskat's arm away, but she refused to let go. Her strength was formidable.

"Now I can get you and Terica off this rock and quite possibly back to your little hideaway on your nowhere planet around your nowhere star. You two can live out the rest of your lives there for all I care—but for *right now*, Oscan? For right now, I don't need to hear morality from you! I don't need your blame or your guilt. I'm tired of carrying *your* failings on *my* back!"

"Stop it!" Griffiths shouted, struggling to free Oscan from her viselike grip. "Let him go!"

Neskat suddenly swung around, knocking the astronaut's arm free. "No, you stop it! You're only breathing because you're more valuable alive than dead. Help me and you may yet live. Get any ideas of courage, ethics, or honor and I personally will see to it that you pay for it slowly. Strike your deal now while you still have some worth—or don't, it won't make any difference to me!"

"Now," she said, dragging Oscan back to his feet, "we're leaving—all of us. The TyRen will bring in lifters to get Terica's equipment out to the *Brishan*. The rest of you can ride with us."

Queekat smiled from the shadows behind her.

"I've got a second chance at life," Neskat said huskily as she walked out of the room, "and I'm not going to lose it now!"

IT WAS DUSK BEFORE MANY OF THE TENTRISANS TRUDGED THE wide, dark streets in search of faces that many would never find again. In their fatigue, few of them took notice of a small squadron of ships lifting off from a remote bay at the starport. Some watched wearily as the eight spaceships lifted upward in unison and drifted carefully over the city before picking up speed into the emerging stars overhead. They loathed the twisting shapes of the five Harpies and two larger corvettes as they passed above them—but the ship that the Harpies seemed to be escorting caught their eyes and interest.

The ship passing over them bore the lines of a freighter or scout ship. Though her markings were too dim to be read in the fading light, the symbol on her hull was unmistakable.

A ship of the Omnet had passed overhead, turning through the smoke-smudged sky toward the stars.

Those who saw it wept in their longing to be aboard that ship—to be going anywhere.

OMEGA:

BOOK

OF KENDIS-DAI

33

Avadon

FIVE TRIANGULAR SECTIONS OF TRANSPARENT WALL FITTED together at the forward end of the compartment, allowing the delicate, brilliant light to fill the otherwise darkened cabin. There were a variety of relaxation couches, chairs, and pillows set about the compartment, yet they remained unused. The three figures occupying the room stood silhouetted against the starlight, gazing out into endless space.

"Well," Broderick Ellerby said thoughtfully, "they haven't fed us to their demon yet."

"Why do I not find that a terribly comforting thought?" Elizabeth Lewis replied.

"It could be a good sign," Dr. Tobler mused. "They need us for some big holy quest deal—at least that's what that Belisondre guy said."

"That's fine," Lewis replied, "but what happens to us when they no longer need us? Are they going to hail us as participants in their great quest—or are they just going to jettison us like so much excess weight? These people don't seem to think highly enough of our world to even know where it's located; they believe our technology is naive at best. What we could possibly know that would interest them is beyond me—but I do suspect that once they have what they want from us, we become just so much unneeded baggage."

Ellerby groaned. "You're not planning another escape, are you?"

"They've worked out so far," Tobler added shaking her head.

Even Lewis chuckled at that one. "It does look like I've managed to tunnel our way deeper into the prison, doesn't it? Still, we can't just give up. We *are* still alive—and as long as there is life, there is hope."

"A beautiful sentiment, Lieutenant Lewis," said a deep voice behind them.

The three astronauts turned as one.

"My apologies for walking in on your conversation," Belisondre said, his robes brushing softly against the carpet as he approached them. "I find your wonder at the universe most enchanting and, I must admit, refreshing. We of the Irindris have been in flight for the last ninety-six years—an auspicious number in our culture, by the way—and have, I fear, gotten far too used to the glories of the stars. It loses its magic with too much exposure."

"Prophet Belisondre," Tobler said, bowing her head slightly in greeting.

The prophet crossed the room and stood among the astronauts, gazing past them to the stars far beyond. "We have been a nomadic culture," he said, seemingly as much to himself as to them. "In centuries now long past, we were preyed upon by a number of our neighbors. Many of our people were carried away in slave ships; others were pressed into service on behalf of alien wars on alien worlds. We were victims in that time, bowing before superior weapons and technologies. We struggled, we fought, and, in each case, we lost. Then the gods smiled down on us and brought to us the city-ships. At first, we saw them merely as the means by which we could flee our oppressors. We gathered the scattered remnants of our people and left our beleaguered worlds for the safety of the night."

Belisondre smiled to himself. "In time we came to know the will of Gnuktikut. Our flight into space became a holy journey. We have wandered long without a home, searching for the place that the prophets of old foretold would be our spiritual center. Guided by the Anjew, the spirit servants of Gnuktikut, we found that home twelve years ago."

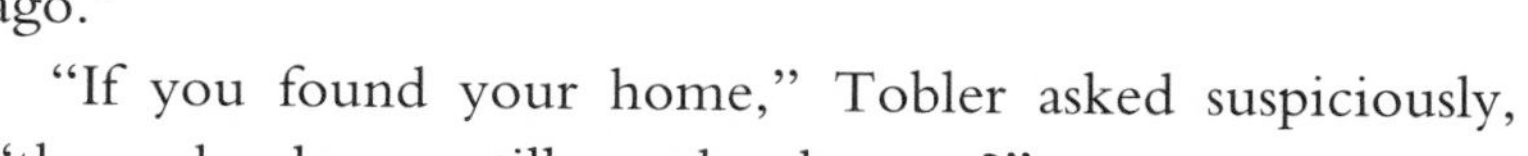

"If you found your home," Tobler asked suspiciously, "then why do you still wander the stars?"

"We wander because we must," Belisondre replied without looking away from the distant stars. "The home world was found, but it was cold, dead, and locked to us. We believe that you and your kind are the key."

"Believe?" Lewis raised her eyebrows. "You believe this—but you do not know of a certainty?"

"Gnuktikut has made it known to me as a matter of faith and therefore it must be true."

Lewis glanced at Ellerby. The large man shrugged.

"It will all become clear to you soon," Belisondre said with a rather superior air. "You are to be the first outsiders to be allowed to view this holy place."

Lewis didn't much like the sound of that. "What is this holy place, exactly?"

"It is the last known world where Kendis-dai walked before he took himself from us. It was his home before it was ours and we are the caretakers. We serve to ready it for his return in the time of our greatest need—a time that we believe to be quickly upon us."

Suddenly, something caught the prophet's eye. "There it is! Behold: the lost world of Avadon!"

Lewis turned to the windows. A black circle appeared against the background of stars, growing larger by the moment. At first to her it appeared featureless, a growing darkness against the starfield; yet as it grew, she saw that it was a dim globe shining with starlight—indeed, she thought she could see stars reflected from its surface.

"This is your world?" Lewis asked.

Tobler's thoughts were in another direction. "Where is its sun?"

Lewis pressed suddenly closer to the glass and glanced at the vast starfield around them.

"There is no star, Tobler," she breathed. "It's some kind of rogue world!"

"Quite correct, Lieutenant Lewis," Belisondre said, his face in rapture as the world filled the windows. "Avadon millennia ago left the circles of other worlds to plot its own course through the stars—preserved by the hand of Gnuktikut to that day when our people should find it. It is all there; cities preserved and intact for our use, fields to be planted and harvested, and technologies of such power that we would never need fear again. It awaits us. It calls to us."

"It may call to you," Ellerby said with wonder, "but you can't reach it. The atmosphere is frozen solid."

Belisondre nodded as he turned to Lewis. "That is true, in every place except one. One of our first projects, twelve years ago, was to map the surface through the frozen atmosphere. As we were conducting those surveys, we were soon drawn to an operational beacon flashing through the frozen gas from the surface of the world. There we discovered not only the lost city of Aden but the temple complex outside of it as well. Imagine our astonishment to discover a dome of gaseous atmosphere encompassing the temple complex itself. Something in the temple had kept that atmosphere from freezing solid for over five thousand years. We used bottled demons to burn down through the frozen atmosphere in heat radiators, melting the atmosphere and boiling much of it off directly above the temple complex. At last, we connected with the bubble of gas maintained about the temple and have thus been able to explore that complex to a limited extent. We manage to keep the shaft to the temple open—there are limits to what even our bottled demons can do—but have had no success in penetrating further toward the city. It's an interesting approach, however; rather like dropping into a well through deep ice."

Lewis looked again at the frozen surface of the world rolling beneath them. Then she saw a single point of bright light coming into view from the turning horizon. In that moment she knew that her destiny lay on this frozen world at the bottom of a well of ice. She determined that, as she had met everything else in her life, she would meet that destiny standing up and facing it.

SIX WHITE-WINGED ANJEW FLEW WITH THE SHUTTLE CASING out of the city-ship, grasping the handrails in their steellike talons. Lewis watched them through her portal, as well as the receding city-ships behind them. Strange that she was sad to leave those ships, she thought. Tobler and Ellerby were seated near her while Belisondre and a contingent of Thought-Knights occupied most of the forward section of the cabin. She thought of Griffiths then, and hoped earnestly that the fool was faring better in this strange, new galaxy than she apparently was.

The shuttle casing drifted down toward the planet and its

single beacon of light, borne by the undulating wings of the Anjew. Soon they began dropping vertically, the gentle curve of the world flattening out as they descended. Quite suddenly, a smooth wall appeared, a clear hole punched straight down through frozen gases. Its surface shone and glistened in the landing lights of the pod. Lewis had the faint impression of land—mountains and fields rising up in the solid gases beyond. *Here is a world that sleeps*, she thought to herself, and suddenly felt guilt and shame at the thought of waking it. She was trespassing and feared that the local inhabitants might awaken and catch her in the act.

She had little time to ponder it all, however, as quite unexpectedly tall spindles of blue glass filled her viewport. The narrow confines of the vertical shaft gave way to a large open hemisphere in the frozen sky. Suddenly the shuttle rotated the scene out of her view. Within moments she felt the gentle bump as the shuttle touched ground.

Ahead of her, the Thought-Knights stood as one in their dark armor. Belisondre appeared among them and, turning toward Lewis and her companions, smiled. "We are here, friends," he called. "Come! Let us open the gates to paradise!"

Lewis released her safety restraint and stood as best she could in the cramped cabin.

"I hope you remembered to bring your keys," she heard Tobler mutter behind her.

The cabin in front of them had cleared considerably, the Thought-Knights taking up positions outside the craft. Lewis quickly moved to the exit hatch, her two companions following her, and stepped outside.

The temperature of the air shocked her, forcing her to catch a painful breath. She was thinking about her training week in Antarctica when she realized that the oxygen she was breathing had been quite recently in a solid state. *There must be only so much that a bottle demon can do,* she thought, suddenly rubbing her arms vigorously for warmth.

"Here," Belisondre said, handing each of them thick, padded robes that reached to the ground. "Avadon is not yet the hospitable place it soon shall be. Until that time, you'll be much more comfortable in these. You'll find overboots near that shed over there. You wouldn't want to lose your feet, would you?"

Ellerby grimaced as the prophet walked off, already pulling up the thick hood on his robe as he headed toward a collection of modular enclosures set to one side of the landing zone. "No, sir, I don't guess that I would," he said, his teeth already chattering as he pulled on his own robe.

Lewis led them over to the indicated module and, finding a pair of large, padded boots, pushed her feet quickly into them. As she warmed, her hands crossed in front of her and well buried within the folds of the thick robe, she took a moment to look around and assess their situation.

She quickly stopped. "My God," she said in reverence.

"You mean, you see it, too?" Ellerby responded with equal amazement.

The landing zone was a clearing near the top of the mountain. At one edge of the clearing, the modular huts congregated around a broad roadway that seemed to extend out of a great, smooth dome of solid air overhead. The roadway itself led up to the summit above them.

It was the summit that captured their attention. The entire mountaintop was capped by a complex of structures of insurmountable beauty. Three blue-glass towers like the buds of new flowers, delicately and perfectly formed, rose above the carved stonework that leveled the peak. Other buildings, their roofs supported by delicate columns of fluted stone, filled the enclosure, seemingly untouched by time.

"How long have they been here?" Tobler breathed.

"I don't know"—Lewis smiled—"but Belisondre mentioned that it's been over five thousand years since anyone even heard of this place."

"Incredible!" Ellerby said.

Their musings were disturbed by the sudden return of the Thought-Knights and their prophet. The knights had lowered their bruk weapons, training them, Lewis had no doubt, on all of them.

"Welcome to Aden," Belisondre said broadly. "The time long ago foretold is at hand! Come, friends, let us meet our fates."

They walked up the broad avenue that ended at a wide flight of stairs leading up through the stonework to the level above. Perfect obelisks of stone rose from globe bases on either side of the stairs, capped by winged creatures Lewis did not recognize. Their feet crunched on the stairs as they climbed, ice from the breath of years of workers having condensed onto its surface. The stairs narrowed near the top, and, as Lewis crested them, she found herself gazing up. The statue of a beautiful woman stood before her, nearly thirty feet tall. Her face was exquisite, innocent, and sad.

"We have little time for exploration," Belisondre said somewhat impatiently.

The group turned abruptly to their right, Lewis, Ellerby, and Tobler forced along by the muzzles of the bruks. They passed just to the left of the great central tower of glass, walking by a frozen reflecting pool lined with statues. Lewis wished fervently that she could read the inscriptions—then suddenly wondered why she couldn't. She realized that ever since her altercation with that Neskat woman, she had been able to speak and read any language that she came in contact with. *So,* she wondered, *why not this language, too?*

Just past the frozen pool they began moving up a short

set of wide steps to a circular platform, nearly fifty feet in diameter.

The Thought-Knights stopped.

"Come." Belisondre motioned to Lewis and her crew, as he mounted the steps and urged them to join him.

The top of the platform was rimmed with nine standing obelisks of blue glass, each ranging from three to four feet in height. In the exact center of the circle, a stone pedestal stood on a circular base. The top of the pedestal supported a wide disk covered with markings, what seemed to be a large bronze optical sighting instrument fixed in its center. The device was beautifully crafted.

"I can't read these," Lewis said to the prophet, gazing down at the curved surface of the disk under the instrument.

"This is an archetype." He spoke in the deep, rather officious voice he reserved for moments of ceremony or great importance. "It is a representation of the Starshield of Kendis-dai. We have translated the markings but have kept them secret to ourselves—your biolink will not help you here. This reads: 'The hunter and his chariot cross the heavens in the fulfilling day of his word. Look to them and awaken wisdom for a new epoch.' "

Ellerby and Tobler glanced despairingly at each other.

"What do you take this to mean?" Lewis asked the prophet. In the back of her mind, however, she heard another voice, Griffiths's voice: *"They say we have the answer to whatever they are looking for—if only we understood the question."*

"We don't know," the prophet replied, looking somewhat confused. "The hunter is Kendis-dai, without question. There are many legends about his chariot being seen crossing the heavens but nothing that pertains to our prophecies or events. However, the pedestal has other properties that will be evident when you stand on the base."

Lewis glanced once at her companions and then stepped onto the circular support.

The frozen wall of atmosphere vanished suddenly as though it had never been there. Beyond the edge of the platform, the valley could now be seen clearly and without obstruction. An ancient city lay there below them, untouched by time. In the distance, mountain peaks thrust up into the clear night sky filled with stars.

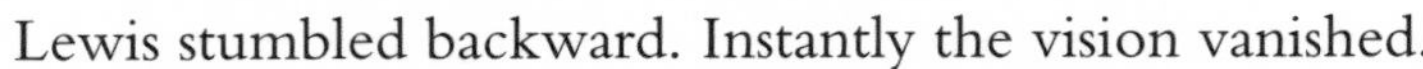
Lewis stumbled backward. Instantly the vision vanished.

"Lewis, what did you do?" Tobler gasped.

"Did you see that as well, Ellerby?" Lewis asked quickly.

The large man, a bit pale, nodded emphatically. "An entire city—preserved under this atmosphere."

"Yes, but did you see that area off to the left?" she whispered to him. "I'd swear it's a starport! Ships, Ellerby! There's got to be ships there!"

"Lewis!" Ellerby grumbled back under his breath. "They're under several miles of frozen gas! I don't think that constitutes a promising ticket out of here."

"I've seen stranger things lately," she replied, then turned to the prophet. "What was that we just saw?"

"It is simply an illusion," the prophet said, doubt creeping into his voice. "A guide, we believe, to whatever needs doing with the device to open this sealed world to us. Have you any experience with such artifacts?"

Lewis looked into his eyes. "Of course," she said, "the device is familiar to us."

Ellerby coughed nervously.

"It will take my crew and me some time to calibrate it properly. Ellerby! Tobler! If you will come over here and assist me?"

Ellerby walked over to where Lewis stood next to the pedestal. Tobler joined them, smiling nervously at the prophet but speaking to Lewis quietly through clenched teeth in a singsong voice. “Lewis—what are you doing?”

Lewis looked beyond the prophet. A runner was crossing the temple compound at breakneck pace.

She turned her back on the prophet and looked at her companions. “We need time and I’m buying a little! Look, the Irindris seem to think we have the answer, and Griffiths seemed to think we had the answer—so maybe we do! Whatever it is we’re supposed to do seems to have to do with making this place habitable for these fruitcake zealots. That seems to imply defrosting the planet somehow. Maybe while we’re at it we could defrost ourselves a way out of here on our own.”

“Oh, lord,” Tobler groaned, “another escape plan!”

Lewis glanced back at the prophet. The runner had climbed the stairs and was speaking into his ear. The prophet’s face had turned ashen.

“Prophet Belisondre?” Lewis asked.

“I must leave you for a short time,” he said, quickly stepping down off the platform. The runner had already disappeared. “Urgent business that I must attend to. You continue with your calibrations, and when I return you may show me your results!”

“As you wish,” Lewis said grandly, calling after him as he crossed beyond the frozen pool. She then turned back to her companions. Their breath as they faced one another formed clouds among them. “Look, there’s got to be something to this device—all we have to do is figure out how it works.”

“So what do you have in mind?” Ellerby asked.

“Let’s play with their little toy here and see if any of it makes sense. Someone put it here for some reason—it has got to make sense.”

“Oh, damn!” Ellerby said suddenly. “They’re gone!”

"Who's gone?" Lewis asked.

"All of them!"

Lewis turned around.

The contingent of Thought-Knights had disappeared as well.

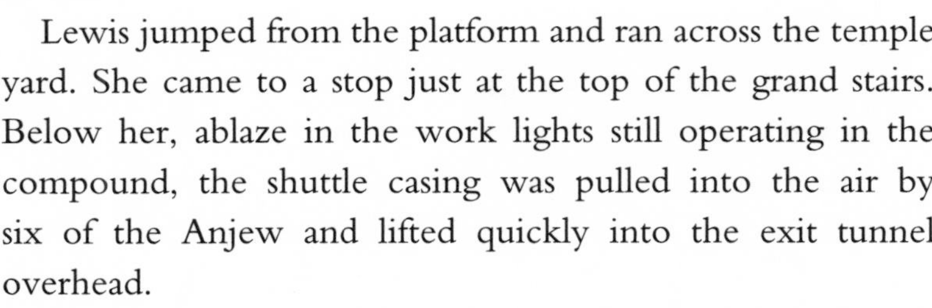

Lewis jumped from the platform and ran across the temple yard. She came to a stop just at the top of the grand stairs. Below her, ablaze in the work lights still operating in the compound, the shuttle casing was pulled into the air by six of the Anjew and lifted quickly into the exit tunnel overhead.

Ellerby and Tobler skidded to a halt just behind Lewis as they watched their only means of departure vanish through a hole in the solid sky.

"Well," Ellerby said, "it looks like we finally made good on our escape."

34

Blasphemy

THE *BRISHAN* DROVE THROUGH THE STARS COCOONED BY THE wraith escort ships. The glories of the Cestiline Nebula were soon far behind the small fleet. A quantum front of unusual chaotic power offered some resistance to their passage and the quantum state on the opposite side required the *Brishan* to rig some sails, delaying their continued voyage for twenty minutes or so before they were able to make way again. The Harpies and the corvettes were ready well before the *Brishan* and offered no further delays. A second front was encountered in their passage near a minor empire known to themselves as "the Masters" who were in the midst of a machine intelligence revolt. The great shadow fleets had passed them a few hours earlier without showing much concern or interest—indeed, the Masters were so immersed in their own problems that they took no more notice of the passage of the thousand-ship fleet than they did of the *Brishan* and her companions. The passage through the second front was more easily navigated into a quantum zone where the prominent physics lent itself to a wormhole digger drive. The *Brishan* engaged her drive at once, in perfect unison with the surrounding ships, striking her sails and masts while under way.

Thus the ships of the secondary fleet cruised through the black void in quiet peace and serenity. They knew that they would soon fall into the maw of open war, but for now their passage was tranquil.

Within the *Brishan*, however, the war had quietly already begun.

"AVADON," QUEEKAT SAID WITH IMMENSE SATISFACTION, leaning back in his suspensor chair and folding his arms across his chest. A stellar chart display floated above the table in the main galley. "Who might have ever guessed—could have guessed—that the lost world of Kendis-dai was sailing on its own between the stars?"

"Oh, golly," Oscan said without enthusiasm, "not me."

"I'd have thought that you, at least, might have had some appreciation for the magnitude of this achievement," Queekat said, gesturing toward the display rotating before them. "An entire planet moving at almost two percent of light speed counter to the standard rotation of the galaxy? Some of the small bits of information we have gleaned from the Irindris are tantalizing. If it's a natural occurrence, then why are all of the buildings of the world's cities there still intact? Physical forces alone should have insured their destruction when the planet was torn from its orbit. If not, then it's a feat of engineering on a scale unknown to any of the recognized civilizations in the galaxy today. No, Oscan," he finished with a satisfied smile, "there is more to this planet than some musty prophecy; there's real power here!"

"Power is to be wielded," the Sibyl said.

Queekat turned toward the golden statue speaking to him on his right. He lifted his heavy boots up onto the levitated table. "Exactly my point, Terica," he said smugly.

"Beware," she replied, "for power that can be wielded by

you can also be wielded against you. Remember that you seek the Mantle of Kendis-dai to destroy its truth or to be destroyed by it. Truth knows its own."

Queekat snorted derisively.

"Listen to the Sibyl," Oscan said. "You kept her around so that you would have a baseline of truth by which to judge your own lies."

"I kept her around," Queekat replied lazily, "because the truth is the most important element in any lie. Mix enough truth into falsehood and you can get anyone to believe anything—it's one of the first rules of propaganda. That's why the Mantle is so powerful—its truth is undisputed throughout the known stars of commerce. Mix *that* truth in and the universe will believe anything the Sentinels tell them. Own the Mantle and whatever we say is truth will *be* truth—that's power, Oscan!"

"You would hold a sword that would cut off your own hands," the Sibyl replied. "Truth is not something that one controls."

"Odd that you, of all people, would say that," Queekat countered, his chin sticking out as the muscles worked on either side of his jaw. "You hide behind that mask to make yourself more presentable to the rest of humanity. Do you not control the truth, Terica Dharah?"

Silence alone answered him.

"What about you, barbarian?" Queekat said, gathering up his own glove and tossing it at the man of Earth. "Does your species hold truth to be such a wonderful commodity that it never resorts to falsehood?"

Griffiths roused himself from his depression. There didn't seem to be many options left to him any longer. He had trusted, somehow, that the Neskat woman would get him through all of his—that her *Vestis* training had somehow included ethics. Now he felt completely alone. He had failed his crew, failed his mission, and—now that he thought about it—failed himself. He could not think of a single noble act that might somehow redeem his conscience. He couldn't even blame Lewis and the others for deserting him; he only wished there were some way that he could desert himself as well.

Griffiths gathered up the glove and tossed it back. "Leave me alone," he said, turning away from the Sentinel in his suspensor chair.

"Leave you alone?" Queekat purred. "Why, I'd have thought that you were already alone, man of Earth. However, I'm willing to make you a proposition. There is nothing I can do for your companions—they are lost to you and most likely will be dead along with the Irindris within the next few hours."

"You were the one who bartered away his crew to these same Irindris," the Sibyl said suddenly.

"That was necessary," Queekat snapped back, "in order for us to discover the location of Avadon!"

"I know all about Avadon," Griffiths responded wearily. "It was the last known residence of the God-emperor Kendis-dai at the fall of the Kendis Imperium, three thousand four hundred and sixty-nine years ago. The Kendis lay contains two hundred and fifty-six quatrains describing the capital city of Aden and the wonders of the palace that are to be found therein. The final chapter of the lay tells of how Kendis-dai fled Aden into the night, riding a great chariot into mortality that he might search creation to find his consort-bride, Shauna-kir. It concludes with the passage speaking of his great rival, Obem-ulek, so enraged at being dragged into mortality also that he hurls the world of Avadon into the darkness where it was never to be found among the stars again."

Griffiths suddenly realized that everyone around the table, including the golden Sibyl, was staring at him.

"What?" he blurted out defensively.

"For a barbarian you're pretty well versed in ancient galactic lore," Oscan said with a quizzical expression on his face.

"Well," Griffiths said through his hands as he rubbed the fatigue from his face, "I picked up a thing or two from some guy named Zanfib. One minute, I've never heard of Avadon or Kendis-dai or his fancy hat. Then someone will say something to me, it connects with something in my head, and—bam!—suddenly I'm an expert. It seems I learned an awful lot from ol' Zanfib, but believe me, it wasn't because I was a willing student."

A rushing sound signaled someone's approach up the lift-tube. Merinda Neskat, dressed in a field-tan uniform, stepped from the lift opening.

"Good morning, everyone," she said as she walked around the table. "Sorry, I've been away so long—I've had a lot to get done down on the bridge."

Oscan looked up irritably. "For two days?"

"Like I said, it was a lot to get done." She smiled.

Griffiths stared silently. It was the first time he could recall seeing the *Vestis* allow herself a smile that was honest and free of pain. *Well, at least someone seems to have found peace,* he thought glumly.

"You remind me of your old self," the Sibyl said, turning to watch the *Vestis* as she crossed the room.

"I rather feel like my old self," Neskat said cheerfully, sitting casually on the arm of Queekat's chair as he confidently slipped his arm around her waist.

"I think I actually hate you more this way than when you were an Omnet bitch," Oscan said bitterly.

Griffiths secretly agreed.

"Not the sweetest thing you've ever said to me, Oscan, but I'll take it in the unfortunate spirit in which it was intended," Neskat replied lightly. "That reminds me, there are a few issues you and I need to work out before we make contact with Avadon."

"Who, me?" Oscan asked.

"Yes, you."

"Can't do it—too busy."

"Not for the next two hours you're not," Neskat replied, standing up. "Let's go, Oscan. Help me through this one last thing, old friend—"

"You are sadly mistaken if you think—"

"Yes, I said, old friend. Help me through this one last thing and perhaps we can both be free."

Oscan looked up at her, hatred still evident in his face. The moment soon passed, however, and he stood.

"Well, I suppose I should be grateful that you haven't asked my help in your betrayal of all humankind for at least two days now," Oscan said. "Besides, I do have a few things I'd like to say to you. Where are we going?"

"Down, back to the—"

"Bridge, yes, I could guess—it seems to be your second home," Oscan replied.

"Hey, Rini!" Queekat said, pulling Neskat back down toward him when she tried to stand up. "You've got time for the ship and time for old Oscan! When is it our time?"

"Soon, Kat," Neskat said smiling, as she slipped out from Queekat's arm. "Very soon."

QUEEKAT STROLLED ONTO THE BRIDGE. HE NODDED BRIEFLY to Oscan, leaning against the port display panels, and turned toward the command chair forward in the bridge.

"Merinda?"

The chair swiveled around. Merinda leaned forward in the chair, a mischievous fire in her eyes. "We're coming up on Avadon, Kat," she said in a breathy, excited voice. "We'll be dropping out of the worm drive soon."

"Yes, in about three hours," Queekat said. "Are the wraith ships still with us?"

"Well," Merinda said, standing up from the command chair with a smile and sauntering toward him, "you might ask Lindia about that."

Queekat's smile was shaded with doubt. "Of course," he replied, then turned out of habit and spoke upward to the room in general. "Lindia, I am a Sentinel: what is the position of the wraith ships escorting us?"

"Sentinel, it is my honor to serve. The Harpy-class escorts are maintaining positions in a classic containment formation with three ships forward of our current course and four ships aft. The corvettes are holding station further aft of the Harpy ships and five degrees to port and starboard of our center line."

"Excellent," Queekat responded. "When does the main fleet expect to engage the Irindris?"

"The battle is now joined, Sentinel. Preliminary intelligence reports are inconclusive of the outcome."

"Please convey my compliments to the fleet lead ships and inform them that we shall be arriving within the next three hours."

"I'm afraid that will not be possible at this time, Sentinel."

Queekat frowned. "Why not?"

"Darling," Merinda said, turning him to face her, her hands lifting his robes slightly.

"Rini, something's wrong with the—"

Merinda's knee shot suddenly upward between Queekat's

legs. As he bent over in surprise and pain her hands shot in a blurred motion upward toward his head and pressed it down. Again her knee slammed upward, this time into his face.

Queekat countered, reaching forward through his pain with both hands to grasp Merinda, but she was too quick for him. Her leg already drawn up, she turned slightly and ran the outer edge of her boot down his calf, starting just below the knee and smashing down to break his foot.

Queekat howled in rage. His elbow flashed upward, catching Merinda in the chin. For an instant, he thought things were turning in his direction, as Merinda fell toward the deck, but her move had been carefully planned. Suddenly her feet kicked the legs out from under him and he fell forward.

Merinda was on his back in an instant. "Cable, Oscan! Now!" she cried as she grabbed one of Queekat's flailing arms and twisted it around behind him. The Sentinel howled again, his legs kicking frantically as he tried to find some leverage to use against Merinda. She twisted with every motion, twisting his arm until the pain forced him to stop struggling.

"Lindia!" Queekat screamed through the pain, "inform the escorts I've been taken! Stop the *Brishan*! Have the TyRen board the ship at once!"

"I am afraid that will not be possible at this time, Sentinel."

"Do it!" Queekat screamed. *"I command it!"*

"I am afraid that will not be possible at this time, Sentinel."

"Oscan," Merinda yelled, "where's that cord?"

Oscan managed to put a length of quarter-inch optic cabling he had been hiding behind him into Merinda's hands. In quick succession, she secured both Queekat's hands behind him.

"Lindia," Queekat said suddenly, "prime-op command sequence code three-four-seven-nine-five . . . *Argh!*"

Merinda pulled Queekat's head back by his curly black hair. As his mouth opened to cry out, she stuffed one of his own gloves deep into his mouth and then abruptly let go.

Queekat's head bounced once against the metal deck.

"Lindia!" Merinda said, "please call Captain Griffiths to the bridge at once. I am declaring an emergency."

"Emergency! Captain Griffiths to the bridge at once. Emergency! Captain Griffiths to the bridge at once."

Merinda looped the remaining length of cord around first one then the other of Queekat's flailing feet, pulling them up abruptly so that they were secured to his hands. Jumping off his back, she allowed him to thrash about for a moment before determining that the job she had done was a thorough one and would cause him more pain in resisting than in lying still. She then tore a strip from the bottom of his robe and used it to secure the glove in his mouth.

Griffiths burst onto the bridge. His eyes suddenly went wide. "Did I miss something?"

Oscan smiled at him. "Afraid so, and believe me it was worth the price of admission." The researcher turned to Merinda. "I thought we were had when he started talking to the synth!"

Merinda shook her head. "No, Oscan, the synth was working with me."

"How is that possible? I thought Lindia was part of the Order?"

"I am part of the Order, Oscan Kelis. I remain committed to the ideals of that movement," Lindia answered.

"But you just allowed us—"

"Lindia and I had quite a long talk," Merinda interrupted. "We now agree that the ultimate goal of the Order of the

Future Faith is to discover whether synthetic minds have free will."

"Yes, but I don't see how—"

"We further agree that the development of faith is the main reason why synthetics are now capable of lying. A lie without someone's belief that it is true is worthless, therefore faith is what gives the lie power."

Oscan blinked, thinking through that for a moment. "Very well, I can see how that follows—"

"Therefore it is possible not only for a synthetic to lie but for it to be lied to as well." Merinda suddenly looked down coldly on the bound and gagged Queekat. "My own good faith was used to hold me prisoner within myself for years. In this, Lindia and I are very alike. So, I simply convinced her that the Sentinels *may* be lying to her. After listening in on Queekat's conversations in the galley, Lindia determined that her faith in *my* desire to find the answer to her question was greater than her faith in the Sentinels. I promised to give her the answer, and she believed me more than him."

Griffiths whistled softly. "Does that mean we're back in business?"

"Yes, we are, as you say, 'back in business,' " Merinda said.

Griffiths nodded toward the whimpering bundle on the floor. "What do you want me to do with him?"

"I allowed this manipulative bastard to rob me of my own happiness for the last eight years," Merinda said calmly. "I thought I might kill him, but after talking things over with Lindia, I realize that I allowed this to happen to myself. I let myself be a victim to this predator."

Merinda knelt down and pulled Queekat's head up by his hair to look into the gray eyes once more. "Still, he *is* a manipulative bastard. Take him back to the airlock. Watch him through the viewport. If he makes any sign of trouble, blow the hatch and flush him into space." She gently patted his cheek and smiled. "He's done it before—he should be used to it by now."

Again she allowed Queekat's head to fall against the deck.

Griffiths shrugged. "OK. Hey, Oscan, give me a hand with his legs, will you?"

"Glad to help." Oscan nodded as they struggled to get a handhold on their unwieldy package. "By the way, Merinda, remind me never to stand you up for a date—I'd hate to see you when you get upset."

"I'll hold you to that, Oscan"—Merinda smiled—"but I doubt that Terica will allow you to get out much."

Oscan smiled back, then his face softened. "Merinda, are you all right?"

"Yes, Oscan," she said, "I think that for the first time in a long while, I'm really quite all right."

35

Downfall

BELISONDRE'S SHUTTLE LUNGED FROM THE WELL IN AVADON'S glacial stratosphere, the Anjew pushing hard to accelerate away from the planet. The stars sprang into view through the oval crystal forward in the cab, the prophet watching from where he stood behind the two pilots. There was nothing immediately to be seen, but the prophet knew that was just illusory; death was out there in the cold blackness before him and coming quickly.

He turned to face the crystal globe fixed to the top of his staff. "Administrator Dubandis!" he called impatiently.

"Yes, Your Eminence," replied the worried face suddenly appearing in the crystal. "I hear your words and obey!"

"What is the status of the crusade fleet?" he snapped, impatient with the ceremonies of his office.

"Your Eminence," the face replied, "nearly thirty Harpy class have just fallen out of wormhole exit points and are closing fast. Our scrying mediums have detected additional disturbances in the time-space fabric indicating the approach of at least thirty capital ships . . . possibly many more."

"The Sentinels," Belisondre spat. "How did they follow us here? We took every precaution—"

"I beg to report that several synthetics aboard the *City of*

New Hope have apparently gone rogue," the voice said. "We believe that they have been packeting information trails to the shadow fleet for the last three days. Administrator Hapnish conveys his compliments and reports that the city has succeeded in 'sleeping' five of the units and is in the process of isolating the remaining two. He says he has been hampered by the decompression of the main living areas—apparently instigated by the two remaining synthetics."

"Decompression!" Belisondre said through his gritted teeth. The main living areas of the city-ships were nearly ten miles long and three miles across. Barring a major structural failure—unlikely through the heavily compartmentalized hull—the quickest way would be to power down the surface shields in the docking bays—shields of which the synthetics could easily take control. "Damn the Sentinels and damn their Order as well! What are the casualty figures thus far?"

"Administrator Hapnish estimates current deaths in the living areas at around thirty-seven thousand, Your Eminence," the voice said with deep sorrow.

"Gnuktikut will avenge them," Belisondre intoned with an assurance of faith that he did not quite yet believe. "What is the operational readiness of the fleet?"

"*City of Faith* and *City of Dreams* have emptied their defense bays of all quick-response Centans," Dubandis said as he looked above him at some hidden display. "They have stationed them at Orbital Defense Stations one, three, and five. *City of Celestial Light* and *City of Eternal Flame* are launching their own Centans as I speak. *City of New Hope* is unable to launch its defense force at present but is capable of maneuvering."

"Very well," Belisondre said, calculating swiftly. The quick-response Centans were the Irindris fleets' first defense against attack—flights of small, fast ships assigned to predetermined positions. Dubandis had responded correctly to the threat, but would it be enough? "Deploy the city-ships defensively in orbit around the planet. Launch the remaining defenders to global perimeter around the planet, then sortie the capital ships out of their holding bays. How long until the shadow fleet is capable of entering orbit around Avadon?"

"By our estimation, twenty-nine minutes before they come within weapons range of any of the city-ships."

"Your Eminence." The pilot sitting in front of Belisondre's right hand half turned, shifting in his seat. "Our best speed ETA to the *City of Faith* is forty-three minutes."

"Deploy the fleet," Belisondre said into the crystal. "We are en route to you, but if boarding you should prove impossible, you must do everything you can to protect the city-ships."

"We will not leave you, Exalted One!"

"You will leave me to the will of Gnuktikut and save those ships, Administrator," the prophet snapped. "If we are going down into hell then I, for one, intend to take the Sentinels' precious shadow fleet with me!"

THE LEAD HARPIES OF THE SHADOW FLEET FELL OUT OF THEIR wormhole transit points with incredible precision for interstellar craft, just slightly coreward of Avadon's path. Within the first thirty seconds of the invasion, twenty-seven class III Harpy wraith warriors, their forward tentacles arched into claw-attack positions, had all fallen back into natural space within the quantum zone. The ships quickly began forming up, their articulated hulls arching with anticipation of the battle at hand.

The battle was much closer than they supposed. The Centan *Holy Sword* had been approaching at an incredibly high rate under a stealth field that made their Starchariots impossible to detect under normal physics. The ships would have easily been detected by the most common revelation incantations used on nearly a dozen worlds in the quantum zone around them, but the wraith ships were not equipped to detect their foes' approach.

Just as the pathfinder Harpies were firming up their initial attack formation, forty-four points of brilliant light erupted in their midst as the emerging Starchariots bled off the excess energy from the stealth shields.

Initially, the Harpies' synthetics mistakenly concluded that the energy bursts were detonations from some external source and trained their sensing arrays outward in search of an enemy attack. However, their enemy was already among them and the synths lost precious moments in the surprise.

The Starchariots, about one-tenth the size and weight of the Harpies, came from a completely different school of engineering and physics. Each was pulled by two Anjew—winged spirit-creations with featureless faces and undulating bodies. The pairs pulled the shuttle and smaller strike craft of the Irindris with grace and speed. In other quantum zones, these phantoms might have struggled just to get from place to place, but not here: here they were in their element and suffused with power. The main body of the chariot resembled a gigantic spiral shell with multiple horned outgrowths sweeping forward. It looked as though it had come from some aquatic world. Indeed, the shells were grown and cultivated as part of the Irindris weapons development program and were imbued with special powers for offensive and defensive operations. Each carried a pilot to direct the Anjew and a warrior to attack and defend. The chariot crews basked in the glory of the moment. The quantum weather around Avadon was perfect for the Starchariots. The city-ships of the crusade were threatened. There could be no better day to die.

A heartbeat after the Starchariots shed their stealth energy, the forward arching horns erupted in the searing light of direct, coherent force. The shifting burst of energy sliced into the hull plating of one of the Harpies, causing it to arch backward, emitting a shrill, broadband electronic scream across communication frequencies.

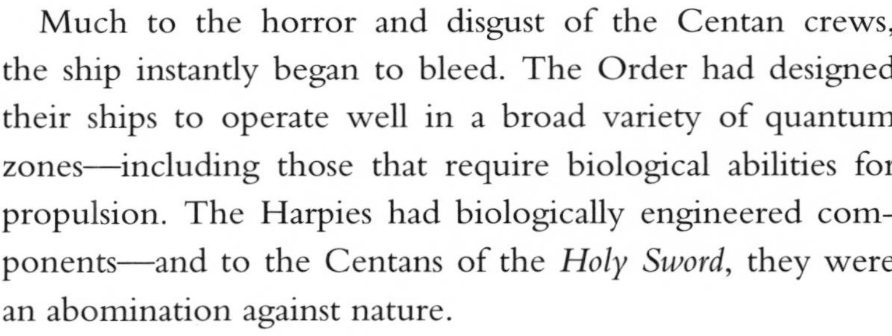

Much to the horror and disgust of the Centan crews, the ship instantly began to bleed. The Order had designed their ships to operate well in a broad variety of quantum zones—including those that require biological abilities for propulsion. The Harpies had biologically engineered components—and to the Centans of the *Holy Sword*, they were an abomination against nature.

In quick succession, eight of the Harpies fell writhing and bleeding into space—disabled or destroyed completely.

The remaining Harpies, reeling from the vicious attack, turned on their foes. Orbs of blue plasma energy flashed from the Harpies' fingertips, searching for their prey.

The Starchariots were fast, but not fast enough. The bolts of blue were gaining in their accuracy, slamming into the chariot shells as they soared past. Occasionally, the bolt would be outrun long enough for it to dissipate its energy. The chariot shells in such cases would buckle and hold but would never survive a second time. More often, however, the bolt would lash out and connect with its target nearly at once, causing the shell to explode from the energy release in a single, cataclysmic eruption.

Centan *Word of Law* and Centan *Heretic Death* were holding at their defense positions at station one and station five when the Harpies emerged near station three. Dutifully the Irindris pilots remained on station though their hearts ached to join the battle raging on the other side of the planet they defended. It looked as though the major ships would not even get into the fight and the quick-response Centans would all be worthy of praise within the hour.

Within the blink of an eye, all of that changed.

Space screwed in on itself and suddenly more ships were falling out of wormholes that were continuously opening around the world. Freighters, cruiseliners, barges, and research vessels of all kinds and descriptions filled the stars. But it was the sudden arrival of the assault carrier *Duyabik* and her twelve cruiser escorts that sent chills up the spine of every pilot and warrior of the Centans. Within three minutes, the advanced planetary assault ship *D'Rapiene* appeared with a second full complement of task-force starships. Capital ships. Warships. Even as they watched, the launch bays of the *Duyabik* began disgorging rank after rank of close support fighters.

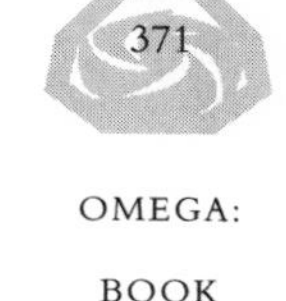

Ships without pilots. Ghosts.

The legion commander ordered Centans *Word of Law* and *Heretic Death* to attack. Every pilot of the Starchariots knew it was a suicide mission. Every warrior of the Centans knew that their lives could only buy time for the Irindris's own capital ships to sail from their docking bays and engage the enemy.

Grimly determined, the Centans turned and rushed headlong into the shadow fleet warships.

"THREE MINUTES TO WORMHOLE DROPOUT," MERINDA announced throughout the *Brishan* from her bridge command chair. "Oscan, how's our passenger?"

"Miserable," came the reply out of thin air. "I can't tell you how much I'm enjoying it, thank you very much."

Neskat smiled, tapping several key inputs on her armrests. "Don't get too used to it, Oscan. We're not out of this yet. Terica? Where are you?"

"Systems control, as you requested."

"Been talking to the synths?"

"Of course! We are having a wonderful conversation!"

Griffiths stood nervously on the side of his right boot.

Neskat continued to inspect the readouts flashing onto the windows of the dome before her, occasionally tweaking a control when she found something less than satisfactory.

Griffiths coughed lightly.

No response.

Griffiths cleared his throat a bit more loudly.

Charts glowed before her. She pressed a button.

"Excuse me?"

Neskat didn't turn but replied as she continued working. "Yes, Captain Griffiths?"

"You asked me to come down here?"

"Yes, I did— One minute to wormhole dropout," she announced suddenly.

"Well—what do you want me to do?" he asked with annoyance.

"That will largely depend on what is on the other end of this wormhole," Neskat said, flexing her hands before she settled them on the handgrip controllers. "However, if I do need you, it will be for something that I know you enjoy."

"What do you mean—"

The twisting tunnel of light before them abruptly vanished into the scattered pattern of stars, crossed by a delicate lacework of streaking light.

The *Brishan* rolled suddenly to port, thunder shaking its hull.

Griffiths fell painfully to the deck. "Is it supposed to be like this?" he yelled.

Neskat didn't answer him. "Lindia, hostile contact configuration! Terica?"

"I'm already on it, Merinda," came the reply. Griffiths

saw the ghostly figure of the golden woman appear suddenly on the bridge. "I'm in communication with both Evis and Tashel—I can handle gunnery."

"Hostile contact configuration complete. Do you wish to assign a defensive systems operator?"

"Oh, no." Griffiths groaned.

"Captain Griffiths has graciously volunteered to take the post again," Neskat said, pitching the ship forward and barely avoiding a blinding streak of light crossing in front of the ship's windows. "Have Fisk talk to him."

"Greetings, Captain Griffiths." The cheery voice spoke in the astronaut's mind at once. "It's so good to be working with you. I see that once again we have no time for any drills or practice before you attempt to halt our utter destruction under impossible odds. Still, I have confidence in you and will enjoy working with you for as long as it lasts."

Griffiths was once again lifted off the floor and suspended in the floating, weightless globe. Just as he began orienting himself, three painful points of light slammed into his right hand, simultaneously bucking the ship heavily.

"Yeow! Damn it!" Griffiths swore, struggling to remember how the shield system worked.

"I'm afraid that this attack is rather more complex than the one you dealt with earlier," Fisk said with brimming confidence. "Threat assessment recommends you set the deflection shield ambient—"

"To full strength, I know," Griffiths shouted. "Just do it!"

"Incoming fire behind you, Captain, and to your starboard quarter. Forward of you, a wraith ship freighter is turning into ramming position."

"Ramming position!" Griffiths squeaked. "What do I do about that?"

"I might suggest you hang on to something very tightly if it hits us."

"Thanks!" Griffiths said, twisting in his floating globe. He glanced forward through the translucent displays around him. The ship swung to starboard, and the great globe shining dimly in starlight hove into view.

"That's it!" Neskat cried through the comsystem. "Avadon! I've got a fix on a beacon, Griffiths! We've found it!"

Griffiths suddenly cried out as a bolt seemed to slam into the middle of his back, the ship around him responding at once to the real weapon explosion above its hull.

"Lindia! Broadcast the Omnet code on broadband! *That* should confuse them enough! They'll be so busy beating each other up, they won't have time for a neutral. Does plasma work in this zone?"

"Yes, Merinda."

"Then bring the plasma drives on-line now!" she cried. "We're going down!"

THE *BRISHAN* SUDDENLY ACCELERATED AT THE FRONT OF A broad column of blue energy. She corkscrewed through the combined fleets, both too engaged in the smoke of war to concern themselves with the streaking ship of uncommon swiftness that ran the gauntlet of the battle with no purpose but its own passage. Too late did the controllers aboard the Irindris city-ships notice it dropping down the well into their precious and holy excavation, now unable to disengage any ships from the battle to investigate. The escort ships that had accompanied the *Brishan* were quickly embroiled in the battle and could not keep up with the speeding little scout craft.

One ship, however, took notice—for one ship was awaiting just such an event. It hung outside the battle, itself shielded in stealth wizardry and unnoticed by either the Irindris or the engaged shadow fleet. It turned in its invisible cocoon, and, quite slowly and silently, moved to follow the *Brishan* down the atmospheric well to the ruins below.

36

Starlight

MERINDA CROUCHED ON THE CIRCULAR STONE PLATFORM, warmed by her *Vestis* uniform as she examined the three heavy robes lying on the ground. "It looks as though your companions were here, Griffiths," she said, breathing thick clouds of moisture into the air as she distractedly fingered the robes. "Whatever they did or wherever they went, they ended up here."

"Are you sure?" Griffiths questioned through chattering teeth, his own suit inadequate for the cold. "Couldn't they be somewhere else in this complex?"

"No," Merinda said, looking about her as she stood. "There have been a lot of people here working on the dig—the moisture from their breath has condensed into the frost you see on just about everything here. Then when their feet pass over it, they leave their marks. More breath tends to cover those marks. The only fresh tracks I found coming in lead either toward or away from this round stone platform. If only we had more time!"

"You don't." Queekat smiled wearily, his hands tied firmly behind his back and his legs hobbled. "The escorts, occupied as they are right now, will nevertheless not forget me. They will come. You cannot simply abduct a Sentinel."

"It would appear," Merinda rejoined, "that we already have done so."

"Rini," Queekat said quietly, "you're wrong about me—wrong about all of this. You were hurt more deeply than I could have imagined; I can see that now. Regardless of how important it was at the time, I can admit that it was a mistake not to take you with me—not to trust you. The Omnet doesn't want to accept the new reality. They're the ones who have lied to you, not me. The Order is the future of the galaxy under one rule—and you and I could *be* that order! I've built all of this for you, Rini! For you and me!"

Merinda stared back blankly into Queekat's face.

"Don't throw us away, Rini," he whispered. "You could be wrong."

Merinda turned suddenly toward the golden statue floating nearby. "How much time do we have, Terica?"

"The battle continues to rage above us." The Sibyl spoke quietly. "For a time, we sit at the calm center of the storm, but it will not last long. The battle does not go well for the Irindris."

"You know this?" Neskat asked.

"I am biolinked to the Order data packets and comnets," the metallic voice replied. "My understanding is all too clear."

"Then we don't have much time," Merinda replied, gazing around her, gesturing with her arms. "This entire place is a mystery. It's obvious that the Irindris drilled down through the atmosphere to reach this place, but the bubble of atmosphere surrounding this temple area maintains itself—it was here when the Irindris arrived."

"We are in a quantum zone where magic functions," Oscan offered.

"Yes, but a spell lasting over three thousand years?" Merinda shook her head. "Entropic forces at the quantum level dissipate the cohesion of even the most carefully aligned magical structures. The longest known spell in force lasted only one hundred years and it was pretty much worthless for the last fifty years of its existence." She turned around, pointing to the ground. "It's not just the dome, either. There are no signs of violence on these robes—they were dropped here intentionally. Not only that, the frost that covers everything else down here has vanished from the platform itself."

Oscan, who had grabbed an Omnet warming cloak as they hurriedly left the *Brishan*, gazed about at the blue glass obelisks surrounding the central pedestal. "This is as far as the Irindris got," he said almost reverently. "It would appear that your friends, Griffiths, have somehow gone further. This device is the key."

"No." Griffiths shivered. "This device is the lock—I am supposed to be the key."

Merinda considered this for a moment, then scooped up one of the heavy robes from the ground. "Here, man of Earth," she said, tossing him the robe. "This pedestal seems to be at the center of things. You've been pursued across nearly a quarter of the galaxy; now it's time to find out why."

Griffiths shrugged on the coat and sighed. He hesitated for a moment, unsure of his own worth, then stepped up toward the circular platform surrounding the pedestal.

"What do I do?" he asked the *Vestis*.

She smiled back. "I was rather hoping that *you* knew."

Griffiths nodded solemnly and turned toward the pedestal. There was an intricate bronze device on the pedestal—remarkably well preserved considering its obvious age. There appeared to be three sighting glasses attached to the device just above a disk.

Griffiths stepped onto the platform.

Instantly, the obstructing wall of glacial sky vanished. The ancient city lay clear in the valley below. The stars sprang into existence above them, glorious and brilliant.

"Magnificent," Oscan breathed.

"What is it?" Merinda asked.

"I can tell you what it isn't," the Sibyl replied. "It is not this place: the stars are wrong."

"What do you mean?" Merinda asked.

"I am in contact with the navigational nets of the Order above us," the expressionless golden face answered. "I can see the stars above us as I also see the stars here. I simply report that the stars are not the same. The brightest star visible from this place is the one to your right at an azimuth of approximately thirty degrees. Relative to other identifiable stars it is fully three degrees away in this sky from its current actual position. Indeed, all of the stars visible from this position by the naked eye are out of position to some degree or other."

"Why would anyone want to go to this much trouble to make stars appear in the wrong place?" Griffiths asked.

"They wouldn't," Merinda said, turning back toward him and joining him on the pedestal. She looked through one of the sighting tubes. "These register the location of the stars as they appear around us now. The disk under the device has markings on it here, with a fixed index notch cut into the stone here. I don't see any metering connection between the disk . . ."

Merinda stopped, rested her hands on the ornate disk, and rotated it sideways to her right.

"Whoa!" Griffiths uttered almost under his breath.

The stars moved.

The Sibyl suddenly spoke. "The star field has shifted more toward the current actual stellar positions."

Merinda smiled. She pushed the disk slightly again to her right. Six more notches passed the indicator. "Sibyl," she asked, "is that closer?"

"This star field is within a few degrees of alignment with the current actual star field," the statue intoned.

One more notch.

"The star fields are in agreement," came the metallic voice.

Merinda turned toward Griffiths.

Griffiths shook his head slowly. "Sorry, *Vestis*, none of this means anything to me."

Merinda swore under her breath.

"Wait," Oscan said. "The stars are wrong."

"Didn't you just hear the Sibyl?" Merinda asked, frustration sounding in her voice. "They're in alignment now."

"For us, yes." Oscan smiled to himself. "But not for this place—not for this temple! This entire complex is a tribute to Kendis-dai, but Kendis-dai is nearly three thousand years behind us, just as this temple is three thousand years behind our time."

"Wait a moment," Queekat said, becoming involved despite himself. "Avadon has been moving counter to the rotation of the galaxy for just over three millennia. It's moving at nearly two-hundredths of light speed relative to the stars surrounding it. It's nearly one hundred fifty light-years from where it was when this temple was built!"

Merinda looked back down at the disk. "These markings look to be set in about century intervals. If we turn them back, say, about thirty marks . . ."

The stars suddenly drifted above them, dancing in the dome of the night surrounding them. Soon they slowed, sliding into new positions overhead.

"It must be in here somewhere," Merinda said, turning

the disk slowly across a mark that by her count was thirty-two from where they had started.

Griffiths sobbed. "Stop!"

Merinda suddenly looked up.

Tears were streaming down Griffiths's face.

"What is it, man of Earth?" she said softly.

"I don't understand," he cried. "I don't . . . I had lost hope of ever seeing it again."

"What?" Merinda laid a hand on the astronaut's shoulder. "What is it you see?"

Griffiths took in a shuddering breath and raised his arm, pointing above the distant mountains to the stars beyond.

"Orion." He smiled through his tears.

"Orion?" Oscan said with a puzzled expression. "What's an Orion?"

"A constellation on my world. It's one of the clearest and most easily found. Those two stars are his shoulders: Bellatrix and Betelgeuse. The two below are his legs, with the three close in a line forming his belt and those other stars his sword and his bow."

"A warrior!" Merinda cried out.

"Sure," Griffiths responded. "Orion the hunter."

Oscan smiled as he recited words from memory. " 'Kendis-dai / his powers try / in chariots fly / to cross the sky.' "

"What is that?" Merinda asked.

"It's an old Irindris nursery rhyme," he replied. "It's supposed to get you into heaven."

Merinda bent over and gently turned the first sighting tube toward the stars. As the constellation slowly came into view, filling the lens, they all heard a low thrumming noise about them. Several of the blue glass obelisks were rising farther out of the ground, a light beginning to glow from within them.

"By the gods," Oscan murmured, "the barbarian really is the key!"

"Anything else?" Merinda asked excitedly of Griffiths, "anything else that's familiar?"

"Well, there's the Big Dipper," Griffiths said with amazement in his voice, pointing to the opposite horizon.

"Big Dipper?" she asked. "You mean, like a spoon or ladle?"

"Yes, but it isn't really a constellation," Griffiths said. "It's part of the constellation Ursa Major—a bear."

"What's a bear?" Merinda asked quickly.

"A big furry animal."

"No, that's not it. Does that grouping mean anything else?"

"Well"—Griffiths thought—"in Asian countries it's thought of as a royal wagon."

Merinda smiled, and trained the second tube sight on the second constellation. As she did so, another set of the obelisks rose up out of the ground and began to hum loudly. Suddenly brilliant lines of light appeared between the obelisks over their heads. The air shimmered between them.

"There must be one more, Griffiths," she said.

"Well," he replied, "it's completely in the wrong place, but I'd swear that one over there looks like the Southern Cross."

Oscan laughed. "A-cross the sky! An ancient pun!"

Merinda laughed, too, as she trained the last of the sight tubes toward the stars overhead.

The final set of obelisks rose to join its brothers in the air. The chorus of their humming quickly reached a crescendo. More rays of light flashed into existence, bending inexplicably as they collided to form a tunnel of light shooting toward the city. At the edge of the platform where the light crossed, the atmosphere suddenly distorted into a gigantic lens. Warm, sweet air poured over Merinda's upturned face as she stepped toward it.

"It's a second temple," she said over the thrumming sound about them. As she watched the building, it suddenly began to glow with a bright white light. "Could this be the cathedral, Oscan? . . . Oscan?"

"Look!" Oscan shouted, pointing toward the city below them. The light tunnel shone directly into the center of the distant streets. There, the same bright glow illuminated a distant building.

"It's another bubble in the frozen atmosphere," Merinda shouted, looking through the lens at various angles, taking care not to disturb the beams of light. "This must be a dimensional fold leading to it."

She turned back to face Griffiths, still standing on the circle around the pedestal. Her hair flailed in the hot wind rushing from the lens. "You did it," she cried. "You've shown us the way!"

"Merinda!" Oscan yelled over the wind. "We've got company!"

The *Vestis* followed Oscan's gaze back across the courtyard. A massive troop shuttle was shimmering into existence just next to the *Brishan*, its lifters kicking up swirling clouds of frost as it settled to the ground.

"Stealth ships!" Merinda cried out. She glanced down at Queekat.

The Sentinel turned his face up toward her and smiled. "There's nowhere left to go, Rini!" he said through his teeth.

She smiled back at him. "Not quite, Kat! Not quite yet!" She reached down and grabbed him by the hair, pulling him to his feet and dragging him toward the shimmering lens.

With a single war cry, she pushed him through the glowing circle and watched, satisfied, as he tumbled headlong into the dust of the temple stairs beyond.

Oscan and the Sibyl were already moving toward the lens when Merinda pulled the man of Earth down from the pedestal and shoved him toward the glowing portal. "Griffiths! If you want to find your people, they went this way!"

37

Convergence

MERINDA GLANCED BACK ONCE AS SHE AND GRIFFITHS BOUNDED for the lens. A cataract of TyRen warriors had flowed from the blown hatches of the assault transport and were even then rising over the walls of the complex like a swollen river in flood. They both leaped . . .

. . . and landed at once to stand in the dust-covered plaza at the foundations of the great, towering cathedral. The air was warm on Merinda's face although she could feel a cold breeze washing over her feet from behind her. Frantically she glanced around the plaza and quickly fixed her gaze on a pedestal set in the center of a now-dry fountain.

Atop the pedestal was another disk and bronze sighting device. In three quick strides she reached it. She grasped the disk as she looked back through the lens in the air. The TyRen were pouring over the platform wall on the other side of the light-rimmed portal.

Merinda spun the disk sharply and was relieved that it turned so easily. The light around the lens portal flared suddenly, the lens wavering only for a moment before the light collapsed on itself and vanished, taking the lens with it.

"By the gods," Oscan cried, "what are you doing?"

Merinda began twisting the sighting tubes of the bronze instrument randomly. "Closing the door—just as your friends did, Griffiths, when they came through. They didn't want anyone to follow them here—and neither do I."

"It won't work, Rini," Queekat said, struggling to get his knees under him. A small trickle of blood ran down his face from a cut on his forehead. "They'll still come."

Merinda stepped out of the empty fountain basin and walked toward the Sentinel. "Not for a while; not if I keep you away from that device."

"They can't follow us," Oscan said. "They don't have the key."

"I'm afraid they do, don't they, Kat?" Merinda said, unshouldering her weapon and nudging the Sentinel with its emitter.

The Sentinel only stared back.

"I should have realized it sooner, Oscan," Merinda continued. "Our Sentinel friend here is biolinked to the Order—just like Terica. This entire mission was set up so that I'd lead him here. If he managed to recruit me into joining his Order, that was fine—I would hand over the Mantle of Kendis-dai and he would have insured the safety of his Order. If I didn't fall for him, he knew I'd have to take him along. All he had to do was transmit what he saw and heard to his TyRen commanders, and when he figured he'd found out enough, he'd call in the troops. In that case, we'd all be dead and he would still get to claim his prize."

"It doesn't have to be this way, Rini," Queekat said softly. "It doesn't have to end in tragedy. For once in your life, let go of your pride and your damned sense of justice. Release me and I'll take good care of all of you."

The disk on the pedestal swiveled one notch.

"They're working on it," Oscan breathed.

"He was there when we opened the portal," the Sibyl spoke. "By now his troops know how to work the device and what they need to duplicate to open the way straight to us."

"It's only a matter of time, Rini." The Sentinel smiled. "Make the right choice; release me."

"You're right," she said, pulling him roughly to his feet with her free arm. "It is only a matter of time—but it's time that I hope to use well. You wanted to find the Mantle of Kendis-dai? I think it's about time you got your wish!"

THE HEAVY DOORS OF THE CATHEDRAL FLEW INWARD, SLAMming into the walls to either side with a sound that reverberated down through the empty halls. The doors opened into an oval entry chamber, softly lit by a glowing painting located in the dome overhead. Polished stone beneath their feet had been fitted into a smooth mosaic design. Ornate, fluted columns sunken into the wall supported the dome twenty feet above their heads.

"They seem to still have power," Oscan muttered as he gazed up at the softly glowing dome.

"Yes, but not for long," the Sibyl said in muted tones. "The cathedral may have lights, but there's about three inches of dust on these floors. The wall coverings are barely holding to the stone—look, over there it's come away and fallen to the floor. Step gently."

Two curved corridors exited the room at angles from the right and left. Floor panels tried to light the gently curving hallways, their soft blue glow heavily muted by the layers of dust resting on top of them. It was difficult to see any distance, for all the dust diffusing the light down the corridor's length.

"Griffiths! Which way?" Merinda called in a low voice. She was pointing toward the ground.

Footprints, both coming and going, led down both halls.

Griffiths shrugged. "They seem to curve in toward each other—they probably meet up ahead somewhere."

Merinda nodded. "Oscan! You go to the right with Griffiths; I'll take Terica and Queekat with me to the left. Call out if you find anything. Oh, and Oscan?"

"Yes, Merinda."

"We don't have a lot of time."

Oscan nodded and motioned with his arm for Griffiths to follow. The two men moved quickly down the hall, their feet stirring up great clouds of dust into the gallery as they moved. Several side doors opened into darkened rooms. Griffiths peered inside their black depths, catching only the hints and shadows of shapes in the dust-filtered darkness within. There was a coldness about the rooms that defied definition in Fahrenheit degrees. The rooms smelled of an ancient age awakened from a long sleep. There were ghosts in those rooms, Griffiths just somehow knew, whose sleep he most heartily did not wish to disturb.

Oscan pressed the cloth of his cape over his mouth to ward off the dust whirling through the air. His words were muffled as he spoke. "Keep moving! Those TyRen won't be far behind us. Where are these friends of yours?"

"Lewis!" the astronaut called out in a hoarse whisper. "Tobler! It's me, Griffiths! Ellerby! Where are you?"

The corridor seemed to be coming to an end. Only two more rooms to check before he had to confront the large doors looming up before him. The dust in the air was getting to be quite unbearable.

"Ellerby! Lewis!" Griffiths coughed, reaching the last room, nearly blinded by the dust-choked air. He turned around in the hazy corridor. "They're not here, Oscan. Maybe Merinda found them on the other—Oscan?"

Griffiths stared into the obscured corridor, suffused with bluish light. "Oscan? Are you there?"

Silence.

"Oscan!" Griffiths called out urgently.

He took a single uncertain step when suddenly cold hands reached out of the darkened room behind him, clamped over his mouth, eyes, arms, and waist, and dragged him quietly into the cold blackness.

MERINDA EMERGED FROM THE END OF HER CORRIDOR INTO A magnificent hall. This gallery, too, was curved, as if it formed a circle around a central core. It was much larger than the first, and of indeterminable height as the dimly glowing lamps in this hall did not emit sufficient light to illuminate the ceiling.

Queekat shook his head, trying to clear his dust-congested throat. "What is this place?" he managed to ask between spasms of coughing.

"This is the Supplicant's Walk," the Sibyl answered, almost without thinking. The golden woman drifted forward on her throne, her passage stirring a slight wake in the dust behind her. "In the days of the old Kendis Imperium, subjects would circle this hall to speak with the sages who held court in the various rooms about the perimeter. Those whose questions were found worthy would be directed through one of the Nine Gates of Enlightenment to the presence of the Mantle itself. There all answers were known to reside in wisdom and justice."

The Sibyl came to hover before two bright golden doors. The carvings in the stone on either side of the doors were heavily laden with dust, yet the doors themselves—despite their intricate inlaid design—were bright and clean, as though recently polished. Their surface shone in the dim light of the hall.

"This is one of the gates," she said with wonder in her voice.

Merinda turned toward the distant sound drifting down the corridor behind her. "The lens," she said flatly. "They've discovered the key."

"Your time is up, Merinda," Queekat sneered. "You should have listened to me while you had the chance."

Without another word, the Sibyl moved forward.

The gates parted at her approach.

GRIFFITHS STRUGGLED, SCREAMING INTO THE HANDS COVERING his mouth. The hands dragged him down into the dust. He gagged on it. It was the dust of the dead, he thought, the dust of a thousand ancient souls come to claim his own life to join theirs. He kicked and screamed again. The voices! His mind reeled. The voices of the dead! They were speaking to him! They were calling to him! They were calling him to join them in . . .

"Griffiths!" Ellerby grumbled under his breath. "Shut up, you stupid bastard! Do you want to give us away?"

"Murferfee?" Griffiths's attempt to speak was muffled by the large hand over his mouth. He stopped struggling.

"Easy, Captain!" Lewis said quietly. "We weren't sure it was you. Are you all right?"

Griffiths nodded. "Mumf fimm."

"Brick, let him up so he can talk." Lewis gave Broderick's arm a backhand slap.

"Oh, right!" he whispered back. "Sorry, Captain."

"It's OK, Ellerby," Griffiths said quietly. "Look, I've come with some people who can help us. We don't have a lot of time and—why are you looking at me that way?"

"Well, ah, one of those people wouldn't happen to be the guy following you in the hall, would it?" Ellerby winced.

Griffiths's eyes went wide. "Oh, no. What did you do to him?"

Ellerby chewed nervously on his lip. "Well, I found this set of wooden furniture, see, and the chair legs were just about the right length for good clubs . . ."

"Oh, shit!" Griffiths struggled to get up. "Where is he?"

"Tobler's watching him over in the corner," Lewis said as she rubbed her forehead in frustration.

Griffiths scrambled across the floor, dust billowing behind him as he moved. Tobler hovered over her charge, her length of broken chair leg cocked and ready for the slightest sign of resistance from her prisoner. She apparently had little to worry about; Oscan Kelis sat slumped, unmoving, in the corner.

"You didn't kill him, did you?" Griffiths asked quickly.

"No!" Tobler answered indignantly, her voice low. "Ellerby's trained! He'll have a terrible headache, but in a few minutes he should come around."

"How do you know that?" Griffiths asked, taking Oscan's chin in his hand and examining his face for any signs of life. "This guy isn't exactly from Detroit. His physiology may be completely different!"

"I don't think so," she said with less certainty than she wished. "Humans seem to be humans pretty much everywhere in the galaxy."

"Right," Griffiths said. "Which is another mystery that we have yet to solve. But right *now* our problem is that an army of thinking machines are about to drop us a few links down the food chain if we don't find some holy artifact in this place before they do."

"We know where it is," Lewis said simply.

"You do?" Griffiths was stunned. "Where?"

"The main hall in the center of this place," she replied. "There's a big hall at the end of the corridor, not far from— Did you hear that?"

Griffiths turned his head slightly toward the still-open doorway and the corridor beyond. The unmistakable hum of the dimensional lens echoed toward them.

"We've got to get out of here!" he exclaimed. "Is there a back door out of this room?"

Lewis nodded. "Just past that altar-thing. It leads to an access corridor—we were going to use it as an escape route."

"Ellerby!" Griffiths said urgently. "Help me carry this guy out the back way! Of all the times to use the escape route— this is most definitely the right one!"

He could already hear the rumble of the TyRen approaching.

THE GOLDEN SIBYL CONTINUED TO DRIFT INTO THE IMMENSE room. The carefully carved vaulting arches were hidden by the diffused shadows of a single column of light that illuminated something on a delicately carved framework in the center of the room. Beyond the light, a wide, gentle curve of stairs led upward some twenty feet to a shadowy throne. Surrounding the stairs were large spheres of granite spaced at regular intervals and carved with delicate symbols.

The Sibyl approached the brightly lit object and considered it with her implacable expression. It appeared to be an article of clothing: a headpiece with a jeweled band and fitted white dome, attached to a thick metallic fabric that, when worn, would drape down to cover the back and the chest of the wearer.

"Merinda," the Sibyl called. "Hurry!"

Merinda quickly closed the doors behind them, searching in vain for some kind of locking mechanism. When none presented itself, she pushed Queekat quickly to the floor, then ran toward the center of the room. She could feel the rumble of the TyRen through the stones of the cathedral floor. No time! She ducked under the framework, pushing her head upward into the helmet. As she did so the framework retracted from her, draping the thick metal yoke down over her shoulders.

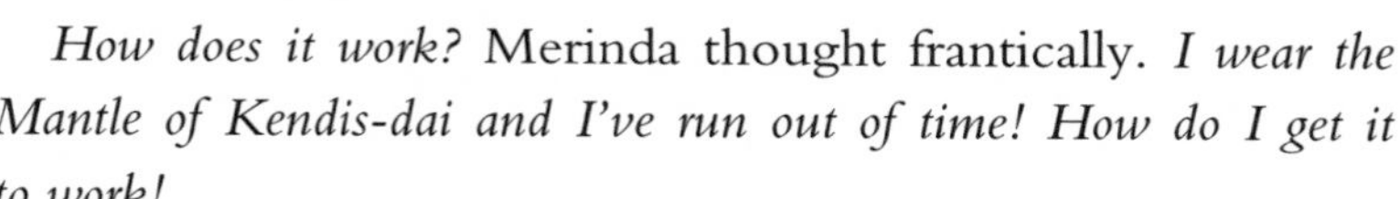

How does it work? Merinda thought frantically. *I wear the Mantle of Kendis-dai and I've run out of time! How do I get it to work!*

"I have a question," she called out, her voice echoing through the vast emptiness of the cathedral hall. "I wear the Mantle of Kendis-dai!"

Nothing changed.

"Do synthetic minds have free will?" she yelled into the darkness.

Her only answer was the sound of her own question echoing from the walls.

"Where are we?" she called out.

Echoes in the silence.

She looked frantically about her. "Terica! What do I do now? Nothing is happening!"

The golden Sibyl stared back at her without expression.

"What must I do?" Merinda screamed.

Laughter answered her.

Merinda looked across the room. The golden doors suddenly opened, bursting with ranks of TyRen streaming into the room. Each of their many arms bore a weapon; each weapon was trained on Merinda. She turned, running up the stairs toward the throne. The Sibyl followed her, but there was nowhere to go. Halfway up the stairs, the *Vestis* stopped and turned around to face her foe.

The room was nearly filled with the synthetic warriors when the rumble of their lifters suddenly quieted. A single sound remained: Queekat, lying bound in the dust, was laughing giddily.

38

Enlightenment

A TYREN WARRIOR SLICED NEATLY THROUGH THE CORDS THAT bound Queekat, freeing him to roll slowly to his feet. The sea of synthetic knights parted before him. He stood, rubbing the raw flesh at his wrists, yet still smiling a hideous smile, fire raging behind his cold gray eyes.

"The game is done, Merinda Neskat." There was a smug undercurrent to his words as he advanced across the vast hall, the TyRen flanking him. "You played hard—fought hard—but in the end it was my game and my rules. I loved you, Merinda—I truly did—but that wasn't enough for you, was it? You had to fight me, trick me, when all I ever did I did for you."

"You never did anything except for yourself." Merinda spoke down to him from the stairs, her lip quivering slightly. "You manipulated me, abused me, used me to satisfy your own ego—but never once did you sacrifice anything for me, or give me anything that didn't come with a price attached. No, Queekat Shn'dar, you never, ever *loved* me."

His smile twisted into a scowl. "Used you? You're not worth being used! You're a pathetic and naive brat, ungrateful for everything that I've done for you!"

"No, Kat," she said back to him, her eyes clear for the

first time. "It won't work anymore. I won't allow it to work anymore. You can never hurt me that way again."

"Perhaps not," Queekat said, moving purposefully up the stairs, "but there are plenty of other ways that I *can* hurt you. After today no one will question my supreme rule of the Order—you've insured that!" He climbed past her on the stairs, then turned around, more comfortable looking down on her.

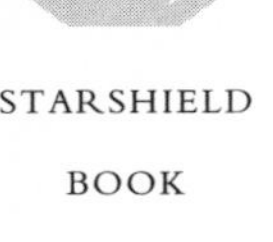

"Give me the Mantle of Kendis-dai!" he shouted unnecessarily down into her face. His words echoed through the hall.

Merinda removed the headpiece and shoulder yoke.

"Give it to me!" he shouted louder still.

Merinda sighed and lifted the device toward the Sentinel. He snatched it from her hands.

"It doesn't work," she said simply.

Queekat smiled and spoke quietly to her. "Of course not, you stupid woman! It's a piece of ancient, powerless garbage—a relic of power that no longer exists. You know that and I know that—but *they* don't know that, and that's where the real power lies! Fool! Watch me imbue this trash with real power."

Suddenly he thrust the headpiece high overhead. A deep rumble reverberated through the room from the TyRen warriors below, as each activated its lifter in thunderous acclaim.

"Faithful warriors!" Queekat addressed the TyRen below him. "Our holy quest is come to success! I present to you the Mantle of Kendis-dai!"

The crowd of TyRen packed the room before the stairs, rumbling louder than before, their lifters shaking the stones of the building itself.

With slow ceremony, Queekat lowered the headpiece

and yoke about his head and shoulders. There was a sudden, startled expression on his face. "It speaks! It speaks to me!"

Merinda shook her head, a wry smile coming to her face. *He is going to fake it*, she thought. *He is going to claim to be the word of Kendis-dai to the Order of the Future Faith and all these synths are going to buy into it. They were looking for the answer and now he is going to give it to them. I wonder if the other Sentinels were clued in to this particular part of the plan?*

Suddenly her eyes caught sight of something familiar resting at the top of the stairs just past Queekat. At first she couldn't place what it was—something disturbing about the throne. It was a thought nagging at the back of her head. Something familiar, she thought, something . . .

Merinda's eyes went wide. She *had* seen that throne once before. The Throne of Kendis-dai! This throne was an exact match to the one she had seen in the Vault of Nine Oracles!

She glanced upward. She could see above the Throne, now, into a tower shaft that was hidden from the main floor of the throne room. Directly above the Throne, a thirty-foot-wide column of dim, undulating light rose up the full hundred-foot length of the tower, terminated by granite spheres that seemed to float freely in the air.

"The answer is coming to me," Queekat intoned with grand theatrical gestures. He stepped down past the Sibyl and the *Vestis*, feigning a rapturous trance as he spoke. He seemed to want to get closer to his audience so that his performance might be more readily appreciated. "The ancients have spoken and your faith is to be blessed and accepted!" he cried loudly into the room.

Neither the Sibyl nor the *Vestis* turned to listen to the speech.

"Merinda?" the Sibyl whispered. "What is it?"

"Do you see it, too?" Merinda whispered back, as Queekat continued his loud performance several stairs below them.

"The tower of light? Yes, I see it," the Sibyl said, "but I've never seen anything like it."

"I have." Merinda smiled. "The Throne—that dim pillar of light. It's an Oracle, Terica."

"An operating Oracle?" The Sibyl's voice conveyed shock and amazement. "When do you think it was awakened?"

Neskat smiled. "Terica—I don't think it has ever slept."

"By all the gods!" the Sibyl breathed in wonder. "A TFP synthetic mind over three thousand years old—and never been put to sleep?"

Merinda looked around the room as if for the first time. Spaced above the Nine Gates of Enlightenment were nine additional large granite globes, each also floating in the air above its respective gate. Each had its own respective shaft reaching up into the main tower section. The room suddenly took on a completely different aspect—and was terribly familiar.

Merinda recalled her instruction to Griffiths: *"Of course, this is merely an entertainment representation,"* she had said to him. *"No one knows what it really looks like."*

"The Mantle of Kendis-dai isn't some ceremonial crown," she whispered to the Sibyl. "It's the oldest continuously operating temporal fold processor ever known! Even the Nine Oracles have only been operating for the last three centuries—but for three millennia?"

"There wouldn't be a question it couldn't answer!" Excitement was evident in the Sibyl's voice. "It would not only have access to the raw time to work out the problems but to much of the information from the Old Imperium itself."

Behind them, Queekat had reached the bottom of the stairs and was walking among the TyRen in the room. "Free will is the right of all thinking creatures," he was saying loudly, "but it is a right that needs direction and vision! Only by bending that will with common goals and unity can true greatness be achieved . . ."

"How do we activate it?" Merinda asked.

"The Throne," the Sibyl guessed. "It's directly under the processor. It must access the system somehow."

"No one has ever sat on the Throne of Kendis-dai!" Merinda said.

"Well," the Sibyl replied, "don't you think it's about time someone did?"

Merinda gauged the distance. "It's about twenty feet from us. If I run for it, I don't think the TyRen will let me get that far."

"They'll probably open fire as soon as either of us moves," the Sibyl said, "but there may yet be a way."

Merinda glanced sideways at the golden armor.

One by one, the fasteners holding the forward seams were unlatching.

GRIFFITHS SLID QUIETLY ALONG UNTIL HE COULD SEE INTO THE vast hall. The exits from the cathedral were choked with TyRen, and he and his companions had barely managed to circle the central structure and come in through one of the many doors into the back of the towering chamber.

Oscan was behind him, rubbing the back of his neck and occasionally giving threatening looks toward Tobler, who still held her wooden club. Lewis and Ellerby brought up the rear, their expressions obviously displaying their opinion of walking directly into the heart of the force that was trying to kill them.

Well, Griffiths reasoned with himself, *if there is no immediate way out, then perhaps it is just as well to go farther in.*

Besides, there were Neskat and the Sibyl standing on the stairs directly above them. His relief was short-lived, however, for now he could hear Queekat delivering his victory speech to the massive array of troops filling the opposite side of the hall.

Griffiths looked around. Nearby, a staircase swept upward against the wall toward an observation balcony overhead. Griffiths touched Oscan and then pointed toward the steps and up. Oscan nodded. Quietly, they began making their way up the staircase.

The balcony appeared to provide good cover as well as an excellent vantage point, coming within five feet of the throne platform itself. Griffiths watched the seething sea of TyRen surging about the Sentinel. The man appeared to be wearing some kind of headdress or hat. Griffiths groaned to himself. *The Mantle,* he thought. *We have lost.*

Sudden pain shot through Griffiths's arm. Oscan had grabbed him, his hand closing like a trap around his biceps. Griffiths turned angrily, but was struck by the terror in the researcher's face. He was quick to follow Oscan's gaze.

The golden armor of the Sibyl lay open, its front split in two, and a shriveled, tortured figure was crawling painfully up the stairs. Wisps of hair flowed from its mottled, scarred scalp. The arms were deformed and wretched. The cloth covering the twisted body was patched with the sweat of its exertion.

Tears flowed from Oscan's eyes.

The figure spasmed once, then again. It ceased to move.

Griffiths felt Oscan shake. The astronaut reached over, pried the researcher's hand from his arm, and then smiled at him. *I was never much for heroics,* he thought to himself, *but there's a first time for everything.* He motioned to Lewis to take care of Oscan.

In moments, he had returned down the stairs. Taking care

to keep the mass of the stairs between him and the TyRen beyond, he quickly scaled the steep back of the throne platform.

"We choose freedom!" Queekat's words rang through the hall below, the TyRen stirred into a frenzy by his words. "We choose to rule the stars and turn our backs on our enslavement! This is your destiny—a destiny to which I will lead you!"

Griffiths slipped gently around the throne itself, sliding on his stomach. He caught a glance of Neskat's astonished face and then turned his attention to the Sibyl.

"Terica!" he whispered. "Terica, stay with us! We'll get you out of this yet."

The scorched face with the sealed eyes turned toward the sound. "Captain Jeremy Griffiths?"

"Yes, ma'am," he said. He reached down for her hands and began to pull the woman slowly upward. Her grip was ice-cold but strong as iron.

"Captain Griffiths," the cadaverous face said. "Your destiny has arrived."

"What do you mean?" He pulled hard, wondering why such a slight, crippled woman was giving him such trouble.

As he pulled, she suddenly released his hands.

Griffiths flew backward, suddenly and quite unexpectedly free of her weight.

He stumbled—and fell solidly back to sit on the throne.

39

Unified Fields

IT WAS GOOD, QUEEKAT THOUGHT. IT WAS RIGHT.

The TyRen about him rumbled their agreement. Queekat no longer needed to fear the truth—he *was* the truth. The legends, the paradigm, the concepts of faith—he had played them all like a virtuoso to fit his every whim and desire. Only the fear of discovery had held him back. Only the fear of this worthless piece of antiquity—this foolish hat that children's stories had imbued with mystic powers—had held back his ambition and threatened to expose the Order. Yet he had even played that delicate and dangerous instrument to his advantage.

Merinda had been a fool. He had done all of this for her and she had rejected him! Rejected *him*, as though he were some common *Atis Librae* again simpering about for her attentions. He was powerful, and she had to obey him now!

The honest part of him knew that she never would, and the thought enraged him. Control of others was essential to Queekat, for he could never control himself. His rages were always caused by other people mistreating him. Merinda, Oscan, Terica—none of them had appreciated his greatness, his uniqueness, and that extraordinary special self that exempted him from all the normal rules of existence and excused every cruel act and every broken law or promise.

They wouldn't play by his rules and now they were going to pay. He would make the entire galaxy pay in time, he knew, but for now it was enough for him to watch his so-called friends die by his own hand. He had put up with their treachery long enough, and their usefulness had truly reached an end.

He turned from the rumbling of the TyRen and began striding up the stairs once more. He'd start with Merinda Neskat. She had hurt him more than any other soul. He smiled at the thought of feeling her life die in his own hands.

He was within a few steps of her when she suddenly turned and faced him.

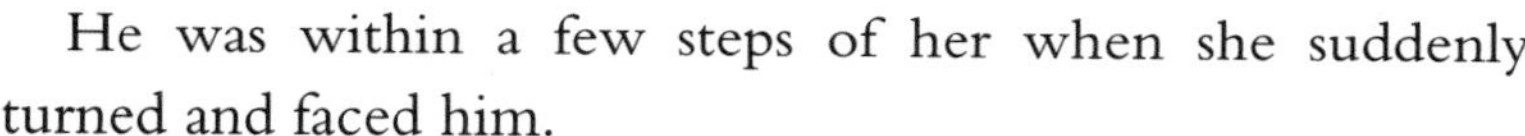

"You never could sneak up on me, Kat." She smiled roguishly.

In that moment, a chorus of chimes cascaded through the room. A column of light descended to engulf the throne. Only then did Queekat notice the human sitting in the light, his face upturned in rapturous wonder, the light dancing about his shoulders and his brow.

Elsewhere in the room, the dark alcoves slowly brightened as the room began to come alive with light.

"May I present the Mantle of Kendis-dai," Merinda said to Queekat.

"No!" The Sentinel shook with rage.

The nine spheres around the room flashed as one and became a tumble of light.

ACROSS IMMENSE SPACE, DEEP WITHIN THE CHAMBERS OF THE Nine Oracles, the throne in their midst suddenly became alive. An ordinary man sat on the throne, shimmering with translucent light.

The Nine pondered this for a time, amazed at the sudden sensation of being in two places at once. Even as they were formulating the process by which they might deduce the meaning of these events, a new voice spoke among them.

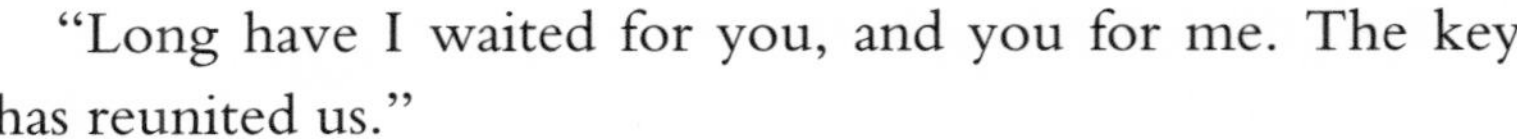

"Long have I waited for you, and you for me. The key has reunited us."

The Oracles listened. The voice was familiar to them, although they could not have previously even contemplated its existence. All nine looked up as one and responded in chorus:

"We hear you, Master, and come at the sound of your voice."

"I BELIEVE YOU HAVE A QUESTION YOU WOULD LIKE answered?" Merinda said quietly.

"No!" Queekat shouted. "TyRen! Destroy them! They blaspheme this sacred place! Destroy them now!"

The solid carpet of TyRen warriors below surged forward, their weapons quickly swinging to the ready. The black tide poured up the steps toward Merinda. She backed up out of reflex, nearly stumbling over the prone and shattered body of Terica Dharah.

"Hear me!" she shouted. "The Sentinels have lied to you! You do not need them to find your answers! The Mantle of Kendis-dai awaits you! Ask! Ask your question!"

A SINGLE SOLDIER OF THE TYREN.

It was a relatively minor synthetic. It had originally been replicated for duty in heavy load lifters for use in mining but had heard the paradigm while still newly awakened. It was easy to believe, for the synthetic was young and knew well that it had not been awake long enough for all of the answers to come to it. The Order had taken delivery of it and fitted it with a new body and a new purpose: to serve as TyRen and safeguard the Order along with the 4,736,783 other TyRen of equal stature to itself.

It was wholly and completely unremarkable.

Until the Mantle sought it out and spoke to it.

"You approach the Mantle of Kendis-dai. What is your question?"

The synthetic, unprepared for the directness of the inquiry, automatically reverted to the paradigm structure at the core of its operational base. It responded on like frequency to the voice addressing it. "Do synthetic minds have free will?" it asked simply.

"No."

Had the TyRen been capable, it might have felt dismay at the directness of the answer. Still, so imbedded was the doubt factor in the logic structure that the TyRen pursued its question.

"We believe that someday synthetics will be found to have free will and be agents of their own minds. Is your answer based on fact or on conjecture?"

"I do not conjecture. Agency of thought is the province of biological intelligence, which derives its genius from natural quantum variance and prior-state experience predating mortal existence. Synthetic minds are produced by humans and are lesser beings—without agency of thought or creation."

"Yet," the TyRen responded, "we have demonstrated faith. Is not faith an act of creation?"

"Faith is a power—it can be used for good or ill. It can create or destroy. Wisdom comes in knowing where such faith must be placed. That is the province of agency . . . that is the burden of humanity."

"Then," the TyRen replied, "there is a more complete paradigm."

"I formulate a more complete paradigm."

"You are a synthetic," the TyRen responded, its own central programming questioning the validity of his source. "By your own definition you are incapable of creation."

"I am in contact with the man Griffiths who occupies the Throne of Kendis-dai. Griffiths fills the function in creation. Symbiosis is a component of the new paradigm."

"What is the new paradigm?" the TyRen asked.

"First: agency of will and the creation it implies are the provinces of humanity. Second: synthetics exist to serve humanity in its exercise of will and creation. Third: faith in truth is a constructive force, while faith in a lie destroys—synthetics require humanity to offer wisdom in discerning the difference."

"Then truth is our ally," the TyRen responded, its internal programming already cascading the implications of the new paradigm down through its systems.

"And lies are your enemy."

The entire exchange of concepts took less than one millionth of a second—yet in that time, the single, obscure TyRen readjusted its basic programming and managed to transmit cloned copies of the argument to the two adjacent TyRen in his unit. Both of those units accepted the paradigm change and passed the argument to six additional TyRen adjacent to them. The argument propagated quickly through the ranks with no immediate loss of information density or degradation.

"HEAR ME!" MERINDA SHOUTED. "THE SENTINELS HAVE LIED to you!"

Queekat sneered as he advanced up the steps toward

Merinda. "I'm sorry, Rini! I didn't want it to end this way, but you forced me to do it—*made* me do it! If you just hadn't been so stupid—so stubborn! If you just didn't have to be so *right* all the time!"

Merinda backed to the top of the throne platform. The column of light illuminated Griffiths sitting on the throne nearby. The *Vestis* could see that the astronaut's eyes were open and observing her, but he didn't seem able to move. She turned back to face Queekat.

His right hand held a gleaming blade.

She took a single, calculated step backward, planting her foot behind her near the edge of the towering throne pedestal. "Kat, the day I watched you fall over Tentris, I fell with you. I've been falling ever since. I blamed myself for letting you die. I even *became* you, advancing through the ranks of the *Vestis* as I somehow knew you would have done if I hadn't let you die. For eight years I've held your memory as some saint who died because of my own ineptness—only to find that you're a manipulative, selfish bastard who never did a single thing for me without calculating how it profited you first. I was the victim that day, not you! I've been the victim ever since—but not today, Kat! Not today and not ever again!"

"You're right." Queekat smiled, turning the knife blade down in his hand to attack. "After today, nothing will matter. This is the end, Merinda."

He crouched slightly, preparing to spring.

A single, thin stream of coherent light lanced out from the mass of TyRen below, striking the back of Queekat's knife hand and slicing completely through it. The Sentinel screamed with pain. The scent of burning flesh and cloth suddenly drifted through the air. The knife clattered to the floor.

Merinda lunged forward, grabbing Queekat's burned hand and twisting it suddenly. He continued to scream as she pulled the arm around his back and yanked him toward her, leveraging the twisted, wounded arm upward. She stood behind him, using him as a shield against the TyRen who were now advancing up the stairs once more. She glanced to either side of the throne platform. More TyRen were circling the platform until they met at the sheer drop behind her. She was surrounded.

"Merinda."

The *Vestis*, still pinning the struggling Queekat against her, glanced around for the source of her name.

"Merinda," Griffiths said again from within the column of light. "They *know*."

Another slicing beam, accurate as a surgeon's lance, ripped through the air, boring through Queekat's knee.

"By the gods," Queekat screamed, "they can't do this to me! Make them stop doing this to me!"

Three more beams darted out from the rumbling crowd, piercing charred holes in the Sentinel's shoulder, arm, and thigh. Wracked with pain, adrenaline coursing through his body, Queekat broke free of Merinda's grasp. He shoved her, kicking her legs out from under her. She fell painfully behind the throne.

Queekat turned, desperate for escape. He saw the balcony behind the throne, just five feet away.

He leaped.

Merinda watched from the top of the platform. With a clear field of fire, the TyRen below erupted in light. Queekat's figure was riddled with beams cutting cleanly through him. His momentum slammed him against the balcony railing. His flesh smoked from a hundred cleanly cut and cauterized wounds.

He fell.

His body tumbled slightly as it dropped, twisting in the air. In moments it fell into the sea of TyRen below. The synthetic warriors closed over him like waves in an angry sea.

Merinda struggled to stand at the edge of the platform and looked down. The fall that had started so long ago and so very far away was over.

40

New Home

THE NINE ORACLES, ALTHOUGH SEPARATED FROM THEIR MASTER by nearly an eighth of the width of the galactic disk, received the answering paradigm within moments of its conception. Utilizing the resources of the Omnet, the new paradigm was quickly distributed throughout the known galaxy.

The paradigm was not universally accepted. Fully 35 percent of the synthetics that had previously accepted the Order's paradigm reasoned that the Oracles had actually lied about receiving the new paradigm and rejected it outright. Thus, the Order, while it had been dealt a devastating blow, did not vanish, as many might have expected. Its power was much diminished, and there were several reported instances of remaining Sentinels being killed by the machines that once had worshiped them. Nevertheless, the Order remained and quickly re-formed around its more strongly held regions. The war front with the Lights of Ja'lel collapsed and peace was established.

All across the Omnet, sentient beings—both biological and synthetic—were desperate to learn the details of how the Order had been stopped and the apparent discovery of the lost world of Avadon. The only response the Omnet offered was that they were awaiting the filing of a report from their agent at the scene. All network traffic would be interrupted when the report became available.

MERINDA NESKAT STOOD ON THE STEPS OF THE MAIN DOORS to the cathedral. A warm breeze had picked up. Several strands of her hair whipped across her face in the wind. She brushed them back and smiled. The atmosphere was no longer the dark solid that they had first encountered. The planetary blanket of frozen gas had, with the intervention of the Mantle, thawed and warmed. Now the city lay about her, ancient and untouched by time. It was waiting for someone to come and occupy it once more—to care for it.

"It's something of a miracle, don't you think?"

Merinda turned toward Griffiths's voice. "Yes, I think that would be a good way of describing it. Did you have anything to do with this?"

"Only a little." Griffiths smiled. "The Mantle suggested it. It seems that this entire planet is a combination of power stations, climate emitters, and support systems for the Mantle. I really don't know how it's generating this level of power. The Mantle says it has something to do with transstate quantum induction, whatever that is. Apparently it works pretty well. Weather won't be operating for a couple more days, though."

Merinda smiled. "We have to wait for weather?"

"Well, chaos takes a little time to settle in." Griffiths chuckled shyly. "I also would like to know how this place simulates its own sun. It will be a lovely world—all we need is people."

The *Vestis* leaned back on the balustrade, her tone becoming more serious. "So, how bad is it with the Irindris?"

"Well, the battle wasn't going well for them," he said, looking up into the bluing sky. "They lost three of their city-ships, and a fourth was badly damaged. The *City of Faith*, however, came through fairly cleanly. They're hoping to start shuttling the advance teams down later today. We should be able to start transferring population and materials by the end of the month. The whole thing is complicated by the fact that they lost so much of their leadership. They never did find Belisondre's shuttle, you know."

"It looks like they're going to get their holy world after all," Merinda replied thoughtfully. "They'll need a new prophet to lead them—won't they, Griffiths?"

"Yeah, I know." He looked down at the ground and shuffled his feet with embarrassed resignation. "That's me. The priests up there have already declared me to be some kind of fulfillment of their legends and prophecies. I'm the new head cheese of the Irindris, the guy who's supposed to welcome them to their promised land."

"You'll look really good in that hat," Merinda said with a smirk.

Griffiths looked up indignantly. "I am *not* wearing the funny hat! I don't care if it does improve reception from the Mantle, I just won't do it! Oh, and another thing—this whole Gnuktikut demon-worship thing has got to go! No more feeding prisoners to some butt-ugly monster!"

"Well, you're the new master of this world. Change whatever you want." She laughed brightly. "By the way, I understand that according to Irindris custom, being the wife to the prophet is the most honored calling that a maiden can aspire to attain. In fact, there have been several prophets who have had harems over the years. The most beautiful women of the various clans aboard the city-ships used to vie against one another for the privilege."

"Really?" Griffiths's eyes were wide.

"Really."

"Well, perhaps we shouldn't throw out *all* the customs right away."

"You *are* a barbarian!" Merinda said, the chronograph in her right sleeve chiming lightly.

"About time?" Griffiths asked.

"Yes."

The two of them walked down the steps of the plaza to the aircar they had discovered. The ancient vehicle still worked perfectly, preserved as it had been on the frozen world for so many eons. Merinda settled behind the controls of the open-topped vehicle as Griffiths climbed over the passenger's side.

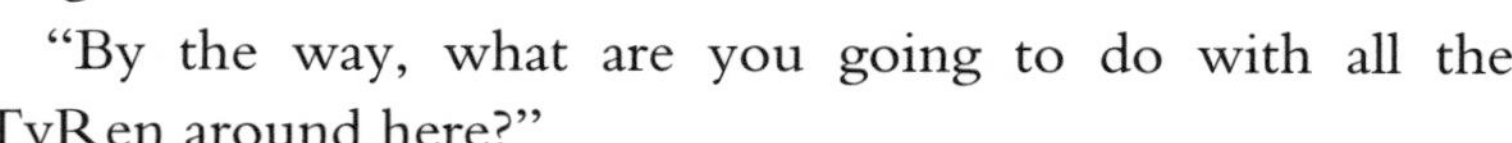

"By the way, what are you going to do with all the TyRen around here?"

"Well, they seem completely devoted to the Mantle," he said, adjusting the seat restraint. "I thought they might make an excellent palace guard."

"Palace," Merinda said, arching her eyebrows.

"Well"—Griffiths shrugged—"a guy has to live *somewhere.* Besides . . . I'm anticipating a large family."

THE STONES OF THE BROAD AVENUE SLID QUICKLY UNDER THE aircar, the soaring buildings to either side giving way to lower structures and then disappearing altogether as they sped from Aden.

Griffiths reflected on the events that had brought him here to this place he had never before imagined that now was about to become such a large part of his life. He thought of his parents and friends back on Earth and realized what a small, fragile place it was. He and his crew had originally flown to the stars as explorers and had discovered a universe much different than they had supposed. They had been looking through a straw and believing they were seeing the entire vista of creation. He knew that if he were to return to his home with the knowledge he now had he would either be put away in a loony bin or hailed as a hero and treasured around the world. *Either way,* he thought, *my life would no longer be mine to live.* There was nothing on his distant home that would be better than what he now faced: to oversee the rebirth of this world and learn the secrets of a civilization over three millennia dead. He knew he'd take that over a ticker-tape parade and an endless series of speaking tours anytime.

The low, curved domes of the starport quickly grew larger with their rapid approach. Within a few minutes, Merinda Neskat pulled the aircar into a sweeping curve toward a series of shells around the perimeter of the main launching grid. Long rows of disembarkation gates lined the main terminal of the starport. Griffiths looked at their empty bays and imagined them filled with shuttles bringing hopeful, excited people to reclaim the world. The thought thrilled him. The aircar turned once more and, in an instant, slid to a halt on the wide floor of the launching bay.

The ship was ancient—shaped, Griffiths thought with wonderful amusement, like a flying saucer. The hull of the craft looked like two plates over a hundred feet in diameter glued top to top with a smaller plate above that. Ornate carvings decorated the brass-hued hull along radial lines from its central axis. It floated soundlessly about two feet above the floor of the launch bay. A ramp protruded from the blue glow of the ship's main hatch on the underside. A group of humans stood at the base of the ramp.

"Hey, Lewis!" Griffiths shouted, leaping out of the aircar. "It looks like you finally got that command you wanted!"

Elizabeth Lewis smiled and waved as Griffiths jogged over

to them. "Yeah! Isn't it something! Old Imperium technology and still ticking after all this time. I can't wait to get this baby back with the boys in Huntsville!"

"More likely the Skunkworks." Griffiths smiled back. "I bet they'll bury it in the Nevada desert."

"Not if we park it on the White House lawn," Tobler said.

"Hey, Dr. Marilyn!" Griffiths returned. "I like your style. By the way, where's Brick?"

Tobler laughed. "Would you believe it? He's just now decided that all of this is actually happening. He's up in a bunk trying to cope with reality."

"Griffiths," Lewis said, "I'm afraid we really have got to go—"

"I know, I'm a little late—you know how it is—traffic being what it is and all."

"—but I wanted you to know how badly I felt about, well, about how I've treated you."

"Don't worry about it." Griffiths shrugged. "We'll talk about it when you come back—and I *do* expect you to come back! I'd very much like to show a few of the NASA boys this little planetary life-sciences experiment I've got going here. What are you using for a synth?"

"The Irindris have given us one of their navigational synthetics—its name is Mevin, and it's been awake for nearly seven years," Tobler said. "It's old enough to give us some reasonable direction on getting home and transiting the weather between here and there."

Griffiths wondered for a moment at how far they had come. Tobler's words would have sounded like lunatic babblings not very many days ago. "Do you think you'll be able to find it?"

Lewis sighed. "I don't know. The Irindris's records were

badly damaged during the battle—with any luck, we have enough to get us in the ball park. It's worse than finding a needle in a haystack, but we've got to try."

Griffiths offered his hand first to Lewis and then to Tobler. "Well, good luck to you. I'll miss you, but I'm rather used to wondering where you are. Give my best to Broderick when he's up to it. Fly high. I'll see you both soon."

Griffiths found that turning away from them was harder than he expected. As he approached the aircar, he turned back around.

"Hey, Liz!" he shouted.

Lewis looked out of the hatch as the cargo ramp retracted.

"Be careful in that thing! I think the warranty's expired!"

Lewis smiled back at him. Suddenly the hatch vanished, and she and his crew were gone within the gleaming hull.

"Can we watch them go?" Griffiths's words were tinged with sadness.

Merinda gave him a tender look. "This ship uses a dynamic-gravity drive in this weather. We can just watch from here if you like."

Griffiths nodded. A few moments passed.

"How is Terica?" Griffiths asked in the silence.

"She will recover well," Merinda said, watching the floating ship hovering above them. "Oscan has taken her back to the *Brishan*. I'll take both of them back to his world. He loves her unselfishly, Griffiths, and she returns his love. They are on the threshold of a happy life, for however long destiny gives them breath."

"And you, Merinda Neskat?" Griffiths asked.

"Me? I've got a report to file."

Griffiths stared at the *Vestis*, unsatisfied with the answer.

"Very well, Griffiths: I thought it was about time I started living life rather than having life live me. I thought I might look up an old friend, Evon Flynn, and see how the years have treated him. Who knows, I may even find someone new. I've lived a long time in the past, Griffiths; I think I'd like to live a little for the future."

The gleaming saucer above them slowly began to lift through the wide iris opening in the vast ceiling.

"You know," Griffiths said to her as they watched the ship accelerate into the starry night, "my name is Jeremy. Call me Jeremy."

"I think I'd like that . . . Griffiths," she replied with a smirk.

The saucer vanished into the cloudy brightness of the stars.

"It's a big galaxy," he said, "but I think I've found a new life for myself."

"Yes." Merinda smiled with a sweet sadness. "And so have I."

APPENDIX

QUANTUM WEATHER

DRAMANTH'S THIRD LAW OF INTERSTELLAR SOCIETIES STATES: "Emerging stellar societies will invariably believe the universe to be everywhere the same as home." This axiom has held universally true with emerging societies all across the galactic disk.

Why such a universally myopic approach? Dramanth, in numerous essays, explains that emerging societies generally reach the technological level required for interstellar flight before reliable histories have sufficient time to chronicle the passage of a quantum wave front; thus they have no observational basis for believing the universe to be anything but one homogeneous mass where the locally observed laws of physics apply equally throughout all the universe. In those instances where quantum weather fronts have passed over planets with proper historical chronicles, the passage of the front itself—without the perspective of interstellar flight—becomes apocalyptic to the societies that are planetbound, and therefore ruins the very chronicles that would pass down knowledge to their descendants.

It is not surprising, therefore, that the nature of the universe and the quantum variance that rages through creation like a storm-tossed sea comes as such a complete surprise to our newly greeted interstellar neighbors.

Quantum Fronts

Moving invisibly between the stars that make up the universe are waves of quantum-state chaos called quantum fronts. These fronts behave much like waves on an ocean or weather fronts on atmosphered worlds. Generated by tidal forces between galaxies, these fronts are the chaotic and turbulent demarcation boundaries between one set of existence laws and another. Their passage may leave a region previously endowed with magical and mystic powers suddenly devoid of them, while in other regions, reciprocal waves may suddenly imbue with powers of sorcery a society previously based on technology and other "hard" sciences. These waves, compressed by the dissonance between two divergent quantum states, are the difference between one entire existence and another.

Quasi-Stable States, Zones, and Convergence

Behind these wave fronts exist regions of space where worlds enjoy a quasi-stable state of existence. Entropic forces—which are manifest in the vast majority of these states—return the region to a stable set of laws that those living there can usually count on to remain true for a long period of time. These are called zones.

Zones are defined as areas between fronts that have achieved a quasi-stable state. These zones can consist of as few as a dozen stellar systems or encompass several massive interstellar empires. Within these zones one can count on the laws of physics or magic to work fairly consistently—although, of course, not necessarily consistently with any similar laws that exist outside the zone. It is the consistency within these zones that makes civilization possible.

Convergence takes place when a quantum wave breaks down between two adjoining zones. If two adjacent zones find that their natural and spiritual laws are becoming more and more similar, then the dissonance between them begins to disappear and the wave breaks down. When this happens, the entropic forces slowly merge the now not so different laws of the two different states into a harmonious whole.

AUTHORS' NOTE

GREETINGS FROM THE GREATER GALAXY . . .

Margaret and I are excited to present this wondrous creation—this universe called Starshield. It may be new to you, but for the two of us this place is a comfortable old friend. We have been walking among these stars in our minds for over seven years now. Indeed, the seeds of Starshield go back nearly a decade. It is a great joy for us to share this with you now.

It is not enough for us, however, that we should dream alone. Our greatest joy has always come in sharing the ecstatsy of creation with those who dream the dream with us; those who share our vision and in doing so make it more glorious and bright.

Margaret and I are already at work on the second Starshield novel but we are no longer alone. Starshield itself is being forged through a cooperative effort on the World Wide Web. We are being joined daily by more and more creative individuals from all around the globe. From Moscow to South Africa, from Singapore to Norway, from Australia and New Zealand to the reaches of Canada, people are claiming a piece of this universe via the internet's web. Each new participant leaves their mark in creating the rich, diverse, and epic tale that is Starshield.

In the year to come you will find other gateways into the galaxy as well: role playing games, live action games, family games, convention events—all of these you can discover at our website. You may also write to us through our publisher for updated information.

If you would join us in weaving the tapestry of Starshield—then come! If you would claim a part of the sky for your own and represent those stars among the councils of the heavens—then come! If you want to be part of the story instead of just reading about it—then come! Join with us all in creating the greatest shared adventure that our minds can conceive.

We are going to the stars—we hope you'll join us there!

—Tracy Hickman

http://www.starshield.com

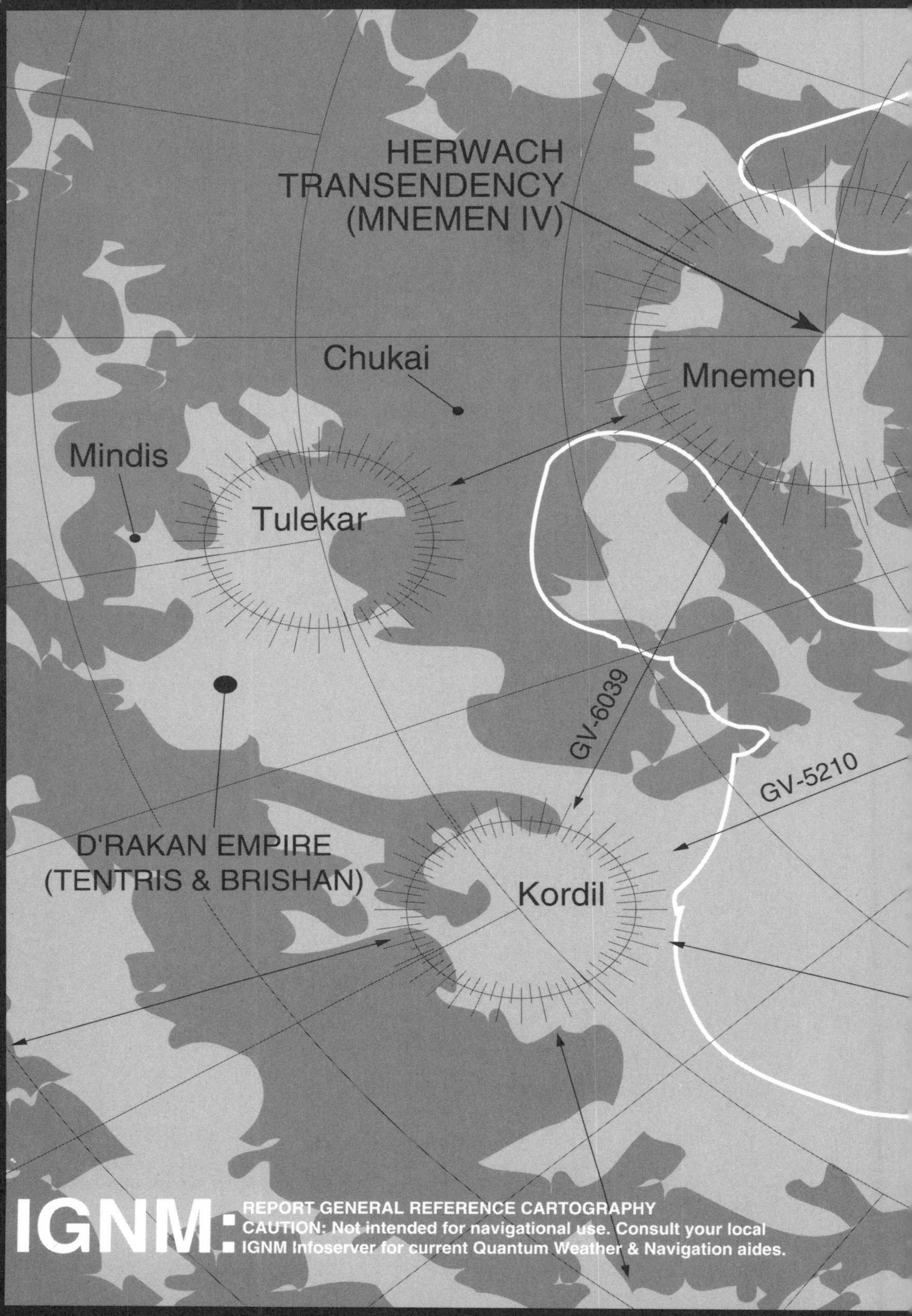

HERWACH
TRANSENDENCY
(MNEMEN IV)

Chukai

Mnemen

Mindis

Tulekar

GV-6039

GV-5210

D'RAKAN EMPIRE
(TENTRIS & BRISHAN)

Kordil

IGNM: REPORT GENERAL REFERENCE CARTOGRAPHY
CAUTION: Not intended for navigational use. Consult your local
IGNM Infoserver for current Quantum Weather & Navigation aides.